THE
**VERSIPELLIS**
MYSTERIES

# DEATH
## IN THE
# SOUND

# RHEN GARLAND

*E Rangi e Papa e te whanau Atua*
*Whakatohia to koutou manaakitanga ki roto i tenei mahi o matou*

*Sky Father and Earth Mother and the family of Gods*
*infuse your blessing upon this work*

# DRAMATIS PERSONAE

| | |
|---|---|
| Elliott Caine/Versipellis | Private Enquiry Agent |
| Giselle Du'Lac/Angellis | Private Enquiry Agent |
| Abernathy Thorne/Shadavarian | Private Enquiry Agent |
| Octavius Damant/O.D | Millionaire Philanthropist |
| Merry Damant | O.D's Daughter |
| Darius Damant | O.D's Nephew |
| Madame Aquilleia Aquileisi | A Psychic |
| Sir Wesley Eade | A Lawyer |
| Lady Leonora Carlton-Cayce | A Baroness |
| Carolyn Nolloth | O.D's Sister-in-law |
| Morten Van der Linde | A Diamond Merchant |
| Dona Carla Riva | A Ballet Dancer |
| Marjorie Lee Colville | A Companion |
| Torrance Burrows | O.D's Secretary |
| Veronique | Thorne's Labrador |
| Vasily Ainu | The Butler |
| Desdemonia Ainu | The Housekeeper |
| Lilith Tournay | Giselle's Maid |

# PRONUNCIATION GUIDE

Versipellis - Ver-si-**pell**-is
Shadavarian - Shad-a-**vair**-ian
Angellis - On-**jel**-is
Aquilleia – A-kwee-**lay**-ah
Xenocyon - Zee-noh-**sigh**-on
Abditivus - Ab-**dity**-vus
Chymeris - Ky-**meh**-ris
Phoenixus - Fee-**nick**-sus

Taniwha - Tani-fah
Pourewa Station - Pow-reh-wah
Lake Wakatipu - Wa-ka-tip-oo
Ngaio - Ny-oh
Manaia – Man-**eye**-ee-a

# The Taniwha

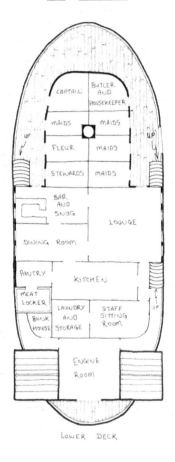

LOWER DECK

# The Taniwha

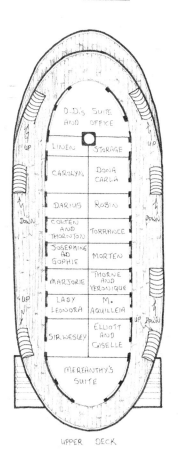

UPPER DECK

○

**Milford Sound, New Zealand**
**9:30am**
**15th January 1891**

Thomas Nibbs hurriedly tucked the item he had just stolen into his deepest pocket and ran for his life through the lush undergrowth of Sinbad Gully, sending up a fervent prayer that the little rowing boat which had carried him to this verdant and deadly place would still be pulled up on the beach where he had left it.

A few short hours ago, when he had landed to start his first day surveying the fertile but narrow valley, he hadn't expected the terrifying turn his day would take. He had to return to the safety of the hotel; once Coll had been informed of what had taken place, and had seen the item, he would become a powerful ally.

Breathing heavily, Thomas ran alongside the babbling stream that threaded its way down the gully, the eye-water-ingly green tree ferns slapping at his face and hands as he headed for the little beach where his boat was waiting.

With a sudden gasp he pulled up and looked behind him…he could hear dogs!

Shouldering his knapsack and redoubling his efforts, he shot along the sun dappled path, past a huge clump of silver beech and onto the shingle strewn shoreline as though fired from a cannon. Yes, he could see his boat! But alongside the little watercraft was a much larger tender, one more than capable of carrying the sizeable number of men and dogs now running him down.

Thundering along the sunny beach, Thomas made it to his boat and threw his pack on board. He paused to catch his

1

breath, before pulling an axe from the pack. Feeling a pair of eyes on him, he slowly turned to look into the bright, button-like eyes of a small, greenish coloured bird; the rock wren was sitting on the edge of one of his oarlocks, judging him quietly. He realised he had only just missed hitting it with his pack.

Thomas nodded at the bird. Scanning the heavily wooded shoreline, he gripped his climbing axe, rushed to the other boat and began to hack at the waterline of the vessel. After what seemed an eternity, a crack appeared in the woodwork and water began to seep in.

Thomas ran back to his boat and with a desperate effort pushed the little craft into the water. As he pulled himself aboard, the small bird flew to a rocky outcrop and watched as he began to row steadily away from the shoreline and into the still waters of the Sound.

No other boats were visible, that meant his pursuers would have to patch up their craft to follow him. As Milford City could not be reached on foot from Sinbad Gully, that would take them much longer than the few hours he needed to reach the safety of the little settlement.

Thomas looked up from his work and saw at least fifteen men with guns, pickaxes, and dogs crowding onto the shoreline. They saw Thomas in the water and immediately headed towards their boat. There was a silence as they took in the damage Thomas had inflicted, then the sudden, sharp crack of gunfire echoed across the water.

One of the men, somewhat larger than the others, grabbed two of the gunmen and banged their heads together. Thomas grinned through gritted teeth as he pulled on the oars. Oh yes, the sound of gunfire carries, especially across water, and even more so on such a still day. Can't have the people in Milford City hearing that!

The large man waved his arms in fury, and pushed the

men towards the slowly sinking remains of their boat. As Thomas settled into a rhythm, he saw several men start to bail water, while others began to patch up the hole he had inflicted on their vessel. The large man, meanwhile, stood on the beach and watched in seething silence as Thomas doggedly rowed his way towards freedom.

The young man threw himself into his work, and after a few tiring hours, he pulled into the little jetty at Milford City. As he climbed out, Thomas cast a look down the Sound. In the distance, a boat was slowly but steadily making its way towards the settlement. He quickly tied his boat up, grabbed his pack, and hurried to the hotel in search of Coll.

Milford City was considerably smaller that its name suggested; established across several decades by visiting sealers and fishermen, the settlement consisted of a functional jetty, a few cottages, and a small but clean hotel that served as a base for visitors and international walkers, a large number of whom were milling around outside the hotel, checking their packs, rolls, and food supplies for their return tramp to Te Anau.

Thomas headed for the front door as Manu, one of the guides from the local Iwi, nodded at him. "Kia ora, Thomas." He paused, taking in Thomas's pallor. "Are you all right, man? You look ill!"

Thomas shook his head. "You would look ill if you had just been through what I have, Manu! Have you seen Coll?"

"Yes: he went on ahead to check the track. He'll meet with us and then return tomorrow."

Thomas blenched. "Christ!"

Manu flinched and Thomas held up an apologetic hand. "Sorry, Manu." Thomas thought rapidly; it wasn't safe for him to take the item to Coll; the men following him knew who he was and where he was staying. He had to get the item and the information to safety…and then get himself out of the Sound. He looked at the wiry young Maori. "Manu, if I give you a package, would you give it to Coll when you meet him?"

Manu nodded. "Yes, of course." He looked at Thomas and frowned. "What's going on?"

Thomas squeezed his friend's shoulder. "I can't say right now, Manu. I'll be right back." Heading into the hotel, he paused at the little reception. Looking around to check no one was watching, he walked into the office area, reached into his pocket and carefully placed the item on the counter. He looked at the object that had caused him so much fear, and with a sudden movement swept it up. He was about to stuff it into his pack when he saw a small figurine of a tui on the counter. Grabbing it in his left hand, he held the object he had taken in his right and judged the weight, shape, and size; they were almost the same.

He placed both on the table before rummaging through various drawers, producing brown paper, string, a post card, and a pencil. Thomas swiftly wrote a note for Coll explaining what he had witnessed in the gully, and what he had done, before carefully wrapping the tui in brown paper and tying it with string.

Taking another piece of paper, Thomas wrote a letter to his half-sister Ngaio, explaining the route he would be taking, and why. Licking the gummed envelope with a grimace, he dropped it, along with a penny for a stamp, into the postal tray that Coll and his wife Rose left for their guests to use.

Picking up the parcel, he walked back outside and handed the package to a curious Manu who tucked it into his pack. "I'll see Coll gets it; we should be meeting up at the first hut."

"Thanks, Manu. Take care on the track."

Manu grinned. "Always." His grin faltered slightly. "Kia kaha, Thomas."

Thomas held out his hand and Manu clasped it firmly before heading to the front of the group and calling them to order. The twenty or so people, who had travelled from as far afield as England, the United States of America, and Canada to take in the untouched natural beauty of Milford Sound, quickly shouldered their packs and began their slow and steady hike behind the young Maori. It would take them a good few hours to weave their way out of the little settlement and up into the mountains, towards the hut where Coll awaited them.

Thomas headed to his room; the late-morning sunshine boded well for him to cover a good distance before the end of the day. Taking only what he would need for a rapid journey; which consisted of his thickest, warmest clothes and his climbing equipment, he made his way down to the kitchen and took enough provisions to sustain him to Queenstown, placing money on the breadboard to cover the cost.

He couldn't run the risk of the men finding him and the item. The mock package was heading south west, so he would head south east and try to reach Queenstown via Gertrude Saddle; a demanding ascent that was a suitable obstacle for those who hadn't prepared for such a climb. The rest of his journey would be a long but fairly manageable valley tramp to Lake Wakatipu, and then he could either continue walking around the edge of the lake, or take one of the station supply boats direct to Queenstown.

Shouldering his pack, the determined young man left the hotel and made for the short track that led to the south east of the settlement.

Pushing through the underbrush, he could still just see the group led by Manu heading up the Milford track. Turning, he looked back towards Milford City and the jetty. There, tying up their listing vessel, were a large number of men with dogs.

Thomas walked away swiftly, his heart pounding. Hopefully, they would follow the walkers to Te Anau…but if they didn't, he would only have a half hour's head start on them; he had to make it count.

He followed the Cleddau River that wound its way deeply into the mountains. The songs of a bellbird and a tui fought for possession of his ears as he headed up the worn track; he knew to take the left-hand path where the river split, and follow the route up to the Saddle. He filled his lungs with the clean, sweet air. In spite of the frightening events of the last few hours, walking alone in the mountains always gave him a sense of peace.

After several hours, Thomas looked up at the slope before him. The light was still bright enough to guarantee him a few hours' safe climbing time. If he could reach the top, he should be able to stop for the night and continue his journey at daybreak.

He was almost at the end of his ascent as the light began to fail. Looking back down the slope, he saw smoke; his pursuers had set up camp for the night in the valley at the foot of the mountain. Breathing a sigh of relief, Thomas continued until he crested Gertrude Saddle.

Even in the half-light of the evening, the view was stunning. The soft purples and golds of the setting sun to his right bathing the white-capped mountains with a burning light that never failed to take his breath away.

Thomas shrugged off his pack and took a deep breath. Behind him, the Sound stretched away into the sunset, whilst before him, the route he had hurriedly planned was being covered by a rapidly approaching darkness. As he stood, his mind focused on the disappearing view, a sudden noise made him turn sharply. A large, shadowy figure clambered over the ledge behind him and lashed out violently, backhanding Thomas across the face and knocking the young surveyor to the ground. The figure roughly sat astride him, and slapped down his pockets. Not finding what they sought, the figure glared at Thomas and snarled. "Where is it? Where?"

Thomas clamped his mouth shut and shook his head. The figure leapt up, grabbed him by the throat, and with a bellow of anger lifted Thomas off his feet and flung him into the air. Thomas screamed and flailed desperately for a handhold as he soared over the cliff edge and plummeted six hundred feet to the dark valley below.

His killer looked down the sheer cliff, then turned their attention to Thomas' pack. Emptying the contents on the ground, they pawed through the few meagre belongings before finding what they were looking for inside one of the carefully darned socks.

Pocketing the item, they stuffed the remaining contents back into the pack and threw it after its owner. Turning from the edge, they climbed back down to their comrades sitting around the campfire in the valley below.

○

## Austria
## Early November 1899

The figure looked at the corpse in the little trunk and breathed a happy sigh. After the temporary postponement of their plans caused by the interference of Versipellis, Angellis, and Shadavarian, they had been forced into rapid flight, taking over ugly, unwashed, and useless bodies. It felt good to take over a new, worthy form that could not be traced back to them...and how much better a body it was than the one they had inhabited for several years!

They paused before the mirror and ran a gentle hand across the unlined forehead and smoothed the springing hair, so soft and full, before allowing their gaze to wander across the rest of their newly acquired form. Yes, a much better body!

This body had called to them partly for its appearance, but mainly for its connection to a certain person. The discovery of its previous owner's personal habits was both an added bonus and such a stroke of luck that it set them to believe in the Fates.

Vague memories were beginning to crowd in now: a happy but dull childhood and myriad love affairs. They smiled and focused on the memories, thoughts, and emotions of their most recent victim as they searched for one particular memory involving the item they sought, and the person connected to it. The image of a face swam into their mind…yes, there they were – and there *it* was!

In their previous incarnation, they had met and done government business with a close friend of this person. They were both highly placed and wealthy, and judging by the thoughts and memories arriving ever faster, one of them was not only the possessor of that which they sought, but they were also utterly corrupted. Due to their predilections, they should prove easy to direct!

The gentle smile widened and twisted as their devious mind sifted through their victim's thoughts; discarding happy memories in favour of the greed, ambition, and licentiousness which their victim had taken great care to hide, but that were now completely exposed to their killer.

Yes, this body had definite possibilities.

There was a sudden light tapping on the door to the little room. The figure's head snapped round, they opened their mouth and their victim's voice spoke. "Yes, who is it?"

A deferential cough sounded on the other side of the door. "It is I. May I enter?"

The twisted smile broadened as their new memories

recognised the voice. Moving swiftly, they closed the trunk lid and arranged a throw and some cushions over it.

They smoothed their expensive evening wear as they moved towards the door. Their last thought before admitting their guest was that this could well prove to be one of the easiest and more pleasurable of their plans.

# The Taniwha

# PART I

Mickey Cable struck the dirty match and held his breath. Would the flame catch this time, or would it blow out like the other two? He stared intently at the flame as it bobbed about on the end of the spindly little matchstick. Would it be third time lucky?

Holding his breath, he carefully touched the burning match to the length of fuse that led into the market square, and away from where he and his friend Billy Jakes were hiding behind a number of well-placed barrels. With a strange fizzing pop, the fuse caught. Mickey and his friend immediately leapt out from behind the barrels for a better view.

The sparking light moved quickly up the powder-covered fuse, looping and winding its way along the cobbled street towards the pile of explosives placed neatly in the middle of the square.

Mickey nudged Billy. "There she goes — I bloody told you I'd get her this time!"

His friend looked at him. "This had better be good,

Mickey. Old Jeremiah paid a lot of money for these bombs and he's damn determined to get his money's worth."

Mickey grinned. "That old bugger'll get more than his money's worth out of these, I can tell you! Got them from the Chinese Quarter I did. They'll be good."

Turning to look at the spitting flame rapidly approaching the middle of the square, the two young men, hardly more than boys, watched in smug satisfaction as the expensive Chinese fireworks shot into the air in a shower of brilliant sparks, then exploded in a profusion of purple and gold light that showered back down onto the harbour and the hundreds of locals who ringed the walls of the tiny marketplace.

As the dock workers and their families oohed and aahed over the beautiful colours and sparkling lights that spread out over the harbour, the working population of Sydney officially began their celebrations as they welcomed in the New Year.

The Chinese fireworks that Mickey had bought with the money and the blessing of old Jeremiah mingled in the air with the even more expensive rockets that the wealthier locals had purchased for their own private celebrations. Up on Cricket Hill, one such celebration was in full swing. A large gathering of several dozen of the Empire's great and good, including actors, diplomats, and members of high society, were gathered at a suitably ostentatious house that commanded stunning views of the city and coastline. Here, five young men were required to do the job that Mickey and Billy had been managing on their own just a few miles away.

As was normal at such soirees, various groups of people had clumped together for mutual support, depending on their political, financial, or religious leanings.

As the guests gazed skywards with similar oohs and aahs to the people at the docks, one such group, made up of two people, was deep in discussion. So wrapped up in the enormity of the situation they found themselves in, they were oblivious to the fireworks exploding with increasingly showier displays of colour and wealth all around them.

"Are you sure?" hissed Number One.

"Quite sure," replied Number Two, looking around nervously. "I checked the safe myself, and it's gone! You know there's only one person mad enough to try to get it, and he's damn well done it!"

Number One paused as a pretty young thing wearing this season's latest fashion walked past. Turning back to Number Two, Number One enquired in a tightly controlled voice, "How exactly did he get in? I'm pretty sure he didn't receive an invitation!"

Number Two looked incredulous. "How the bloody hell should I know? I'm not in charge of security, you are — I'm just the secretary!" Number Two looked around and spoke more quietly. "It's your job to find him, and your job to see that what he's taken is returned!"

Number One stared at his colleague with a searching expression. Number Two frowned. "What's wrong?"

Number One took a deep breath. "That's exactly what he said to me the last time I saw him: "what was taken must be returned."

Number Two shook their head. "Well, it's your problem, my friend. You're going to have to tell the boss, and I'm damned glad I'm not you!"

The pair stood in silence in the middle of the immaculately tended garden, surrounded by noisy partygoers, and gazed at the hideously expensive display of lights without actually witnessing any of the wonders of modern Chinese firework manufacture.

## Sydney Docks
### 12:15am

Malachy Featherstone limped through the crowd of watchers by the docks, his damaged leg doing him no favours in his hurry to reach the safe house on the quayside.

Anyone watching might have been curious about the package he gripped in his left hand, but the docker's hook in his right would persuade any would-be thief to search for a victim elsewhere.

Well past middle age, with a thick sweep of grey hair tied back in a waist-length plait, and piercing green eyes that could see through any attempts at subterfuge, he was an easily recognisable presence on the docks. You didn't approach him unless you had good reason. If the reason was acceptable, he would help, but if it were unjust, prepare for the consequences. His reputation was that of a hard but fair man, whose reaction to being used was both swift and painful.

The main thought passing through Malachy's mind as he walked along the dockside was that this time, he might well have bitten off more than he could chew.

Hurrying as quickly as his leg would allow, he made his way through the main entrance to the quays, and past the fishing vessels that had moored for their crews to enjoy New Year in the many brothels, opium dens, and cheap taverns that littered the area.

Approaching one such place now, the unmistakable scent of the harbour assaulting his nostrils, Malachy paused. They knew some of his safe places: one had been raided a few days earlier. Perhaps it would be safer to go somewhere they wouldn't expect. Somewhere, perhaps, a little closer to home?

A vicious grin split his tanned face. He turned sharply and began the long trek towards the more affluent side of the city.

After nearly an hour's mostly uphill walk that utterly wrecked his knee, he stopped outside a palatial villa that, on the outside at least, was the height of propriety — unless or until you knew who it belonged to, and understood its true purpose.

The beautiful and opulent building was the home of the infamous Tai-Pan Club. Not a place for either the highly moral or the shrinking violet; although some of the highly moral had been known to enjoy an occasional fall from grace within the perfumed boudoirs on the other side of the yellow stucco walls.

Faint music came from within the stately building as Malachy straightened his back and walked through the grand open porch towards the ornate front door where a huge, dark-haired man wearing evening dress sat on a ridiculously small chair.

As Malachy approached, the huge man's face split into a beaming smile. Rising to his full six feet eight inches, Johnny Cussler, prize fighter and occasional bouncer, held out a ham-sized hand to Malachy. "Mister Malachy, we's not seen you in here for ages!" A frown furrowed the massive brow above docile, ox-like eyes. "Everytin' all right, Mister Malachy?"

Malachy shook his head. "No, Johnny, everything is most definitely *not* all right! Is Simone in?"

"Yeah, she'm in the office doin' the books. Is there anytin' I can do, Mister Malachy? If there was, you know I would."

Malachy gripped the young giant's hand. "I know you would, Johnny, but things are rather more dangerous now. If

I did get you involved, and even if we both survived, chances are your young Annie would kill us both!"

Johnny gave Malachy a sheepish grin. "You'm probably right." Leaning towards the massive oak door, he pushed hard, and the door that led into the ornate lobby of the Tai-Pan Club swung open.

With another beaming grin from Johnny, Malachy walked through the door into a fragrant and rather noisy paradise. The Tai-Pan Club was not for the average paying client, but the connoisseur. Gentlemen, and indeed ladies, came to ride with the dragon and enjoy the company of a selection of expensive and well-trained escorts of both sexes.

In the main reception room, the members-only New Year's Eve party was going with a swing. Here the great and the good, rather less dressed than their more conservative counterparts at the house on Cricket Hill, were ringing in the New Year with the sort of bang that didn't require fireworks!

The bodies dancing in a horizontal fashion to the American ragtime band were clad in colours, masks, and outfits that would have sent their more refined family members into fits. However, they suited their equally opulent and ornate surroundings: Chinese silk in rich shades of red and purple covered the walls, while fluted columns of green marble held up the ceilings which were covered with intricate mouldings of satyrs and nymphs behaving in a most disreputable way. Their rich covering of gold leaf failing to disguise their blatant behaviour, instead drawing even more attention to their lewdness.

This room, however was nothing compared to the Room of the Golden Harvest, which was covered in decorative motifs from Sir Richard Burton's infamous "Kama Sutra".

The men and women who could afford the privacy and discretion the Tai-Pan club offered might play out any fantasy they wished within the hallowed walls, with one or two notable exceptions. Once, one of the wealthier and more obnoxious club members had asked the proprietress, Simone, to procure him an eleven-year-old girl. With a gracious smile, Simone had acquiesced, furnishing him with a date and time because "such things do take time to organise".

As the member approached the rendezvous, which, oddly, was not at the club itself but one of their lesser-known private establishments, he saw a small figure standing by the front door. Believing this to be the child procured for him, he advanced and addressed the slim figure, which silently held out its hand. The diplomat, believing this to be a rather peremptory gesture for payment, handed over the agreed amount, and to his horror, suddenly found himself surrounded by surly police officers and gleeful reporters. The child turned out to be a lithe young man of some years' experience, who disappeared before he could be arrested. The diplomat was charged with attempted sodomy, for which he was rewarded with two years' hard labour in Sydney gaol, the total annihilation of his political career, and his expulsion to the Motherland in disgrace on completion of his sentence.

With a grimace at the weakness of others, Malachy pushed through the crush of bodies writhing on what was euphemistically referred to as the dance floor, made his way across the opulent room and through an intricately carved door almost hidden behind a decorative screen. Beyond was a long corridor with several other doors leading off to the left and right, but the door he needed was the one at the far end.

He stood still, listening to the sounds around him. Apart from the noise in the massive room he had just left, in the distance were the usual sounds of such a place. The moans of the opium addicts, whose rooms were through the door to his left and down a flight of steps guarded by Johnny's equally large brother, Will, could barely be heard. That was how Simone preferred it, believing it safer for her escorts. Then there were the articulations of those rarefied creatures themselves: soft laughter and other sounds as they entertained their private clients behind the myriad doors on his right.

Malachy limped down the long corridor and stopped at the doorway leading to Simone's private rooms. He smoothed his hair, and without bothering to knock, swept the heavy door back with a flourish. "Good evening, my darling, I'm home!"

The statuesque and beautifully dressed brunette seated behind the desk at the far end of the room didn't bother to raise her elegantly coiffured head, but instead finished adding up the column of figures in the black ledger before her. Closing the book with a satisfied smile, she carefully removed her gold Pince-nez and turned to look at the somewhat moth-eaten figure in front of her. Wrinkling her nose, she smiled. "For the love of the Gods, Mal, you bloody stink!"

Malachy grinned. "So would you, my love, if you'd been where I've been!"

Simone looked at him with a quizzical but amused expression on her exquisitely made-up face. She leant back in her chair. "Go on then, husband, where have you been?"

Malachy poured two large whiskies from the well-stocked bar and handed one to Simone. Standing by his blue armchair next to the fireplace, he grinned at the woman who had been his wife for over twenty years as he took a long sip from his drink. "I've been in *his* house, up on Cricket Hill!"

Simone's perfectly drawn dark eyebrows snapped down over her nose. "Are you crazy, Mal? What the hell were you thinking?"

Malachy put his drink down and crossed the room.

Kneeling by her chair, his bad knee protesting volubly, he took her hand and kissed it gently. "It will be fine, my love, it will." He looked up at her. "My contact was right, Sim; he had it, it was there…it was all there! And I took it back!"

Simone stared at him, a sudden look of hope on her face. "Oh, Mal, can I see?"

Malachy sat back on his haunches, and reaching into his pocket he produced the package. Opening it, he passed the treasure it contained to Simone who gazed in silence at what had led them halfway across the world. He smiled at his wife. "We have to get out of the country quickly and begin the next stage of our plan. And then, when that is finished and behind us, my beautiful wife, then we can go home!"

"Home!" Simone smiled, a look of happy relief on her face. "It's been a long game we've played, husband…and it's nearly done." She placed the package on the table and sipped her drink thoughtfully. "I think we can leave Australia tonight. The Aethernautica vessel, the Dale Castle, is set to fly to New Zealand at dawn with three of my girls and a protector on board. The captain is a client of the club, and he owes me a favour. We can pack and be at the aetherdrome before she is due to leave; that will get both us and the package away from here quite rapidly." A frown crossed her face as she looked at her husband. "But if we leave now, how will we know where our target will be, or how to get to him?"

Malachy took a sip from his glass. "My contact has agreed to keep us informed of his travel plans for the next few months. Because of their…closeness to him, they will know exactly where he is."

Simone nodded slowly. "What did you promise them in payment, Mal?"

He shrugged. "Money, what else? If we pull this off, my love, we will have everything that is ours by right! And he —

that utter, bloody bastard — he will have nothing!" He finished his drink in one gulp and looked at Simone with a strange expression. "Time for a change, my love, are you ready?"

Simone smiled. "We have been here long enough, husband. It's time to go home!"

○

### Malachy and Simone's private residence
### 03:30am

The front door reverberated with the heavy-handed knocking of the man outside. He didn't wait to be admitted, but instead pushed the door open and walked in. The man's name was Juggernaut; seven feet tall and a force of nature from India, he had worked for Simone for over ten years as both an enforcer in the club, and as a protector for her girls when they travelled aboard airships and sea vessels for their work.

Carrying a rolled-up rug tied with string over one shoulder, and two carpet bags in his free hand, he nodded at Malachy, then dumped the rug on the floor and placed the bags next to it. Undoing the knots, he unrolled the rug to reveal the huddled remains of a middle-aged couple.

Malachy looked at Simone's huge enforcer with a carefully blank expression. "You didn't…?" He gestured at the bodies.

Juggernaut shook his head and spoke, his Missionary English accent clipping the words tightly. "They were in the morgue; I simply removed them. Have you everything you need?"

Malachy nodded, holding up the bedraggled looking pack he had used for years on his travels with Simone. "All I need is Sim and the contents of this bag. No, wait…scissors." Rummaging in one of the dresser drawers, he produced a pair and shoved them in his pack. "Speaking of Sim, where the devil is she?"

Juggernaut looked up from the bodies on the floor. "She said she would meet us at the aetherdrome, there were things she needed to attend to at the club."

Malachy nodded as the enforcer carefully placed the body of the woman in Simone's armchair, then set the man's corpse in what had been, up until now, his comfortable wingback. "Ready?"

The huge man nodded. Removing two large earthenware bottles from one of the carpet bags, he handed one to Malachy and proceeded to throw the liquid around the little room; the unmistakable smell of paraffin filled the air as Malachy went upstairs to do the same. He walked back down the well-scrubbed stairs and looked at Juggernaut. "Finished?" The huge man looked at him and nodded.

The two men checked the street outside was empty before gathering up their packs, with the few belongings they were taking with them.

Malachy looked at the front of the little house that he and Simone had lived in for nearly fifteen years. There were many happy memories in that house. With a sigh, he struck a match and lit his cigar. He stood by the gate and took a long, deep pull before throwing the cigar through the open door.

Turning, he shouldered his pack as he and Juggernaut headed towards the aetherdrome on the other side of the city, while behind them, the tidy little cottage burned.

### Milford Sound
### 1st January 1900
### Midday

Octavius Damant; business magnate, millionaire, and philanthropist watched his daughter with a smile as she played with the excitable puppy. He turned to Coll. "Such a kind and thoughtful gift, Coll. Merry does love animals."

His friend smiled. "I thought it would be appreciated."

The two men looked on as the young woman happily celebrated an early, and very furry, twenty-first birthday gift as they wandered along the shoreline of Milford City. Only a handful of houses dotted the little settlement, the stone and wood buildings gleaming in the sunshine that had broken through the earlier rain.

All those who travel to that remote part of the world agree that the brilliance and peculiar beauty of the early autumn light is very specific to New Zealand; all it touched looked as new to the world as though just created. It spread its light down the green, blue, and silver length of Milford Sound, gilding everything with a golden light that set the huge, three-storey American paddle steamer sitting at her moorings ablaze; her brilliant white woodwork and polished brass balustrades glowing in the lustrous, mid-morning sunshine.

Coll looked at his friend. "Have you received any more threatening letters?"

Octavius, known to his intimates as O.D; gave him a sharp look, then sighed and shook his head. "Just the ones in England and Australia. None since we have been here, thank God!" He smiled. "It's been a breath of fresh air to know that we are finally safe." The smile disappeared as his tanned face hardened. "I just hope it stays that way!"

Coll nodded, looking back to where Merry and her maid were playing with the little pup. His gaze took in the gentle young woman who had been her father's only light since her mother's death ten years earlier. He sighed, not looking forward to what he felt he had no choice about. Well, it had to be said, and better it came from a friend. He turned to O.D. "And what of Merry? How does she feel about being here?"

O.D frowned. "How do you mean?"

Coll sighed again, this time with a touch of exasperation. "You know exactly what I mean, O.D! She's nearly twenty-one and she has no friends of her own age, no entertainment, no suitors. How is the poor lass to get married if you keep her in exile down here?"

O.D's thick grey eyebrows set in a line across his nose. "She does have entertainment! She has Mar, and her time with Jane and Fleur, and now she has your gift—"

Coll cut him off with a smile. "A governess turned companion is not a friend, O.D. Marjorie might have been with you for years but she is still a paid companion, nothing more. And Jane is Merry's maid, not a friend! If someone offered her a better-paid position she would go, and rightly so. That might also apply to Fleur; she is your captain's daughter, after all. If he leaves, so will she, and that would leave Merry with no female companionship at all." Coll paused. "But I'll agree with ye, a pup is a fine companion for a young lass!"

The two men continued their wander along the water's edge, both watching Merry in silence as they made their way towards Coll's hotel. As they entered the solid building, they headed to the little bar and sat down. O.D looked at his friend and spoke in a quiet, almost plaintive voice. "I don't want her to be on her own, Coll. I'm an old man and when I am gone…" He sighed and straightened his shoulders. "What would you suggest I do?"

Coll considered. "Well, now…firstly, it's to be her twenty-first birthday in a few months. That gives you plenty of time to organise a wonderful surprise party. Young lassies love parties!" As O.D leaned forward Coll held up his hand. "Don't interrupt me! Secondly, that's when she will come into her inheritance, yes?"

O.D nodded. "Well, part of her inheritance. She will come into her mother's money."

Coll gripped his friend's shoulder and carried on. "It's to be a special time for her, so make it a weekend party with lots of silliness – entertainers, music, and the like. She'll have a splendid time, with good memories made!"

O.D nodded slowly. His face changed as he thought more about the idea, becoming suddenly eager. "Yes! Merry has always spoken of her enjoyment of legerdemain and the such…maybe an illusionist, or even a psychic! Yes, that's a very good idea! Will you assist me in the organisation?"

Coll smiled at him. "I would be honoured! And now, a drink to celebrate!" He got up and poured two large drams. That had been rather easier than he had thought! He handed one of the tumblers to O.D and held his glass aloft. "To young Merry, in this, the beginning of the rest of her life!"

As the men drank, Coll's wife Rose entered the room and with a tolerant smile handed her husband a pile of letters. She turned to her husband's friend. "There's one for you too, O.D."

O.D put his glass down and took the letter Rose offered him. Looking at the printed writing on the envelope, his face blenched.

Coll asked sharply, "What is it man?"

O.D stared at the letter. "It's from him; he's found us!" He looked at Coll, the happiness of a few moments ago wiped from his face. He suddenly appeared much older. "I can't open it — it will be the same as the others."

Coll held out his hand. "I'll do it, man, hand it here."

O.D hesitated, then handed the little envelope to Coll who examined it. A plain, cheap envelope with heavily inked capital letters, addressed to Octavius Damant, c/o Coll's Rest, Milford City. Interestingly, it bore no stamp. He opened the letter and read the contents with a growing sense of anger. He looked at the man he had known for nearly ten years and in a deceptively quiet, tightly controlled voice he bit out, "You never told me what was in the letters, and I never asked. You said they were threatening and nothing more. These aren't just poison pen letters, O.D, this is an abomination — accusing you of murdering your wife and your business partner because they were committing adultery!"

O.D closed his eyes. "I didn't know at the time that they…" He paused and swallowed hard. "I loved her, Coll… but it wasn't enough. I didn't know about them until after she and Burrows were kidnapped and murdered at the mine." O.D stood up, walked towards the snapping fire in the grate, and turned to Coll and Rose. "I paid the ransom! I paid it – and they killed her and Alexander anyway!" He closed his eyes and faced the fireplace as the façade of ten years crumbled. Coll looked at his wife, who nodded and left the room. Manly support was her husband's place, but she could offer a good meal, and Merry and the others from the Taniwha could offer company.

Coll looked again at the letter. "They never found those responsible?"

O.D wiped his eyes and shook his head. "They found nothing. All they knew was what the ransom note demanded: £25,000 in cut diamonds to be left in the site office and they would be released. Cordelia and Alexander were taken to the mine, and murdered when the kidnappers sealed it with dynamite. The supports were too damaged to allow any attempt at rescue. They might only have been injured, but…" He bowed his head, unable to go on.

Coll thought hard. He had only known O.D for ten years, but he prided himself on his ability to read people, and he believed O.D to be a good man. He cleared his throat. "I might know someone who can help you discover your poison-pen author. They work in a — well, a private capacity, you understand? It's been quite a while, but I think I still have their details. Would you like me to see if they can help?"

O.D looked at Coll with hope in his eyes. "Do you think they would? It's not me I'm worried for, Coll, it's Merry. One of the previous letters…they threatened Merry!"

Coll gritted his teeth and nodded. "Aye, I think they might. It'll take a while for them to get here, though. The last I heard they were in England, so that's a good month and a half of travel."

O.D frowned. "They could get here far quicker by airship."

Coll smiled. "Oh, no…the one I'm thinking of used to have a bit of a problem with such things and I doubt he's changed that much!"

O.D suddenly shook his head. "But how will I explain their presence to my daughter?"

Coll thought, then snapped his fingers. "Simple: they can be invited to her party!"

"But they won't be people she knows."

Coll looked at O.D with a strange expression. "Oh, don't you worry about that. They're very good at changing their appearance, if need be!"

## London
## 2nd January 1900

Lapotaire smiled at Bunny and kissed her.

The gathered guests applauded as Lapotaire and his beautiful bride turned to face the massed ranks of family and friends who had gathered to witness their wedding.

The family chapel was hidden in the grounds of Lapotaire Howse; a stately town house on the edge of Piccadilly that had been the Lapotaire family's London residence for over five hundred years. Rather small for a London house, she possessed only a few rooms: no more than thirty…not counting the servants' quarters.

Bedecked with green boughs and brightly coloured hothouse flowers ordered specially for the occasion, the chapel glowed in the winter sunshine that streamed through the medieval stained-glass windows, touching the altar, pews, and assorted guests with splashes of red, blue, and gold light.

As the bridal procession began its short walk along the little path back to the house, several of the guests murmured about the undue speed of the wedding. Lord Lapotaire, a dedicated bachelor, had only met Lady Ellerbeck, as she had been, some few months earlier at Marmis Hall. But perhaps the less said about the events of that particular weekend, the better!

If some of the wedding guests who had been at Marmis Hall during the weekend in question had looked closely at the stained glass windows in the little chapel, they might have been surprised to see two faces which bore an incredible likeness to the two police officers who had investigated that case. But the chapel windows were over five hundred years old…

Bunny smiled at her husband as they wandered back to the house where she would now be chatelaine. So much had happened so quickly, but all she felt was happiness. Her aunt's tragic murder had finally been solved, the killer had been exposed and punished, and now she and Vyvian were married.

Lapotaire walked alongside his wife, his mind roving between his personal happiness, how beautiful his wife looked, and a telegram he had received just that morning from New Zealand. It had been addressed to his father, dead these past ten years. Lapotaire had studied the contents between bathing and dressing, and with only a few moments to spare before the ceremony, had given the telegram to Vanamoinen with instructions to carry it to the true addressee.

Vanamoinen had happily accepted the order. His duties that day had mostly been fulfilled, since they were little more than dressing his master for the ceremony and ensuring he would arrive on time.

Vanamoinen headed onto the main road. Flagging down a hansom cab and giving the driver the address, he settled back into his seat; it would take a fair while to cross London and reach his destination.

As Lord and Lady Lapotaire continued their short walk back to the house, the young lord remembered the rather awkward discussion a few weeks earlier, when he had been forced to explain to a highly irate Commissioner Bolton that a certain duo would not be returning to their employment at Scotland Yard for the foreseeable future.

○

## San Francisco
## 16th February
## 9:30pm

Preston and Lydeard Bowyer acknowledged the ecstatic applause of their audience with gracious aplomb and escorted their star assistant off the stage.

The patrons of the Hotel Majestic were in raptures over the illusionists' performance; legerdemain being one of the few entertainments that both high and low society enjoyed equally. The cheap seats had been entertained enough not to throw their bottles at the stage, and the boxes, hopefully, had been sufficiently entertained to throw some bookings their way.

Preston, the younger of the two by some few years, smoothed his springy mop of brown hair and turned his dark eyes to his brother. "Not too bad, Lyddy, not too bad at all."

Lydeard, almost the exact opposite of his brother, being several inches taller with wheat-blond hair, grinned. "Hopefully the takings will be good enough to get us to our next booking. It's a birthday, isn't it, in New Zealand? Private events can sometimes be a little awkward, but I hope this one won't be. It certainly promises to pay well!" He frowned suddenly. "Speaking of money, have you seen our dear manager?"

Preston nodded. "He said he would return after counting the takings. If he isn't in our dressing room, he should be in the office."

The two young men made their way down to the poky little room that had been their home for eight long weeks. There was no sign of their manager, Albert Marks — or his luggage. They exchanged worried looks before they made their way to the third floor and the grand office where the hotel manager Gretel Alsace sat behind her ornate desk. Approximately three foot nothing, Madame Alsace ran the Hotel Majestic with an iron fist, a brusque manner, and a large chair booster to ensure that people saw eye to eye with her.

As the two young men knocked briskly on her door and walked into her office, she raised a warning hand. "I know what you are going to say. The takings were slightly down on what we predicted, but your manager said it would be good enough. So, there are no problems, yes?"

Preston and Lydeard scanned the room but could see no sign of their manager. Preston cleared his suddenly dry throat. "Madame Alsace, where is Marks?"

She looked from Preston to Lydeard. "This is a joke, yes? I do not do jokes. You know where your manager is. He took your money to your dressing room, yes?"

Lydeard shook his head. "No, Madame Alsace, he didn't. We haven't seen him since before the act, and his luggage has gone!"

Gretel stared at him and flipped open her ledger. Running her wrinkled finger down the columns, she paused at the entry for the Magnificent Bowyers and tapped her nail against the total. "He has taken the total income for your performance here."

Preston swore as Lydeard slammed his hand down on the desk. "Are you saying that we have no money from this evening's show?"

Gretel shook her head and settled back in her chair. "No, I am saying that he took all your money from your entire two month booking! That was just over three hundred and fifty pounds." She paused, thinking. "It was a little strange. When you first arrived here, he asked me to pay *him*...not you, your takings after each performance. He said you had agreed to this in your contract, so I did not bother much."

Preston's face blenched as he turned to his equally ashen brother. "Lyddy, he's taken everything! That was the money we needed to get to our booking in New Zealand! Oh Gods, what are we going to do?"

Madame Alsace shook her head. "I do not know what you are going to do, but your performances here are finished. Your manager has your money, so go and talk with him. You will need to vacate your rooms for the next performers; they arrive tomorrow morning!" And with a gesture from her boosted throne, she shooed them out of her office.

The brothers stumbled into the dimly lit corridor in silent shock, the realisation of their predicament rendering them both speechless. Preston swallowed hard and looked at his brother. "We need to find another job, Lyddy, and fast!"

As they stared at each other, a beautifully gowned and coiffured young woman appeared from the far end of the corridor.

Recognising the star who had assisted them in their final grand illusion, the brothers immediately assumed the charming, fake smiles that dedicated entertainers learn before all else, to cover their true feelings.

The lovely young woman smiled back at them. "Gentlemen, I couldn't help but overhear your difficulties. Some friends of mine might be able to assist. Please join us for a little late supper." Linking her arms through theirs, she guided the feebly protesting brothers towards the finest suite the hotel had to offer, and knocked on the door.

The man who answered was tall, with dark-blond hair and a Van Dyke. Immaculately dressed in evening wear covered by a velvet dressing gown of an eye-watering paisley design in violet and chartreuse, he smiled and stepped away from the door to invite them in. Seated behind him was a dark, bearded gentleman holding a red Malacca cane, also resplendent in simple but expensive evening wear covered by an exquisite Chinese silk dressing gown embroidered with burgundy and gold details. A smart, red-headed maid poured wine at a table laden with food, which was in turn being stared at hopefully by a leggy black Labrador ensconced on a silken bed by the window.

Giselle smiled as she gently nudged the two young men into the room and closed the door.

### Somewhere in Sydney
### 16th February
### 9:30pm

Carolyn Nolloth studied the manicure her maid had furnished her with, picked up the glass vase of pink roses, and flung it at the young woman who stood shaking by the door.

"I said I wanted points, not ovals! Get out, you idiot!" Carolyn swept her arm across the surface of the table, spilling the manicure paraphernalia onto the carpet.

The man standing by the window laughed as the terrified young maid fled. "You do realise that's another one who will leave? You're getting through maids like most people get through tea!"

Carolyn smirked. "They need to know their place. If they weren't so useless, I would keep them longer." She held her slim, pale hand up to the light. "She didn't do that bad a job, though." Turning to look at her lover, she arranged her peignoir to best show her legs and fluffed her chestnut curls. "Well, what do you think?"

Morten Van der Linde smiled. "You know very well what I think!"

Carolyn laughed. "Not about that! About the letter from Octavius: the invitation to my darling niece's twenty-first birthday!"

Morten moved to the dressing table and caressed Carolyn's neck. "I think it has…possibilities."

Carolyn caught his hand and gave him a hard look. "What do you mean, possibilities?"

Morten perched on the edge of the dressing table. "I have a proposition. Think about it before making a decision."

She narrowed her eyes. "This sounds ominously like one of your plans, Morten. But go on."

He took a deep breath. Time to strike! "Mereanthy will be twenty-one, yes?"

Carolyn smirked as she turned back to her mirror and smoothed one exquisitely drawn eyebrow. "I just said that, darling. Well done!"

He ignored her remark. "Twenty-one is when she will come into her inheritance from her mother, yes?"

Carolyn's smirk was replaced with a look of bitterness that twisted her full-lipped beauty into an ugly mask. "My sainted sister! I will never forgive that bitch for cutting me out of her will. After everything I did for her! I even gave my brat of a son Damant's surname to ensure the sacred family name would continue!"

Morten hid his delight. This was too easy! He took her hand and kissed it. "An idea, my darling — you might not be keen, but don't dismiss it out of hand. Mereanthy will be of an age to marry. As far as I can see, there are no suitors paying court to her in the barren wastes of Milford Sound… and that is where I come in. What say you?"

Carolyn stared at him in silence. "Are you suggesting that we — that is, you — court and marry my niece?"

Morten nodded. "We can take control of her inheritance. Then I shall divorce her, marry you, and we will have the money that should rightfully be yours! My dear, what do you say?"

Carolyn looked at him blankly for a few moments, then very slowly, a malicious smile appeared on her face. "Why divorce, when there are so many far more interesting options available?"

Morten stared at her; this was moving in a direction he had not foreseen. "How do you mean?"

Carolyn picked up her hairbrush and lightly fluffed her hair. "She has always been like her mother, going for moonlight wanders on her own, that sort of thing. Perhaps an accident — in the Sound? An "Oh my God she's gone overboard" kind of accident." She leant back in her chair, a triumphant look in her blue eyes. "Well, my dear, what say you?"

Looking at her, Morten had a sudden feeling that despite his extensive criminal experience, in this particular instance, Carolyn had the drop on him.

Hiding his unease behind a well-practised and charming smile, he wandered over to the bell pull and tugged it. After a brief wait the butler arrived, and Morten looked at Carolyn. "Champagne to celebrate, my dear?"

Carolyn nodded at her butler. "See to it, Marshall!"

The butler bowed his head and left the room as the two began their plans for the seduction, marriage, and murder of Mereanthy Ozanne Damant.

## Elsewhere in Sydney
### 16th February
### 9:30pm

Sir Wesley Eade, Queen's Council and saviour of the theatrical world for his philanthropical work in preventing poor but talented actors from starving to death in theatres worldwide, smiled at the little troupe he had gathered in his magnificent office and nudged a lobster sandwich from the buffet towards their spokesman.

Thornton Rust, whose heavily edited and thus utterly untrue résumé gave his age as fifty, waved his plump, well-manicured hand towards the heavenly creation, and in his carefully modulated English baritone, which had taken years to perfect, murmured, "No, no, I truly couldn't eat another morsel. Oh, but, if you insist…"

Sir Wesley smiled again and insisted. He left the heaving buffet table and sat back in his chair, taking in the magnificent Sydney shoreline and the well-tended trees at the end of his beautiful gardens that kept the more squalid areas of the city hidden from view.

The troupe, two men and two women, were part of a larger group better known as the Macquarie Players' Dramatic Society, all dedicated thespians, and all in desperate need of paying work: Thornton Rust had tried his hand as both an actor and manager over the years and had failed, quite spectacularly, in both fields. Colten Kayfield, nearly three decades younger than his colleague and a far better actor, was also in dire need of cash. His dark hair, liberally striped with grey, framed a tired, thin face that looked far older than his thirty years. Sophie Havercroft, who had begun her career many years earlier as a "boy" on stage and was now pushing thirty from the wrong side, sat with a hopeful, slightly pouty expression on her face as she judged the little canapé she held in a dainty grip. Would eating it destroy the diet her doctor had prescribed? And Josephine Carter, forty years of age, with a mane of strawberry-blonde hair, a bright, lively smile, and an unashamedly full figure. Unlike Sophie, Josephine cheerfully balanced a plate that seemed to contain three of everything and tucked in with relish.

Sir Wesley judged that the time had come to deliver his news. "Ladies and gentlemen, may I have your attention?"

The actors immediately settled into their 'polite and intrigued' stock positions as Sir Wesley explained why he had invited them to lunch. "A very dear friend of mine has a daughter who will soon be celebrating her twenty-first birthday, and I wondered long and hard what kind of gift would be appropriate. Mereanthy — that is her name, but her intimates call her Merry — she loves the theatre, so I have decided to hire your little troupe to organise and perform a surprise entertainment during her birthday weekend."

Thornton puffed himself up. "It is most flattering that you immediately though of our little company, Sir Wesley."

Sir Wesley smiled, his eyes flicking over his guests. "I have an eye for spotting talent, Mr Rust. And I have to say, a very good friend of mine has seen all of you perform on the stage…both here, and in Europe, and was very taken with your abilities, so I am quite aware of just how good you are." He paused. "Where was I? Oh yes, I forgot to say it's a weekend house party; we will be arriving mid-morning on the Friday and staying until after lunch on the Sunday…you know the kind of thing."

The assorted group of actors nodded sagely, though none of them had been invited to a weekend house party in their lives.

Sir Wesley continued, "There is limited space, so just the four of you would be enough for the performance."

Three of the troupe turned to look at Thornton, their eyes signalling him to say, "Yes please," and "How much?"

Thornton swallowed the last few crumbs of lobster sandwich and stood up. Placing his plate on the side table, he intoned, "What type of entertainment were you thinking of, Sir Wesley? A little light Shakespeare, perhaps? A reading from Dickens?"

Sir Wesley permitted himself a smile. "Perhaps I was not clear, Mr Rust. I wish you to put on a little play, that would start after dinner and conclude the following morning."

Thornton frowned. "I still don't—"

Sir Wesley held up his hand, opened a small drawer in his desk, and removed a slim hardback book which he handed to Thornton. "I would like you to use the plot of this trifling little story to create a short mystery play and enact it during the evening. It is rather a good yarn of its type. You know the sort of thing: two people do something a little naughty and are caught out, accusations fly, and a corpse or two is discovered. Very entertaining for a young girl — and for everyone else too, I should think!" He smiled at Sophie, who simpered in response.

Thornton stared at the man before him. "But Sir Wesley, we cannot: not without the author's approval and permission and that can take a great deal of time." He shrugged uneasily.

Sir Wesley smiled and pressed his fingertips together as he looked at the uncomfortable actor. "I have already secured permission from the author, Mr Rust. As I myself wrote the book some years ago, you may take it as read that the contract has been agreed and signed."

Thornton held out a conciliatory hand. "Well, in that case, of course. But there is still the issue of our presence. If, as you say, you want this to be a surprise, how would the presence of a group of strangers be explained to the young lady?"

"Good question, Mr Rust." Thornton preened slightly. "Her father and I have some business to discuss, so you will be two of my business associates and their charming wives, who will return to Auckland after the weekend pleasantries."

Colten looked up, his grey eyes questioning. "Auckland? The job is in New Zealand?"

Sir Wesley nodded. "My friend and his daughter live a very secluded life in Milford Sound, on rather a large boat. It is an incredible craft, O.D had her shipped over from America in pieces to be built in Picton; The captain travelled with her from America and oversaw it. I believe that type of vessel is referred to as a sternwheeler paddle steamer, and she is quite stunning: O.D spared no expense. The weekend will be spent aboard her." He paused. "But it is rather remote, I'm afraid. Pretty much one way in and one way out, unless you count the Milford track, and that is — well, not the way I would choose to travel!" He saw their expressions and hurriedly continued. "But your passage to and from the Sound will be by private airship, obviously! And via the Auckland Aetherdrome: quite civilised, I assure you." He paused again. "There is a final, simple request from me. It is perhaps a little silly but the symmetry appeals to me. The story in the book revolves around four people. I would like Miss Havercroft and Mr Rust to play the couple, if you please, and Miss Carter and Mr Kayfield the two other roles. When you read through the play you will see that I have given you your parts accordingly. You may use your own names or the character names, as you see fit. That is all, other than to say if you accept, you will each be paid the sum of fifty pounds for the weekend. What are your thoughts?" He paused, and uttered the magic words. "All expenses paid, of course."

The four actors looked at each other. A trip to New Zealand, a weekend party on a boat, fifty pounds, and expenses!

As one, they turned to the philanthropist. "Agreed!"

○

**Milford City**
**Wednesday 21st March**
**11:00am**

Mereanthy Damant gazed out of the open window of her sunny private sitting room and hummed under her breath as she watched the fur seals splashing in the shimmering water a few dozen feet away from her enforced viewpoint. She sighed heavily. It was far too lovely a day to be trapped indoors, watching her friend Fleur trying to conjugate verbs — learning verbs in any language was always a painful process, never mind German! But here she was, offering her friend moral support while dreaming of swimming!

Marjorie Lee Colville paused in her determined efforts and watched the daydreaming young woman with a faint smile. "I understand that German isn't to everyone's taste, Merry, but if you could just be silent for a short while, it will soon be over and then you and Fleur will have the rest of the day to spend at your leisure."

Merry's head snapped back from her study of the sun-drenched outside world. She smiled at the woman who had been with her since birth, first as her nanny, then as her governess, and now as a knowledgeable lady's companion. She cast a quick look at her friend Fleur, the target of the German lessons, as she continued to valiantly fight the good fight against the German language. Merry looked at Mar. "I'm sorry…it's just such a lovely day. I think Manaia needs a stretch of his legs. Don't you, Manaia? This last remark was addressed to the English Cocker Spaniel pup sprawled snoring next to his mistress on the lavender-coloured settee.

Mar raised her left eyebrow with an amused look and Merry hurriedly fell back to her book and waited for Fleur to finish her lessons.

As Merry read and Fleur focused on her studies, on the far side of the Sound, a mixed group of walkers and horses appeared on the crest of the Milford Track. They were tramping from Te Anau to the only hotel in Milford Sound; Coll's Rest. One of their number, a tall, dark-haired woman in well-worn travel clothes, paused to gaze at the paddle steamer with vibrant, violet-coloured eyes, before she continued her trek towards the small settlement that sprawled across the narrow slice of land between the forested mountains and the glassy, teal coloured water of the Sound.

### Auckland Aetherdrome
### Wednesday 21st March
### 11:00am

Built atop one of the largest extinct volcanos in New Zealand, the Auckland Aetherdrome was considered one of the most spectacular airship ports in the world. A steady stream of private airships, air-carriages, cargo carriers, steam-junks, and the grandest of all; the Aethernautica Clippers, flew in and out of the area every day, carrying people and freight from all over the world.

The Pourewa Station itself sat at the entrance to the main platform; a massive cast iron and plate glass building that had been designed to closely resemble the Crystal Palace in

England. The colossal building was home to exclusive shops, highly expensive restaurants, and luxury luggage companies who ignored the existence of their competition in the politest way possible: Signs were restrained and almost invisible within the fabulously lavish and plushly opulent edifice; the only way of knowing the whereabouts of a particular shop was with advanced, inside knowledge.

Several different platforms sprung from this parent level; air-carriage companies were on one outer edge of the building, while on the inner section, overlooking the crater, warehouses full of timber, wool, and heavily guarded strongboxes loaded with gold awaited collection. On the north-east side of the platform, various cantilevered air-jetties projected out over the outer edge of the volcano, offering stunning views of Waiheke Island to the individuals wealthy enough to afford a private mooring for their vessel.

In one of many such docks set aside for private airships, a disparate selection of travellers waited and studiously avoided eye contact or any other form of communication. They had not as yet been formally introduced, so any forwardness might be misconstrued as an attempt at friendship, and that would never do.

As the silence became oppressive, they were joined by a carefree, chattering group. This second, much smaller collection was made up of two young men, a young woman with a maid, and two porters struggling with several very large trunks. Both the young men were also manhandling large cases, while the taller of the two was also trying to control a leggy black Labrador who was having none of it.

The dark-haired young man bearing a red Malacca cane paused to look at the silent group and decided with a faint smile that attack was probably the best option. In his beautifully modulated voice, he introduced himself and his brother. They were the Magnificent Bowyers, Preston and Lydeard, illusionists and magicians. He and Thorne had agreed beforehand that using the names of the true Bowyers would be more sensible than trying to create new identities for themselves. The vivacious redhead with them was introduced as the renown opera singer, Giselle Du'Lac.

At this point a shape swaddled in a thick fur cape at the back of the quiet group suddenly folded a corner of the covering away from their face. "Giselle? My God, Giselle!" The cape was flung to the ground as the figure leapt to their feet. Giselle's jaw dropped as the suddenly revealed woman headed towards her at high speed and enveloped her in a crushing embrace; engulfing her in a cloud of perfume, furs and diamonds that was utterly unsuitable for any form of travel outside of first class. "Carla?" She managed to squeak.

The leggy beauty laughed as she released her death grip from Giselle's neck. "But yes, Carla! My darling, it has been too, too long." The woman gestured expansively at the opulent buildings with a mocking smile. "Who would believe the greatest singer, and the greatest dancer of our time would both be found here, in this damp and…what is the word I am looking for…? Temperamental? No…temperate? Yes! That is the word…temperate region of the world. I so miss the warmth of Brazil!" She lowered her voice. "But, my darling, I need the money! So, when I am invited for a weekend party I say of course, how much, and when?" She shrugged elegantly; the top button on her tightly fitted silver fox jacket gaped slightly, exposing her gleaming ebony neck. "But I did not think to ask where! That might have been a little mistake!"

Giselle smiled and turned to Elliott and to Thorne, who was still trying and failing to control Veronique. "May I present Dona Carla Riva, whom I met at the Amazonas Theatre in Brazil? Dona Carla, may I present the Magnificent Bowyers; Preston and Lydeard."

Carla held out an elegant, red-lacquered, jewellery-clad hand to Elliott, who gallantly kissed it. Thorne did the same with panache, considering the canine sulk in progress at the end of the leash.

Carla's full, painted lips split in a broad grin. "I was dancing "Giselle", of all things! Ah, the days of my youth." She noticed Lilith standing behind Giselle and her wickedly arched brows lifted as she nudged past her friend. To the shock of the first group, who were studiously not looking, she introduced herself to the maid in a voice that was almost a purr. "And who might you be, my fiery redhead?"

Lilith met the dancer's eyes and smiled. "I am Lilith Tournay, Dona, Mlle Du'Lac's maid."

Carla's eyes narrowed. "Tournay?" She glanced at Giselle. "The same Tournay?"

Giselle's face set as she gave a brief nod.

Carla leant back with a thoughtful expression, then smiled at Lilith. "You were not with your mistress at the Amazonas — I would remember seeing you!" She turned and flung an expressive hand towards the still silent group behind her, who jumped. At least one person showed a sudden desire to try and leap from the end of the air-jetty they were corralled at to avoid her all-encompassing gesture. "Well, darlings, if they won't, I will! May I present Sir Wesley Eade and his very good friend, Baroness Carlton-Cayce?" The term "very good friend" was murmured with a waggle of her eyebrows. Giselle hid a smile as Dona Carla continued. "And that is the sum of my knowledge. Sir Wesley I know for his generous patronage of the arts, and the baroness for her stupendous collection of jewels. Of the others, I know nothing!" Carla sat back down on the little bench she had previously claimed as her own and accepted her maid's deferential re-draping of the cape with grace; but her eyes never once left Lilith's face.

Sir Wesley coughed, and with the manner of a member of high society approaching the gallows, he approached the group. He extended a firm hand to both Elliott and Thorne, and with a delicate grip, waved a light kiss in the general vicinity of Giselle's right thumb. With a slightly less effusive hand gesture than Dona Carla's, he indicated the rest of the small flock. "May I present the Baroness Carlton-Cayce; my business partners, Mr Thornton Rust Esquire, Mr Colton Kayfield, and their wives; and my secretary Robin Ellis. Dona Carla Riva, I believe you already know."

The baroness graced the group with a faint smile. Hers was a Scandinavian beauty; a tall and slender white blonde with brilliant, almost painfully blue eyes set in an alabaster skin. She was framed to perfection by a floor-length confection of deep-red astrakhan, crowned by a matching hat perched archly atop her smoothly pinned hair. As Elliott and Thorne approached her, she lifted her hand languidly as the customary greetings were exchanged.

Thornton Rust blustered in his finest Canterbury Music Hall fashion as he finally introduced his "wife" Sophie, his business partner Kayfield, and *his* good lady, Josephine.

Robin Ellis, the man who had attempted to commune with the underside of the air-jetty to avoid Dona Carla's introduction, stood and gripped his attaché case at the end of the quay. He scanned the dull grey sky and called, "Sir Wesley, I believe the airship is arriving."

Sir Wesley looked up at the damp sky. "Good! I hope it's dry aboard." He addressed the others. "It's a two-day journey from here to the Sound. O.D informed me that we should arrive on Friday morning."

Further discussion was prevented by the approaching airship's horn, and the disparate group of travellers turned to watch the vessel pull into the dock.

The large, two-storied airship slowed to a graceful halt at

the end of the air-jetty, her two massive propellers slowly turning to guide the vessel into her prearranged berth. As several aethernauts leap off the craft, tied her up, and deployed the ramp, a sturdy young man in a dark blue uniform swiftly disembarked, and scanned the travellers with a practised eye before introducing himself to Sir Wesley as the airship's captain, Ralph Marcheston. He turned to the rest of the group and held up a sheaf of papers. "I have your names and your allotted cabins here. When I call your name, please step forward to take possession of your key."

The young man began reciting the names on the list, handing out cabin keys to those called. Eventually everyone present had their cabins, and led by Sir Wesley, began to encourage their maids and valets to gather up their belongings and board the vessel.

The captain paused. "I believe we are waiting for four more: two guests and two new servants."

As he spoke, a carriage pulled up at the end of the jetty and a smartly dressed couple descended and approached with their luggage. The man had short, clipped grey hair and bright green eyes that seemed to look straight through the group; the woman was dark, attractive, and very well dressed.

The captain looked at his name list. "Mr Morten Van der Linde and Mrs Carolyn Nolloth?" The man smiled and shook his head. "Mr and Mrs Vasily Ainu. We are the new butler and housekeeper." The captain looked slightly embarrassed and quickly handed them their key.

Another carriage pulled up, and a harried-looking young maid disembarked with a speed suggesting she had been ejected from the vehicle. Morten Van der Linde, sharply dressed and knowing it, stepped off the carriage and held out a hand to the person within. After a fashionable pause, a slim hand touched his and Carolyn made her first appearance before the group. Wearing a royal-blue gown under a tailored, floor-length ocelot coat, her matching blue hat was festooned with sapphire hatpins that complimented her choker. Carolyn, like Dona Carla and Lady Carlton-Cayce, was dressed for the best of first-class travel.

Elliott leant towards Giselle. "Last to arrive, and quite the entrance!" Giselle nodded. "I've heard of her. She's a society hostess in Australia: beautiful, but deeply unpleasant to those she perceives as her social inferior. Lilith knew one of her many former maids. The stories she could tell!"

The baroness eyed the approaching couple from her position on the chilly marble bench and spoke, her voice had a languid quality. "Dear Carolyn. Perhaps she should have brought her better jewels, rather than placing her hopes on larger but lesser gems!"

Elliott shot her a look and murmured, "Class trumps race, but money trumps both."

The baroness stared at him with her painfully brilliant eyes, paused for a long moment, then stood, turned her back, and gestured to her maid, who swiftly collected her possessions as Sir Wesley took her arm and they boarded the airship.

Morten offered his arm to Carolyn and the two of them walked towards the craft, the maid trailing a few deferential feet behind as they left a valet to deal with the many trunks piled atop the little carriage.

As Elliott opened his mouth to introduce himself, the couple didn't slow down, but continued towards the airship. Morten snapped his fingers at the captain. "Mrs Carolyn Nolloth and Mr Morten Van der Linde. Mrs Nolloth, as you should know, is Mr Damant's sister-in-law, and as her representative I demand that she is given the best cabin aboard this flying wreck!"

The man's attitude and the slight smirk on Carolyn's face

caused Elliott's eyebrows to lower as Thorne's eyebrows rose. He shared a look with Thorne and Giselle; it was bad enough that he had been forced to accept the offer of travel by airship, but with the terrible duo of Van der Linde and Nolloth, it could well turn out to be a very long and painful journey!

## The airship
## After dinner

The airship sailed through the darkness, heading slowly towards her ultimate destination. Captain Marcheston sat in the wheelhouse and scowled at the chart before him. He checked the airship's position before throwing the pencil down with a grumbled oath and instead thought back to the events that had occurred earlier; lunch had been an unmitigated disaster, and it had gone downhill from there. If this was how the weekend was shaping up, he was very much looking forward to handing the assorted guests over to the Taniwha's captain on Friday, and heading home to Nelson! Carolyn Nolloth had begun to complain before the vessel had even left the aetherdrome, and had continued her verbal onslaught through lunch and right up to the cocktail hour: her cabin was grotesque; it was too small; it stank; there was no room for her wardrobe to be fully unpacked. Her list of complaints was endless.

Captain Marcheston had explained very politely that there were no other cabins to be offered as alternative accommodation. At that point Mrs Nolloth had revealed an almost operatic talent for screaming her demands at the top of her voice, possibly believing that a louder request would be met. It was not.

Then Morten Van der Linde had duly arrived (as prearranged), he insisted that Mrs Nolloth's demands be satisfied, and accused the captain of being less than a gentleman in his refusal to accommodate the simple requests of a lady guest. As the flustered young man apologised again and insisted that there were no available cabins, Morten made a show of removing his gloves. As his open hand swung sharply back, Morten felt a sudden pressure around his wrist as Elliott, who had been sitting quietly by the window with Thorne and Giselle moments before, suddenly crossed the room and grasped his wrist before the blow had a chance to land.

Morten stared at Elliott in shock as he realised his planned attempt to dominate the captain had failed. He twisted in Elliott's vice-like grip, but failed to gain release. "Let me go! How dare you lay your hands on me, you…you unclean oaf! Unhand me! Eikel!" Elliott tightened his grip and leaned in so that only the angry Dutchman could hear. "This vessel has been generously laid on by our host, and the cabins are more than adequate for a two-day journey. I suggest you escort the lady back to her room to rest." He released the man's wrist and walked back to his table where, without a backward glance, he continued the conversation he and Giselle had been having with Thorne about Veronique's penchant for stealing slippers, and the damp and chewed state of said items upon their return.

Morten rubbed his wrist and cast an eye around the room. Sir Wesley and the baroness appeared engrossed in a game of piquet; Sir Wesley's business partners and their wives were equally engrossed in their game of bridge and were also politely ignoring the set-to. Dona Carla Riva, however, was watching with bright eyes as she sipped her second cocktail.

Carolyn looked at Morten and her perfectly painted

DEATH IN THE SOUND

scarlet mouth snapped shut as she realised that her highly vocal theatrics were not achieving the expected results, and her demands would not be met. Turning, she stormed in a fragrant manner towards the door and with a dismissive sniff, left the room. Some minutes later her maid entered, an angry red mark clearly visible on her left cheek, and quietly informed the young captain that her mistress would be taking every meal in her cabin.

Captain Marcheston studied the face of the young woman: a quiet, unassuming girl barely in her twenties, her gaze directed at the floor. He confirmed the request would be carried out, starting with dinner that evening.

The maid nodded, and as she turned away her eyes met his. Captain Marcheston felt a strange sensation in his stomach; her eyes were so pale a grey they were almost white. A delicate flush touched her cheeks, almost covering the welt her mistress had dealt her. She glanced back at him as she left, a tentative smile on her lips.

He turned back to the room, mildly stunned, and saw Dona Carla watching him with a grin. To his shock, she winked at him.

Trying to stop his jaw from hitting the floor, he turned and with a carefully constructed blank face headed back to the wheelhouse. There he was guaranteed peace and quiet, a large whisky, the passenger lists to discover the maid's name, and time to consider just what had happened to him...and what he could do about it!

## Friday 23rd March
### 06:00am
### Milford City

Coll wiped his hands, stacked the clean plates in the dresser, picked up his steaming cup of black coffee, and left his private rooms for the open front door. Pausing on the threshold, he breathed deeply and drank in the view that had been his for over thirty years. The clear morning sun was on his right as he gazed down the brightly lit Sound. The vibrant colours of the punga ferns, his wife's carefully tended roses, and the brilliant blue of the water combined to create an illusion that the world was clean and new, freshly created that morning purely for his delectation.

Coll heaved a happy sigh and headed back into the hotel to deal with the daily business. One of O.D's guests had unexpectedly arrived under their own steam on Wednesday, and asked for a room. Coll smiled. Many of the new, modern women reckoned they had gumption, but this one actually did. Walking the Milford Track in a mixed group, with no maid, and guiding her own horse. Coll's smile widened and he chuckled, it was nothing his own Rose hadn't already done decades earlier when she travelled alone to New Zealand from her old home in England, but it was the done thing these days to act shocked and outraged about such forward behaviour.

After the initial surprise of an unchaperoned woman's arrival on their doorstep, Coll had checked her credentials with O.D over the new-fangled telegraph he'd had installed a few months earlier. O.D had confirmed her invitation and invited her to the boat early, but she had politely declined, stating that she needed to rest before the weekend to ensure her abilities were suitably refreshed. Rose had escorted her to her room in the female-only section of the hotel. Access was through a small door that led off Coll and Rose's private rooms, to ensure their lady guests were guaranteed peace and safety. Coll took a deep gulp of his coffee and considered their guest. She was an unusual woman: beautiful in a handsome way, with black hair, strong features and strange, slightly tilted violet eyes set in almost translucent skin, with an expression on her mobile face that Coll knew his old mother back in Berwick would have described as "fey".

He knew who she was, of course – how could he not? Her fame in the Southern Hemisphere was legend. She was the psychic whom O.D had hired, no expense spared, for his daughter's birthday weekend. The Flatworld Witch herself; Madame Aquilleia Aquileisi.

# Milford Sound

**PART**
**II**

### The same Day
### 12:25pm
### Aboard the Taniwha

Captain Marcus Peach watched from his wheelhouse as the airship carrying O.D's guests slowly lowered herself into the still waters of the Sound and moored at the jetty.

American, in his late thirties, and with a smooth grace that was almost feline, Captain Peach made his way down to the main deck. He paused to flash a quick smile at his daughter Fleur, who was sitting with Merry on the starboard sundeck, suffering the daily joy of needlecraft and history with Mar.

Fleur rolled her eyes good-naturedly at her father and continued to try and understand the difference between a running stitch and a herringbone, and Prussia and the French issue, while also attempting and failing to prevent Merry's new puppy, Manaia, from chewing her pencil.

Captain Peach continued down another flight of stairs and stood at the main entrance of the Taniwha to await the shuttle that would ferry the guests, their collections of various physical and emotional baggage, and their slightly stressed servants from the jetty to the Taniwha.

The Taniwha was the ultimate paddle steamer. She had

been designed in America, to the absolute requirements of the man who was paying, and then shipped to New Zealand piecemeal for building: gleaming white woodwork offset by dark-stained decks, orange silk drapes radiant between the open wrought-iron arches and balustrades, ornate open staircases enabling access to all three floors, and a top deck with the wheelhouse to the fore and a part-covered observation platform with potted plants aft.

Standing by the low brass gateway on the starboard side of the vessel, Captain Peach watched the approach of the laden shuttle. Casting a glance at his pocket-watch, he permitted himself a slight smile. Even Mrs Nolloth couldn't complain: 12:30pm to the minute!

Captain Marcheston had sent O.D a telegram from his vessel detailing the demands of Carolyn Nolloth and her execrable associate, Morten Van der Linde. If Mrs Nolloth thought she would get away with such behaviour aboard the Taniwha, she would be rapidly stripped of that belief. O.D had read the telegram in his private rooms and cursed his former sister-in-law in at least three different languages, before issuing his captain with an edict to throw said lady and her questionable companion overboard at the deepest point of the Sound if either of them attempted to cause trouble.

Captain Peach had also been privy to the conversation between O.D and his nephew Darius. Darius Damant also lived aboard the Taniwha; employed as he was in his uncle's Southern Hemisphere mining concerns. It was easier for him to deal with his uncle's most pressing business matters from aboard the Taniwha, working both as a trusted family member and a most capable manager. Darius had been horrified and embarrassed but not altogether surprised by his mother's behaviour. He hadn't seen her for several years, and was quite voluble about preferring to keep it that way, but he understood that meeting and mixing with her that weekend was unavoidable as her invitation had come from Merry, who wanted to see her aunt in hopes of bringing about a reconciliation. Darius had managed not to laugh in Merry's face; his cousin meant well, but she was quite naïve…the bridges she hoped to rebuild had been razed out of existence many years ago! The presence of Morten Van der Linde was also something neither he nor his uncle were happy about, but O.D would have to deal with that particular abuse of his hospitality.

The small shuttle approached and pirouetted into position. The young mate threw the line and the captain of the Taniwha tied the vessel to a solid cleat then undid the latch of the gate and secured it. The two vessels steadied and the shuttle's mate carefully slid the gangplank across the narrow gap.

As the guests gathered on the deck, Captain Peach allowed himself a few moments of quiet observation. His parents had always told him not to judge a book by its cover, but several years of dealing with the shenanigans of passengers had taught him that first impressions were usually correct.

A young woman with fiery red hair who was the focal point of attention for an impeccably dressed dark young man with a walking stick; a tall blond man in a somewhat loud travel suit, who was fighting an obstreperous black Labrador; a vibrant woman swaddled in a sumptuous fur cape whose laughter carried across the Sound, and an upright, smartly dressed man in late middle-age who was so much the epitome of the English country gent that Captain Peach immediately marked him down as Sir Wesley Eade without further thought. This tastefully understated gentleman was escorting a woman of unusual, pale beauty; even at that distance her glamour was palpable; two terribly correct, upper-middle-class couples who seemed out of their depth in that company; and, finally, a sulky-looking, well-dressed woman whom the captain took to be Carolyn Nolloth…which meant that the overdressed, sharp-looking man next to her simply had to be Morten Van der Linde. In the face of the joie de vivre that emanated from some of the other guests, their forced brilliance was glaring in its very dullness, and he suspected they felt it too.

Noting the collection of maids, valets, and general luggage lumpers, he found himself hoping they had enough cabins to go around. Several of the cabins were suites with servant accommodation built in, and there were a few spare servants' beds down on the main deck, but all the suites and guest cabins were full to capacity.

Scanning the sheet of paper he'd had the foresight to bring with him, he checked the list against the people milling on deck and breathed a silent sigh of relief. It appeared that the numbers were correct, even counting the lady guest who had been staying in Milford City, and who had come aboard earlier that morning. There should be no issues regarding guest accommodation – unless Mrs Nolloth tried to create one! He flipped the list over; the two names on the back were new employees, a butler and housekeeper. He scanned the large group again as the guests began to gather around the little walkway. He caught the eye of one of the men, rather commanding with grey hair and green eyes. The man nodded at him and taking his rather ravishing lady by the elbow, guided her across the gangplank towards the captain. Holding out his hand, he intoned, "Vasily and Desdemonia Ainu: we are the new butler and housekeeper."

Marcus shook the proffered hand, wincing at the knuckle-cracking firmness of the other man's grip. "Captain Marcus Peach. Welcome aboard. Your cabin is the first on the port side of the main deck: your name plaque is on the door and your keys and a plan of the vessel are within. Mr Damant has also left instructions for the weekend in your room." The man nodded his thanks, and the couple headed for their cabin.

The steward Trevenniss, and his second appeared on the deck and caught the captain's eye. Marcus inclined his head in response and turned back to the gathering throng as Morten Van der Linde pushed through the crowd and boarded the boat, a mocking smirk on his face as he tutted at the captain and wagged his finger. "What on earth do you think you are doing? It is always guests before servants! Rest assured, Captain, I shall report you to your employer for your disregard of the social niceties!" He smoothed his heavily oiled hair. "Mrs Carolyn Nolloth is, as even you must be aware, Mr Damant's sister-in-law, and I must insist that—"

"You must be Mr Van der Linde," said Marcus, with a polite but distant smile. "Mr Damant has informed me about you…sir." Ignoring the indrawn breath and deathly silence that issued from the man, he raised his voice and addressed the company. "Ladies and gentlemen, if I may have your attention! Welcome aboard the Taniwha. I am Captain Marcus Peach and these are your stewards, Trevenniss and Callahan; during your stay they will see to your needs. If you will please come aboard, we shall settle you into your cabins, set sail, and then the weekend's festivities will begin." He bowed from the waist, stepped back from the gate and swept his hand towards the open staircase that led from the main deck to the private suites and cabins one deck up.

The two stewards, who were also carrying copies of the same passenger list, were joined by a number of neat, tidy, and highly efficient maids, all armed with a polite manner and an ability to smooth even the most ruffled guest.

As the myriad guests swarmed aboard, they were organised and ushered towards their individual cabins with minimum fuss — all except Carolyn, of course, who had already started in on the strange smell aboard the beautiful and very new vessel. Her strident objections faded into the distance as she and Morten Van der Linde were ushered up the stairs to their respective cabins.

Marcus breathed an unprofessional sigh of relief that ended in a cough as he realised that a handful of guests were still standing behind him. As he turned towards them, he heard a voice calling from the head of the steps. He turned back and saw Darius Damant heading down the stairs at speed. "Captain, now that all the guests have arrived, my uncle has given the order to set off as soon as possible."

"Yes, Mr Damant, but there are still these guests—"

Darius held up his hand. "I'll see to them."

"Yes, sir."

As the captain headed back up the stairs towards the wheelhouse, Darius gazed at the four people left on the deck. A vibrant redheaded woman and an equally red-haired and smart-looking maid were standing next to a tall blond man struggling with a Labrador who seemed to realise that lunch would not be happening just yet and so had decided to attempt a surreptitious chew at the corner of one of the large trunks beside her owner. At the front of this small group was a dark-haired young man who suddenly stepped forward. His dark-brown eyes crinkled at the corners as he smiled, his oddly long canines flashing in the sunlight.

Darius smiled back. "Please excuse my staring. I am Darius Damant; O.D is my uncle. You must be the Magnificent Bowyers. My cousin is so looking forward to your act."

Elliott took in the young man's appearance: of medium height, with dark hair and a smiling, engaged face. Luckily, he seemed very little like his mother! "How do you do, Mr Damant. Forgive me for leaping straight in, but if I were to say to you that nowadays, people know the price of everything…"

Darius's eyes widened and an expression of understanding crossed his face. "I would respond: and the value of nothing." His smile broadened. "Mr Caine, I presume! An absolute pleasure. My uncle is waiting for you in his office; I have orders to take you to him on arrival."

He turned to look at Giselle, Thorne, and Lilith, and Elliott followed his gaze. "For the duration of this weekend we will be known by our…working names, you understand. Allow me to formally introduce us all. I am Elliott Caine, but for the duration of our time with you my name will be Preston Bowyer. This is my good friend Abernathy Thorne, who will be my brother Lydeard. As you so rightly understood, we are the Magnificent Bowyers. This is my wife, the truly magnificent Giselle Du'Lac, and her maid Lilith Tournay."

Darius nodded, feeling suddenly out of his depth as he shook Elliott's proffered hand, then Thorne's, and bowed over Giselle's. He noticed Elliott gripped the middle of a red Malacca cane with a peculiar handle, the design was that of a snake eating its own tail. Then he frowned as he realised what had been said. "Wife? That information wasn't passed to us, Mr Cai — I'm sorry, Mr Bowyer!"

Elliott held up his hands and the red cane flashed as he smiled. "The fault lies entirely with us, I'm afraid! The opportunity to marry presented itself, and we obliged." He leaned towards Darius and murmured, "I trust it won't upset the balance of the cabins? As I understand it, the suite allocated to my wife has more than enough room for a spouse and comes with its own maid's accommodation, so Thorne will therefore be on his own in the room I was to share with him. All quite acceptable, hmm? Oh, and a few little things; my wife has decided to keep her professional title, so is still addressed as Mlle Du'Lac. The luggage bound in blue contains personal effects for our cabins, but the larger trunks bound in red are for our various acts; I'm not quite sure where you would prefer them to go."

Darius collected himself. "That should be fine…Mr Bowyer. If you will follow me, I'll show you to your cabins and then take you up to Uncle's suite." He turned and gestured at the large trunks that the lads from the shuttle were struggling with. "Please take the blue trunks to the cabins and the red trunks to the lower storage room. Mlle Du'Lac, Mr Bowyer, Mr Bowyer and Labrador!"

Thorne grinned. "Veronique!"

Darius smiled in return. "Veronique. I hope she gets on well with Merry's new puppy! If you'll follow me?"

The small group headed up the stairs and walked past a number of cabins before Darius stopped and opened one of the doors. "This is Mr Lydeard Bowyer's room. Your key is on the dressing table, and your luggage will be brought up shortly."

Thorne nodded and ducked into the room. As he closed the door and let go of the lead, Veronique immediately leapt upon one of the plush single beds and knocked the feather-stuffed pillows about until she was quite comfortable. She closed her eyes for her usual afternoon nap as Thorne opened his battered leather case and settled on the other bed. He had time for a few moments with a penny dreadful before he would be called for their meeting with O.D. He leant back on the well-fluffed white pillows and froze as a strange feeling came over him: almost a vibration in his stomach. He pressed a hand to his middle, then shook his head…probably lack of food: lunch shouldn't be that far off. He picked up the next four sheets of the story and reacquainted himself with the lady in peril, the evil godfather, and the poverty-stricken but dashing swain who had just discovered his family's financial ruin had been deliberately orchestrated by…his fair lady's wicked godfather, the cad! He couldn't wait to read part sixteen!

As Thorne was perusing high literature in his cabin, Elliott, Giselle, and Lilith were shown the suite of rooms that were to be their accommodation for the weekend. Sizeable, with a private bathroom and a small separate bedroom for Lilith, the suite had been well designed, with plenty of storage and large windows either side of the door.

Darius hovered in the doorway. "I trust everything is acceptable?"

Giselle entered the bathroom, looked at the full-sized bath, and beamed. "It's perfect!"

Elliott smiled; he knew what his wife was like when it came to her ablutions!

There was a knock on the open door and several young men walked in carrying various items of luggage.

Darius turned to look at Elliott. "Perhaps you would like a little time to freshen up before meeting my uncle. If I return in, say, thirty minutes, would that be suitable?"

Elliott looked at Giselle, who nodded. "That would be lovely."

"Very well." He waited until the porters had finished bringing in the luggage and left the bright room, quietly closing the door behind them.

Elliott smiled at his wife. "Thirty minutes…I don't think you can manage a bath in that time!"

Giselle laughed. "Not a soak, perhaps, but definitely a light refreshing. Lilith, my robes, please."

Lilith had already begun to open her mistress's trunks and put away various items of clothing. She immediately lifted Giselle's lavender silk peignoir from its resting place on the bed and started to draw a hot bath. Opening several of the ornate bottles beside the bath, she gave each a dismissive sniff before settling on one plucked from Giselle's own luggage.

The gentle but pervasive scent of attar of roses filled the cabin as Giselle sank into her bath with a happy sigh; Lilith laid out several fluffy towels and her mistresses' robe before returning to the unpacking. Elliott reached into his Gladstone bag, removed a small, green jade box and opened it; the unusual locking mechanism that guarded its contents was based around a spindle, so the lid of the ornate box was simply pulled gently and turned to reveal its secret; an exquisitely carved bust of both Versipellis and Angellis. The carving had been a wedding gift from his father. After the loss of his wife, he had kept her wedding ring within the precious gift, waiting for the day he could finally return it to her. Elliott gently ran his fingertips across the carving of his wife's face before placing it on the bedside table. Turning, he sank into one of the armchairs. His mind relaxed as he breathed the soft scent his wife always used, and he drifted into a light sleep.

Alone in the sumptuous bathroom, Giselle lay back in the scented water. Closing her eyes, she allowed her mind to return to the journey they had undertaken to Astraea, to finally retrieve her memories.

### The journey to Astraea

After the events at Marmis Hall and Sir Hubert's London house, Elliott and Giselle had initially returned to their own separate homes in London; but now they had finally found each other, their desire to stay together proved too strong to ignore. Within a month they were married, which raised some eyebrows amongst those unaware of their shared history – which meant everyone in the Greater London area!

Shortly after their wedding, their first Christmas as husband and wife loomed. They threw themselves into purchasing gifts while creating a shared home together; Elliott had given up his accommodation with Thorne and Veronique, and Giselle had given up her apartments in Piccadilly, to share a suitably large villa in Richmond.

Thorne had continued to stay at the rooms he had shared with Elliott, and enjoyed pretending mild grief to his land-lady at the loss of his housemate. However, both he and Veronique were rather pleased at the extra room. Veronique in particular was very happy, having decided that Elliott's old room was now hers, leaving Thorne to stay in his smaller bedroom whilst his spoilt Labrador revelled in the cosiness of a double bed with a silky eiderdown topper.

Elliott and Giselle had settled into their new life together with aplomb. As Christmas approached, Giselle's presence in particular was in great demand in high society, the social whirl of charity balls, Christmas parties, and recitals filling their time in the weeks before Christmas Day. Elliott had decided to take a step back from his work, to spend more time with the woman he had finally found after so many years of desperate searching. He was content to simply be with her now, understanding her as Giselle, the woman she was, not only as the wife he had lost so many years before.

Although Elliott was prepared to face their future together without reference to their shared past, Giselle still brooded that though she was happy, she lacked the memories of her previous existence as Angellis: memories she had shared with Elliott, and which she knew would help her understand more about herself, her abilities, her husband, Thorne, and what they had discovered in the cellar at Sir Hubert Kingston-Folly's London house.

A few days after Christmas, she had raised the subject with Elliott. He had been concerned about informing her of their past and how she had been taken from him, for fear of forcing her into a decision. However, as she would not stop asking, he had explained that her memories could be returned, but only at a particular place, and that because of the nature of her history and what had actually happened to her, it would cause her great pain…physically and emotionally, this last fact was the reason none of her previous incarnations had been prepared to undertake the journey to Astraea with him.

Giselle had spent several long days considering this, and finally decided that regardless of Elliott's concerns, she wanted to regain her memories of who she truly was. So, on a sunny day in early January, Elliott, Giselle, Thorne, Veronique, and Lilith travelled from London to Somerset.

After several hours' journey by train, which had not induced a good mood in the sulky, and slightly queasy Labrador, they finally arrived at the town of Wiveliscombe. There, they bought some provisions, hired four horses, and made their way north. Trotting through several small settlements, they finally arrived at the small hamlet of Kettlemead, which consisted of one inn, two small farms, and a tumble-down thatched cottage. To the left of the cottage, an overgrown path led away from the hamlet and into Thornedyke woods. They followed the path into the woods. It was more a forest than a wood, massed with oaks, beech, and by the narrow little stream, thickets of willow.

Even in the bare month of January, the heavy foliage of holly, ivy, and other evergreens made the forested area appear lush. The watery winter sun shone through the leaves and added a dappled deep green light to their journey as they followed the path alongside the small stream, which in turn, led them to a river. After nearly an hour of following the larger watercourse, a faint roaring sound could be heard. As they made their way around a bend in the path, the river opened up before them and fell in a sudden, straight drop to a lake nearly one hundred feet below: a hamlet, a river, a waterfall, and a lake that were not on any map.

Elliott and Thorne dismounted. While Giselle and Lilith stayed on their horses and Veronique snuffled in the damp undergrowth, the two men led their horses along the river-bank towards the drop. Some fifty feet from the edge, Elliott nodded at Thorne, who walked over to Lilith's horse. "You can go no further, Lilith. We will set up camp and wait; they shouldn't be too long." He turned and gave Elliott a hard stare. "Will you?"

Elliott smiled. "He will take as long as he needs to take, my friend. You know what he's like…and he doesn't get much company these days. We'll be back." He turned to Giselle. "You must lead your horse, Giselle; your feet need to be in the water."

Giselle slid off her horse and held the reins as Elliott covered their horses' eyes. They carefully led the animals into the river and made their way to the water's edge, the noise from the waterfall thundering below them.

She turned to Elliott, a look of trepidation on her face. "What now?"

Elliott smiled gently, his canines flashing in the early afternoon light. "Many things are about to become clear. Do you trust me, my love?"

Giselle smiled back; her blue eyes steady. "Yes."

"Then hold the reins tightly, take my hand, and follow me."

She gripped his hand, and as she did so, Elliott turned to face the waterfall. He tilted his head upright and with a firm foot, stepped over the edge, taking Giselle and the horses with him.

Lilith screamed and ran to the falls as Thorne tried to grab her. She stood in silent shock as she saw her mistress, Elliott, and the two horses walking at a ninety-degree angle down the face of the waterfall. As she and Thorne watched, the foamy base of the falls parted to reveal a long, dark tunnel beyond. Giselle and Elliott led their horses into the tunnel as the water slowly drew over them like a curtain, and the falls returned to their natural state.

Speechless, Lilith turned to Thorne who was stroking Veronique's ears; Lilith's sudden scream had caught the dog unawares and she had run back to her master to grump at the young maid. Thorne gave Lilith a tentative smile. "We did say we were a little odd!"

Lilith shook her head firmly and wagged her finger at him. "What the two of you said to my mistress I took for — how do you say — jokes, yes? The trying of a man to impress a woman! I did not believe — how could I possibly…pfft! I need a drink!"

With a flounce the young Frenchwoman headed back to their horses, muttering under her breath in French, followed by a slightly concerned Thorne and a rather peckish Veronique, who had decided her stomach was entirely over the unfortunate incident on the train and she could now manage a little light lunch.

Several hundred feet below them, Giselle and Elliott were walking through the watery tunnel under the surface of the lake. Elliott watched Giselle's expression flicker from fear to curiosity and finally to excitement as they led their skittish animals through the strangely blue light, towards what appeared to be a huge silvery mirror that filled the entire tunnel.

Elliott turned to Giselle. His face was pale, and faint specks of green light appeared in his brown eyes. "You know why we have come here; once we present ourselves to him, there is no turning back." He gently touched her face. "Giselle, there are some things I haven't told you about your past…our past. You will need to see those things to understand them, and it will be painful." He blinked rapidly and cleared his throat. "The thought of seeing you in pain again makes me feel ill. But I understand that this must be your decision. What I am asking is, are you still sure?"

Giselle reached up and caught his hand. "I understand, and I am sure. I need to know who I am, and who you are. I love you too, Elliott; I'm not going anywhere." She kissed his hand and gestured at the shimmering portal before them. "The question I would really like you to answer right now is how we get through." Elliott smiled faintly. Walking towards the barrier, he reached out and gently stroked the surface of the glistening doorway. The smooth sheet of water slowly parted, revealing a mirror image of the entrance behind them, complete with a frothing waterfall that this time, led up.

Giselle looked, and took a deep breath; there was no going back now!

As she stepped through, she became aware of a subtle difference in the feeling of the land beyond the waterfall, compared to the place they had just left. A feeling of deep peace enveloped her as she and Elliott walked up the water-fall and into the river at the top of the cliff.

Here, they paused. As she turned to look at the view, Giselle gasped. Beyond the falls, was a forest of lavender and teal trees that stretched away into the distance, interspersed with lakes and waterfalls in shades of blue, green and violet. Looking down, she realised that the lake they had just walked from was itself a brilliant turquoise that glowed in the golden sunlight.

Elliott smiled and nodded towards the lake they had just

passed through. "That is our portal. All the lakes here are doorways; each couple has a different one."

Giselle looked at him, a questioning expression on her face. "There are others like us?"

Elliott squeezed her hand. "Oh yes, quite a few! It's still an hour or so travel from here, and you might see things that are a little...unexpected, shall we say? Don't worry, nothing can hurt us here."

Giselle and Elliott removed the covers from their horses' eyes, remounted, and set off at a gentle walk down the verdant green meadow, which led to a little pathway beside a babbling, lavender coloured stream.

Giselle's mouth dropped open as a small glowing creature no bigger than her thumb floated in front of her. "Elliott!"

He turned to see, and smiled. "It's all right, they're perfectly safe."

Giselle pointed at the creature and stared hard at her husband. "It's a faery!"

Elliott shook his head. "Not quite. They get out sometimes and enjoy themselves a little too much; that's where most of the legends come from." He looked at her, a faint expression of worry appeared on his face. "It's not too far now."

Giselle dragged her eyes away from the tiny chortling creature and settled back into her saddle. Things had definitely taken an interesting turn. A sudden guilty thought caught hold of her as she wondered how her maid was coping with the shock of the last few hours. Lilith was a strong woman, but some things could be too much to bear! Chewing her lip, she cast a look at Elliott. She knew him, she had always known him. and very soon, all her memories from her life as Angellis would be returned to her...

The path suddenly opened into a meadow that reminded her of estate parkland. Giselle saw English oak and weeping willow growing on the banks of the stream that meandered towards a large outcrop of pale pink rock. In front of this impressive natural feature sat a building of butter-coloured stone surrounded by a rampant rose garden.

As they approached the building, Giselle realised the alien nature of the architecture; she had never seen that style of structure before. It was a blend of English and Moorish, Aztec and Egyptian and many others between, the different styles blended to yield a beautiful, perfect building set across many levels, with balconies, open stairs, and partial courtyards.

As Elliott swung himself down from his horse and assisted Giselle from hers, a tall, bearded man with jet-black hair and warm brown eyes stepped out of an open doorway and approached them. As he came closer, Giselle's first thought was that he looked somewhat melancholy. Then he smiled, and his face showed an inner light that made her realise she was in the presence of an "Other" just like Elliott and Thorne — and very soon, just like her.

The man spoke, his voice rich and warm. "Versipellis! Welcome home. I take it you had a good trip?"

Elliott nodded as the two men clasped hands. "Yes, thank you, Abditivus." He turned to Giselle. "May I present Mlle Giselle Du'Lac, also known as Penelope Lake and—"

Abditivus took her hand with a gentle, welcoming smile. "Angellis, of course." His smile deepened. "You are most welcome. There is nothing for you to fear here; we are safe in this place. It is our own private little universe, and sadly, all that is left of our homeland…although that may change with time, and the more of our people we find and bring home." He glanced at Elliott. "You must be famished after your journey. I have prepared a meal for us." His brown eyes sharpened as he looked back at Giselle. "It's never a good idea to endure a recollection on an empty stomach. Follow me."

Giselle's stomach was definitely telling her otherwise as they entered the dwelling. They were politely guided towards the bathrooms before being urged into the dining room, where a large wooden dining table sat by an open window whose views showed the stunning gardens leading towards the pink stone hill at the back of the beautiful house.

Giselle's attention fell to the table as Abditivus showed her to her seat, then nodded to Elliott. "Please feel free to start. I have a bottle of champagne chilling. I shall return."

As he left the room, Giselle turned to Elliott and whispered in a slightly panicked tone. "Elliott, tell me again… what happens next?"

Elliott placed his hand over hers. "First, we eat. Abditivus is right: you can't face a recollection without food. Your body needs something to ground you here, to let it know you need to come back."

Giselle held up a hand, her eyes questioning. "I know I chose to face this, Elliott. I know you haven't told me everything about what happened the day we were separated, and I understand why: you want me to see what happened with my own eyes, not yours. I also understand there will be pain, but Abditivus just used the word "endure". What exactly does he mean?"

Elliott knelt beside her and took her hand. "When you decided that you wanted to recall your memories, I sent word to Abditivus asking what I should tell you about the recollection and the day we were parted. He said that I should tell you as little as possible about both. For you to be able to understand what happened, you have to face this day without any instructions."

Elliott's eyes flicked to the door; Abditivus still hadn't returned. "Usually in a recollection there is no physical pain, but remembering pain caused by others can be unpleasant. You will remember how and why we were separated." He took a deep breath and continued. "Several people died the same day as you, Giselle, due to the actions of someone who was with us at Marmis Hall. That person ultimately killed Sir Hubert and took his place. You chose to face this recollection, Giselle, but you didn't have all the information…" Elliott paused, his face pale. "Physical pain can be extreme…but emotional pain can be overwhelming. It was for me the day you were taken, and I have spent over a thousand years trying to find you. Sometimes I was too late, and you had passed on to a new life. On two occasions your incarnation refused to face the pain of the recollection. On the last occasion I found you, you were married to Lord Marmis and you wouldn't leave him, even though you recognised me. Then, nearly one hundred and fifty years later you reappeared there, and I finally found you." He grasped her hands and kissed them, tears coursing down his cheeks. "And this time, I will never let you go."

Giselle smiled through her own tears and flung her arms around Elliott's neck as Abditivus re-entered the room clutching a bottle of champagne. In a slightly embarrassed tone, he inquired, "Er, shall I leave?"

Elliott wiped his face and smiled. "No, Abditivus, that won't be necessary."

Giselle blotted her eyes with a napkin, then smiled tremulously at Abditivus as he poured a generous helping of wine into her coupe. She lifted her glass to her husband. "To us, and to memories…soon to be remembered."

Elliott and Abditivus raised their coupes in response, and Giselle took a sip of her drink: that was actually rather fine! She drained the glass and placed it on the table.

Elliott sat back in his chair, then pointed at one of the loaded plates. "Is that a lobster?"

Abditivus grinned. "I was wondering when you would

spot that. Yes, it is; I remembered they were your favourite many years ago!"

"They still are! Thorne isn't going to speak to me when he hears about this!"

Abditivus topped up Giselle's glass as Elliott cracked open the shellfish and placed some of the pale-pink meat on Giselle's plate. As she stared at the plate and wondered if she could function on a stomach full of alcohol but no food, Abditivus placed her refreshed coupe in front of her. "You must eat something, or the ritual cannot take place. Now, eat a little and drink a little. You will survive this, Angellis, and return to who you were born to be, with eternal life in both this world and all the others." He turned to Elliott. "Where did you leave Shadavarian?"

Giselle looked bemused as Elliott hurriedly finished his mouthful of lobster. "He is with Giselle's maid, Lilith, on the other side of the waterfall; they should be fine there."

Abditivus nodded. "He has yet to find his Other?"

Elliott's face darkened. "Yes. But we will continue our search. Finding Angellis has given him hope of finding Aquilleia."

"Good." Abditivus turned his gaze on Giselle, who was tentatively chewing on a slice of bread and butter. "I think it is time."

Giselle's face paled, but she nodded, swallowed the last few crumbs of her bread, and took a healthy gulp of champagne as she stood up and smoothed her green tweed travelling dress. "I'm ready, I think!"

Elliott gently kissed her hand, his face as pale as hers. "I will be here." He turned to Abditivus. "Take care of her, please."

Abditivus nodded with a gentle expression. "As though she were my own." His face twisted slightly as he offered Giselle his arm. The two of them left the bright, sunny room through the open doors and headed through the garden towards the pink rock.

Elliott sat back down, his eyes blank to the spread before him as his mind travelled back to the day many years before when he and Angellis had been forced apart, along with so many others — and all because of one man!

Abditivus guided Giselle towards a small wooden door at the base of the outcrop. Symbols were carved on the door: symbols she recognised from Elliott's cane and the wooden chest they had found at Sir Hubert Kingston-Folly's house in London all those months ago, the ouroboros: the symbol of eternity.

Abditivus opened the door and led her down a narrow corridor that stretched for many yards into the pink stone, and that ended at a narrow door at the far end. Abditivus turned to her. "I cannot promise that there will not be pain; our feelings can be our most brutal torturers. But I can promise you that if you see this through, Giselle, all the glorious memories of your life with Versipellis and the others of Astraea will be returned to you. Now, I ask you this: do you choose to enter this door of your own free will?"

Giselle took a deep breath and felt her heart thumping. "I do!"

He nodded, and pushed the door open. Giselle paused on the threshold and gasped; the cavern beyond was vast. Hundreds of feet wide and at least one hundred feet high, it was lit with a pink glow that emanated from the very walls. As she gazed at the incredible chamber, Giselle realised that the outcrop was solid rose quartz, the golden sunlight outside transforming the crystal into a blazing pink beacon. Steps led from the door to a raised dais that bore a carved, high backed stone chair and an ornate plinth that held the cracked and broken remains of a large crystal.

Abditivus led her to the dais and gestured at the seat with

a gentle smile. Giselle settled herself on the chair; as she placed her hands on the arms, she saw the faint tracings of ouroboros carved into the stone.

Giselle tried to relax and looked at Abditivus, who smiled encouragingly at her. She realised that his face was not that much older that Elliott's. "You lost your Other, too?" His smile wavered and he looked down at his feet; when he looked up, the melancholy she had noticed earlier had returned.

Giselle caught her breath. "I am so sorry!"

A sad smile touched his lips. "My golden lady and I were separated from each other at the same time so many others were forced from theirs. They were evil times. You will see why, and—" He stopped and shook his head. "But I shall say no more! You will see the truth, and perhaps you will be able to help those of us who are yet to find our Others. There is one more thing; when you arrive, your memories will be those of Giselle. It will take a while to regain Angellis' memories, so take your time and do not rush. You will make yourself ill if you force them to return too quickly." He gently brushed her hair back from her face. "When it begins…and you will know when it begins, you must look into my eyes." He turned and walked to the foot of the dais. Facing her, he held his arms at his sides, elbows bent, palms up, and began to hum gently. The lustre in the chamber walls pulsed and slowly began to move through the stone, the soft light entering the cavern and flooding the massive space with waves of pink and gold.

As the notes changed in tone, Giselle felt the compulsion and gazed into his eyes, the brown now mixed with a golden, spinning light. She felt the room begin to move; the blood pounded in her head as she heard voices calling her name from far away. Air shuddered in her lungs as she tried to breathe, and then…nothing.

With a sudden gasp she sat up in the bed. The light filtering through the heavy cream curtains was the watery light of early morning, not afternoon, as it had been at Abditivus' house.

She realised she was not alone, and turned to look at the figure lying next to her. Elliott, he looked…a little younger. As she sat, trying to deal with the impact of regression and the discovery of her very naked husband in her bed, someone knocked on the door. She gasped and pulled the covers up to her eyes as a sleepy voice next to her called out. "Go away, Shad! I told you, no interruptions!"

There was a pause, then a familiar but slightly embarrassed voice called through the woodwork. "Pel, you know I wouldn't interrupt you for the world, but there is a bit of an issue that needs your personal attention."

The body next to her groaned, flipped the top of the covers down and glared at the door. "Why? What is so difficult that the High Elders couldn't—"

"It's Phoenixus, Pel. He has attacked another couple…and this time he has killed them both!"

Versipellis flung back the blankets and leapt from the bed. Giselle tried — but not too hard — to ignore her naked, muscular husband as he flung items of clothing at himself.

Giselle pushed back the covers just a little and looked at him. "What is happening?"

Versipellis looked at her, then sitting on the edge of the bed, he kissed her. "Good morning my beautiful wife. It is Phoenixus, he has attacked again." He paused and gently stroked her face. "Please listen to me, Angellis. Whatever happens, it is not your fault. You made your choice, and my brother made his! You stay here; Phoenixus is many things, but I doubt he'd be foolish enough to attack you while Aquilleia is in the house." He dragged a hand through his unruly mop of dark hair. "I know it's not quite the proper start to our married life, my love, but I shall be home as soon as I can. I love you."

Giselle smiled. "I love you too. Please be careful!"

"I shall, my love." He swung the door open; on the doorstep, a little younger but still favouring clashing colours, was Thorne. Standing next to him was a leggy, jet-black dog. "Ready, Shad?"

Shadavarian nodded, shouldering an unpleasant-looking edged weapon as Versipellis pulled the door shut with a gentle smile.

Giselle sat in bed, her mind spinning. It had worked…she had regressed to the time when she was Angellis, but inside she was still Giselle. She thought about what she had already learned; she and Versipellis were married, his friends called him Pel, and they were only recently married; Thorne was Shadavarian, Phoenixus was attacking people, and he was Versipellis' brother. She frowned. What had her husband meant by "You made your choice, and my brother made his"? She sat up in the bed and thought hard. He had also said that someone called Aquilleia was in the house, she had heard that name recently but couldn't quite remember where.

Giselle climbed out of bed and cautiously opened one of the little doors on the opposite side of the room. No, that looked like a water closet…aha! This one was more hopeful. Rummaging through the wardrobe, she found clothing the like of which she had never seen before — where were the stays, the corsets, and the bustles? Biting her lip, she pulled on what she hoped would do, and devised a plan of action.

Opening the door, she looked down a short corridor that was painted a soft yellow. Closing the door behind her, she walked towards a flight of stairs; as she descended, a sudden scuffling came from somewhere below. A sense of unease came over her as she reached the foot of the stairs and opened the first door on her right

It was a kitchen. Standing at the stove was Versipellis, and lying on the floor before him was a woman Giselle did not recognise. A wealth of thick blue-black hair spread in a silken pool around her body, her deathly pallor highlighting the ugly bruise forming over the entire left side of her face.

Versipellis turned and smiled at her. "We got him — finally!"

Giselle looked at the woman lying on the floor and a wave of sickness hit her as a memory suddenly revealed itself; the woman on the floor was Aquilleia, Shadavarian's wife!

Versipellis frowned. "My darling, are you well?"

Giselle shook her head. She leant against the well-scrubbed kitchen table as memories suddenly began to crowd in on her; faces, places, people, their work…and Veronique! Giselle took a deep breath; Veronique was also an Other, and her true name was Xenocyon! More and more memories poured back into her mind, threatening to over-whelm her…including the knowledge of just who, and what, Abditivus was.

Versipellis came over and slid his arm around her back, guiding her to a chair by the fireside, then poured her a glass of water from a pitcher. He handed her the glass and smiled as she took a sip. "There now, is that a little better?" He leant towards her and kissed her hard on her lips, and as he did so he plunged the dagger he was holding deep into her side.

Giselle screamed in pain as she fell to the ground, she stared at him in horror as she lay bleeding on the earthen floor.

He laughed as he stood over her, and with a smile began to gently stroke his face. Almost imperceptibly, his features changed back to his true likeness. Her mind whirled as Giselle and Angellis' memories finally merged together and she remembered all that had happened. This was not Pel. This was Phoenixus, his twin brother.

As the rest of his face settled into his usual expression of bitter contempt, the eyes that looked so like Pel's fixed her with a malicious glare. "Don't worry, my blessed brother isn't dead. I don't actually have to kill someone to take their place; it just makes it easier! And this would have been so very much easier if you had just accepted me and not him." He crouched next to her on the floor. "Did they really think that putting Aquilleia here would stop me coming back to take what I wanted? My brother is such a fool! It was ridiculously easy to get past Aquilleia. All I had to do was think about you, and her gift told her I was Pel, your loving husband!" Reaching down, he tapped a finger against the knife in her side. His smile deepened as she cried out in pain. "So, you see, Angellis, it's all your fault. The pain, the deaths, and what I shall do next — it's all your fault!" He laughed. "You really should have said yes to me, my sweet!" He stood up and stared at her for a moment, then walked through the door and away down the lane.

Giselle pressed a trembling hand to her side and pulled the knife free, she dragged herself across the floor to Aquilleia and shook the woman's arm, to no avail. With a sob, she realised that Shadavarian's wife was dead.

She leant against the table leg and tried to take shallow breaths. As the room began to fade the outer door was flung open, and Versipellis, Shadavarian, and Xenocyon ran into the kitchen.

Shadavarian fell to his knees beside his wife. In utter silence he gathered her up in his arms and wept as Xenocyon threw back her head and howled.

Versipellis ran to Angellis and knelt beside her, his face ashen as he held her and stroked her face. "My love…my love."

Her eyes flicked towards him as she whispered, "It was Phoenixus...he looked like you, but I knew it wasn't. I love you, Pel."

His arms tightened around her, and as the spirit of life left her body, the last thing she heard was his voice. "I will find you, my love...I will find you!"

○

## Abditivus' house

Giselle slowly came to and realised she was back in the Rose Hall. Her eyes flickered as she registered that she was wrapped in Elliott's arms. Leaning back, she looked into his eyes and touched his face. "Pel!" Elliott stared at her, then tightened his arms around her in a hug that made her ribs creak before kissing her. Giselle held him tightly, her mind spinning as all her memories returned, including those of her other incarnations. She finally understood that theirs was an eternal bond...he had searched for her for over a thousand years, and he would never let her go. Memories of her life with Versipellis were now firmly implanted in her mind: their home, the places they had lived, their friends and family...and Phoenixus.

She touched his face again, her own face set. "He murdered so many. He killed Aquilleia, and then he killed me — because I rejected him! I will never be parted from you again, Pel, never! I understand now what we lost, what was taken from us — what he took from us, and why...and I reject him again, utterly!" She started to weep as she and Elliott clung to each other.

Abditivus walked towards them. "You have regained all your memories, Angellis. Welcome home!"

○

## Back at the river

Lilith looked up from her perusal of the food stores as Thorne stoked the little campfire. "Will they be long, do you think?"

Thorne shrugged wearily. "I really couldn't say, Lilith. The man they have gone to meet takes his time over such things. But we should be back in Wiveliscombe by nightfall. We passed a rather nice-looking coaching inn on the Square. After Elliott and Giselle return, it might be an idea to head there for the night."

Lilith nodded. "Then I shall make us a little…well, not a supper but a little…" She stamped her foot. "What is the word — a meal after lunch but before dinner?"

Thorne grinned as he sat back against the tree. "After-noon tea?"

Lilith nodded. "Yes, afternoon tea. I shall make a little afternoon tea, and we shall leave theirs for later." Rummaging through the bag, she began to put together a simple spread of bread and cheese, a slab of honeyed ham, and a large fruit cake that immediately became the object of Veronique's hopeful gaze.

Lilith's attempt at an English afternoon tea was nearing completion when Veronique cocked her head to one side and began to bark. Lilith and Thorne turned as they heard the sound of approaching horses.

Thorne walked to the edge of the waterfall, smiled, and turned back to Lilith. "It's all right, it's them! Trust Elliott to arrive in time for food!"

The two blindfolded horses reappeared over the water's edge and Elliott and Giselle led them back into the little camp.

Thorne raised an eyebrow at Elliott as they untied the blindfolds and removed the packs, which looked full to bursting.

Elliott nodded to Thorne as Giselle approached her husband's oldest and most loyal friend with a smile. "I remember you now, Shadavarian. And I remember Aquilleia. Pel found me; we *will* find her!" Giselle stroked Veronique's ears. "And I remember you too, Xenocyon. We will find your mistress."

Thorne's eyes glistened as he nodded. "Have you eaten? Lilith's setting up high tea."

Elliott smiled. "We had a light lunch with Abditivus and he loaded our packs with food for the return trip." He leaned towards Thorne. "We have lobster!"

Thorne's eyebrows shot into his hairline. "We need to come here more often!"

Elliott handed him a package. "Enjoy, my friend."

The four of them tucked in to the large meal as Giselle explained to Lilith what had happened. Bearing in mind her earlier temperament, the young Frenchwoman took it very well. She turned to Elliott with a curious expression. "What do I call you now? I met you as Detective Chief Inspector Elliott Caine, but now I know you are Versipellis. I met Detective Sergeant Abernathy Thorne, but I now know him as Shadavarian. Veronique is also Xenocyon. And what does my mistress call herself? She was born Penelope Lake, and became Giselle Du'Lac, but she is really Angellis."

Elliott nodded. "Yes, Lilith, you're right. It is a little confusing, to put it mildly!" He looked at Giselle, smiling at the woman he had loved for so long. "I think it best that you continue with your stage name of Giselle Du'Lac, and the best option for Thorne and me is to continue as Thorne and Elliott until such time as we are required to change that. Lilith, of course, shall remain her fiery Gallic self."

Lilith nodded graciously as she placed a morsel of fresh bread roll dripping with butter into her mouth.

Giselle looked at Elliott. "So, where now?"

Elliott thoughtfully took a bite of bread. "What say you to a trip to the Antipodes?" He wiped his fingers, reached into his inside pocket and flourished a battered-looking envelope, then looked at Thorne. "Do you remember Coll Langen?"

Thorne hurriedly swallowed his mouthful of lobster. "How could I forget him? He was a nice lad, desperate to travel, so he went to sea and that's where we met him." He frowned. "But why are you asking about Coll? That was a long, long time ago."

Elliott smiled. "Yes, it was. This was sent to us via Lapotaire. You remember we gave Coll our details before we parted company in Australia?"

Thorne nodded. "But that was well over forty years ago, Elliott. How on earth did he know we would still be around?"

Elliott coughed and tugged at his collar. Thorne's eyebrows rose, then he sat back. "What did he see, Elliott?" he asked, his tone sharp.

Elliott looked sheepish. "Me, changing back from impersonating the ship's captain. Oddly enough, some people hold on to things like that! At least he didn't try blackmail. He just asked for a favour in the future, and now he's called it in. A few days ago, Vanamoinen appeared at the door."

"The big Finn? What did he – or should I say, what did *Lapotaire* want?"

Elliott handed Thorne the telegram. "Read this."

Thorne glared at the inoffensive piece of paper.

VERSIPELLIS STOP URGENT STOP DEBT BEING CALLED STOP FRIEND UNDER ATTACK DAUGHTER THREATENED STOP PLEASE HELP STOP COLL LANGEN STOP

Elliott looked at Thorne. "Bearing in mind that none of us have any burning plans for the next few months, I immediately popped out to the telegraph office and sent a reply requesting more information. This is what came back. Poor Coll, I hope his wealthy friend paid for these. There's quite a number, and all the way from New Zealand!" He pulled out a thick wad of telegrams and read aloud, handing each to Giselle when he had finished.

VERSIPELLIS STOP FALSE ALLEGATIONS OF MURDER IN ATTEMPT TO BLACKMAIL AND TAKE CONTROL OF MINING COMPANY STOP

VERSIPELLIS STOP DAUGHTER THREATENED IF FATHER WILL NOT STAND DOWN STOP AGGRESSOR BELIEVED TO BE SOMEONE CLOSE STOP

VERSIPELLIS STOP THREATS MADE PREVIOUSLY PAUSED THEN RESTARTED STOP

VERSIPELLIS STOP 23RD TO 26TH MARCH HER BIRTHDAY WEEKEND YOU ARE INVITED STOP MILFORD CITY NEW ZEALAND STOP

VERSIPELLIS STOP COME IN DISGUISE AS PERFORMERS STOP TRUST YOU REMEMBER HOW TO CHANGE YOUR APPEARANCE STOP

VERSIPELLIS STOP IF YES AUCKLAND 21ST MARCH RIVERSTONE HOTEL STOP PRIVATE AIRSHIP FROM AUCKLAND AETHERDROME WILL BRING YOU HERE STOP

VERSIPELLIS STOP NAME YOUR PRICE STOP

83

Elliott pulled out several more pieces of paper. "This gentleman, whom Coll goes out of his way to avoid naming, appears to be a wealthy man who owns a mining company. Due to previous threats, he decided a boat in the middle of Milford Sound, New Zealand was the safest place for him and his daughter. The person or persons responsible for those threats may or may not be the ones responsible for these new aggressions. It would be up to us to discover the nature of these threats, find those responsible, and hand the information over to the correct authorities. Now, I told Coll that I would discuss these points with you and be guided by your decision, so…what say you?"

Giselle looked at Elliott and smiled. "Perhaps a little more background information is in order? From what you have said, and based on information gleaned from my travels in society, the wealthy man sounds very much like one Octavius Damant. British by way of South America, his main business is mining; the DB Mining Company is one of the largest mining concerns in the Southern Hemisphere. His wife died several years ago in an incident at a diamond mine, and he has a young daughter. He is an exceptionally successful and wealthy businessman — his worth is measured in the millions — and he is known as that most unusual of fish, a decent and likeable millionaire who does a great deal for charitable concerns." She paused. "But I am not invited to this performance; the gentleman has asked for the two of you."

Elliott caught her hand and kissed it. "Do you honestly think I would go anywhere without you now that I have finally found you?" He turned suddenly. "That is, if Thorne is also willing."

Thorne smiled around the last of the lobster he had tried to eat before Elliott or Giselle noticed and dabbed at his lips with a napkin. "Thorne is willing, but I will have to bring

Veronique. When she gets bored, she sulks, and when she sulks, she chews things! Mrs Hardcourt would not be happy!"

Elliott turned back to his wife. "What do you say, my love? In at the beginning and at the kill, as it were?"

Giselle laughed, her even teeth gleaming in the soft sunlight. "It sounds lovely to me. Lilith, do you fancy a jaunt to the far south to investigate a crime?"

Lilith produced one of her best Gallic shrugs. "Another stamp on my passport, more arrangements, hotels and amusements. Yes, it sounds entertaining."

Elliott smiled with relief. "Excellent — because I took the liberty of sending this response!" He whipped out another piece of paper.

COLL STOP WILL ACCEPT CASE STOP MR ELLIOTT CAINE MR ABERNATHY THORNE AND MLLE GISELLE DU'LAC WILL ARRIVE STOP

"I'm sure Lapotaire won't mind us dropping our titles now we are no longer police officers." He paused with a happy smile. "We are now private enquiry agents, and according to Abditivus, the Espion Court are more than happy to accept that." He took a bite from his slice of bread and continued. "Now, going on the date today, that gives us roughly seventy-eight days to travel from London to Auckland, then on to Milford Sound in time for the young lady's birthday weekend. This could be a smidge tricky!"

Thorne smiled. "Do you remember that smart remark of yours about Commissioner Bolton sending us to the far Antipodes?"

Elliott grinned back. "I really should have kept my mouth shut. Well, at least we're not after Jack the Ripper again."

Thorne grimaced. "Thank the Gods! That was a messy business."

Lilith stared hard at the two men before deciding it was perhaps better not to know!

Thorne paused and looked at Elliott with a devilish grin. He rummaged through the telegrams until he found the one he was after. "Ah, yes…here it is…" He cleared his throat and read the missive in his fruity voice.

VERSIPELLIS STOP IF YES AUCKLAND 21ST MARCH RIVERSTONE HOTEL STOP PRIVATE AIRSHIP FROM AUCKLAND AETHERDROME WILL BRING YOU HERE STOP

He looked at his old friend, leant forward and carefully enunciated the word. "Airship! Passage aboard an airship from Auckland Aetherdrome…and you agreed to it!" He pursed his lips. "The Auckland Aetherdrome is supposed to be one of the most opulent aetherdromes in the world, perfectly placed for the Pacific-Indian Ocean Route from North America to South Africa via China, Australia, and New Zealand." His grin widened. "That's a long journey, my friend!"

Elliott frowned slightly. "Yes…well, don't rub it in. The jury is still out on just how trustworthy those things actually are, but if the bookings have been made, then who am I to say no to a spot of free travel." Elliott's dark brows snapped down over his eyes as he shot a sharp look at both his wife and Thorne. "But I will most definitely *not* be travelling from England to New Zealand on one of the dratted creations!"

Giselle laughed as she bit into her slice of cake. "Well, need to head to Auckland, and as you say, that might take us a while. I think we will probably have to travel via the Americas. The quickest route, not counting airships, would be a steamship from London to New York, the train to San Francisco, and then another steamer on to Auckland. I made a similar trip when I performed in Sydney some years ago, and as I recall, it was quite easy to get passage in first class." She frowned as she remembered. "It is however, rather expensive. My previous agent complained volubly about Lilith going as my companion…he actually tried to put her in steerage until I put my foot down." She took a sip of water and looked at Elliott. "Needless to say, he ceased to be my agent that same day."

Elliott looked at her with a smile. "Well, at least one of us already has an exemplary history as an entertainer of note, with good reason to be invited to a weekend birthday party thrown by a reclusive millionaire. We shall simply have to find a suitable guise for Thorne and myself."

Thorne nodded firmly. "I agree. We're rather a long way from London and it will take some time to return, so I suggest we head back to Wiveliscombe for the night, catch the train to Taunton tomorrow morning, and then back home to pack, search out a ship to New York, and go from there. Hopefully we will be able to come up with a suitable disguise before we reach New Zealand!"

* * *

### Back aboard the Taniwha

As Giselle slowly returned to the bright, richly appointed bathroom aboard the Taniwha, Lilith walked back into the room and picked up a large towel which she shook in a peremptory manner at her mistress. With a smile, Giselle stood up and allowed her maid to wrap her in the wonderfully thick material.

A few minutes later, Elliott was woken from his nap as

Lilith re-entered the cabin and threw the damp towel into the woven basket by the door. She flicked through several outfits in an open trunk before settling on a frothy lavender blouse and grey tweed skirt and disappearing back into the bathroom. Some minutes later, a fully bathed, dressed and smiling Giselle walked out. Elliott took her hand. "Better?"

"Much! Your turn."

He collected a light silver-grey suit, entered the little bathroom, and had a damp few minutes with a flannel and a sink full of hot soapy water before redressing and combing a little oil through his springy dark hair. As he wandered back into the cabin a few sharp taps sounded at the door. He raised his eyebrows at Giselle. "Timing is everything! Ready?"

"Ready!"

Elliott flung open the door with a smile and fixed his eyes on a slightly surprised Darius. "Mr Damant. Is it now time to parlay with your uncle?"

The dark young man smiled. "Absolutely. If you'll follow me."

Elliott and Giselle left Lilith to continue her rampage through their luggage and followed the young man to Thorne's room, where several items of luggage were still sitting by the door. After several attempts at knocking achieved nothing, Elliott finally opened the door and found Thorne fast asleep, the penny dreadful open at a particularly lurid illustration. Veronique was no guard dog as she opened one tired eye, saw Elliott, and promptly closed it again.

Elliott shook Thorne's shoulder. "Come on, Thorne. You're making us look bad, old chap!"

Thorne groaned as he grudgingly stood up and stretched. Heading to the door, he dragged in his luggage, then digging out a selection of Veronique's favourite toys and her food bowls, he put down clean water and a selection of nibbles.

Giving her ears a gentle squeeze, he headed to the door, and the four of them made their way to their first meeting with Octavius Damant.

○

## O.D's Office
## 1:15pm

O.D sat in the massive oak chair behind his desk. Taking a sip of his coffee, he wrapped his fingers around the bone-china cup and stared at the far wall. His "special" guests should be arriving shortly; his secretary, Torrance Burrows, was on watch in the outer office, ready to let him know the moment they appeared.

O.D had a sudden spasm of doubt. Surely there was an easier way to deal with the situation? Was he perhaps over-exaggerating the issue? He sighed and rubbed his face; he knew damn well he wasn't! He was a hard-nosed businessman with years of experience in dealing with the great, the good — and the evil.

The letters had been bad enough when they threatened him and his company. Now they threatened his daughter, and that – that was something he wasn't prepared to take!

Standing up abruptly, O.D placed his cup in its saucer with a jarring clatter. He walked over to the huge window that opened onto his private veranda and paused by the rich red curtains. Reaching out to touch the silky material, he permitted himself a slight smile. The material and a sizeable quantity of the furnishings had been chosen by Merry. There was plenty of colour: perhaps sometimes a touch too much. He had offered her the interiors of the rest of the boat but had held sway in his suite, his office, the dining room, and the lounge. Ah, the dining room and the lounge; two of his favourite rooms aboard, resplendent in Pompeiian red, old gold, black, and white. The dining-room walls were covered with an Athenian-style fresco created by an artist from Athens, who had travelled to New Zealand specially to recreate the artistic style of the vase painter, Andokides. In the lounge, ornate display cases on three walls showcased the most exceptional pieces from his myriad collections, including a complete set of samurai armour on a full-sized mannequin. Truly, a statement room!

At a sudden knock on the outer door, he took a deep breath. "Yes?

The door opened and his secretary Torrance entered quietly. Tall and very thin, with large knuckles and a prominent Adam's apple, Torrance hovered by the door, his ill-fitting clothes hanging off his frame in an obvious display of the amount of weight the young man had recently lost. He cleared his throat; his voice, oddly unsuited to his appearance, was smooth and curiously compelling. "Mr Damant? The guests you have been waiting for have arrived. Shall I bring them in?"

"Yes, Torrance, thank you. Oh, and some tea, and perhaps some cakes…we might be a touch late for lunch."

Torrance nodded, his oil-slicked dark hair gleaming in the light from the large windows. "Yes, Mr Damant." He turned, and holding the door open, raised his voice. "Mr Damant will see you now."

Darius led Elliott, Thorne, and Giselle into the opulent office as Torrance stepped out. Walking back to his desk, he sat down, flicked the switch on one of the speaking tubes mounted on his desk, and blew down the mouthpiece. After a few moments, his whistle was answered by one of the kitchen maids, who took his order for tea. Hanging up that particular tube, Torrance opened the one immediately to its left. This tube was connected to the desk in Mr Damant's office, and by dint of its position could afford the listener a way to carry out any amount of eavesdropping…as long as said eavesdropper had the foresight to remove the plug from the other end, as he had done earlier that morning. Torrance sat back with a pad and pencil and began to jot down the private conversation in shorthand.

In the office, utterly unaware of their secret listener, Darius had introduced everyone under both their true and weekend names. O.D nodded and gestured at the armchairs around his desk. "Please take a seat. I was afraid our meeting might take us past the lunch hour, so I took the liberty of ordering some light refreshment. It should arrive soon."

Thorne's ears pricked up. Refreshment might mean cake!

Elliott placed an armchair for Giselle, then sat in the chair next to her and gazed at their host. Late fifties, he would say: longish grey hair, but still trim and upright. A firm face, not one to suffer fools – unless there was good reason.

O.D sat back in his chair and smoothed his cravat. A hesitant expression crossed his face before he addressed his nephew. "You might well hear some things that may shock or worry you, Darius, but please do not interrupt proceedings. I have decided that, in the light of certain events that have occurred, some things need more specialised knowledge than I possess, and that is why I have invited these gentlemen and Mlle Du'Lac here this weekend."

Darius looked intrigued. Casually crossing his legs, he settled into his chair, then suddenly sat bolt upright. "Uncle, the cheques for the Grizenburg Mine – they have to be sent today at the latest! I completely forgot. If you sign them now, I can take them to be posted immediately."

O.D waved his hand in a dismissive manner. "It isn't an issue, my boy. Just do what you do with my signature and post them tomorrow. What's happening to my daughter is far more important than mere company paperwork!" He unlocked a drawer in his desk, removed a sheaf of papers, walked over to Elliott and handed him the topmost document. "Coll wrote this before he realised a telegram would reach you more quickly. I suggest you read this before I say anything else."

Elliott took the letter, Thorne leant over, and Giselle read over her husband's shoulder.

1st January 1900
    For Versipellis
    Care of Lord Lapotaire

Old Friend,

I hope you will remember me after all these years – I certainly remember you! And, of course, your good friend Shadavarian.

If you recall, after the events that led up to a certain captain being reduced in power, you made me an offer of future assistance if certain things I had witnessed were forgotten in the ensuing investigation.

I accepted your offer and continued on my way, travelling many oceans in my journey before marrying – yes, Versipellis, I have married – and I am content. For the last few decades my wife and I have made a home for ourselves here in Milford Sound, in New Zealand's South Island.

It is a beautiful place, the peace and serenity we have here is unsurpassed…at least, it was until this last evening.

A friend of mine is the victim of persecution and terror by person or persons unknown. He has received letters accusing him of the murder of his wife and business partner some ten years ago. The letters demand that he turn himself in for a crime he did not commit and relinquish control of his company, or they will cause the death of his only child, a daughter named Merry. She is a lovely girl, gentle and kind, without any artifice in her nature.

My friend knows I am writing to you and he hopes you will be able to help him; he is deeply concerned for his daughter's life.

It is his daughter's twenty-first birthday on the 25th of March, and I have encouraged him to arrange a weekend birthday party, starting on the 23rd and finishing sometime after lunch on the 26th.

I had an idea that the two of you could arrive as – well, as you are not known to Merry, perhaps you could pass yourselves off as entertainers of a sort? She loves illusion and magic trickery; her father has already made contact with the greatest psychic in the Southern Hemisphere and asked her to grace us with her insight for the weekend.

Your presence here, investigating this hideous mess, would be most welcome.

Please help us, Versipellis. I place my hope and trust in you both.

Your friend.

Coll Langen

Elliott passed the letter back to O.D. "Coll covered most of this in his telegrams, and quite thoroughly…including your daughter's love of illusion." Elliott's canines flashed as he grinned. "I would have dreaded the charges incurred during the sending of those messages — certainly no expense spared!" He handed the letter back to O.D. "Now we are here, perhaps you can tell us everything from the beginning, omitting nothing?"

The muscles in O.D's jaw clenched as he gripped the edge of his desk.

A soft, deferential knock sounded at the door and Torrance entered, holding the door open for two young maids who were each carrying a loaded tray: one filled with a light selection of sandwiches, cakes, and scones, and the other with a large teapot, a water pot, milk, sugar, and various items of crockery. The maids set out the tea and left as quickly as they had entered, with Torrance closing the door firmly behind them. As the maids left the outer office, he sat back down at his desk and continued his eavesdropping.

O.D stared at the victuals as though he couldn't place where they had come from. Giselle sat up and said brightly. "Shall I be mother?" She checked the contents of the pot and began to pour, pausing only to dimple at her husband when he heaved a sigh of relief that the tea on offer was black and not green.

With the tea poured and various nibbles loaded onto plates, O.D cleared his throat. "I…" He gave an exasperated sigh. "I really don't know where to begin; it all seems so bloody ridiculous! Oh, I do beg your pardon, Mlle Du'Lac!"

Giselle hid a smile and waved a manicured hand that gripped a cucumber finger sandwich. "Not at all, Mr Damant. Emotions always run high when those nearest our hearts are threatened." She placed the remains of her sandwich on the little plate, sipped her tea and set the bone-china cup in its saucer. "Perhaps it would be best to start at the very beginning? The letter states that the original threats contain some libellous accusations regarding the deaths of your wife and your business partner. Perhaps you could start there and work your way forward?" She looked at him with an understanding expression. "And Mr Damant, we must insist on candour, no matter how painful. In return, we promise absolute discretion." As Giselle spoke, Thorne unobtrusively removed a notebook and several pencils from his pocket and began to take notes.

"Yes, yes of course," said O.D. "Coll was very...reassuring about your abilities. Well! As you can understand, this is rather difficult for me. Talking about such personal things is not in my nature. Indeed, if my enemies heard what I am about to tell you, it would be the end of my standing in business — amongst other things!" He cleared his throat. "Many years ago — twenty-three to be exact — I met a young lady. Her name was Cordelia Ozanne. I was forty years old; she was twenty-five and quite the loveliest woman I had ever seen. I set about courting her, and after a correct amount of time had passed, I asked her father for her hand in marriage and was accepted. A little over a year after our marriage, our daughter Merry was born and we moved to Brazil, where one of my fledgling mining concerns was showing great promise. My business partner, Alexander Burrows, and his young son were already living there, and the area was rather remote, so it seemed the easiest thing in the world to engage with them more. You know the sort of thing: dinners, charades, boardgames and such. Alexander's wife Nanette had died several years earlier in childbirth, and my wife had just had Merry. She enjoyed spending as much time looking after his son as she did our daughter..." His voice trailed off as he thought back to those times.

"We were happy for quite some time. Several years, in fact, in spite of having to deal with wary tribes, corrupt authorities, and marabunta: army ants, you know — they eat anything and everything — completely ruined the garden! However, our business, the DB Mining Company, was doing splendidly and we had a run of luck. Our company's value increased massively." He frowned. "Unfortunately, so did people's knowledge of our financial worth. Over the course of several weeks, three of our mines were vandalised. The attacks were small, and mostly inconsequential: windows smashed, sluices damaged, that sort of thing. It was an irritation more than anything else."

He lifted his cup. "Then, very suddenly, things escalated. One of the explosives sheds was broken into, several pounds of dynamite were stolen, and I began to take the attacks rather more seriously. One of the first sites to be vandalised was one of our most productive diamond mines, and due to the rash of attacks there, I decided I had no option but to go and deal with the aftermath myself. When I returned several days later, the atmosphere at home had changed: my wife could no longer bear to be in the same room as me or Alexander, and he would no longer come to the house."

O.D took a deep breath, and a muscle began to twitch in his jaw. "The evidence was obvious to all but myself; Cordelia and Alexander had become closer than they should. Looking back, I realised they were trying to do the right thing by staying away from each other, but I just couldn't see it." He stared at the little cup in his hand, and carefully placed the untouched tea back on his desk. "There was another attack at the Amberley Mine, a small site several miles from our little settlement, and again I left to deal with it. The situation there was so bad that I decided to close the mine temporarily to see if that would deter the villain. I went straight from closing the mine to the town, informed the workers of the temporary closure, and guaranteed them all a return to work once the issues had been resolved." He gritted his teeth. "Upon my arrival home I discovered my wife missing, and a note on my desk telling me that unless I handed over twenty-five thousand pounds in cut diamonds she would be murdered!"

Elliott held up a hand. "Did you keep that note?"

O.D slid a piece of paper off his desk and handed it to

Elliott. "That is the note. I did what it said: I took the sum they had asked for in cut diamonds, I took it where they told me to, and I did not call the police."

> Mr Damant. We have your wife. Do what we say, and she will be released unharmed. £25,000 in cut diamonds to be placed inside a small satchel and taken to the top end of Viagem Valley. There you will find a man waiting. Throw the satchel to him and leave immediately.
>
> Do not attempt to interfere with him. Do not engage in conversation with him. Do not turn around. Do not involve the police.
>
> If you disobey, she will die.

Elliott handed the note to Thorne, who held it up to the light that streamed through the large windows. "Water-marked, good quality…looks like vellum, torn at one end. Rather an expensive and easily traceable type of paper."

O.D shook his head. "Unfortunately not. You noticed the tear; here's why. He handed Thorne another sheet of paper from his desk. Thorne held it up and nodded. "Same water-mark, vellum…" He grimaced. "And a very nice header for the DB Mining Company across the top. That explains why it was torn." He handed the piece of paper back and continued with his notes.

Elliott took a sip of his tea, added a lump of sugar and a splash more milk before he looked at O.D. "What happened at Viagem Valley?"

O.D looked at the little cheese scone he had absent-mind-edly picked up, and dropped it back onto his plate. "As I took the diamonds from my safe, Merry, Darius, and Alexander's son suddenly arrived in my office—"

"Darius was there?" asked Elliot.

"Yes, it was the last holiday Darius had with us before—

Well, I will leave Darius to fill you in on another, equally sordid part of our family's history. Because Darius was staying with us, we had also invited Alexander's son to stay at the house…he enjoyed having another boy to talk with. Where was I? Oh yes, the children returned. Merry, Darius, and Alexander's boy had been taken to Alexander's house earlier that morning by Nanny. The children had gone out to play in the garden and Nanny had travelled on into town to do some shopping, but when the children returned to the house for lunch, Alexander wasn't there, and neither was his housekeeper as it was her day off, so the children decided to return early. I knew Nanny wouldn't be back until nearly dark, as it took a few hours to travel into town, and I knew Carolyn wouldn't be prepared to help as she was leaving for Europe later that day, so I settled the children in with our cook and went to the agreed meeting place with the diamonds."

O.D stood up abruptly and walked to the ornate marble fireplace. Gazing into the unlit grate, he continued. "A figure stood beside the road. I held up the satchel and moved to get off my horse, but they pulled out a gun and threatened me! They obviously wanted me to stay on my horse, so I threw the diamonds to them. They checked the contents, then threw a package back and made a sign that I should open it. It contained a rock, to make sure it carried through the air, and a note informing me that my wife and my business partner were being held at the Amberley Mine, and I was allowed to retrieve them as long as I gave the kidnapper twenty minutes' grace. As I was reading this note, he walked to the end of the valley and disappeared. I waited twenty minutes, then rode my horse back to the main track." He paused, gritted his teeth and dragged his hand through his hair. "Mr Caine, he was already gone! He must have had a horse hidden because I couldn't see hide nor hair of him. I wanted to follow him; you understand? But I had to find my wife. And I had no idea that Alexander had also been taken. I rather thought that…" His voice tailed off and Elliott finished the sentence for him. "You thought that the figure might have been Alexander himself?"

O.D nodded. "Yes," he whispered.

Elliott tapped his fingertips together. "Please proceed, Mr Damant."

O.D pinched the bridge of his nose. "The Amberley Mine was some miles from the valley; it took me three hours to get there. As I pulled up to the head office a massive explosion shook the ground and the mine entrance disappeared in a ball of flame and smoke." O.D's jaw clenched as he turned away from the others, and he drew a shuddering breath. "As the mine was closed, I was the only person there. I managed to get into the office and send a call through to the site manager, Perry, who was in the town. He returned with several mine workers, and the police, who were angry that I had not contacted them before heading out to try and save my wife."

O.D walked to his drinks cabinet and poured himself a large brandy, then waved the decanter at his guests. "Anyone?" As Elliott began to shake his head, Giselle nodded and said brightly, "That would be lovely, thank you." O.D poured the drinks, handed them round, and sat back down at his desk, his brandy glass coddled between his large hands as his eyes gazed back at what he had witnessed that day.

"The lads started to dig out the opening, but the sheer force of the dynamite rendered the mine too dangerous for the men to go any further than twenty feet in. They tried, but there were further falls and I had to give the order to get them out. Just in time: the weight of the overhang could no longer be borne by the damaged shorings and the front of the mine collapsed under its own weight." A single tear trickled down O.D's cheek. "On the advice of my manager, I decided to abandon the rescue attempt and leave the mine as my wife's final resting place. I had the area blessed by the local priest and set a tombstone there…a tombstone bearing both their names."

Silence fell in the plush office as the inhabitants thought over the last ten years of sorrow and loss.

Darius shook his head, his expression one of confusion. "Uncle, why do you think this would cause you to lose standing in the industry? It wouldn't at all; this is common knowledge." He paused, "Well, aside from Aunt C and Alexander's behaviour, that is…"

O.D looked at his young nephew and the ghost of a smile crossed his face as he shook his head. "It doesn't end there, Darius. The police report said they believed the dynamite that had previously been stolen was used for the explosion. The fact that it had been taken some days earlier suggested premeditation." He sighed. "Apparently Cordelia and Alexander were not as discreet as they should have been. Alexander's housekeeper was aware of their…closeness, as were several others. The officer in charge of the investigation was very much of the belief that I had discovered my wife's adultery, and had planned to remove both her and her paramour. The police determined to have me hung, drawn and quartered before the week was out. Luckily I managed to get word to Mar and she contacted the company lawyer."

Elliott looked at him. "Mar?"

O.D nodded. "Merry's nanny, as was: Marjorie Lee Colville. She became Merry's governess and is now her companion."

"She's here?"

"Yes, of course." O.D smiled faintly, "She doesn't need to teach Merry any more, but Merry cares for her a great deal.

And Captain Peach's daughter, Fleur, is only fifteen and in need of a governess, so Mar stayed."

Elliott contemplated the iced bun that sat innocently on his plate. Biting into it, he turned his eyes towards the magnate, who had the sudden impression that a green light had flashed behind the warm brown eyes. Elliott finished his mouthful. "Is there anyone else on this vessel who was there at the time of your wife's death, Mr Damant?"

"Aside from Darius, Mar, and Carolyn, you mean? No, no one that I can recall. Our cook was elderly and she retired to Canada to be with her daughter…no, no one." He paused. "Except Torrance, of course."

Thorne looked up from his notes and raised an eyebrow. "Torrance?"

O.D nodded. "My secretary, Torrance Burrows. Alexander was his father."

Thorne's eyebrows shot into his hairline as he made several scribbled additions to his notebook.

Elliott and Giselle looked at each other silently, then at O.D who met their gaze. "I have known Torrance since his birth; he was a babe in arms when he lost his mother and only fourteen when he lost his father. I took it upon myself to finish his education, protect his share in the business and offer him a job in the company his father and I had started." A strange look came over his face as he gazed at the little group. "Alexander had…almost a sixth sense for finding the right type of mine. I knew very little about them at the time, but I had a little money, so we went into business together. I also knew his wife, Nanette. She was a strong woman, but I can still hear her screams on that one night at our very first mine when a small charge failed to detonate correctly, and Alexander went to see what was wrong. He held out his hand just as the damn thing went! Blew his left hand clean off! Nanette took us into the town on our cart and the doctor dealt with his injuries…he couldn't save his hand, but he did save his life. Nanette loved him greatly; the loss he felt when she died was savage! Please don't misunderstand me; Alexander loved his son very much, but Torrance's birth left his father alone. The loss of a loved one is too painful to be understood by one who has not suffered it."

Elliott and Giselle exchanged glances. Giselle flicked a swift glance at Thorne, whose hand trembled as he wrote. Elliott cleared his throat loudly. "So, to clarify. Several of your mines were attacked and one suffered the theft of several pounds of dynamite; your wife and business partner were having an illicit relationship, they were kidnapped and held to ransom; you paid the ransom, but they were still killed; their murderer or murderers were never found, and there are four people aboard this boat, other than you and your daughter, who were there when it happened; your daughter's companion, Marjorie Lee Colville; your sister-in-law, Carolyn Nolloth; your nephew, Darius Damant; and your secretary, Torrance Burrows. Yes?"

O.D slumped in his chair. "Yes."

Darius shook his head again. "But I still don't understand, Uncle. You did no wrong."

O.D leant back in his chair and sighed. "It was what happened afterwards, Darius. The police refused to drop the case against me, even with a total lack of hard evidence, so the company lawyer, God help me, paid the police officer in charge to…to lose whatever evidence they thought they had and close the case. Shortly after, the site manager made a spirited attempt at blackmail. He was, I'm afraid to say, bought off, and removed from the company payroll."

Darius' face blenched as he ran his hand through his hair. "Good God, Uncle! Who else knew?"

"I thought that either of these two men could have sent the anonymous letters, so I employed a private detective to find them both. The police officer in question, one Capitão Mateus Guedes, was very easy to find. He had taken the money, left the police force in Brazil, and retired to a quiet life in England. Bristol, to be exact, where he lived under the name of Matthew George…and where he died three years ago after being struck by a tram. He was interred at Arnos Vale Cemetery. The site manager and attempted blackmailer, Perry Undercliffe, however, has completely eluded me for the last ten years."

Giselle took a sip of her drink, looked at O.D over the rim of her glass and arched one eyebrow. "And what of the company lawyer, Mr Damant? Where is he?"

O.D looked even more uncomfortable. He plucked at his silk cravat and grimaced. "Ah, well, you see, that would be—"

There was a sudden knock on the door and Torrance Burrows appeared. In a flustered voice, he announced, "Sir Wesley Eade, sir!"

Sir Wesley entered the room as though ready to preside over the summing up of a felon, his attire changed from his pale-grey travel suit to a spectacular suit of heather-coloured tweed.

Torrance hovered by the open door, his face deathly pale. "I apologise, Mr Damant. I know you said you were not to be disturbed, but Sir Wesley insisted."

O.D raised his hand, cutting off Torrance's flow of apologies. "It's quite all right, Torrance. I don't think we will be needing another cup…I very much doubt that Sir Wesley will be with us for long."

Torrance nodded jerkily and closed the door. He collapsed into his chair, jammed the stopper back into the speaking tube and put his head in his shaking hands. All his plans, all that time and effort, for nothing!

Back in his employer's office, Sir Wesley regarded O.D with a calm, almost bland expression. "If I were you, O.D, I would say no more. You can still go to gaol, you know, even after ten years."

O.D's face hardened. "You overheard? Ah, of course, Torrance's penchant for listening in to private conversations. Eavesdroppers seldom hear anything to their advantage, or that shows their personality in a good light!" He turned to face the others. "Lady and gentlemen, I give to you the company lawyer, who is exceptionally adept at covering up all manner of unfortunate incidents...for the right price!"

Sir Wesley smiled, the expression failing to meet his eyes as he smoothed the front of his suit and studied each of the room's inhabitants in turn. His voice was matter-of-fact as he addressed them, that curiously detached smile still on his face. "If any word of what has been mentioned in this room goes beyond these walls, no judge or jury will be able to save you — any of you!"

With the faint smile still on his lips he turned, opened the door and left the suite, walking straight past the silent Torrance.

O.D gripped the edge of his desk, his breath hissing through his teeth. "Who the hell does he think he is? Threatening me and my guests in my home!"

Elliott looked up at the incandescent philanthropist. "Well, you did employ him to pay off two men who thought you had murdered your wife and business partner, Mr Damant." He settled back in his chair. "Is it possible that out of spite or malice, he might attempt to cause you harm?"

O.D uttered a short bark of laughter. "Sir Wesley? If there were money or position to be had, he would burn us all! Now, if you will excuse me, I feel rather ill...I think I have said enough for a lifetime, let alone one afternoon!"

Elliott held up his hand. "Mr Damant, we understand that there have been more recent letters threatening the safety of your daughter. I trust you will show us these letters before you leave us?"

O.D ran his hand though his hair. "Yes, of course…forgive me. He removed an envelope from one of his desk drawers Opening it, he shook several letters onto his desk. He put them in order and handed them to Elliott, who read the contents with a grimace, Giselle looking over his shoulder, before handing them to Thorne.

I KNOW WHAT YOU DID. YOU WERE SEEN, CONFESS YOUR SINS.

YOU MURDERED YOUR WIFE AND YOUR BUSINESS PARTNER. CONFESS, MURDERER!

SELL YOUR COMPANY AND CONFESS, OR I WILL TELL YOUR DAUGHTER WHAT YOU DID TO HER MOTHER!

CONFESS TO YOUR CRIMES OR YOUR DAUGHTER WILL SUFFER!

CONFESS! MURDERER, LIAR, CHEAT, THIEF! SHE WILL DIE BY YOUR OWN PERFIDY!

YOU HAVE CHOSEN MONEY AND POSITION OVER YOUR OWN CHILD. YOU HAVE CHOSEN HER DEATH!

MURDERER, I AM COMING FOR YOU BOTH!

Thorne scanned the torn-off pieces of paper and their strangely angular writing with a practiced eye. "Short and to the point, and written in capitals…the standard approach for a poison pen writer or blackmailer without access to newspapers, and it would be somewhat difficult for them to get hold of a ready supply of newsprint down here. Again, standard wording along the lines of 'Give me what I want or I will take what you value most: in this case, your daughter.' He wafted the letters under his nose and sniffed. "Lime blossom, I think…perfume, or perhaps hair oil."

He held the letters out to O.D, who waved his hand. "Keep them, for your investigation. Now, if you will excuse me…" He walked towards the door behind him and turned, his face bleak. "Can you help us, Mr Caine?"

Elliott looked at Giselle and Thorne, who both nodded. "We will help, though we can't promise miracles…well, perhaps we can! Take heart, Mr Damant; we will do whatever we can to get to the bottom of this and discover what truth there is to find."

O.D passed a shaky hand across his face. "Thank you – thank you all! Now, if there is anything else you need to know about the guests or the Taniwha herself, please ask Darius. Oh, I almost forgot; several dossiers arrived yesterday. They came from the Government, and are for your eyes only. There was a cover note stating that they could only get information on a handful of guests in time for your arrival. They will wire anything else they find as and when it arrives. The documents are here, on my desk. Now, if you will please excuse me." He left the room, closing the door quietly behind him.

Elliott, Giselle and Thorne looked at each other. The silence in the plush office was heavy as Darius tried to come to terms with what he had just heard.

Thorne took the opportunity to sample a few more things from the victuals tray. Placing his plate on the desk, he collected the files that O.D had indicated then settled back into his seat, taking a healthy bite out of a rather nice slice of seed cake.

Darius angrily shook his head. "I don't care what you might think, but I know my uncle would never—"

Elliott held up a calming hand. "I know, and from what I have seen of your uncle so far, I agree with you. Now, what else can you tell me about Marjorie Lee Colville, and Torrance Burrows?"

Giselle topped up the tea with more hot water and pressed a cheese savoury on the young man as he sat in thought.

"Um, well, Mar first, then. Mar has been with us since before Merry was born. She was a friend of Aunt C's, and when she and Uncle were married, Mar stayed on as a companion of sorts for Aunt C. As Uncle's job took him to some rather remote places, they decided that her companionship would help Aunt C with any homesickness. When Merry was born, she immediately became her nanny as well as Aunt C's companion; then when Aunt C was killed, Mar ran the house for Uncle. She's a lovely person…" Darius sat forward slightly with a smile. "Years ago, when Aunt C was still alive, I travelled down to Uncle's house in Brazil with my parents for Christmas. Mar had created a beautiful doll's house for Merry, complete with little posable figures she'd made from lead sticks and linen. It was so real!"

Giselle looked at him. "She never thought to leave and seek out a life or family of her own?"

Darius looked at her sharply. "That is a very personal question, Mlle Du'Lac…but I suppose I should answer it. Mar had been married some years previously. He was a few years older than her, a military man: one of the 16th, the Queen's Lancers. I'm afraid he…well, he and Mar came out to visit Aunt C and Uncle, and he became rather authoritarian and decided they should return to India. Mar didn't want to and they had a blazing row about it. He abandoned her and returned to India…he probably didn't appreciate her thinking for herself. That's when Aunt C asked her to live with them — if she hadn't, Mar would have been left destitute." He paused, thinking. "It's actually *his* uniform on one of the mannequins in the lounge. Mar made the dummies for uncle to display his collections."

Giselle frowned. "Her husband abandoned her, but she kept his uniform? Surely he would have needed it in India?"

Darius shrugged, seeming slightly uncomfortable. "As I understand it, he was retired from the military. Apparently, he not only abandoned her but also the military: a bit of a blackguard, really! He disappeared into the wilds of the subcontinent, and there I presume he remains to this day."

Thorne discarded his now blunt pencil, picked up a fresh one, and continued with his notes.

Giselle placed her cup and saucer back on the table and looked at the young man. "What about Torrance?"

Darius was silent for a moment, then sighed. "I think Uncle covered most of Torrance's history. After his father's death he stayed with us. Uncle paid for him to finish his education, then employed him as his secretary immediately he left college. His personal money is tied up in his share of the company and according to his father's will, he gets full control of that income when he turns twenty-eight. That's a few years away yet." Darius shifted uncomfortably and looked at Elliott. "I think there has been something on his mind, though. Over the last year or so, he's lost a great deal of weight. Something has been bothering him, but I couldn't say what: we aren't as close as we were."

Elliott walked to the massive windows that looked out over the private deck, and thought about the various pieces of the puzzle that were beginning to emerge; there were rather a lot of pieces in this particular case, and it should prove to be most entertaining. He turned back to the young man, who was studying a cream éclair with interest. "As we are in a sharing mood, Mr Damant, what can you tell me about your mother?"

Darius coughed as the mouthful of pastry tried and failed to make a clean exit down his gullet, he took a healthy swallow of his now lukewarm tea. "My mother? What do you wish to know?"

Elliott shrugged in his best Lilith fashion. "Oh, whatever you think we should know. But the question of import is this: if we ask the lady a question, will she tell the truth? And the second…just out of interest, was there any animosity between your mother and her sister?"

Darius looked at Elliott and stood up. He went to his uncle's drinks cabinet and poured himself what appeared to be a treble whisky. Staring at the multitudinous bottles, glasses, and shakers, he took out an ornate ice pick, opened a small, lead-lined cupboard, and chipped a few slivers from the solid block of ice held within.

"To answer your first question Mr Caine, I am sorry to say that, unless the outcome was guaranteed to be in my mother's favour, she would not tell the truth." He gave a short bark of laughter. "I honestly don't know if she ever has! As for your query regarding any animosity between my mother and her sister, there was, God help us, far too much!" Turning back to the others, he swallowed a mouthful of his drink and mustered a smile. "What else can I say about my mother? Nothing very kind, I'm afraid. She wasn't really cut out for motherhood, but she married and naturally I arrived shortly thereafter. My father died when I was twelve. After Aunt C's death, Mother left Brazil — and me — to enjoy her life on the Continent. Again, Uncle took in the abandoned waif and stray and I was sent to the same school as Torrance."

He gestured with his glass. "I visited Uncle, Aunt C and Merry several times before being taken in permanently. It was a happy household — far, far happier than the one I lost! He took another gulp of his drink, and a bitter look appeared on his young face. "My mother's maiden name was Ozanne, and her married name, my father's name, was Nolloth. After my father died, Mother insisted that I be removed to my uncle's care, my surname be changed to Damant, and that I be written into my uncle's will as his sole heir, or she would abandon me in a workhouse without informing the family where I was! Naturally Uncle was horrified, for two very different reasons; for his sister-in-law to threaten such cruelty to her only child appalled him…and besides, Merry was, and still is, his heir. He refused to even consider Merry being left penniless, so, he and Aunt C made an arrangement with my mother. In return for her agreeing to allow my formal adoption by Uncle, the changing of my surname to Damant, and my inheritance of a small but more than adequate legacy from Uncle's will, Aunt C agreed to leave all her personal wealth to her sister. My mother agreed, signed the documents, and was on the earliest available boat to the Continent the very next day!"

He paused, a thoughtful expression on his face. "Mother abandoned me and left for Europe the same afternoon that Aunt C was kidnapped." Darius swallowed the last of his whisky, returned to the cabinet and topped it up. His face registered anger, sadness and disgust in equal measure. "But my aunt was to have the last laugh! After Aunt C's murder, my mother returned for the reading of the will, where she shed copious crocodile tears…right up to the point where the executor revealed that Aunt C had left everything to Merry! My Mother's tears dried almost immediately, and she showed an almost naval capability for swearing that made even my uncle, with his experience of working with miners, blench!"

Darius's face bore a faraway expression. "Until the

reading of the will I hadn't seen my mother since the day she walked out on me a few months previously. As she entered the room, she looked at me, looked away and said nothing. She didn't even acknowledge my presence!" The muscles in his jaw clenched. "I was nearly thirteen when my mother abandoned me for the second time, and I swore I would not allow her to cause me harm a third time! After the reading she declared that Aunt C's will had voided the rules of their agreement, and that I should be returned to her, with all the entitlements that I had become accustomed to signed over to her; the money for my education, my allowance and my future expectations in uncle's company, or she would follow through on her previous plans and send me to the work-house!" He took a sip of his drink, a faint smile appearing on his face. "Uncle laughed in her face. He informed her that he had hired a private enquiry agent to follow her and gather information to prove her criminality, her immorality, and that of her associates, and that based on what the agent had found, he would not let her take me away. Once she saw that she had lost the game, she left. That was nearly ten years ago. This is the first time I have seen her since, and nothing has changed." He sat back down, avoiding their eyes, his face pale and his nostrils pinched. Then he enquired, with a false light-ness of tone, "Is there anything else you wish to know?"

Thorne looked up from his notes, leant over to snaffle a finger sandwich, and cleared his throat. "What can you tell us about your mother's business partner, the delectable Mr Morten Van der Linde?"

A touch of colour brightened Darius's pale cheeks. "Van der Linde is a Dutch diamond merchant from Amsterdam. He and my mother have been business partners for several years." He paused, his colour deepening. "Possibly more — I couldn't say." He cleared his throat and continued, anger showing on his face as he spoke. "There is something you should know. Uncle wasn't sure that you should be told, since he didn't think it germane to the affair at hand, but in the light of what I have heard today, I think I should inform you. When Uncle sent out the invitations for this weekend, he only invited my mother; there was no "and guest" included. She sent a telegram agreeing to come, and indicated that she would be bringing her 'dear friend and business partner' with her. To say that Uncle was not happy would be an understatement!"

He took a sip of his drink, glowering. "Then things took a deeply concerning turn. Merry received a letter, utterly unsolicited I hasten to add, from Van der Linde himself, saying that her aunt had spoken a great deal about her, how much he was looking forward to finally meeting her, and what a shame it was that they hadn't met sooner. Merry… well, she's an innocent. She took the letter to Mar and asked for her opinion. Mar was very diplomatic about it and suggested a polite but distant response. Merry agreed, but Mar immediately informed Uncle of the matter." Darius inhaled sharply and pulled at his collar. "Mar kept a watch on the letters, and sure enough, several more arrived for Merry from Van der Linde. Judging by the sheer amount of post, I believe he was writing to her every other day! After a few weeks, Merry became somewhat reticent in sharing…she stopped showing the letters to Mar, so I'm afraid we became conspirators and headed Merry off at the post, so to speak. The mail addressed to the Taniwha is held for us by Coll at Milford City and we send a lad to collect it every few days, so for over a month now, Mar, and I have been intercepting her letters."

He stood up suddenly, and walking to his uncle's desk, he slammed his hand down. "That execrable man has actually been attempting to court my cousin by letter! Merry is a child — yes, I know she's of age — but she is a complete innocent! The letters are an utter travesty of genuine affection, and if Merry had any knowledge of that side of human nature, she would see through his and my mother's grotesque charade." He saw Elliott's raised eyebrows. "Oh, mistake me not, my mother is behind this; I can smell it! Use, abuse, cheat, steal, leave and destroy — that's her motto, it should be on her crest!" He took a deep breath. "Uncle has seen the letters we withheld from Merry." His face twisted in disgust. "They became more insinuating, more brazen, until in the last letter he actually had the temerity to ask her to marry him and run away with him this weekend!" He dragged a hand through his hair. "Needless to say, that will not be happening. I look on Merry as more a sister than a cousin. What he asks would utterly destroy her reputation, even if he did marry her…but that is only one of the issues."

Elliott settled back in his chair. "Pray tell, Mr Damant, what is the other issue?"

Darius sighed, collapsed into his armchair and made a steeple with his fingers. "What Uncle and I believe to be the *real* reason for Van der Linde's interest in my cousin. At the age of twenty-one, Merry takes control of the money her mother left her, the money my mother believes should be hers. It is Merry's twenty-first birthday this weekend. If, God forbid, she elopes with him, Morten Van der Linde will, as her husband, take control of her not inconsiderable fortune — which means that control of Merry's money will ultimately fall to the aunt who loathes her for taking what she believes to be 'her' inheritance!"

Giselle leant forward. "Do you believe either your mother or Van der Linde to be capable of threatening your cousin's life in order to achieve their ends?"

Darius swallowed and nodded. "Yes, I'm afraid I do!"

### Thorne's cabin
### 6:45pm

Thorne shook his head at the reflection in the mirror and carefully smoothed his freshly trimmed Vandyke. "That's all you're getting, so make it last!"

From her seated position by the bed, Veronique turned her huge brown eyes onto her master and her jowls trembled as she alternated between gazing imploringly at Thorne and her now utterly empty food bowl.

Thorne straightened his cravat. "I did say: one dinner and one dinner only!"

There was a faint whine in response and a clatter as she hit the bowl with her paw.

Thorne turned, held up one finger and raised his eyebrow. "What did I say?"

The response was another clatter as Veronique's paw again came down and smacked the empty dish across the room. She flung herself into her bed, laid her nose on her eiderdown and with a look of reproach, kicked at her cushions in protest.

Thorne smiled. "Sulking is not an attractive quality, Veronique!" He opened one of the small trunks in the corner of his cabin. As he did so, Veronique's ears pricked up and she raised her head from its prone and obviously starving position on her bed. Thorne turned and waved a quantity of discreetly folded newspaper at her. "Come along, walkies!"

After several minutes wandering the deck, Veronique completed her necessary after-dinner habits, which Thorne disposed of overboard, and they returned to their cabin where Thorne, with a flourish, presented her with the large mutton bone he had managed to procure from the kitchen.

He wagged his finger again. "Be good! I'll return in a few hours."

Veronique looked up from her treat, wagged her tail, and returned to the more important matter at hand — or paw!

Thorne closed the door and wandered past the cabin that was between his and the one shared by Elliott and Giselle. Again, the strange sensation returned to his stomach. He took a deep breath and waited. As the feeling faded, he reached into his inside pocket, pulled out his monocle and gave it a swift wipe, then with a grin, returned it to his pocket for later use. Walking to the edge of the deck, he leant on the handrail and focused on the incredible views of the Sound as the day began its journey into night. The brilliant blue of the sky in the east dimmed to the colour of periwinkles, while in the west, gleaming ribbons of gold and lavender stretched out their fingers to paint the sky with the last glow of light, before dusk fell behind the magnificent sea cliffs at the edge of Milford Sound, blocking the final descent of the sun from his view.

### Carolyn's cabin
### 6:50pm

Carolyn fluffed her carefully curled fringe in the mirror and smirked. "You know as well as I do that there is no way out. You will do what I say, or certain information will find its way to both O.D and the authorities. You, and all you value, will disappear the moment you try to cross me! So, you see, you have absolutely no choice but to assist me!"

The figure she addressed regarded her silently as Carolyn stood up with an expression of triumph and entered the bathroom to see to her final pre-dinner ablutions, slamming the door behind her.

Her victim stared at the closed door for some time before leaving the room without a word.

○

## Elliott and Giselle's Cabin
### 6:55pm

Elliott fastened his gold cufflinks and smoothed his collar. Facing the full-length mirror in the little cabin, he ran a thoughtful eye over his evening dress. He turned to look at Giselle, who gave him an approving nod from where she lounged in the little green armchair by the door, her lavender gown glowing in the same gaslights that set her red hair to flame and her diamond and amethyst choker to brilliance. He smiled back. Yes, they would both do very nicely.

There was a knock at the door. Lilith glanced up from her sewing and looked inquiringly at her mistress, who nodded. Putting down her embroidery, Lilith opened the door to admit Thorne, resplendent in his broadcloth and linen evening dress with a chartreuse cravat, matching cummerbund, and a gleaming gold monocle clenched in his left eye.

Elliott grinned at the spectacle. "Let's hope nothing untoward happens tonight, my friend. If your eyebrows rise too high, you'll lose that monocle!"

Thorne assumed a tragic air and removed the monocle with a flourish. "As you wish. The gong announcing the cocktail hour should sound in a few minutes, and the bar is in the snug, which is just off the lounge...so if we wander down now, we can be first in line!"

Giselle laughed. She rose from her armchair and smoothed the front of her gown as Elliott picked up her stole and carefully draped it across her shoulders. She smiled at her husband. "Shall we?"

Elliott nodded. Collecting his Malacca cane, he offered his arm to his wife, and the three of them headed down to dinner.

Lilith watched them descend the stairs, and closed the door behind them. She paused, then reopened the door and checked to make sure they had gone before she stepped out of the suite, and made her way towards another cabin on the same side of the boat. Pausing outside the door, she straightened her shoulders and knocked. There was silence; then the door opened and the figure standing before her slowly smiled. "I *was* wondering...come in."

Lilith stepped into the cabin and the door closed behind her.

○

### 7:15pm
### The Lounge

Thorne smoothed his dark-blond hair as he cast a jaundiced eye around the bright room. His hopes of being among the first down for the cocktail hour had been dashed the instant they set foot in the lounge; the world and his wife seemed to have had the same thought, at the same time!

As they entered the lounge, they hadn't even made it to the bar before their host O.D had greeted them and introduced them, under their stage names, to his daughter.

O.D gestured towards the rest of his party. "May I also introduce Marjorie Lee Colville, known to us as Mar, the most irreplaceable member of our little family?" Mar laughed gently as she acknowledged O.D's kind words; in her late forties with dark eyes and a wealth of brown hair neatly pinned into a braided bun, Mar was the epitome of a capable woman. O.D continued. "Darius, Torrance, and Captain Peach you have already met, but I don't think you have been introduced to our captain's delightful daughter, Fleur." The very young blonde girl dropped a neat curtsy and in her soft, Deep South accent murmured, "Pleased to meet y'all, I'm sure." O.D waived a hand towards the last of the group. "And of course, you know Sir Wesley Eade's secretary, Robin Ellis." The rather stiff-looking man gave them a sharp nod, looking as though he wished he were somewhere else entirely.

Merry looked at Elliott and Thorne with a faint blush on her cheeks. "Thank you for coming this weekend. I have heard so much about your performances in America and Australia: you are legendary here in New Zealand. I have been looking forward to meeting you ever since my father told me you were coming — I find the art of illusion mesmerising! Two years ago, my father and I were in Los Angeles and we went to see Mr Houdini perform at the Orpheum. It was both terrifying and spectacular."

Elliott smiled, allowing his canines to flash. "Houdini is indeed a master of the craft; I remember telling him so not that long ago!"

Merry's jaw dropped slightly; turning her wide eyes to Elliott she stammered, "D-did you actually meet Houdini?"

"Several times, but we crossed paths with him most recently in America; I believe he was traveling to London as we were heading here."

Merry bit her lip and smiled brilliantly, her hazel eyes glowing.

Mar looked at O.D with a slight smile. "I believe it's time for us to take to our table." She turned to Elliott, Giselle, and Thorne with a polite smile. "It was a great pleasure meeting you all. If you will please excuse us."

Captain Peach extended his arm to Mar just as Torrance

extended his to Fleur. With Robin Ellis bringing up the rear alone, the five of them left the lounge.

Giselle watched the small party head out of the room. She turned to O.D with a slight lift of her eyebrow. "I thought both companions and captains were acceptable at table, Mr Damant?"

O.D turned to her with a slightly embarrassed look on his face. "They are! Mar always dines with us, as do Captain Peach, Fleur, and Torrance. But they are all very…proper about it when we have guests."

Merry cleared her throat. "I have informed Mar that she, Fleur, Captain Peach, and Torrance will all be expected to dine with us tomorrow and for the rest of the weekend: I refused to take no for an answer!"

O.D smiled. "Excellent."

Merry frowned slightly. "But Mr Ellis said it would not be appropriate. I didn't want to cause offence, so I accepted his refusal."

"Very well, my dear. Mr Bowyer, if you will please excuse us, we need to circulate before the dinner gong."

Elliott nodded graciously. "Yes, of course."

O.D took Merry by the arm as they and a rather quiet Darius moved around the room. Elliott turned his attention to his wife, and Thorne, feeling a little like a gooseberry, wandered into the snug in the hope of finally receiving a drink before dinner.

Many of the guests were already ensconced in the more comfortable of the velvet-upholstered settees and armchairs, clutching colourful cocktails and engaging in that most civilised of pastimes: the art of small talk, most of which revolved around the ostentatious displays of wealth in the magnificently appointed room.

The displays were many, varied, and extremely expensive. Aside from the several glass-fronted cases containing several decades of O.D's collections of jewellery, assorted incunabula, and objet d'art, there were also three life-sized mannequins: one dressed as a Maori elder in a kahu kiwi — the kiwi feather cloak — and bearing a stunning, intricately carved greenstone mere — a short, teardrop shaped hand axe; another wearing a full and incredibly ornate set of samurai armour, including an elaborate kabuto; and a third in the florid uniform of a member of the 16th The Queen's Lancers, decorated with many medals.

Thorne presented himself at the bar and was served by the steward Trevenniss, who skillfully created the requested gin sling with speed and aplomb.

As the collection of people was swelled by the arrival of a handful of other guests who had taken the fashionably late route to dinner, Thorne's attention was caught by a woman standing by the doorway to the outer deck on the port side, her satin-clad back turned to him. Her thick blue-black hair was artfully coiled around her head and held in place by gold pins set with sapphires, the glittering stones an exact match for her stunning gown.

A strange feeling crept over Thorne as he gazed at her back. His stomach started to jump, just as it had earlier. A sudden sense of certainty came over him. He gulped the remains of his gin sling, slid the glass onto one of the many small tables dotted around the snug, and began to walk towards her. As he was halfway across the room, he felt a sudden hand at his elbow. Turning sharply, he found himself face to face with the butler Vasily, who smiled in a chilly manner. "Excuse me, sir, if I may just get past…"

Thorne nodded distractedly. "Er, yes, of course." He moved out of the way of the limping butler and turned back to the woman, but she had gone. Thorne scanned the small room, his green eyes flicking from face to face, but she had completely disappeared.

Vasily, now no longer blocked from his pre-planned route, walked towards the massive gong that stood between the samurai armour and the uniform of the 16th Lancers, and with a practised aim struck a note so loud that it rendered several of the guests speechless and caused Josephine Carter to jump, flinging the contents of her glass in Thornton Rust's face.

Mint julep dripping down his chin, Thornton extracted his handkerchief and manfully mopped at the ruination of his carefully applied eyebrows, murmuring soothing plati-tudes to his fellow actor as he surreptitiously glanced at his silver cigarette case to check the damage done to his reflection.

Josephine bit her lip. The sound of the gong had made her jump, but the sight of a sodden Rust dabbing at the bits of mint hanging from his chops was almost too much for her to bear. Desperately trying not to laugh, she avoided catching Colten's eye and turned away to try and compose herself. As she did so, she realised she was looking at their host's party. They had been introduced to O.D by Sir Wesley shortly after arriving aboard and she had picked up on the tension between the two men. She had also been quite taken by the renown and somewhat reclusive magnate. Josephine decided that she liked what she had seen and so allowed herself a little impolite staring. As O.D chatted with his group, she noticed the shy-looking young lady she understood to be his daughter, while to his right, a handsome, dark young man in his early twenties whom she took to be his nephew. O.D turned to his daughter and caught Josephine's eye; he nodded to her with a smile. Josephine nodded back, a slight flush on her cheeks as she turned back to her companions.

O.D whispered something to his daughter, who removed several slips of paper from the little reticule that matched her pale-blue frock and moved around the room, handing them to the gentlemen who took note of what was written thereon: the name of the lady they were to escort into dinner.

Josephine heard a sudden choked oath come from behind her. Turning in surprise, she saw a tall blond man with a neat Vandyke staring at his piece of paper. She realised it was Lydeard Bowyer, one of the illusionists who had been hired for the weekend's entertainments. He looked as though he had suffered a terrible shock; his face was ashen, his elegant hands shaking as his slender fingers plucked at the little piece of paper.

She was about to walk over to him when his brother Preston appeared and whispered to him. Lydeard held the note out to his brother, who read it and gripped his arm. A sudden smile appeared on his face which was mirrored by Lydeard, the terrible shock suddenly replaced by an equally terrible hope.

Oblivious to the reaction the slip of paper had caused, O.D caught Vasily's eye and nodded. The butler bowed, and from his position by the dining room door intoned, "Ladies and gentlemen, dinner is served." With a smart bow from the waist, he held out a hand towards the entrance to the dining room.

There was the necessary pre-dinner pause as the gentlemen searched for the ladies they would be escorting. O.D held out a deferential arm to Lady Carlton-Cayce, resplendent in a spectacular gown of cloth of gold; Merry was escorted by Sir Wesley, whose earlier attitude had been replaced by that of a benign uncle; Darius looked rather overwhelmed as his arm was taken in a somewhat possessive grip by Dona Carla Riva, whose feline smile resembled that of a cat that had not only got the cream, but who had also taken delivery of the entire dairy herd.

A thin, dark man suddenly appeared before Giselle and

with a slight bow addressed her in what was quite possibly the most beautiful and melodic voice she had ever heard. "Mlle Du'Lac? I am Colten Kayfield, your escort to dinner."

Giselle smiled, and gathering her stole gave her husband a slightly arch look as she was escorted through to the dining room.

Elliott turned to Thorne. "I need to go and find my lady. Go and find yours, my friend — and I pray it is she!"

Thorne nodded, his jaw clenched as he scanned the room, while Elliott walked to where Josephine Carter was sitting and introduced himself. She smiled at him as she took his arm.

Thorne's eyes took in Carolyn's deathly expression as Thornton Rust, complete with minty facial attachments, bowed and presented her with his arm, even as Morten, suavely smoothing one eyebrow, escorted a simpering Sophie into the dining room.

Thorne realised that he was now alone in the lounge. His heart hammered in his chest as he realised the lady he was to escort must be the woman he had seen by the door, and that she was no longer there.

Merry appeared from the other room. "Mr Bowyer, can you not find your lady?"

Thorne shook his head. Clearing his throat, he managed, "No, she isn't here."

A maid suddenly appeared from the door that led through to the kitchen. Merry caught her eye. "Mary, would you please go and look for one of the guests?"

Mary bobbed. "Yes, Miss Damant, which guest?"

"Madame Aquilleia. She may be in her room or on one of the other decks, and failed to hear the gong. Try her cabin first."

"Yes Miss Damant." The young maid bobbed again and headed off.

Merry smiled at Thorne. "Hopefully all is well. Would you like to wait a moment before we go in, just in case?"

Not trusting his voice, Thorne nodded. Merry immediately re-entered the dining room, explained the slight social hiccough to her father and rejoined Thorne in the lounge. She smiled at him. "Madame Aquilleia was the last of my guests to accept her invitation. I was so happy that she agreed to come…she is the foremost psychic in the Southern Hemisphere!"

The maid suddenly reappeared. "Begging your pardon, Miss Damant, the lady was in her cabin. She says she has come over with a headache and begs to be excused from the evening's entertainments."

Merry nodded, her young face thoughtful. "Thank you, Mary. That will be all."

Mary bobbed again; she was rather proud of her bob. She left the lounge as Thorne mechanically held out his arm to escort his host's daughter into the dining room, his mind full of one thought and one thought only: Aquilleia was here!

## The Dining Room
### 7:30pm

O.D was exceptionally proud of his dining room. In style it was the sister room to the lounge, the beautifully carved oak dining suite stained in deepest stygian black, the walls and ceiling covered in wooden panels and hand-painted with frescos in Pompeiian red and old gold with highlights of black and white.

Vasily had now been joined by the stewards Trevenniss and Callahan and several maids who gently eased the guests into their places around the table. Desdemonia had been tasked with organsing the seating arrangements for the weekend: she had spent a great deal of time and thought studying the individual guests and their precise rank in society to better judge where to place them; she was quite aware that a baronet was somewhat below a widowed baroness — even if that baroness was the aforementioned baronet's companion, and that getting a untitled millionaire's former sister-in-law to accept where she was placed without complaint was a delicate situation that required extreme planning, grace, and some very carefully arranged seating. Her first plan had been sabotaged when Sir Wesley had sent a telegram personally requesting the seat at the opposite end of the table to his host because he preferred to sit facing the window. She had gone back and forth to O.D with several suggestions before he had ended the discussion by telling her, "Place them all where you feel is best…they can like it or lump it!"

Desdemonia watched the social ballet going on in the dining room from her hidden perch in the kitchen, the huge fresco on the wall between the rooms containing various spy-holes to ensure the servants could spot any issue as soon as it arose.

Thorne took his leave of Merry at her chair, to the immediate left of Sir Wesley, and took his place directly opposite Elliott. As the gentlemen waited for the ladies to sit, Thorne avoided Elliot's eye, allowing his gaze to wander around the room. In spite of the recent shock to his system he realised that, regardless of the elevated levels of gaiety at the table, several guests looked a little strained.

Thorne took a deep, shaky breath and decided to focus on the job in hand. He forced his mind back to the paperwork that had arrived for their perusal. The files from the government had actually been sent by Lapotaire. He had furnished them with detailed dossiers on several, but not all of the invited guests; documents that covered their professions, families, and private lives — including some juicy little items that might have come under the heading 'gossip'. Thorne had read through one or two of the more salacious files with enjoyment. His love of a good penny dreadful was legendary, and investigating the real thing, as it were, was one of the many things he enjoyed about the line of work that he and Elliott had chosen.

The first file that he had read after their meeting with O.D was that of the stunningly beautiful Lady Leonora Carlton-Cayce. She was the highest-ranking female guest, and as such, sat on the immediate right of their host, O.D; her file was mostly of interest for the startling number of dead husbands plucked from among the great and the good that littered her life — eight at the last count!

Her life had begun under somewhat unfathomable circumstances. A place and date of birth was the usual start of any investigation into a person's past, but in the dossier that particular piece of information was marked as 'unknown' — and if Lapotaire couldn't find it, it was very well hidden indeed. Her secret past had carried her to the dizzy heights of Italian high society, where she first appeared at the approximate age of twenty, shortly before her marriage to a prince some forty years her senior who had not survived their wedding night. Her other husbands had shared a similar fate, her marriages and repeated widowhood all taking place over a period of fifteen years. Her most recent husband, the eighty-seven-year-old Baron von Schmetterling, had died less than three months after their wedding, leaving her even richer and therefore in even greater demand for society events where wealthy older gentlemen were in ready supply. She had taken to her reaquired widowhood with extreme sangfroid. Reverting to a previous and preferred surname, she had sold all of the

Baron's holdings and was currently the 'companion' of Sir Wesley Eade, that bastion of charm, currently holding court from his requested position at the opposite end of the table from O.D.

Sir Wesley, too, was interesting. His family were quite unusual for not following convention in the slightest, although they had made their fortune in the usual way: an enterprising young commander had, in the early days of the Regency, furnished finances for a cause close to the king's heart…and had also furnished his wife for the king's bed! The arrangement had been well received and the family had been graced with a title and more land. The title was somewhat less than the commander and his wife had expected, but a sudden jump from untitled middle son to a baronet was good enough!

Sir Wesley himself had been born in late 1850, the sole child of his mother, Lady Mary Eade, and his father, Sir Harbottle Eade, who had died some few years later, leaving his son with rather less money than he himself had inherited. In fact, the Eade family estates were somewhat short of funds, and Lady Carlton-Cayce was generous in her support of her dear friend…and his living expenses.

Sir Wesley had managed his self-chosen path in life rather well. Thrown into the usual boarding schools, he had decided quite early on that he preferred money he could see and count, rather than the daily slog of managing the lands of his title and seeing very little recompence for his labours, and so had decided to follow his grandfather into law, as opposed to his father who had gone into tea in India and failed miserably before being shipped home in disgrace to an arranged marriage and his inevitable fading away within the family estates. On leaving school and joining a suitably placed firm in London, Sir Wesley had climbed the ranks with aplomb, managing to do so with what appeared to be very little ill-grace from others…unless, as with his connections to O.D's secret past, such concerns were kept hidden behind closed doors. He had been the DB Mining Company's lawyer since its inception nearly thirty years previously.

A peal of laughter came from the top end of the table; Dona Carla Riva was clearly enjoying herself.

Thorne pondered the file on the Brazilian ballet dancer. She had been born in 1870 to a well-respected family of coffee growers in the Paraiba valley, Sao Paolo. Her grandfather had been a jeweller in the city until he realised that the demand for coffee covered a far wider market of both the rich and the poor; the poor being far more willing to part with their hard-earned money for coffee beans than they were for expensive trinkets. Dona Carla's abilities were soon noticed and she was sent to the Teatro Colón in Argentina to study, only leaving when it was closed in 1888 for restoration works — which were still ongoing. Her joie de vivre, sheer magnetism, and spectacular abilities on stage had enabled her to dance with the best companies in Moscow, London, Paris, Vienna, and New York.

There was little information about any romantic attachments, although it had been alleged that she had caused a separation between husband and wife in Paris — but that was Paris!

The only other interesting thing to note was her habit of appearing in performances where rather expensive items of jewellery belonging to the guests had disappeared. But then, the very wealthy often lost, dropped or otherwise mislaid costly baubles and simply bought another to replace that which was missing. However, she *had* been present at the infamous event in New York City when the magnificent Larkspur Diamond had been stolen from its display case and its owner, the reclusive millionaire Nathaniel De Coeur, had vanished…

That was all the information Lapotaire had sent them. As Thorne considered the lack of dossiers on the other guests, his mind focused on one guest in particular: as Aquilleia had only recently accepted the invitation, her file must be one that would be arriving soon. The lines of his face hardened; if it was his Aquilleia, and she wished to remember them, he would never lose her again!

A terribly polite cough sounded at the top of the table.

Thorne looked around the table and noted that all the ladies were seated. Sliding elegantly into his seat and flicking his linen napkin across his lap, he fumed silently. Aquilleia was on the Taniwha, and instead of finding her, he was trapped in a hell of social niceties! He tried very hard not to focus on the empty chair on his immediate right, and forced a polite smile at Elliott, who was directly opposite and not a little concerned for his friend.

Thorne braced himself for the evening's entertainment as the steward poured him a glass of Champagne.

O.D stood, smiled at everyone and raised his glass. "Honoured guests, welcome to the Taniwha on this, my daughter Merry's twenty-first birthday weekend. Thank you for travelling so far to help us celebrate a very special occasion." He sat down and nodded to Vasily, who immediately raised his hand.

The first dish was brought to the table: soupe jardinière. It came and went without much to-do, other than everyone trying not to make a noise while drinking it — one or two failed!

The soup bowls were cleared and the fish course arrived: salmon in lobster sauce. The conversation started to get louder as the stewards refilled the champagne coupes and retired to the kitchens for a break before the next course was due.

Dona Carla savoured a forkful of the salmon, then taking

a sip from her glass, she caught the eye of Lady Carlton-Cayce and smiled. Leaning forward, she allowed the massive emerald choker at her throat to gleam in the flicker of the gaslights that also illuminated her outrageously low-cut orange satin gown. Her ruby-painted smile widened slightly. "Do you see anything you like, Lady Carlton-Cayce?"

The Scandinavian beauty opposite raised her vivid blue eyes from Dona Carla's rather scandalous décolleté and smiled in response, but said nothing, her long white fingers playing with the ornate necklace draped around her throat: a glowing, golden serpent wrapped around a huge oval ruby.

O.D sat between the two ladies, a slightly pained expression on his face. Dona Carla was an exceptional dancer whom he and Merry had seen perform on several occasions. Her invitation had come from Merry herself, though the financial incentive to acquiesce had come entirely from O.D.

Lady Carlton-Cayce was, however, an entirely separate kettle of fish; she was there solely because of her connection to Sir Wesley. O.D frowned. He still hadn't forgiven Sir Wesley for his earlier remarks; he would take him to one side later that evening for a polite discussion.

To the immediate right of Lady Carlton-Cayce, Colten wore an amused expression as his eyes and ears took in the conversations and expressions around him, while keeping a dry and witty exchange going with his conversational partner.

Giselle, seated to his right, caught Dona Carla's eye and smiled as the spectacular Brazilian winked at her and continued to purr at Lady Carlton-Cayce.

Darius sat in a stunned silence between the vivacious Dona Carla and the rather quiet Sophie, who had barely touched her soup or salmon, choosing instead to push the tender morsels around her plate without actually tasting them — quite unlike Dona Carla, who had thrown herself into enjoying her meal with every ounce of her being.

Darius, though not a shrinking violet by any means, felt slightly out of his depth with the highly ornamental yet really rather terrifying woman on his right. He tried not to let his jaw drop at a highly irregular and very naughty remark she flung at Lady Carlton-Cayce; Dona Carla truly was quite spectacular!

To the left of Darius, Sophie sat in a mood of mild to moderate unhappiness. Her doctor had insisted that if she truly wished to lose weight, then she had to continue with his banting plan and not eat anything that he had not explicitly allowed; that meant she was currently existing on water, sherry, champagne, and air, and she was now rapidly beginning to feel the effects of no food and too much alcohol. She turned to her left, suddenly realising that her escort had asked her a question. In a bit of a fluster, she asked him to repeat himself. Morten smiled suavely and did so with good grace; Sophie smiled back and without thinking took another sip of her champagne before she replied. Such an attentive, attractive, charming man!

Directly opposite Morten, Thornton Rust was attempting to entertain Carolyn with absolutely no success whatsoever. Having managed to finally disentangle the last of the offending herb garnish from his whiskers, he tried to turn his quite inconsiderable charm on the lady who had suffered his rather damp escort into dinner, but the comments he received in response were monosyllabic at best and rude at worst. His best mixed-company music-hall jests hadn't even elicited a smile, let alone a laugh!

Carolyn sat in a state of extreme and bitter fury, her soup and salmon untouched and her posture so rigid that she was in danger of doubling as a replacement for one the mannequins in the lounge. Her mind weighed the slights that had been afforded to her position and dignity in the last few minutes alone. To be escorted in by an oafish nonentity and seated in the middle of the table was an absolute insult. *She* should have been escorted in by Sir Wesley, the honour should not have been given to that simpering brat, Merry! She ground her teeth in impotent rage. She should have expected such treatment from her sainted brother-in-law… the utter, utter bastard! And to cap it all, Morten had decided to ignore her and employ his charm on the vapid bitch he had escorted in! She felt all-consuming anger threaten to overtake her; she took a deep breath and with a carefully steadied hand picked up her coupe and took a long sip of her champagne. Placing the glass back on the table with as much care as she had lifted it, she smiled suddenly. The evening wasn't without merit, nor was it over yet. There was still the meeting she had arranged with a somewhat interesting and possibly lucrative party later in her cabin. Her smile widened as she finally lifted her fork to sample the salmon.

To her immediate right, Elliott had heard the slight grating noise as her teeth ground together. He raised his eyebrows at Thorne, who frowned slightly, followed Elliott's sideways glance and realised what he was hearing. He rolled his eyes and focused on his plate, still studiously ignoring the vacant chair beside him.

Elliott turned his attention to Josephine, who was seated between Thorne and Sir Wesley. She was certainly enjoying her evening, discussing the art of the theatre with Merry and Sir Wesley, and trying to cajole a silent Thorne into the conversation, whilst showing as much enjoyment of her meal as Dona Carla.

Josephine was in her element; she and the other members of their little troupe had decided their backstories, and hers involved a long and much-loved association with amateur dramatics that had continued after her "marriage" to Colten. She cast a quick glance up the table. Her "husband" certainly seemed to be enjoying himself; Giselle and Dona Carla were both quite lovely. As she took in the other guests, her gaze again fell on O.D at the head of the table. As she studied his face, he looked up and caught her eye. A blush immediately covered her cheeks and she turned her attention back to her glass and her end of the table.

As the remains of the fish course were cleared the entrée arrived; veal cutlets, curried fowl vol-au-vents and savoury rissoles accompanied by even greater quantities of champagne, which was when Sophie finally decided that what her doctor didn't know, wouldn't hurt him. She proceeded to apply herself to the superb meal before her with as much gusto as Dona Carla and Josephine.

The evening continued, the chatter around the table grew, the air of strained enjoyment was dispelled and there was much laughter, but not from Carolyn.

As the entrée was removed and rum punch to cleanse the palate arrived, Morten caught her eye with a suave smile and tried to reach her ankle with his foot. He winced and choked on an oath as her right foot swung in a sudden sharp kick that caught him squarely on the inside of his right ankle.

The table shook and the crockery and glasses clattered and rang as he shot backwards. An equally loud silence descended as everyone turned to stare at Morten, who was now standing by his overturned chair, clutching at his leg and muttering under his breath in Dutch.

O.D looked at the man with very real dislike. "Are you quite well, Mr Van der Linde?"

Realising he was the centre of attention, and not for a good reason, Morten plastered a smile on his face as Vasily swiftly replaced his chair. "It is nothing: merely a touch of the cramp" He looked at a bewildered Merry. "Malaria, you know…from my work in South Africa; it comes and goes. Perhaps I could have a glass of tonic water?"

O.D caught Vasily's eye. He disappeared and returned in less than a minute with a crystal tumbler of tonic water on a silver salver.

Vasily was about to place the tumbler on the table when Morten took it straight from the small tray. Vasily paused, his expression unreadable. He was about to leave the table when Sir Wesley, in a quiet undertone, committed the utter social faux pas of telling another man's servant to be more polite. Vasily looked at Sir Wesley, turned in silence, and swept into the kitchen. As he did so, O.D, barely hiding his fury at his guest's impertinence, faced his lawyer and in a tight voice said, "We must talk business this evening before the entertainments begins, my old friend!"

Sir Wesley smiled and sipped his champagne.

In the kitchen, Vasily walked to where his wife was organising the battery of attendants in getting the next course ready for delivery to the table. He placed the salver back on its little velvet pad with extreme care and looked at his wife, his green eyes snapping. "I really don't like that man." Desdemonia smiled as cook gave the next course a critical look before scattering a little more watercress around the roast pheasant. "If he knew who you were, husband, the feeling would definitely be mutual!"

Vasily checked the time on his fob watch and gestured to the stewards to carry the main course in and present it to the host: roast fowl aux Cresson with matchstick potatoes and a green salad. The conversation around the table paused as the guests also happily accepted the offer of a fully charged glass of Côte de Nuits to accompany the dish.

As the meal progressed, several more courses faded into what was, for most of the guests, a warm and slightly fuzzy champagne-fuelled haze. The game course was supplanted by a light sorbet which in turn was followed by the entremets, all complimented with an almost endless supply of champagne. A dessert of iced apple pudding came and went, along with port and Madeira; then finally, coffee was offered in the lounge for those who wanted it.

O.D stood up and again offered his arm to Lady Carlton-Cayce, who took it in a light, almost non-existent grip as they walked back into the lounge, followed by Sir Wesley escorting Merry, then various of the guests. The scent of perfume, alcohol, and affluence wafting around them as they made their way back into the exquisite room for the completion of the evening's entertainment.

Carolyn, with a distant smile at her escort, refused his offer of a drink, touched her head, and with a pained expression excused herself to ascend to her cabin for some aspirin to deal with the beginnings of a headache. As she swished onto the outer deck, Josephine turned to Sophie and murmured, sotto voce, "I'm not surprised she has a headache. The way she was grinding her teeth during dinner, I'm truly astonished she has any left!"

Sophie looked shocked. "Josephine, really!"

Josephine smiled. "Yes, dear, really! Didn't you notice the daggers she was aiming at you and Morten at table? I dread to think what her companion will face after we retire for the evening! Now, I truly could do with another drink."

Sophie's face took on a stunned look. "Companion? I didn't know! Are you sure?"

Josephine nodded firmly. "Yes, I am sure, you utter ninny! But then, being called a ninny is somewhat better than being called a loose woman…again! Now, more champagne; to the snug, and let's be quick about it!" Josephine managed to catch Vasily's eye and two fully charged coupes were waiting for them when they arrived in the snug. On their way back to the lounge, Morten intercepted them and engaged Sophie in conversation. Josephine rolled her eyes and paused, contemplating where would be best to take her ease, before seating herself at the same table as Lady Carlton-Cayce.

O.D came back to the same table, and presented Lady Carlton-Cayce with the drink she had requested, as Sir Wesley guided Merry to the same settee. The two men looked at each other as they settled the ladies in. Sir Wesley murmured. "Shall we have that conversation now, old friend?" O.D nodded, his face a careful blank as he bent down to inform his daughter. Merry looked disappointed as the two stiff-backed men walked away; she sipped her mint cordial with a faint expression of mulishness.

Josephine saw her expression. Leaning forward, she touched Merry's hand. "Whatever is wrong?"

Merry looked at the kindly woman with some doubt, cast a glance at Lady Carlton-Cayce, then blurted. "I think Papa and Sir Wesley have had a falling-out."

Josephine raised an eyebrow at Lady Carlton-Cayce, who took a sip of her champagne and nodded, her brilliant eyes steady. "Go on."

Merry took a deep breath. "They've been friends for longer than I have been alive, but something…something from the past has come between them. I don't know what to do!"

Josephine again touched her hand, and Merry looked up into a face that was kind and understanding. "Men are interesting creatures. Many upsetting things occur, and they either choose to ignore those occasions or it affords them no concern at all…but they can take changes to their household quite hard. Has anything else occurred that could have upset your father?"

A slightly guilty look crossed Merry's face, together with a touch of her previous mulishness.

Josephine's smile deepened; she recognised that look. "Is it — are you perhaps…courting?"

Merry gulped and nodded. "I think so — yes!"

Josephine put her head on one side and her eyes narrowed. "You…think so?"

Merry twisted a little gold ring on her left hand and both Leonora and Josephine noticed the flash of a stone that had been turned inwards, towards the palm.

The two older women looked at the young girl sitting before them, their thoughts following similar lines that had led them to vastly different outcomes: Leonora's mind turned to her early years; by the time she was Merry's age, she had already been married once, widowed, and had begun a second courtship — and that wasn't counting the many and varied friendships she had enjoyed before she had met her first husband. Merry was of a ripe age for marriage, but she was emotionally young and far more naïve than she herself had ever been! Josephine, meanwhile, remembered how wonderful it was to love and be loved in return. Until the outbreak of the Anglo-Egyptian War in 1882 and the death of her beloved husband, killed in the Battle of Tell El Kebir, she had been exceptionally happy. She sat back with a sigh; the pain became easier to manage with each passing year, but it never truly left.

Leonora took a sip from her champagne and looked at Merry with hooded eyes. "And what does your gentleman say, hmm? Would he say you were courting, or would he say it was already a little more serious than that?"

Merry stared at her in silence.

On the other side of the room, Elliott, Giselle, and Thorne sat in quiet discussion, picking apart the various conversations they had overheard or been a part of at dinner, whilst trying to ignore the possible above-stairs presence of a rather important part of their past: Aquilleia.

The conversation turned to Morten and the rather painful incident at table. Elliott looked at Thorne. "What do you think, Thorne? I don't believe it was cramp, it looked more like a dead leg to me!"

Thorne nodded as he looked at his pocket watch. "Who do you think kicked him?"

Elliott smiled. "My money would be on the charming Mrs Carolyn Nolloth. Yours?"

"The very same. Talking of which, the good lady is taking her time about getting some aspirin, isn't she? She should have returned several minutes ago."

Giselle nodded and took a sip of her champagne. "I wonder what she's up to?"

◯

### Carolyn's cabin
### 10:00pm

Carolyn entered her cabin and locked the door. As she turned, she noticed a piece of paper on the carpet that had obviously been posted through the gap at the bottom of the door. Picking it up, she unfolded the missive and scanned the contents. She leant against the door and allowed herself a self-satisfied smirk. Excellent: her plans had been confirmed by her confederate, and it had all been so easy!

Morten had taken her at her word for the entire set-up with Mereanthy. That criminal, foolish, and rather boring cretin had been worth her effort for a short while, but his usefulness had started to drop as his willingness to spend *her* income rather than his own had risen. Then, just as she had finally decided to leave him, a far better and rather more entertaining idea had presented itself!

Using him had been part of a long-term plan for revenge

that had been several gruelling years in the preparation. She and her accomplice had spent much of the last few years studying and planning the downfall of O.D and his daughter. It simply wasn't enough to just kill them — it had to be nothing more or less than their utter destruction.

Her previous, murderous suggestion to Morten was almost her entire plan — almost. What she hadn't divulged to Morten was his part in it. He had believed the plan was to woo the girl after arriving, but unbeknownst to him both she and her confederate had been in contact with Merry for the last few months by letter: pretending to be Morten and presenting him as an ardent suitor. Each letter moved them a step closer to the planned outcome: that of causing the maximum amount of pain to O.D. A secret relationship and a hidden engagement with a man of questionable family and society, and with obvious criminal connections, could well tip O.D over the edge.

The idea of the love letters had been a spark of true genius, and all done without any input from Morten. Several letters had been sent without his knowledge before they had even left Australia, wooing Merry from afar in his name. Carolyn smiled. Her accomplice had continued the ruse from the boat after the mail had been intercepted, sending letters every other day. Merry's girlishly naive replies, including her effusive acceptance of his courtship, were currently in a small ribbon-tied bundle hidden in Carolyn's writing case for future use. And the pièce de resistance had been her confederate's act of placing a diamond engagement ring in Merry's cabin…Carolyn smiled, the malice twisting her lips, she had seen the ring on the brat's finger at the dining table. Such a shame that pathetic little diamond was the only item of jewellery Merry would ever wear.

She had enjoyed writing the first few letters to her niece, knowing that she was killing two birds with one stone. Soon she would be free of Morten's suffocating possessiveness and roving eye, and then that simpering brat and her insufferable father would both be dead. Securing her rightful inheritance was all that kept her going — that, and the support of her collaborator.

Poor, foolish, greedy, gullible Morten! He was utterly unaware that he had never been her accomplice, and that she was framing him for the murder of her niece. He could consider it his just reward for that short-lived dalliance with a cheap music-hall actress some years ago. Well, he would, if he lived long enough to do so, which wasn't part of her plan!

The final, excellent piece of forgery had been a gift from her confederate and was currently tucked away in her writing case: Morten's signature on a suicide note. This detailed his offer of marriage, Merry's enthusiastic acceptance, her subsequent rejection on the grounds of his lack of social standing and money, his decision to kill her, and the sudden remorse that led him to throw himself off the boat. The note would be planted in his room shortly after her niece's tragic murder and Morten's almost immediate death. She and her accomplice had considered poison, but that would be difficult to furnish aboard a boat, so they had agreed that a blow to the head and the old heave-ho overboard was the best and cleanest method for both Merry and Morten.

Carolyn smirked at her reflection in the mirror. Did Morten actually think she was stupid enough to believe he would stay with her after marrying her wealthier, younger, and easier to manipulate niece?

Her niece's trust fund had been so helpful; the lawyer she had hired to look into the matter had been almost apologetic as he'd explained that if Merry died a spinster before her twenty-first birthday, her entire inheritance from her mother would pass to her, the patient aunt.

Setting Merry up for a dramatic fall from grace had been so easy. The revelation of her death and disgrace would cause O.D pain and humiliation, and if that didn't kill him… well, perhaps out of heartbreak and loss he too would take a tumble overboard.

Carolyn laughed out loud; the game was hers to win!

She sighed a deep and happy sigh as she walked to her dressing table, perched on the padded seat and patted her artfully arranged hair. Then she turned her mind back to the present. Her new maid was satisfactory, her background a trifle not, but she would do until her return to civilisation, when hopefully she could discover a servants' bureau who had neither heard of her nor banned her. The cheek!

Carolyn looked critically at her make-up, and her smile faded slightly as she leant forward and lightly pushed at the skin on her face. She ran a smoothing hand across her barely rouged cheek and cast a small frown at one perfectly drawn eyebrow. It was quite late and she was rather tired, but there was the little matter of playing the game. Perhaps a light refresh and a change of gown before returning to the lounge with an expression of pained yet martyred suffering at the hands of a boorish escort, a selfish companion, and the beginnings of a migraine. Might that be a suitable approach to finishing the evening's entertainment? Carolyn smiled; she would not stay up too long…she and her accomplice had much to organise to ensure the death of Mereanthy before the brat's birthday on Sunday.

Leaning across the table, covered with bottles, jars and various unguents to keep age at bay, she rang the little brass bell. The little door of the maid's sleeping room opened swiftly and her maid, Ngaio Lattimer, entered. She bobbed at her mistress and stared at the floor. "Yes, madam?"

Carolyn toyed with the idea of a spot of abuse before discarding it on the grounds of the amount of assistance she required to remove her latest fashion acquisition. If the lump became upset, she invariably ran. Stays were rather impossible to undo on one's own, and she was in no mood to offer relations to Morten in return for his assistance. She stood and peremptorily raised her arms. Ngaio quickly began to disrobe her mistress, draping the items over the Japanese dressing screen that stood before the curtained window.

When Carolyn finally stood in her chemise, the maid silently hung the clothing in the large built-in armoire and waited as Carolyn ran a thoughtful eye over the contents before pointing to a blood-red velvet gown. Ngaio removed the gown and laid it out on the bed, then removed the matching shoes. As she turned, her mistress suddenly raised her voice. "I require peace, Lattimer. Leave now, and return in not less than twenty minutes to dress me; then you may spend the rest of the evening in the staff quarters. I will send for you when I am ready to retire. Go!" The maid nodded, and entered her little room, she returned with a blanket and then left, closing the door quietly behind her.

Carolyn locked the door behind her maid and smiled; it really was all too easy! Now she had privacy to refresh, rest, plan, and gloat.

Reopening the armoire, she rummaged until she found her black peignoir. Slipping the silky item around her, she headed to the table, which held a pitcher and bowl, lifting the white porcelain jug, she poured a small amount of water into the matching bowl. She paused and walked to the little drinks table by the door, where she poured herself a generous tot of whisky. Returning to her dressing table she added a touch of water to her drink, leant over the wash bowl and gently splashed the cool water onto her face; the best way she had found to renew her dewy complexion was liberal splashes of cool water followed by equally liberal amounts of cold cream, a touch of powder, and the lightest possible reapplication of rouge

As the cool liquid hit her skin, Carolyn sighed, patted a little more around her eyes, lips and jaw, and took a sip from the glass. She choked, and coughed. That was wrong: it felt hot! The burning sensation in her mouth and throat spread to her face and hands as she gazed in horror at the mirror, where the smooth, evenly toned skin on her face was turning an angry red. Her immaculately drawn eyebrows and the carefully arranged curls on her hairline began to melt as the lye solution in the basin started to eat into her mouth, face, and hands, and she began to scream.

### The Snug
### 10:10pm

Thorne looked at the piece of paper in his hand. How much would Aquilleia remember of them? Everything...or nothing? He turned back to the little bar and with a grimace ordered another whisky. Vasily, who was now permanently manning the large selection of drinks, noted his expression and poured him a double.

As Thorne knocked his drink back in one, a hideous scream suddenly exploded from the deck above, the noise flooding through the small room like a malignant wave.

A unnatural silence descended as the guests gaped at each other like gaffed fish. Thorne choked out an oath and dropped his glass as he and Vasily turned to face the door to the port-side deck. They were quickly joined by Elliott, Colten, and a white-jowled Thornton.

As they made their way towards the door, Desdemonia and the two stewards appeared from the kitchens. Vasily held his hand out to his wife and spoke in an authoritative voice. "Stay here. Trevenniss, Callahan, stay with the ladies. The rest of you gentlemen, with me."

The five men headed out as the screams continued, each piercing shriek seeming to redouble its efforts in an attempt to convey the suffering of its owner.

Giselle stood up and made to follow. Merry looked up, her eyes huge in her pale face. "Where are you going?" Her voice held a note of hysteria.

Giselle knelt by her chair. "I think it's your Aunt Carolyn. Where is her cabin?"

Merry took a deep breath, attempting to marshal her thoughts. "Through the snug onto the deck, up the stairs, turn immediate left…it's not the cabin before you, it's to the left of that, just before the store cupboard."

Giselle squeezed the girl's hand. Josephine moved to sit closer to the young girl, who clutched at her.

Giselle gathered her skirts and turned to leave. As she did so, she caught Lady Carlton-Cayce's eye. The Scandinavian beauty held her glance as Giselle continued on her way to Carolyn's cabin.

As she swept up the stairs, she could hear the screams beginning to weaken. She walked faster, but before she reached the top of the stairs, she heard Elliott's voice calling to someone. "It's lye! Vinegar! For the love of the Gods, we need vinegar!"

Colten suddenly appeared, thrusting her aside as he ran down the stairs towards the kitchen, his usual dry demeanour supplanted by one of utter horror.

Giselle reached the first deck and found Thornton Rust gripping the rail, his well-rehearsed blustering manner forgotten as he vomited over the side of the boat. A feeling of dread consumed her as she approached the open cabin door where a silent and shaking Sir Wesley stood, his eyes desperately averted from the hideous scene in the room beyond, but his ears could not block out the sounds; Carolyn's screams had lessened in strength but had become more unsettling: wet, rasping sobs that were far worse to hear.

As Giselle reached the doorway she took in the broken lock and splintered wood that showed it had been locked from the inside before being forced.

Thorne appeared from within the room, his face deathly pale. He grasped her by her wrists; his green eyes blazing with a violet light as his otherness fought to control his shock at what he had witnessed. His voice, usually light and sardonic, was low and harsh. "No, Giselle — don't go in!"

As they stood in the doorway, the moaning sobs ebbed into a hideous, gurgling rattle.

Deathly silence filled the air, then suddenly, O.D's shaking voice. "She's dead, thank God, she's dead!"

○

**The Snug**
**10:25pm**
**Immediate aftermath**

O.D stood by the bar in the snug and shakily tried to pour himself a large brandy. Vasily, realising what he was trying to do, walked over to his master, removed the decanter, and with a supremely steady hand poured two trebles, handing one to his employer and taking the other for himself. O.D didn't even blink as his butler drained the glass and disappeared into the dining room.

Silence fell; no one looked at each other, then everyone jumped as an equally silent group suddenly appeared in the doorway.

Josephine, sitting with an exhausted Merry, took in the

new arrivals with detached interest. The only one she recognised was Captain Peach. Of the others, there was a mature woman who carried the 'Capable Lady's Companion' look to perfection, albeit in a deathly pale fashion; behind her, a very tall, almost gangly young man who tugged incessantly at his collar; behind him came the captain of the vessel with a very pale, frightened young girl clinging to his arm.

Josephine looked over as the two Bowyer brothers and the singer Giselle Du'Lac came through the snug door, made their way to O.D, and stood in a tight huddle, talking quietly.

Josephine thought hard. Something strange was going on. Not just the death of Mrs Nolloth — it was more than that. Why was a millionaire philanthropist behaving in such a deferential manner towards three working guests? She cast a glance around the room. Two guests were missing: Sophie, and Morten Van der Linde.

Josephine closed her eyes and groaned silently. She and Sophie had performed together over many seasons and in several countries, and a minor tendresse had often rendered her associate temporarily...well, useless would probably be the best word. The last encounter had led to Sophie being threatened with ejection from her position in the Grüne Bucht Theatre in Salzburg on a charge of immorality. Josephine pressed her lips together...it had taken a great deal of effort on her part to persuade the management that Sophie had been guilty of nothing more than poor judgement, but they had still been forced to leave the revue. Luckily, however, the management had agreed not to place black marks against their names as long as they left the country; she and Sophie had been so taken aback by the request, they had decided to go one step further and left the entire continent of Europe to seek their fortunes in the New World instead. She sighed; perhaps the events of this evening would help her friend see sense...a death had never occurred on any of the previous occasions Sophie had allowed her better judgement to be overruled by her heart, and where Sophie was foolish, she, Josephine, was not!

Josephine smoothed the front of her painfully expensive hired gown, and was about to go in search of her compatriot when the starboard door opened and a smirking Morten appeared, escorting a pink and smiling Sophie.

As everyone turned to look at them, Sophie's expression became rather flustered as she saw their expressions. Then she spotted Josephine, and a relieved look appeared on her face. She nodded politely at Morten, disengaged her arm from his, glided across the room, and sat next to her friend with a slightly dazed expression.

Josephine leant toward Sophie, her lips moving rapidly as she informed her friend of the events that had occurred whilst she and Van der Linde had been incommunicado. The younger woman's vapid smile slowly disappeared and her eyes widened as Morten made his way to the bar, stood next to O.D and rang the service bell.

O.D glared at him. "Where have you been?"

Morten raised an eyebrow. "Something wrong?" He turned back to the bar and again rang the bell. "The service aboard this vessel is somewhat lacklustre, I must say."

O.D gripped his shoulder. "Damn you, where have you been?"

Morten twisted his shoulder away and smirked. "A gentleman never tells, Mr Damant! If you will excuse me, I believe I shall have to get my own drink." He flipped open the counter top and entered the bar, collected a bottle of Edradour and a glass, and headed back to the lounge.

Realising what was about to happen, Thorne attempted to grab O.D's arm, but missed, as O.D followed Morten into the lounge, spun him round and punched him squarely in the face.

Morten staggered backwards, hitting one of the mannequins that stood sentinel next to O.D's jewellery collection before landing on his elegantly clad backside next to the display. The nearly full bottle of whisky hit the polished wooden floor and smashed, spreading its pungent contents and glittering shards of glass far and wide. The samurai mannequin collapsed about Morten with a crash, the armour clattering across the floor as the stunned diamond merchant lay on his back in the midst of the whisky-soaked mess.

Merry, standing next to a shocked Mar, burst into tears and ran from the room just as Vasily reappeared in the dining room doorway and took in the bruised and whisky sodden state of Van der Linde with one sharp-eyed glance. Mar stared at Morten in wide-eyed silence, glanced at the damaged mannequin and murmured, "Fleur, please go with Merry; I'll see to this." She swept out of the room as Morten staggered to his feet, a bloodied handkerchief clutched to his nose. Rage and shock routed Van der Linde's usual control and his accent was thicker and far more pronounced than usual as he shouted at O.D, "Have you taken leave of your senses, man?"

O.D clenched his fists. It had been quite a while, but that had felt good! "I'll ask you again, Van der Linde; where have you been?" he growled.

Morten dabbed at his damaged face. "What business is it of yours?"

The muscles in O.D's neck bulged as he stared at the diamond merchant. With effort, he reined in his anger, responding in a clipped and precise tone as though explaining to a dotard. "Because there has been a death."

Morten paused in his mopping and frowned. "But what is that to do with me?" He waved his hand dismissively as he patted at a whisky-scented damp patch on his evening dress.

"It is very sad, I am sure." He turned a faintly spiteful smile on O.D. "But that still does not give you the right to treat a guest in such a rude and common manner."

Elliott laid a hand on the older man's arm. "If you will allow me, Mr Damant?"

O.D inclined his head and headed back to the bar, where Vasily silently handed him another treble.

Elliott looked at the diamond merchant and tried very hard to override the intense dislike he had felt from the first moment he had set eyes on the man. First impressions were usually correct, but they played havoc with socially enforced politeness!

He decided the best course was to address the issue formally. "Mr Van der Linde, I regret to inform you that it is your business partner, Mrs Carolyn Nolloth who has died. From the manner of her demise, I'm afraid there can be no doubt that she was quite brutally and deliberately murdered."

His words were greeted with quiet from the rest of the company, except for Sophie, who gave a faint, stifled shriek before slowly sliding from her seat onto the floor. Josephine hurriedly knelt next to her friend and rummaged in her reticule for her smelling salts as Morten Van der Linde stared at Elliott in stunned silence.

### Carolyn's cabin
### Saturday morning
### 4:45am

Thorne wheeled his equipment trunk out of the now photographed and fingerprinted cabin and nodded at Trevenniss and Callahan. The stewards entered the room with a stretcher and reappeared a few moments later, both pale and in need of a drink, bearing Carolyn's sheet-wrapped remains between them.

The two stewards made their way to the coldest room on the vessel: the meat locker just off the kitchen, where Desdemonia had cleared space for the unexpected and unprecedented delivery.

Elliott watched the removal of the body before turning to Thorne. "Let's get the evidence and our equipment to your cabin and then head to the bar. I don't know about you, Thorne, but after what's happened here, I need a damn stiff drink! We should wait until morning to conduct a thorough search of Mrs Nolloth's suite; the photographs are enough for now."

Thorne nodded. "Agreed. I could certainly use a drink before we investigate any further!"

Moving quickly, they took the trunk and plates to Thorne's room. Elliott ducked into the cabin he shared with Giselle and informed her of their plans before going back to Thorne's cabin to help set up the baths for the photographs. He also joined Thorne in impressing on Veronique the importance of not interfering with the interesting, and somewhat smelly trays of liquid now jostling for space on the dressing table. Thorne gave her a biscuit and a back-scratch before the two men headed down to the bar, where Giselle was already ensconced. The bar being unstaffed now, she had decided to claim a bottle of champagne, which sat patiently in its ice filled silver bucket awaiting her husband's attention. Giselle was more than capable of opening the bottle herself, but she knew Elliott enjoyed the sound.

Elliott grinned at his wife, popped the cork as discreetly as he could, and poured the frothy wine into the coupes that Giselle had thoughtfully provided. He handed Giselle and Thorne a glass each and flung himself into an armchair, draping one leg over the arm. "So, let's think…in the few minutes before her death, who wasn't in the lounge or snug?"

Thorne sipped his drink and thought. "Let's start with who was there. You, Giselle, and I were together to begin with, then I went to get another drink, so we can vouch for each other; Vasily can also place me at the bar, which conversely makes me his alibi; Lady Carlton-Cayce and Merry Damant were sharing their settee with Josephine Kayfield, so they can also vouch for each other; Colten Kayfield and Thornton Rust were sitting opposite the ladies, who were trying to ignore Rust's…well, charm, I think he would call it! And the housekeeper and the two stewards were in the kitchen, along with the cook and several other servants who can vouch for them."

Giselle nodded thoughtfully. "So that leaves O.D and Sir Wesley, who were apparently having a little set-to in O.D's office; Morten Van der Linde and Sophie Rust, who had gone for a post-meal perambulation…" She paused. "Slightly odd behaviour for a married woman! Even one married to such a man as Rust! However, back to the matter in hand. Darius Damant and Dona Carla Riva were also not in the lounge. Marjorie Lee Colville, Captain Peach, his daughter Fleur, Torrance Burrows, and Robin Ellis were to all intents and purposes dining together in the servants' quarters, with various other staff members popping in and out, both serving their meal and eating with them. Not counting assorted maids and valets in various cabins and staff rooms, across all decks."

Elliott took a sip of his drink as he looked at his old friend. "And of course, there is Aquilleia."

Thorne returned the look. "Yes, there is Aquilleia."

There was a heavy silence. Giselle shook her head and placed her drink on the table. "The presence of Aquilleia is something we must deal with in time…but we also have a murder to deal with. We know that it was the lye in the wash jug that killed her, not an actual, physical assailant. It could have been put there at any time during the day or after she left her cabin for dinner."

Thorne studied his drink in the flickering gaslight. "In that case, we're looking for anyone who had access to Mrs Nolloth's cabin between — what? Late morning to very nearly ten pm?"

Elliott nodded with a rueful smile. "It's a large window of opportunity, I'll admit. We need to speak to her maid to confirm the times she wasn't in the room. And, of course, to check her alibi."

Thorne groaned; he had hoped they would manage to escape the drudgery of paperwork in triplicate. He looked hopefully at Elliott. "Can we do this in a private capacity, do you think? Investigate, solve, tidy up, and hand over to the correct authorities without the need for, you know, The Espion Court or official paperwork?" He closed his eyes and shuddered dramatically. "I don't think I could ever face paperwork in triplicate again!"

Elliott laughed as he picked up the bottle of champagne. "We'll see what we can do, my friend! After the discretion and tact we employed in the last case, Lapotaire owes us a little…leeway, shall we say?"

Thorne raised his glass with a smile.

Giselle picked up her drink, stared into the empty glass and waved it at her husband. "I have to say that if it *was* her maid, I wouldn't have blamed her!"

Elliott blew out his cheeks as he topped up his wife's glass. "But in that manner? An incredibly strong solution of lye in the wash jug of a woman known for her perfect appearance? That suggests not mild dislike, but genuine hatred. Who hated Carolyn Nolloth enough to cause her that much suffering?"

Thorne looked up. "Darius?"

Elliott considered. "Hmm, he certainly has a motive. Means and opportunity, however — well, we shall have to see. It has been a very long day and an even longer night; I'll inform O.D that as we have already dealt with the Galton's details and photographs of the crime scene, we shall start our search of the cabins shortly before lunch."

Giselle frowned up from her armchair. "Do you suppose he will accept our jurisdiction?"

Elliott shrugged as he placed the empty bottle of champagne on the bar and opened the cold store for a second. "I don't think he has a choice. I know it's late, but I'll wander over to his suite and inform him of our decision." He paused. "It might also be a good idea to inform the wider world of our problems. A private vessel of this size must have the necessary communications equipment; I'll contact Lapotaire to inform him of events and get official authorisation to continue." He looked at Thorne with a grin. "In a private capacity, of course!" His smile faded as he looked at his wife and Thorne. "We came here to repay an old debt, find the author of a fairly dry series of poison-pen letters, and defeat a vague threat to harm an innocent young girl. We are now confronted with a vicious and quite evil murder…and not of the person apparently in danger. Under the circumstances, I don't think our government connection will mind extending us room to manoeuvre!" Elliott gripped the neck of the bottle as he popped the cork. "But for now, a top up."

Thorne held out his glass as Elliott did the honours and they set about finishing the excellent bottle of champagne.

When they had drained the last of their drinks, they wandered back to their respective cabins, where Elliott delivered Giselle into the safekeeping of a very concerned, and therefore very French, Lilith, before continuing to O.D's cabin.

Thorne watched Elliott walk towards the large private suite at the fore of the boat. Once Elliott had disappeared from view, Thorne spent several minutes hovering between his cabin door and Aquilleia's, before finally letting himself into his own room. There he was struck at knee height by a concerned Labrador. Veronique's brown eyes were huge above her favourite dolly, gripped tightly between her jaws and brought as an offering to her favourite person in the world.

Without a thought for his evening dress, Thorne sat down on the floor, his back against the thin wall that separated him from Aquilleia. He caressed Veronique's silky black ears and sat in quiet thought as she chewed her toy.

○

### O.D's cabin
### 5:45am

Elliott straightened his cravat, smoothed his hair and knocked sharply on the door.

After a short pause, the door was opened by O.D, his waistcoat undone and his cravat askew. On seeing Elliott, his face relaxed and he waved the younger man into the room with a hand that was clutching a sheaf of papers.

Elliott decided that honesty and forthrightness would be the best approach. So almost before the door was closed, he laid out, in a polite and not too deferential manner, that O.D was no longer in charge and that he, Thorne, and Giselle, as representatives of Her Majesty's Government, would be taking over the case. As such, they needed to utilise the radiotelegraphy transmitter and send a message to their contacts in London, posthaste.

O.D ran a hand through his hair as he looked at Elliott. "I

wanted to have a word with you in private; I was about to come to your cabin to let you know that we have another problem."

Elliott narrowed his eyes. "Go on."

O.D pulled at his collar. Elliott detected the unmistakable air of a man rapidly approaching the end of his tether. Dropping the handful of documents onto his desk, O.D attempted to fasten the buttons on the front of his waistcoat, before giving up and gripping the two lapels like a Yorkshire mayor about to deliver a speech. "There are actually two things. Firstly, have you noticed how quiet it is?"

Elliott listened, then pinched the bridge of his nose before inquiring in a deadly calm voice, "What has happened to the engines?"

O.D shrugged hopelessly, his waistcoat in great danger of being torn as he gestured expansively. "According to the engineer, several parts have just vanished! We can't even use the whistle!"

Elliott's eyes snapped open. O.D thought he saw a green light flickering in them — but that was absurd! He continued, his voice wavering. "Secondly, both our transmitter and our telegraph machine have been damaged: we can neither send nor receive any form of signal."

Elliott ground his teeth and gripped his cane. "So, just to clarify: there has been a murder, we have ceased to move, and we have no means of calling for assistance. Is that what you are trying to say?"

O.D swallowed. "It's, ah, a little worse than that, I'm afraid. We haven't actually ceased to move. We are still moving — the tides are pulling us out to sea!"

Elliott stared at him, incredulous. "Then drop anchor, man!"

"We can't! The seabed is too far down: our anchor is only for the bay near Milford City."

Elliott clenched his jaw. "Are you saying that you brought this vessel out here with no means to prevent her and us being swept out into the open sea?"

"Not at all! We were relying on the engines—"

"Which someone has now damaged!" Elliott swore under his breath. "Can the engines or the transmitter be repaired?"

O.D sat back at his desk; he looked tired. "I don't know. The engineer is searching for spare parts that might work as a temporary fix, and Torrance is working on the telegraph device."

Elliott frowned. "Torrance?"

"Yes, he's a bit of an expert when it comes to these newfangled machines."

Elliott sat in the chair opposite O.D and scowled at the philanthropist. "That puts us in a predicament, Mr Damant, since I need to get word to my connections in London to guarantee our jurisdiction here. As it now stands, I think we shall have to make it up as we go along!" He raised an eyebrow at O.D. "Can I count on your support in this matter?"

O.D nodded firmly. "Yes, of course. Anything you say to the guests, I will absolutely confirm." He paused. "But you will be honest with me in return — agreed?"

Elliott smiled. "Absolutely agreed. Now, on to the issue at hand. Is there anywhere we can drop anchor now?"

O.D leant forward; his expression worried. "Not into the water…but Captain Peach had an idea."

"And?"

"It's a little extreme."

"How so?"

O.D fiddled with his pen. "He's suggested that we use one of the lighter ropes and, well, actually send someone out in the little boat to moor us to one of the rocky outcrops."

Elliott tapped his cane on the polished wooden floor. "It might work, at that."

O.D looked incredulous. "I can't believe that you, too, are countenancing it!"

Elliott's ears pricked up. "Ah, so who else thinks it a good idea?"

O.D tugged at his cravat then ripped the offending article off and threw it on the settee behind him. "Sir Wesley bloody Eade! He was here when that young idiot Torrance ran in ahead of Captain Peach and blurted everything out."

Elliott's eyebrows rose again. "Really? That rather suggests that Sir Wesley wouldn't mind us being marooned for a while, doesn't it? But then, being anchored to something solid is somewhat more practicable than resigning ourselves to courting certain death at sea!" He consulted his fob watch. "It is rather late, or rather early, depending on your point of view. Sleep is no longer an option as far as I am concerned, so may I suggest we find a stouthearted volunteer prepared to assist with the necessary heroics? I think I have just the one — to the cabin!"

## Elliott and Giselle's cabin
### 6:05am

Pausing to allow O.D to tidy his somewhat mussed appearance, the two men made their way to Elliott and Giselle's cabin, where they were admitted by Lilith.

Thorne and Giselle were seated at one of the little tables, thoughtfully laid by Desdemonia with a substantial early breakfast which was being eyed by a dozing Veronique, curled up on her eiderdown-topped cushion beside the bed.

Thorne was addressing himself to a thick finger of toast

generously smeared with anchovy paste. As he bit into the crispy morsel, Elliott smiled at him from the doorway. Thorne caught his friend's eye, swallowed the mouthful, and stared. "I know that look, Elliott! What have you done?"

Elliott placed his cane in the rack by the door and kissed his wife, who smiled at O.D. "Can we offer you something, Mr Damant? A toasted crumpet or a little kedgeree, perhaps?"

O.D shook his head. "No food for me, Mrs – I mean, Mlle Du'Lac. Perhaps a cup of tea though, thank you."

As Giselle dealt with the teapot, Elliott surveyed the offerings on the table before settling on the aforementioned toasted crumpet. He slathered a liberal quantity of salted butter across the crisp surface and bit into it with relish. Butter dribbled onto his plate as he addressed Thorne. "Two things, Thorne. Firstly, have you been to see her yet? And secondly, are you up to a spot of swimming?"

Thorne, who had just taken a sip of tea, choked. Clutching his cup and saucer as a drowning man might clutch at a rescuer, he blinked a few times and glanced at a nonplussed O.D. "Er, no, I haven't yet, it is rather early…" He frowned. "And what on earth do you mean by 'swimming'?"

Elliott took a sip of the tea Giselle had poured for him, perfect! He explained to Thorne and Giselle the suggestion that Captain Peach had put forward. Giselle looked thoughtful, while Thorne's expression was incredulous. "You're suggesting that I…?" His voice rose with his eyebrows as he declared in no uncertain terms that Elliott, Captain Peach, and their kind host — here, Thorne stood and bowed to O.D — could all take a running jump into the Sound!

Giselle hid a smile as she looked out of the cabin window towards Milford City. At the far end of the Sound, the sun was rising: a soft, watery light that resembled fresh apricots, shading into a deep and cloudless blue.

"I think it will be a lovely day for a swim," she said. "We will all be in your debt, but if you are going to do this, I suggest you do it now — we seem to be a trifle closer to the sea than we were! You did remember to pack your bathing suit, didn't you?"

Thorne opened and closed his mouth several times before filling it with the mortal remains of his toast. He swallowed the offending mouthful with the assistance of a gulp of tea, and addressed Elliott in a tone of reproach. "So, I am to be volunteered? Very well, then in the event of my untimely death by drowning, pneumonia, or becoming lunch for some large aquatic creature, I bequeath to you, Elliott and Giselle, my fair-weather and somewhat peremptory friends, all my most valuable worldly goods…" Here he paused. "Which at this point consist solely of Veronique, and possibly a certain person whom I have not yet had the courage to address. If you will excuse me, Mr Damant, it appears that I must change my attire." Thorne stood up and brushed crumbs from the front of his evening wear. As he turned to leave, he put a hand to his stomach with a gasp as the sensations that had affected him earlier suddenly returned tenfold. Veronique leapt to her master's side and whined as he leant against the table.

A soft knocking sounded at the door. Thorne, his stomach churning, looked at Elliott, who shot his friend a worried look before gesturing to Giselle to move away from the door. As she and Lilith entered the bathroom, Giselle promptly removed two sharpened ivory hair sticks from her washbag and gripped them in a fighting stance. Lilith pulled a singularly unpleasant looking hatpin from her apron, and both women faced the door.

O.D, feeling as though he had wandered into some grim Gothic tale of valour, blocked the doorway before them as Elliott drew his sword stick and nodded at Thorne.

Thorne, still clutching his stomach, approached the closed door. He took a deep breath, flung the door open and stopped dead as the woman who had knocked stared at him.

Societal niceties, the done thing, and etiquette disappeared as Thorne reached out a trembling hand to touch her porcelain face, a face he hadn't seen for so very long. His voice broke as he whispered, "Aquilleia!"

The woman smiled; her glowing violet eyes brilliant with tears. "Shadavarian!"

○

**Main deck**
**7:15am**

Timmy Beam, the Taniwha's twenty-year-old stoker, who rarely saw the light of day beyond what little filtered through into the engine room, nodded at Captain Peach and swung the heavy coil of rope across his body. He attached one end firmly to the anchor chain before descending to the little rowing boat at the foot of the ladder.

The fit young man had been volunteered for the task after the reunion of Thorne and Aquilleia. Elliott and Giselle both realising that Thorne's attention would in no way be focussed on an attempt to anchor in the Sound now that the wife he had lost so long ago had returned to him with all her memories of their past life together intact.

Thorne and Aquilleia were ensconced in Thorne's cabin with Veronique, who had nearly knocked Aquilleia over in joy at seeing her again. There was much talking to be done; so many years had passed, but their love was still there. And then there was also the little matter of explaining just why Elliott, Giselle, and Thorne happened to be on the Taniwha in the first place. Before Thorne and Aquilleia had taken to the cabin, Elliott and Giselle had suggested bringing her into their investigation. Aquilleia and Shadavarian had been as inseparable as Versipellis and Angellis. It made very little sense to keep things from her, and as her gift of sight had been astounding in Astraea, it could, hopefully, be utilised in their current case.

Out on deck, various early-bird guests and servants were watching the actions of the young stoker with interest. Dona Carla had decided to make an event of it: reclining on a well-positioned folding chair with a large pot of coffee, an equally large bottle of champagne, a scandalously scanty green peignoir, and a thick fur throw. With a set of brass and mother-of-pearl opera glasses clamped to her dark eyes, she looked on with enjoyment as the athletic young man begin to row towards the outcrop of rock that would hopefully prevent them from being carried out into the Abel Tasman Sea.

After several minutes of strenuous activity, Beam pulled up to the outcrop Captain Peach had suggested and carefully moored the boat. Moving quickly, he wrapped the length of rope around the solid point of rock several times and tied her off, then clambered back into his little boat and returned to the Taniwha.

O.D turned to the captain. "I want all the guests marshalled in the lounge at ten am, Captain Peach. Many things need to be explained: I invited these people here, and now we are trapped with a killer. I think I owe them an explanation."

Captain Peach nodded. As a concerned member of staff, with a young daughter, he too was looking forward to hearing what was going on. "Yes, sir."

## The Lounge
### 10:00am

O.D scanned the room with a sense of relief. All the guests and a number of the servants were present; at least they wouldn't have to hunt people down. He winced; an unfortunate turn of phrase, given the events of the last twenty-four hours. He turned to Elliott and raised his eyebrows. Elliott nodded, and O.D turned back to the room. "Ladies and gentlemen, might I have your attention, please?" The general chatter died down as they turned to look at O.D. Several faces were open; several looked as though they wished to be anywhere but there…and would have said so, if the social niceties of being reliant on their host for food, accommodation, and protection hadn't been an issue!

O.D cleared his throat. "You are, by now, all aware of the death of my sister-in-law last night. I regret to inform you all that her death was no accident, but murder!"

Silence fell. Most of those present had been there when O.D had engaged Van der Linde in the unfortunate set-to that had ended with that charming diamond merchant colliding with the samurai display; one or two guests cast a swift glance at the mannequin that had been damaged in the fracas. Placed neatly back on its plinth, with the katana belted at its side, it appeared that Mar had made good on her promise to mend it.

"Some few months ago, I had need to request the presence of three people to investigate certain…unpleasant events that first occurred in England, the nature of which I shall not divulge. I am very relieved to say that they are here and more than capable of investigating this appalling affair. Ladies and gentlemen, the Magnificent Bowyers are in fact

Mr Elliott Caine, and Mr Abernathy Thorne. The third guest is Mlle Giselle Du'Lac. They are investigators who work on behalf of the Empire, and they have absolute jurisdiction to investigate this brutal slaying."

O.D ignored the faint smile that crossed Elliott's face at his bald-faced lie; he had no doubt that as soon as word could be sent to London, the investigators he had hired would be given official approval, so why should a little thing like jurisdiction or authorisation stand in the way of sorting out the mess that had landed on his doorstep?

Several of the guests started to talk over each other, and Sir Wesley glared at O.D. "Am I to take it that we have been invited here under false pretences?"

O.D looked at his company's lawyer with open dislike. "Not at all. You were all invited to celebrate my daughter's twenty-first birthday, but one amongst you has abused my hospitality and committed murder in my home!" He turned. "Mr Caine?"

Elliott stood up, propped his walking stick against his armchair, and faced the curious audience before him. He could see that both Sir Wesley and Thornton Rust were working themselves up to attack, so he produced his most attractive smile, allowing the full wattage of his glamour and charm to strike various guests in turn.

Sophie sighed and settled back in her chair, Josephine rolled her eyes at her friend but relaxed a little, Aquilleia smiled from her seat next to Thorne, who held her hand as though he would never let it go; Dona Carla took a sip from her champagne glass — the sun was over the yardarm some-where! Vasily and Desdemonia stood by the door to the servants' quarters and paid close attention; Merry sat next to Fleur, the two girls holding hands as they listened raptly; Mar sat in an upright chair by the door and stared at O.D, her face deathly pale; Leonora studied her nails as Sir Wesley stood by her side, stony-faced and ramrod straight; next to him, his secretary Robin Ellis looked as though he wished to be anywhere but there; Colten ignored Thornton's attempts at blustering and paid Elliott his full attention, his grey eyes intent; Morten stood by the window and stared out across the Sound, his face blank; Torrance gazed at his hands, blinking rapidly; and Darius sat in utter silence, the Persian rug beneath his feet receiving his full attention.

Elliott began. "Ladies and gentlemen, there is no need for me to go into the full and terrible details; however, last night Mrs Carolyn Nolloth was cruelly and willfully murdered by someone who deliberately tampered with the water in her wash jug, turning it into a strong solution of lye."

Josephine blenched, and against her will, she imagined the suffering Carolyn must have endured. What a truly awful way to die!

Elliott's voice rose above the renewed rumble of conversation. "Today, my colleagues and I will require you all to give statements relating to your whereabouts yesterday, both during the day, and into the evening. I trust you will all accept this request, as the quicker we can get to the truth, the quicker we can catch this miscreant, and the safer you will be."

Sir Wesley, who had opened his mouth to argue, closed it again with a snap.

Elliott continued. "We will begin the interviews shortly, and we will also be speaking to your servants. Please be advised that we will also need to search your rooms in your absence before those interviews can begin—"

Sir Wesley exploded, his usually pale face a mottled shade of puce. "How dare you! You do not have the right to carry out interviews or search our rooms, you insolent pup! I will not be a party to this abuse! O.D, you go too far! Just who is this man, that he believes himself to have the right to rifle through our personal possessions? Investigators for the Empire? Pah!" Sir Wesley snapped his fingers in Elliott's face.

As the noise from the other guests in the room rose sharply, led by a blustering Thornton Rust, Elliott raised his hand and after a slight pause the noise level dropped. So too did Thornton, straight back into his chair.

Elliott approached Sir Wesley, a green light flashing in his eyes. In a voice that only Sir Wesley could hear, he murmured, "Sir Wesley, are you aware of the name Lord Vyvian Lapotaire?"

Sir Wesley looked at Elliott, his expression of self-right-eous indignation faltering somewhat, since the man before him spoke a name whose high position in the Empire he recognised. He nodded guardedly. "Yes, I am aware of Lord Lapotaire…and his work."

Elliott smiled, his canines flashing. "Oh, I doubt very much that you are party to most of the work of our good friend Lapotaire! Would you then accept his choice of investigator in this case?"

Again, Sir Wesley nodded. "Yes, of course, I…" He paused and looked at Elliott, an expression of vexation appeared on his face. "It is you?"

Elliott nodded with a faint smile. "It is I. Now please be seated and let us continue our work here. As I have previously said, the quicker we solve this hideous crime and catch this fiend, the sooner things will return to normal, and the safer you will be."

Sir Wesley sat down next to Lady Carlton-Cayce, a picture of confounded irritation.

Elliott continued. "Ladies and gentlemen, if you will kindly stay in the lounge, Vasily and the stewards will bring you refreshments while my associates and I search your cabins. You may return to your cabins after we have completed our entire search. We shall then visit each of you in your room for a private interview. Please understand that this will take some time, and the interviews may well have to continue tomorrow. Thank you." He turned to the quiet, self-effacing steward Trevenniss. "Please keep the guests here until we have finished searching their rooms." Trevenniss nodded, his benign, slightly plump face blank in the manner of the unflustered servant. "Very good, sir."

Amid the immediate elevation in noise level, and before Thornton Rust could make good on his pompous attempt to wrest control of proceedings, Elliott, Thorne, Giselle, and Aquilleia left the lounge and headed to the cabin deck to start their search, beginning at the scene of the crime: Carolyn's cabin.

### Carolyn Nolloth's cabin
### 10:20am

The broken lock had been carefully repaired by one of the engineers at O.D's behest to ensure the room's security, but some of the damage to the splintered doorframe was simply too much to fix. Elliott produced the key and gingerly swung the door back on its one undamaged hinge. They entered the silent cabin and took in the room where O.D's sister-in-law had met her painful death.

Giselle looked at the dressing table and mirror, both of which were covered with bloody handprints. She closed her eyes and swallowed hard; Carolyn had died seeing what had happened to her lovely face. She turned away from the mirror, set her shoulders and looked at the rest of the cabin with professional eyes. It was tidy, after a fashion, but rather cold. There were no photographs or personal items on display; only the open wardrobe door, exposing the expensive clothes within, and the various jars and bottles that had previously littered the dressing table and were now spilling their contents on the thick carpet, showed that someone had once inhabited the room.

Thorne surveyed the room and scowled. "Where do you want to start?"

A voice came from the doorway. "Look in her writing case."

They turned to look at Aquilleia. Elliott raised an eyebrow. "Writing case?"

Aquilleia nodded firmly. "She was thinking about the case at dinner. That, and how angry she was at being slighted."

Giselle looked at her. "You can remember your gift?"

Aquilleia smiled. "Yes, I remember my gift...throughout all my lives here, it has never left me."

Elliott walked over to the writing desk and checked the little mahogany case that rested on it. He sighed and turned to his wife. "Locked...my love, would you mind?" As Giselle considered the small case on the desk, he turned to face Aquilleia with a quizzical eye. "Slighted?"

Aquilleia nodded again and sat in the little armchair by the door. "She was very easy to read. She thought *she* should have been treated as the mistress of the house and escorted to dinner by Sir Wesley...she was full of rage against her niece."

The three of them watched as Giselle took a pouch from her ornate reticule, removed two small pieces of bent metal, and quickly opened the lock. Replacing the items in her bag, she moved away. With a somewhat forced nonchalance, she sat before the stained mirror and began to go through the contents of the powder-covered dressing table as her husband rummaged through the writing case.

Thorne spoke from beside the bathroom door. "Could she have been the one threatening Merry?"

Aquilleia frowned. "I'm not sure. I know she was planning something, but she was careful to keep that hidden away — even in her own mind — as though it unnerved her to even think about it in front of other people."

Elliott leafed through the papers in his hands. "Rather standard communications. Bills, more bills, a letter from a servants' agency informing her she has been 'removed from their books for the protection of their girls' — she wasn't liked at all, was she?"

Elliott was about to turn from the case when something caught his eye; dropping the papers, he removed a penny knife from his pocket and carefully prised the false bottom of the writing case open. "Aha!" He triumphantly waved a bundle of letters above his head. Moving to the table he opened the first few envelopes and scanned through the missives. "Letters from Van der Linde to Merry, and her letters in response — oh dear!"

Giselle looked up from her perusal of the dressing table. "But I thought Darius said they had intercepted the more recent letters?"

Elliott handed some of the missives to his wife. "It looks like they didn't catch them all. Reading these, I have to agree with Darius; Morten Van der Linde is an extremely unlikable man!" He frowned at his wife. "But what would these letters be doing in Carolyn's room? Was she trying to hold them over her lover's head, or Merry's?" He scanned a few more of the letters. "Well, now…how very strange."

Thorne looked over. "How so?"

Elliott looked up, the green light flashing in his eyes. "When we left the lounge, I take it I was not the only person to see Van der Linde standing by the window and Merry sitting on one of the settees?"

Thorne frowned. "And?"

Elliott held out one of the letters. "Because, according to

this letter, Morten Van der Linde feels extreme remorse and wishes to confess to the murder of Merry Damant due to her rejection of his marriage proposal…he also hopes that his suicide will make amends for his crimes, and he begs her father for forgiveness! Well, well…they both looked to be in exceedingly good health — for corpses! And bearing in mind that Van der Linde's 'suicide note' is signed, it must be a forgery — which raises the possibility that these other letters may also be fake."

Giselle sat back in her chair and looked at Elliott with an appalled expression. "Is that what Carolyn was planning? The murder of her niece and the framing of her own lover? But why?"

Elliott tapped the letter against his lip. "Inheritance, perhaps…did she think there was still a chance she would inherit her sister's fortune?"

Giselle shook her head and continued to rummage through what was left on the surface of the dressing table. She picked up a slip of paper that had slid under the mirror and read it. With a gasp, she turned to the others and held out the note. "Look at this!"

All is going to plan. Hold steady, and all that you desire will soon, rightfully, be yours.

She thought, her blue eyes glittering. "If Van der Linde was being set up and knew nothing of her plans, then this note suggests someone else was helping her — but who?"

Thorne sat on the edge of the bed and frowned. "Torrance, Mar…Darius? A long shot, but what about O.D?"

Elliott scoffed. "O.D? Collude with his hated sister-in-law to murder his own daughter?" He paused, a slightly baffled expression on his face. "Hell, my friend, stranger things have happened…it could be any of them! But right now, Van der

Linde is a strong contender for Carolyn's murderer. If he discovered her plans it would make sense for him to kill her, in order to protect himself…" Elliott paused and shook his head. "But that doesn't work; why would he leave all the evidence pointing to Carolyn's framing of him? He would have destroyed it, not left it for us to find." He sighed. "We need to gather this evidence and continue with the search. If we've finished here, I think we should go on to the next room — what say you?"

Thorne nodded. "We just need to check the maid's bedroom and then we'll be done here." He opened the narrow little door that had been hidden on the other side of the wardrobe at the far end of the room, allowing the cabin guest to believe they were the only person in the suite until they required their servant's assistance. The room beyond the door was extremely narrow, the cramped two-foot-wide bed taking up most of the space, and a tiny chest of drawers topped with a wash jug occupying what little room remained. Thorne looked through the drawers before picking up the thin book on the pillow: a tidy edition of King Solomon's Mines. He opened the book, turning to the title page, on which a strong, masculine hand had written in deep black ink:

December 1887
    Merry Christmas to my dear little sister Ngaio.
    Enjoy the adventure.
    Your loving brother,
    Thomas

Thorne returned the book to its resting place and closed the door behind him.

Elliott raised his eyebrows. "Anything?"

Thorne shook his head. "A standard, very narrow maid's

room, nothing untoward…very few possessions: a book that was a Christmas gift from her brother thirteen years ago, but other than that, nothing."

Elliott nodded and checked the list of names he had requested from the steward. "Very well. I think we should continue in an anti-clockwise direction, which makes our next port of call…Darius Damant's cabin." He smiled brightly. "Let's get started, shall we?

### Darius Damant's cabin
### 10:40am

Pushing the unlocked door open, they trooped in and set about their task. After a few minutes Thorne called from the bathroom where Aquilleia was assisting him, "Are we sure anyone actually lives in this room? There are barely any personal belongings!"

Elliott nodded as he opened and closed various drawers and studied the contents; the folded clothes and other possessions so neatly stowed as to be almost non-existent. "He certainly believes in tidiness. Anything over there, Giselle?"

His wife shook her head as she checked the contents of the dressing table. "Nothing…no letters, no bills, even for personal items, and no photographs either: very strange."

Thorne shrugged as he walked back into the snug little cabin. "Perhaps he is just very, very tidy in his habits." He looked down at the waste bin. "Well, he didn't want to keep that piece of paper!"

Elliott raised his eyebrows. "What piece of paper?"

Thorne picked up the bin and showed Elliott the

contents: a small quantity of charred material at the bottom. "It's too damaged to read…I wonder what it was?"

Elliott pursed his lips. "Let's take it with us anyway; it might come in useful at some point. I think that's it for this cabin, let's lock it and move on."

### Colten and Josephine Kayfield's cabin
### 10:50am

The next two cabins were those of the married couples: Colten and Josephine Kayfield, and Thornton and Sophie Rust. As they entered the first cabin, they realised there was a total lack of any feminine presence in the room. Elliott frowned at the twin beds against the far wall. Flipping back the pillows, he looked at a rather splendid set of mustard-yellow pyjamas. Turning to the other bed, he exposed a more agreeable set in pale blue. "This resembles more a room shared by two gentlemen, rather than a married couple. Hmm…Thorne, would you check the next cabin."

After a few moments, Thorne returned. "The next cabin is definitely that of two ladies. What are they up to?"

Giselle turned to Aquilleia. "Any thoughts?"

The psychic smiled. "All I know is that they are not married to each other and they mean no harm. They are as frightened as most of the others."

Elliott opened the small cupboard between the two beds and discovered two small writing cases. One bore the initials C.K, the other, T.H.R. He handed one to Thorne and sat on the bed to rifle through the other.

Thorne rummaged through the chest bearing the initials T.H.R, which contained several letters of introduction from theatres in Australia, all addressed to Mr Thornton Havelock

Rust, Esquire. One of the letters went into great detail about a private birthday party for which the writer was interested in hiring part of Mr Rust's acting troupe; it was signed by Sir Wesley Eade.

Thorne held up the letter. "This is interesting; it would appear that Thornton Rust, Colten Kayfield, Mrs Josephine Carter, and Miss Sophie Havercroft are actors hired by Sir Wesley to put on a performance for Merry Damant's birthday." He picked up a thin hardback book that was also tucked into the case. Flicking through the small volume, his eyes widened. "Listen to this: 'But sir, I know not where your wife and business partner are, only that they were not there when the children arrived home.'" He turned to Elliott. "That sounds like the disappearance of Cordelia Damant and Alexander Burrows to me."

Elliott took the volume from his friend and flicked through it, noting the name inscribed on the bookplate: Sir Wesley Eade. "I think this is something that needs to be clarified by the four people sharing these rooms…and Sir Wesley Eade!"

Once Elliott had pocketed the small volume and the letter, they spent several minutes rummaging through Josephine and Sophie's cabin. The main room consisted of a large shared wardrobe, a dressing table, and two beds; one neatly made, with a photograph on its bedside table showing a young Josephine with a rather dashing young man in military uniform and bearing the inscription, 'Mr and Mrs C Carter 1880'. The other bed was covered in what appeared to be an explosion in a hosiery factory. The shared bathroom contained a cabinet with two shelves: on one shelf, a single half empty bottle of good quality jasmine bath oil and matching soap, whilst the other shelf bore multiple bottles of unguents in luridly illustrated bottles and a pamphlet on banting addressed to Miss S Havercroft.

They continued to the next suite, that of Marjorie Lee Colville.

○

**Marjorie Lee Colville's cabin**
**11:00am**

Upon entering the room, they immediately noticed the large number of photographs of Mar with Merry and O.D, taken in various far-flung settings including London, Sydney, and San Francisco.

Giselle pursed her lips. "Obviously she travels well in her position as companion: wherever they go, she goes."

Thorne nodded from the bathroom doorway. "Very neat in her habits, too…not as tidy as Darius, but at least there are signs of human habitation!"

Aquilleia entered the bathroom and rummaged through the scant items on the side of the bath. "Lavender bath oil and carbolic soap — that's a mixture you don't often find!"

Elliott smiled from his position at the dressing table and continued to rummage through the various drawers. Pausing, he picked up the wastepaper bin and prodded the contents. "Someone else with a propensity to destroy with fire. Ash…looks like paper; I wonder what she burnt?" He carefully removed the scraps of charred paper and placed them in a small envelope which he tucked in his pocket. "On we go to the next cabin!"

## Lady Carlton-Cayce's Cabin.
### 11:10am

They opened the next cabin door and halted as a billowing cloud of scent wafted out, the strength of which rendered Elliott temporarily speechless.

Giselle waved a hand in front of her face as she coughed. "Lady Carlton-Cayce is obviously a firm believer in the school of 'more is never enough' — that scent is certainly heavy on the musk!"

Aquilleia entered the cabin and gently rifled through the many bottles and jars of expensive creams, unguents, and perfumes on the dressing table. She picked up an exquisite gold glass bottle and sniffed the contents. "She also likes ambergris. I've never seen so many different bottles of perfume outside of a perfumery: Jicky, Malmaison, Special No.127, Eau de Guerlain…there are more bottles on this table than there were in Carolyn Nolloth's entire suite!"

Elliott stood by the open door for a few minutes, breathing in clean air; the overpowering scent in the opulently feminine room was making him feel queasy.

Giselle smiled. "Perhaps you gentlemen would like to go on to the next cabin? Aquilleia and I can search this room."

Elliott cleared his throat. "Well, my darling, if you insist! Thorne, to the good Sir Wesley's suite."

The two men wandered next door as Giselle and Aquilleia smiled at each other and continued their search.

Aquilleia entered the maid's room and found it very similar to the one in Carolyn's cabin; a tiny bed and chest of drawers with almost no hint of the personality of the person sleeping there — not even a penny thriller or knitting reticule to be found!

Giselle sat next to the dressing table in the main cabin and opened the top drawer where several expensive pairs of silk knickers jostled for space with their matching chemises. Giselle turned her attention to the next drawer and discovered several very expensive corsets. Built with the intent of whittling a woman's waist down to little more than a handspan in width, these articles were slightly different from the usual corset in that the front of each was very slightly padded. Giselle frowned as she held one up to the light, and turned to look at Aquilleia. "I know Lady Carlton-Cayce is slender, but I didn't realise she padded her corset!"

She turned back before Aquilleia could respond, missing the strange look on the psychic's face as she carefully placed the undergarments back in their drawer and transferred her attention to the wardrobe. She opened the door and stood back, an appreciative look on her face. "My, my!"

Aquilleia's jet-black eyebrows rose as she too took in the sumptuous collection of gowns, shoes, boots, jackets, and matching reticules. She turned back to the bedside cabinet, and opening the cupboard beneath, discovered a large, locked pigskin jewellery case with the initials L.L.C.C stamped on the front in gilt. She thought for a moment and then called, "Giselle, would you mind?"

Giselle smiled and removed the lock picks from her reticule. A few minutes later the case was open and the two women stared at the contents in awe. Giselle blinked. "Bloody hell! That's a lot of diamonds!"

Aquilleia nodded as she touched the sparkling rings at the top of the case. "And sapphires, emeralds, rubies…" She carefully lifted the top tier out and placed it to one side, exposing a magnificent purple gemstone that lay glittering on a bed of deepest black velvet. Aquilleia turned her violet eyes to Giselle. "What is that gem? It isn't an amethyst."

With trembling fingers, Giselle carefully extracted the

exquisite, unset purple stone from its soft nest. When she spoke, her voice was slightly unsteady. "It's the Larkspur Diamond, I'm sure it is! How on earth did she get hold of it? It's been missing for years!" Giselle and Aquilleia looked at each other. "We need to tell Elliott and Thorne about this," Giselle said decisively. Let's finish our search, then go next door." She carefully placed the stone on its bed, replaced the top tray, and locked the case, pushing it back into the bedside table.

After a few minutes' companionable silence had passed, Giselle asked, "So, how go things with Thorne?"

Aquilleia smiled and sat on the edge of the bed. "Very well, thank you."

Giselle looked down at the documents she was flicking through, and in a more serious tone asked, "What do you remember, Aquilleia? Anything at all? You must have some memories as you still bear the same name."

Aquilleia's pale face was solemn as she looked at the concerned woman before her. "I remember everything. I never lost my memories...with each rebirth I could still remember my name, and my past, but not how to return home to Shad. That day in Astraea, the day we both died...I remember Pel asking me to look after you. I remember someone who looked like him entering the kitchen and hitting me; then you entered the room, they attacked you... and I died."

Giselle looked at Aquilleia, tears in her eyes. "I am so sorry I couldn't do anything to stop him."

Aquilleia held out her hand to Giselle, who clasped it. "You have no need to apologise to me, Angellis. Phoenixus was set on that path from birth. At that point in time, there was nothing you, I, Pel, Shad, or even Phoenixus himself could have done to prevent what happened."

Giselle nodded, not trusting herself to speak. She could

still see the dying form of Aquilleia on the kitchen floor all those years ago. She cleared her throat and gestured at the cabin. "Well, Lady Carlton-Cayce seems to keep a tidy if rather over-scented apartment! Other than an improbably sized and very stolen diamond, I see nothing of interest in here: do you?"

Aquilleia shook her head. "To be honest, the amount of perfume in here is starting to give me a headache. Perhaps we should go next door, let them know what we've found, and see what they've discovered?"

The two women left the cabin and closed the door. As they entered Sir Wesley's cabin, they were unaware of the form which ran swiftly across the deck behind them and into Lady Carlton-Cayce's cabin. The figure closed the door and turned to look at the empty room. With any luck, they had two minutes before the four investigators reappeared…and that should be just enough!

### Sir Wesley Eade's cabin
### 11:30am

Thorne looked up as they entered and smiled at Aquilleia. Elliott, sitting at the rather austere dressing table that was doing sole duty as a writing desk, looked up at his wife. "Anything at all?"

Giselle smiled. "Aside from a fabulous collection of scent, some stupendous gowns, and a heavenly selection of padded matching frippery, very little. Her jewellery case was locked too, but considering her penchant for collecting valuable gems, perhaps that was sensible."

Elliott detected a gleam in his wife's eye. "It *was* locked?"

Giselle's expression was innocent as she looked at her

husband and partner in crime. Then her smile widened. "Yes, it *was* locked…until I opened it! Good Gods, Elliott, that woman has some gems with her…" Giselle paused for effect. "Including the Larkspur Diamond!"

Elliott's eyebrows nearly rivalled Thorne's as the two men stared at the smiling women before them. Elliott rose from his seat. "Where is it?"

"We put it back in the case, locked it and returned it to the bedside cupboard."

Elliott nodded. "Then back to the good, or indeed, not-so-good lady's cabin. Thorne, what have you found?"

Thorne turned, and in his hand a small gun glinted. "It's a Browning. It's loaded and there's a box of ammunition in the same drawer."

Elliott frowned. "I'm not sure I like the idea of the good Sir Wesley trudging the deck with a gun at his hip, but nothing we've found so far ties him in with Carolyn's death. Put the blasted thing back in the drawer, Thorne, and let's give the valet's room a quick squint before heading next door. I have to say, I feel rather relieved that we brought our own weapons with us!"

They checked the little sleeping compartment and found a room with rather more personality and character than they had expected; several books on the subject of chess, and a large collection of letters and telegrams, full of arcane chess references, that suggested their owner had decided their lack of a permanent address would not hinder their passion for the ancient game of strategy.

Elliott looked through some of the letters, making notes of the dates. "He's a very good player, possibly even a Master — intriguing! Right, let's see what Lady Carlton-Cayce's jewellery case has to say for itself."

## Lady Carlton-Cayce's cabin
### 11:35am

The four of them trooped back to the cabin next door. Elliott paused, gesturing to the others to stop as he stared at the cabin door. "Did you close this door on your way out?"

Giselle moved to his side. "Yes, I made sure of it. I didn't lock it because I knew we would be returning quickly, but it was definitely closed when we left it. Why?"

Elliott gently prodded the door, which slowly swung open. Giselle spat an uncouth word under her breath as they entered the cabin and saw the bedside cabinet open, with the jewel-case sitting in almost the same place they had left it — almost!

Elliott lifted the small chest out and looked at the now broken lock before carefully opening the lid. The myriad sparkling gems twinkled at him, but their gleaming light was somewhat shadowed by the lack of the largest gem. The Larkspur Diamond was gone!

Thorne banged his fist on the little cabinet. "Damn, we've lost it! I don't think Lady Carlton-Cayce or Sir Wesley are going to be very happy about this, Elliott!"

Elliott closed his eyes with a groan. Giselle touched his hand and began to speak; he opened his eyes and placed a finger on her lips. "This was not your fault; someone was obviously watching us. But how, when we told the steward to keep them all in the lounge?"

Thorne stood up from the small and now decidedly empty little cupboard. "All the guests are supposed to be in the lounge, but where are the servants and the other staff? We didn't put a watch on them. It could be a disgruntled maid, an angry valet, or the head steward himself." He shook his head. "The Larkspur Diamond…bloody hell!"

Aquilleia looked at them, a thoughtful expression on her face. "The diamond is important…and for reasons I can't yet see." She looked at the glittering tray of rings. "But why would the thief leave the other gems?"

Giselle sat down on the chair by the dressing table. "They must have been after the one gem in particular…so it is likely it was stolen to order." She sighed. "The Larkspur has a history, a legend, and several myths behind it, not to mention a curse — all the best gems do these days! It belonged to the notoriously mysterious and still very missing millionaire art dealer Nathaniel De Coeur. It was stolen from him during one of his exceptionally extravagant parties in New York. The crème de la crème of American East Coast society was there and it was quite an evening, I can assure you…some quite spectacular costumes and rather brazen behaviour, as I recall! It became even more interesting when halfway through the evening a scream came from De Coeur's private suite. Everyone rushed in to find…nothing. No Nathaniel De Coeur, no Larkspur Diamond, no furniture, nothing. He and all his possessions had simply disappeared." She settled back with a grim expression and looked at her husband. "I will tell you this now because it's the right time to do so…or it may perhaps be a little too late: but someone on the Taniwha has wanted that diamond for years, and if they knew it was here, it would only be a matter of time before they acquired it."

Elliott looked at her sharply. "Who?"

Giselle cleared her throat and wafted at the heavy scent around her. "The Fox."

Thorne's jaw dropped. "The Fox! The most notorious jewel thief of the last ten years is on this boat? Impossible! Only the crew, guests, and servants are aboard."

Giselle smiled grimly. "The Fox is one of the guests! We

saw them at the aetherdrome in Auckland, and they have been aboard since we arrived on Friday."

Elliott looked at his wife, a faint smile on his lips. "You know who the Fox is?"

Giselle pursed her lips and inclined her head. "Yes."

Elliott leant forward, and placing his lips against his wife's ear, murmured a name, then stood back.

Giselle looked at him in admiration. "I'm impressed, husband! You are quite right, but they're in the lounge with the others. I don't know how they could have left that room, entered this cabin and stolen the diamond without being seen: it simply isn't possible!"

Aquilleia half-raised a hand. "Unless they had a partner. As Shad said earlier, what about one of the servants?"

Elliott tapped his lip with an overlong fingernail and mused. "It would appear to be the only way for the theft to have occurred. We shall have to add this charming little conundrum to the all-encompassing chaos of our current investigation: murder and theft — involving a diamond stolen at least twice, no less!"

Aquilleia looked at them. "I think we should go back to Sir Wesley's cabin; there is still something to be found."

Thorne looked at her closely then shot a glance at Elliott, who nodded. "Very well, back to Sir Wesley's room."

They returned to the cabin and they began the second search. Aquilleia sat by the doorway and watched quietly. Her gaze flickering towards one of the bedside cabinets, she was about to draw their attention to it when Giselle turned away from the dressing table and addressed the small item of furniture. Opening the front, she removed a small, locked case and began to work on it. After a short while, the case was open and the contents, predominantly photographs, became visible.

Giselle knew a little of the world: she was in no way a

loose woman, but she had observed things at events, parties, and masquerade balls that would cause the average wallflower to drop in a dead faint. The contents of the case, however, while not increasing her knowledge of the behaviour of humans when the lights went out, sent her eyebrows rocketing upwards purely on the grounds of the social damage they would cause if the images were exposed to public scrutiny. She cleared her throat. "Er, Elliott? Would you mind awfully coming over here?"

Her husband looked up from the top drawer of the dressing table and caught his wife's eye. He frowned, joined her, and gave the contents of the case a cursory glance that became a stare. "My, my, my!"

Thorne's blond head swiftly appeared around the corner of the bathroom door. "Anything interesting?"

Elliott coughed and tugged at his cravat. "Possibly not the sort of thing for mixed company."

Thorne grinned. "Oh, that kind of interesting: do let's see!" He left the bathroom and peeked over Giselle's shoulder, and there was a short silence as his jaw dropped. He pointed at one of the photographs, his voice incredulous. "Is that Sir Wesley…with Lady Carlton-Cayce?"

Elliott nodded as he too considered the two very naked subjects in the photographs. Sir Wesley and Lady Carlton-Cayce certainly seemed to be enjoying each other's company, in spite of the presence of the photographer recording their exploits. And there was something else: there was rather more to Lady Carlton-Cayce than the average woman could claim to possess. He exchanged glances with his wife, who nodded. "Yes, I noticed that too…rather difficult not to, really! It certainly explains the padded undergarments we found in her room…"

Thorne looked at the images. "It appears a little Greek to me."

Giselle studied the photographs. "It would certainly appear so; padded corsetry to create a shape she doesn't actually have." She pointed to an ornate stained-glass panel in the background of one of the photographs. "There...what does that say?"

Thorne screwed in his monocle and peered at the photograph. "The...Order of...Chaeronea." He sat back and removed the eyeglass. "That explains a great deal about the photographs."

Giselle nodded. "I've heard of it, it's a society created to enable such men to meet in safety." She frowned. "But these were taken with the knowledge of both Sir Wesley and Lady Carlton-Cayce — that much is obvious. Why on earth would Sir Wesley put his position at stake by having these photographs taken at all? If they fell into the wrong hands then not only his career but his freedom would be forfeit, and the Gods alone know what would happen to Lady Carlton-Cayce!"

Aquilleia spoke from her chair. "Perhaps Sir Wesley and Lady Carlton-Cayce believe themselves above societal reproach or punishment?"

Elliott looked through the rest of the photographs. "This case is certainly developing!"

Thorne gestured at the images. "What should we do with these? Do we leave them here?"

Elliott shook his head. "I think it might be best if we took them with us. If they fall into the wrong hands, things might become worse than they already are. I think we should take these to our cabin for safekeeping, along with the scraps of charred paper and the letter and book from Kayfield and Rust's room." He turned to look at them. "I'm loath to protect Sir Wesley — the man is a cockroach! But we need not bring attention to Lady Carlton-Cayce's...differences. She's obviously made it this far in life with her secret well kept, and I have no desire for it to be brought out into the open on our watch…unless it has a bearing on the case. Agreed?"

Giselle, Thorne, and Aquilleia nodded. Giselle stood up and smoothed her skirt. "In that case, onward to the next cabin?"

Elliott nodded. "Yes, the next cabin, which I believe is young Merry Damant's."

They trooped out of the room and locked the door.

As they walked away from the now safely closed room, Giselle took the opportunity to chide herself silently; that dratted diamond had been the talk of clubs and dinner parties for years…and not just for its rare colour and complete lack of flaws. Its theft had not only terrified several of the richest families into taking out over-inflated insurance policies to protect their prized possessions, but it had also boosted the use of paste copies tenfold overnight! She had a sudden idea, and made a mental note of just what might be done about the Fox, and their unknown assistant. Realising that the others had already at Merry's cabin, she hurried after them.

As Elliott, Giselle, and Aquilleia entered the suite, Thorne headed back to Elliott and Giselle's cabin, where he quickly hid the paper fragments, the book, and the case of photographs before locking the door behind him. He paused outside his cabin and carefully peeked through one of the windows. Veronique was sprawled on his bed, belly up and snoring. He smiled, and made his way to Merry's cabin.

## Merry Damant's Suite
### 11:50am

The airy, brightly decorated room was much, much larger than the guest cabins, denoting Merry's rank as mistress of the vessel. The lavender curtains, green settees, and lightly stained wood a total contrast to the dark, heavily ornate, and obviously masculine main rooms below.

Elliott looked at the room with approval, pausing before a large watercolour of the town of Picton that bore the young girl's signature. "She has a very good eye. Her colour schemes and furnishings are lovely, and her artwork is quite splendid!"

Aquilleia called out from the bathroom, "She certainly doesn't believe in overdoing the scent either, thank goodness; lily of the valley bath oil, matching soap…and nothing more."

Elliott cast his eyes over the photographs that stood on the little piano: several of Merry with her father, a handful of her with Mar, and several of a little girl with a younger-looking O.D and a beautiful blonde woman whom Elliott took to be her mother, Cordelia.

Thorne wandered towards the maid's room, opened the door and stared in surprise. The room was smaller than the guest cabins, but far bigger than the other servant accommodation aboard the vessel…and it had its own bathroom!

As Thorne rummaged through the maid's possessions, Elliot gazed out of the massive aft window that allowed unhindered views of the stunning Milford Sound.

Giselle cleared her throat and he turned. "Elliott, I think you should see this." She had opened a large cupboard and was looking at the contents with a thoughtful expression.

Elliott walked over to her and looked at an array of small, scented waxy cubes, neatly spaced on a wooden tray. He raised his eyebrows. "What are they?"

Giselle pursed her lips. "I would say this is home-made soap."

Elliott smiled. "Home-made soap…and why are we staring at it?"

"Because, my darling, home-made soap uses the basic ingredients of clean water, oil or fat, fragrance…and lye."

Elliott's eyebrows knitted. "I see."

"It's quite easy to make — all you really need is patience, and somewhere to store the soap while it is curing."

Elliott looked at her. "Curing?"

"Hmm. It gives the lye time to neutralise so you don't end up looking like Carolyn Nolloth."

"How do you know all this?" asked Thorne.

Giselle grinned as she settled by the dressing table and began rifling through the contents of the top drawer. "My mother was very proper about such things. 'Ladies' toiletries should always match', she would say, and the best way of ensuring that is to make such things yourself. She enjoyed making soap, and she enjoyed teaching me." She paused, a beautifully embroidered reticule in her hand. "Actually, it *is* generally something a female family member would teach a girl. A mother, a grandmother, an aunt—"

"A companion?" asked Elliot.

"In lieu of the others — and I cannot believe that Carolyn Nolloth would have bothered — yes, I would think so." She opened the little bag and removed the contents; a slim, linen-bound diary and a little pouch containing a single lock of golden-blonde hair. Giselle carefully replaced the lock. "I think this is possibly a lock of her mother's hair. The diary, however, is definitely Merry's…" She read for a few moments before turning to her husband, a horrified and angry look on

187

her face. "I take back any sympathy I might have felt for Carolyn Nolloth! She actually had Merry believing her lies! I can't read this." She almost threw the book at her husband, then stood up and looked at the photographs on the piano. A protected and well-loved little girl had grown into a protected and well-loved young woman, who had become the target of a greedy and vicious aunt, dedicated to her own malicious and tawdry ends. But her plans had gone awry, with the intervention of timely death thwarting her evil schemes.

Elliott scanned the pages and read a handful of heartfelt passages, written by a gentle, trusting young woman who could see no wrong in the people around her. His eyebrows drew together over his nose as he too re-evaluated his opinion of Carolyn Nolloth's death. Like his wife, his immediate reaction to her brutal murder had been one of compassionate sympathy, in spite of her appalling behaviour on the airship from Auckland. Now, given the information they had about her plans, the conduct of her paramour Van der Linde, and the possibility of another, unknown associate assisting in her Machiavellian schemes, Elliott considered her death as rather well timed, preventing as it did the planned murder of Merry, the attempted destruction of Van der Linde, and the success of her wicked plan to claim what she obviously still believed to be her inheritance.

Elliott snapped the slim volume shut and placed it back in the reticule. "We have no choice but to investigate this case. The more I discover about Carolyn Nolloth, the less inclined I am to refer to her as a victim! The Gods alone know how many people she and her associates destroyed over the years." He paused, "That's the other thing bothering me. Van der Linde thought he was her partner, but he was mistaken; he was actually an unwitting and unlikable future victim. So, as we said earlier, her true associate must be aboard. They were obviously assisting her in carrying out her plans, but who are they? And now that she's dead will her wicked plans for Merry and Van der Linde die with her? Or will her associate continue to the bitter end? I think we need to find that other person…and the sooner the better!"

Thorne nodded thoughtfully. "A rather nasty triumvirate, where one of the party was unaware of the presence of another player. If, as Van der Linde's partner for so many years, she still managed to keep the identity of her true associate a secret, then say what you will about her; she was exceptionally gifted at lying and perfidious behaviour."

Giselle glared at him in angry disbelief. "You sound as though you admire her!"

Thorne shook his head firmly. "Absolutely not. But look at it from her side, just for a moment. We have a queen in charge of the Empire, but women, even those who are high-born, generally have no power over things that the average man takes for granted, such as marriage, money, and position. Carolyn faced certain hard facts about her position in life and decided they were not to her liking, so she changed the rules to better suit her own sensibilities. She lied, connived, stole, destroyed, and played one person against another to create the life she wanted for herself. She didn't care who she ruined to get what she wanted; she chose to play the game to its extreme end. Other women have tried and failed to progress beyond marriage and motherhood, yet she managed both, on her own terms and no one else's, before setting out on a life as far removed from what we would call "womanly" as she could get, because it better suited her temperament. Say what you will about her choices: in a man's world, she succeeded in achieving her desire for wealth and position."

Giselle angrily shook her head, her flame-red hair straining against the confines of its neatly pinned bun as she bit one of her immaculately manicured fingernails. "I have managed my own life as a woman, a professional singer, and an enquiry agent without the destruction of my morals or other people's lives, and I have achieved success! Carolyn Nolloth's behaviour towards her niece was disgusting and utterly immoral. It was pure hatred and greed, nothing more!"

Thorne nodded. "Exactly: the two of you are, separately, highly successful women. The difference — and my point — is that you are not a psychopath. I believe that's the fashionable term for it these days: someone who does things for themselves only, and is prepared to sacrifice any and all to achieve their ends." Thorne spread his hands. "How many businessmen who preach moral behaviour display the same ruthless one-track-mindedness as Carolyn, but are excused because they are male and 'good' businessmen? Ultimately, she would have sacrificed her other associate as swiftly as she planned to do away with Van der Linde, if it paid her well enough to do so." He paused. "We must find that other person: they may well attempt to continue with Carolyn's plan and try to harm Merry."

Giselle ruefully looked at the ruination she had made of her fingernail. Lilith would definitely inflict her most suitable Gallic look for the damage she had caused to her manicure! She looked at Thorne, who smiled good-naturedly as he returned to rummaging in the bathroom.

Giselle turned to Elliott, who had stood in quiet thought as his friend had been talking. "The next cabins are ours — are we going to search them?"

Elliott shook his head. "I would fear for the health of anyone who tried to enter our cabins, with the threat of Lilith in one and Veronique in the other!"

Aquilleia laughed suddenly. As the others turned to look

at her, she smiled. "Something just occurred to me…it's no matter for concern."

Thorne pulled out the piece of paper with the cabin allocations and frowned at it. "Right, from here the next cabin is Elliott and Giselle's, then Aquilleia's, then mine and Veronique's…" He looked at the others. "I would rather not bother Veronique if she's sleeping. She was rather upset about the events of last night; it took hours to get her back to bed!"

Aquilleia looked over his shoulder and prodded the next name on the list. "Then the next cabin is that of Van der Linde…can we at least try not to take out our indignation at his behaviour on any of his personal possessions?"

Thorne smoothed the front of his waistcoat. "I promise nothing! Shall we go?"

They left the cabin, locking the door behind them as they walked round the aft deck. They passed the flight of stairs that headed up to the top deck, with its folding chairs, and massive pots full of silver ferns, English roses, and a beautiful specimen of Clematis Jackmanii that trailed its flower-covered tendrils around the rails and down the staircase.

As they approached the door next to Thorne's cabin, Giselle pulled a face. "I need to correct the damage I've done to my fingernail! I'll meet you in Van der Linde's cabin in a few minutes."

As the others continued along the deck, Giselle turned and entered the cabin she shared with her husband. Pausing on the threshold, she realised that Lilith was not in the cabin, she must be with the servants in the staff quarters on the main deck. Giselle breathed a sigh of relief: that meant Lilith wouldn't see the damage she had caused to her manicure until after she had tidied it up. She entered the little bathroom and rummaged in her vanity case, removing several items before realising that her manicure set wasn't there. Giselle walked back into the main cabin and looked at Lilith's bedroom door. As she entered the little room, her gaze settled on Lilith's modest vanity case which was sitting on the bedside table. Picking up the small case, she placed it on the bed and opened it. Her breath caught in her throat and her eyes widened in shock as, for the second time that day, she stared at the sparkling perfection of the Larkspur Diamond, sitting on a square of flannel in the middle of Lilith's vanity case.

Giselle's mind whirled; how on earth had the gem materialised in her maid's cabin? Had someone hidden it there for safekeeping, or had they planted it on Lilith? Or could Lilith herself have taken it – but if she had, why?

Giselle paused at a noise outside. The others would be waiting for her; but after what had happened earlier, she would take no chances this time! She removed the gem and hurriedly put the case away, her attempts to tidy her manicure forgotten as she swiftly closed the door to Lilith's cabin. Standing in the middle of the room she shared with her husband, she thought hurriedly before again entering the little bathroom, grabbing her pot of cold cream and stuffing the glittering gem within. Wiping the cream from her trembling fingers, she screwed the lid back on, dropped the small pot into her reticule, closed the bathroom door and left the cabin, locking the door behind her. She hurriedly walked towards Van der Linde's suite, her embroidered bag and its precious contents clasped in a death grip.

Despite her hopes, Giselle faced the cold reality of the situation. She was now sure she knew the identity of the person who had stolen the jewel from Lady Carlton-Cayce's cabin; she just needed to know why.

## Morten Van der Linde's cabin
## 12:10pm

As Giselle entered the cabin her nose wrinkled. Elliott nodded and grimaced. "Another one for whom 'too much is never enough'! I think Van der Linde and Lady Carlton-Cayce between them own majority shares in several perfume houses!" He frowned. "Are you all right, my love?"

Giselle shook her head, reached into her reticule, and pressed the pot of cold cream into her husband's hand. The smile on Elliot's lips died as he saw the expression on her face; he twisted the lid off and stared at the fabulous purple gem inside the pot. "Good Gods!"

Thorne popped his head around the bathroom door. "What is it?"

Elliott pursed his lips. "Oh, somewhere between three and four hundred thousand pounds, I would guess…give or take a sovereign!"

Thorne's eyebrows shot up as they all gazed at the contents of the little pot in awed silence. The vivid, pear-shaped stone, a little over an inch and a half long and a stunning shade of deep violet, appeared almost unreal in its flawless perfection. The glittering gemstone sparkling in the sunlight that shone through Van der Linde's cabin window, its myriad facets flickering with a purple flame that seeming to glow and wink at them from the depths of the thick white cream that cocooned it.

Elliott puffed out a sigh and handed the pot back to his wife. "Where?"

Giselle took a deep breath; she felt slightly sick. "It was in Lilith's vanity case."

Elliott stared at his wife. He knew the shared history of

his wife and her maid; both their fathers had been murdered by the same gang of bank robbers in France. Giselle's mother had also been attacked and had died of her injuries several months later, while Lilith's mother had died by her own hand: throwing herself into the Seine on the day of her husband's funeral. The two young women had stayed in touch, and when Lilith had fallen on difficult times, Giselle had taken her in. Most people thought of her as a maid, but she was more akin to Mar in her position within their family: a companion and friend, capable of extreme levels of honesty and withering sarcasm.

He gently took his wife's hand. "Before we make any assumptions, we should talk with Lilith. It could have been planted there."

Giselle shrugged miserably. "I honestly don't know, Elliott...I tried to imagine someone else stealing the stone and putting it in our suite, but all I could see was Lilith. It was the only way; all the guests were in the lounge, watched by the stewards, but the servants were unguarded in the staff sitting room."

"Then it could have been *any* of the servants, not just Lilith. After we've finished the search, we will go to Lilith and ask her."

Giselle nodded, and taking a deep breath, squared her shoulders. "Very well. Is there anything interesting in Van der Linde's cabin?"

Thorne shook his head, a slightly disgusted expression on his face. "Other than the overpowering scent of cologne and a large selection of French postcards that would get him a decent bit of gaol time, the only interesting things are a few books on his specialist subject: diamonds." He looked at Elliott with a raised eyebrow. "Could he have something to do with the Larkspur's reappearance?"

Elliott shrugged. "Anything is possible."

"No," said Aquilleia, "he knows nothing of the diamond being here. He knew of its disappearance in New York, but he is not involved in the reappearance of the gem. Nor does he know of Lilith's involvement." She looked at Giselle with some sympathy. "It *was* Lilith who took the stone, but she had a reason."

Giselle paled. "What possible reason would justify the destruction of our friendship?"

Aquilleia's face was grave as she looked at Giselle. "The possibility of discovering who was responsible for the death of her parents…and yours."

Giselle gasped; she swayed on her feet before Elliott gently sat her down on the edge of the bed and knelt beside her as Thorne poured a stiff brandy from the cabin's drinks tray and pressed it into her hand. She stared at the glass as Aquilleia continued. "Lilith was promised a favour in kind. If she would take the stone, the person requesting her assistance would help her by using their connections to discover the identity of the person ultimately responsible for the attacks that killed your parents and hers." A faint blush touched Aquilleia's cheeks. "There is also a…friendship between Lilith and the person who asked her to take the gem."

Giselle took a shuddering breath. "Who?"

"You spoke of them earlier. The jewel thief known as The Fox — or as we know her: Dona Carla Riva."

Thorne's eyebrows had long since finished their attempts to climb any higher and were currently residing at their peak position in his hairline. In lieu of any further eyebrow movement, he gave a long, low whistle. "Of course! The greatest dancer in the world, invited to society's finest dinners, balls, and events. She would be perfectly placed to judge the pieces and take what she wanted…it's the perfect cover."

Elliott nodded as he rubbed Giselle's hands. "If that's the

case, we shall keep the diamond with us at all times! I do wish we knew what had happened to its previous owner Nathaniel De Coeur; it would be so much easier if we could simply return the property to its rightful owner."

Giselle looked at her husband, her eyes thoughtful. "He completely disappeared without a trace…no one knows where he went. But I have an idea: because of her obsession with the stone, it's possible that Dona Carla might know his whereabouts — if he's still alive. It's a long shot, I'll grant you, but it is a possibility."

Elliott looked at her. "Would she tell you?"

She shrugged tiredly as she pressed a hand to her forehead. "There's no reason for her not to. I just need to make sure she doesn't know we have the Larkspur Diamond. If she finds out, she'll either try to take it again or request it in exchange for the information, but it's worth a try."

Elliott looked at her. "Very well, my dear. Back to Aquilleia's suggestion of what Dona Carla promised Lilith. *Could* she know who was responsible for your father's murder?"

Various emotions flickered across Giselle's face as she looked at her husband. "I don't know…possibly. She has many and various connections: some are legitimate, and others are highly criminal. She may have discovered something…or someone. Yes, it's possible. But why tell Lilith and not me?"

Elliott looked at Aquilleia. "You say there's a friendship between them; what do you mean?"

Aquilleia's blush deepened and she looked at Giselle helplessly.

Giselle smiled faintly. "Both Lilith and Dona Carla are more at home with the works of Sappho than those of Sophocles. I've known about Lilith's predilection for several years, and Dona Carla is exceptionally honest about her preferences…" Giselle paused. "But that is not to say she would be averse to dabbling in other waters if the opportunity arose."

"Oh!" Elliott's eyebrows approached Thorne's in height. He pursed his lips and scanned the rest of the room. Apart from the questionable postcards, they had found nothing of interest. He cleared his throat and checked the list. "Very well, on to the next cabin, that of Torrance Burrows."

○

### Torrance Burrow's cabin
### 12:30pm

The room belonging to O.D's secretary was almost as empty as that of Darius. A few items, however, showed a little more personality: a small selection of books, one of Merry's water-colours depicting a white house with two small figures in the garden, and a framed photograph of a dark-haired man with a much younger Torrance.

Giselle picked up the photograph. "This must be his father, Alexander." She studied the image. "He was certainly an attractive man."

Aquilleia took the photograph from Giselle and frowned slightly. "There is someone here who would disagree…but I can't see who they are."

Elliott rummaged through the wastepaper bin and Thorne checked the contents of the bathroom. Nothing questionable to be seen, other than a nearly empty jar of scented hair oil. He gave the contents a tentative sniff: lime blossom, not too overpowering. He grinned; he was becoming quite the scent snob!

Elliott shook his head. "There's nothing much here. The next cabin belongs to Sir Wesley's secretary, Robin Ellis."

### Robin Ellis' cabin
#### 12:40pm

They trooped next door and began their search, Thorne headed into the bathroom as Elliott and Giselle settled into their position by the dressing table. Aquilleia sat by the door and smiled as Thorne rummaged through the negligible contents of the small room, while Elliott emptied the little bin and Giselle fished around the dressing table. Nothing, not even a photograph or a book, just clothes.

Elliott looked around the characterless little cabin. "Right, penultimate room...Dona Carla."

### Dona Carla Riva's cabin
#### 12:55pm

Elliott, Giselle, Thorne and Aquilleia entered the clothing-festooned cabin and began their search. Elliott headed for the bathroom as Thorne settled in by the dressing table, and Giselle and Aquilleia tucked into the rather splendid contents of Dona Carla's travel accoutrements. Her wardrobe was only marginally less fabulous than Lady Carlton-Cayce, but her choice in perfume was far more limited; here, they had only the slightly spicy, musky scent of Jicky to contend with.

Elliott called from the confines of the bathroom. "I have never seen so many different types of bath oil in my entire existence! I feel that I have led a very sheltered life!"

Thorne grinned as he began rummaging through the contents of the jar-covered dressing table. One or two of the items of clothing made him pause, and on one occasion he discovered something that made him cast a surreptitious glance at Aquilleia and Giselle.

Elliott wandered over to him. "Anything?"

Thorne took a deep breath and showed his friend the contents of the top drawer. Elliott's eyes also widened. "Obviously a lady of certain tastes! Anything else?"

Thorne shook his head. "Not really. I'll just check the maid's room." He entered the tiny area and searched the scant belongings. A small suitcase that still contained several items of clothing and a spare uniform lay open upon the neatly made bed. He checked the chest of drawers, they were empty. Frowning he returned to the main cabin and explained his findings to the others. Giselle smiled. "I doubt very much that the bed in there has been slept in, Thorne. I told you: Sappho, not Sophocles!"

Thorne turned pink. "Ah...of course." He thought for a moment. "Won't that be a problem for Lilith? I mean, if she and Dona Carla are friendly, I can't really see Dona Carla's current companion stepping aside without a word, can you?"

Giselle frowned. "I see what you mean...no, I can't." She looked at Elliott apprehensively. "I know what Lilith is like; things could get rather interesting!"

Elliott smiled, his canines flashing. "Well, I think we've seen all we need to here. Now for the last one...O.D's suite."

○

## O.D's suite
## 1:05pm

The four of them entered the suite. It was sizeable, slightly larger than Merry's suite, and had the added bonus of containing both O.D's and Torrance's offices.

They began in the small room used by Torrance. The speaking-tube network was of great interest to Thorne, who made several notes as to its use as he rummaged through a large selection of highly sensitive business papers, including several blank cheques made out for a combined worth of over three thousand pounds. While deciding just how honest he was prepared to be, Thorne turned and caught Aquilleia's eye. She smiled as he swiftly stuffed the pile of papers back into the top drawer and they joined the others in O.D's main suite.

The last time they had been in the room, O.D's force of personality had almost filled the masculine space. Now, without his presence, the rooms seemed somehow smaller and less personal.

Elliott scanned the contents of the larger of the two bookcases that filled one wall in the private sitting room: Charles Dickens, the Strand Magazine, Punch, and several volumes dealing with Brazil and the Yoruba peoples of Western Africa. He turned to O.D's desk which was covered with correspondence, mining reports, and several photographs in silver frames: O.D with Merry, Merry with Mar, Merry and Darius, and a very young Merry with an equally young Torrance, who was actually smiling. There were none of O.D's wife, Cordelia.

In the bathroom, Giselle surveyed the scene of O.D's ablutionary habits: two bars of lemon scented soap and a bottle of matching beard oil, but very little else. She walked back into the bedroom, where Thorne and Aquilleia were checking the wardrobes and chest of drawers. Good-quality tailoring and well-made shoes jostled alongside some very worn and patched tweeds and battered galoshes.

Thorne smiled. "A gentleman who doesn't wear his best to go fishing or walking…sensible!" He looked at Elliott. "There doesn't seem to be anything odd here, aside from several blank cheques for large amounts sitting in Torrance's office."

Elliott looked at his pocket watch. "In that case, it's very nearly time for luncheon. We have a few minutes to refresh ourselves, and then I'm sure the other guests will simply adore sharing their repast with the people who have just spent a happy three hours rummaging through their most personal and private possessions!"

They returned to their respective cabins, Elliott to change his shirt, and Giselle to dab with rose water and apply a touch of balm to her lips. Thorne headed to his cabin to feed the starving Veronique, who now positioned as a draught excluder against the door, her black nose twitching in her snuffling attempt to catch the scent of her master. Aquilleia, meanwhile, retired to her room and sat in quiet contemplation, waiting for the others to collect her before heading towards the dining room…and the wrath to come!

## The lounge
## 1:30pm

As Elliott, Giselle, Thorne, and Aquilleia entered the packed room, the other guests, sipping a little sherry before their meal, paused in their social discourse, and the general atmosphere became rather frosty.

Elliott caught O.D's eye and made a slight bow.; O.D nodded and raised his hand to Vasily. Elliott held out his arm to Giselle and smiled graciously at the other guests as Vasily struck the gong. They walked into the buffet luncheon, ready for the dubious joy of stilted, one-sided socialising with people who knew their very personal secrets were no longer their own.

# PART III

### The Interviews Begin
### The dining room
### 3:00pm

Thorne rolled his eyes at Aquilleia as the rest of the guests left the chilly atmosphere of the dining room and adjourned to the lounge for coffee, sweeping past the four enquiry agents without a word.

Elliott looked around the empty room with a rueful smile and sat back in his chair. "Was it something we said? Never mind…now the interesting part begins! Let us continue with the next level of fun: the interviews! Who should we terrify first?"

Giselle looked rather worried. "I know we need to talk to Lilith, but perhaps we should wait until after we have spoken to Dona Carla."

Elliott nodded, and his humorous expression was replaced by a more understanding one as he looked at his wife. "Very well, then shall we conduct the interviews in the same order as we searched the cabins? That means we will be starting with Darius Damant." He frowned. "Now, where shall we do this? I know I originally suggested the privacy of their cabins, but I think I would prefer a more neutral territory."

Giselle nibbled at her nail. "Perhaps the snug? Then people can return to their rooms and see what we have — or have not — found. It might shake one or two of them up a little."

Aquilleia smiled. "That sounds like a good idea."

Elliott nodded. "Right, let us announce our intentions. To the lounge!" He flung the connecting door open with vigour: the sudden noise making several of the guests jump. Elliott smiled to himself, there were occasions where he did rather enjoy his job!

He looked at the gathered guests. "Ladies and gentlemen! As you are aware, we have finished our search of your cabins, and we shall now begin the interviews. Mr Darius Damant, will you please join us in the snug. The rest of you are free to return to your rooms, but please be aware that we shall be calling you to interview for the rest of today, and possibly tomorrow. We thank you again for your patience." That last remark was directed at Sir Wesley, who once again seemed a little agitated. His mouth snapped shut and he glared at Elliott before offering his arm to Lady Carlton-Cayce and escorting her from the room, muttering under his breath as they went; Elliott managed to catch some of the irritated man's language as he swept past.

Darius looked deathly pale as he stood up and walked to the doorway that led to the snug, while the rest of the guests left the lounge in silence.

As they followed Darius into the snug, Elliott leant towards Giselle and murmured. "I did like Sir Wesley's use of the term 'upstarts', didn't you?"

She smiled and whispered back, "Don't be too smug, Elliott. Just wait until he realises what's missing from his and Lady Carlton-Cayce's cabins…his language may become a trifle fruitier, my love!"

○

## Interview with Darius Damant
## The Snug
## 3:05pm

Elliott escorted Giselle to a chair and Thorne did the same for Aquilleia. As she gracefully sat down and arranged her skirts, Thorne whispered in her ear. She glanced towards Darius and nodded, sat back in her chair, and closed her eyes.

Elliott waved a languid hand towards an armchair and Darius sat down; his hands clasped in his lap as he gazed at Elliott with the expression of a wide-eyed young rabbit who had just spotted an approaching weasel.

Thorne took his seat and produced a notebook and several pencils which he placed on a small table. Choosing one of the pencils, he licked the point and began his notes.

Elliott hid a smile as he turned to the young man. "Mr Damant, whilst it may cause you deep distress, I'm afraid we must ask you to inform us of your movements yesterday, Friday the 23rd of March, during which time your mother, Mrs Carolyn Nolloth, was murdered. If you answer our questions truthfully, the quicker we can bring her murderer to justice."

Darius swallowed and nodded jerkily. "Of course, yes, of course." His voice was husky, and his fingers plucked at his green silk waistcoat.

"Now, what were you doing between the hours of, say, six and ten o'clock last night?"

Darius swallowed again. "At — at six o'clock I had a bath, then a little after half past, I began to dress—"

"Is there anyone who can vouch for you?"

Darius flushed. "I am not married, Mr Caine!" he snapped.

Elliott smiled, his canines flashing. "I meant a valet, Mr Damant."

Darius' flush deepened as he realised his mistake. "No, n-no, I have no valet."

Elliott inclined his head. "Very well. Please continue."

Darius cleared his throat. "At seven o'clock I met with Uncle, Merry, Mar, and Torrance in the lounge. We were the first there, as is customary and proper. As we awaited the arrival of the guests, I mixed drinks for Uncle and Merry… Mar and Torrance don't drink. We were joined by Sir Wesley's secretary, Robin Ellis shortly after. The guests began to arrive at — well, I think some were on time, others arrived around ten past the hour, some a little later still. Then at half past seven the butler struck the gong and we went in to dinner."

Thorne's glance flicked towards Aquilleia. Her eyes opened, and she smiled at him. A wave of happiness hit him as he smiled back: like his friend, his life had been empty — simply searching and waiting for his Other — and now that they had been reunited, nothing would keep them apart. He realised that Darius was still talking and lowered his eyes to his notepad as he scribbled furiously, while Aquilleia's smile deepened.

"Dinner continued, as you know, until I think a quarter to ten, and then people began to leave…"

Elliott noted his hesitation and pounced. "Do continue, Mr Damant. People began to leave…"

Darius stared at the carpet, a muscle twitching under his left eye. "I…I went onto the deck. It was a nice evening… there was moonlight…"

Elliott recognised the signs and allowed himself a quiet sigh; Darius's terror of admitting a slight breach of the social niceties seemed to be rendering him almost mute. "Were you alone in your communion with the moon, Mr Damant? Or were you perhaps sharing the romantic moonlight with someone else?"

Darius stared at Elliott, then sat in miserable silence before passing his hand across his eyes. "I was with…I was… oh God, please don't ask!"

Elliott rolled his eyes at Giselle. "A lady?"

Darius nodded unhappily.

Elliott shrugged. Finally! "Well now, let's play name the lady: I was seated with my wife, Giselle; Lady Carlton-Cayce, Merry Damant and Josephine…Kayfield were seated in the lounge; Madame Aquilleia Aquileisi had excused herself from dinner and retired to her room; and if you will pardon my bluntness, the pretty but slightly vacuous Sophie Rust was believed to have been perambulating with Mr Van der Linde on the starboard side of the deck. So, by a process of elimination, I deduce you were with the lovely and rather fabulous Dona Carla Riva…am I right?"

Darius glared from under angry brows, his spirit seeming to have returned again. "Damn it all, man — a lady's reputation!"

A sudden laugh like a peal of bells came from a high-backed armchair facing into the far corner. Then a grinning face suddenly appeared as the catlike body of Dona Carla unwound itself from the nest of pillows and blankets in the chair and walked with exquisite grace towards them. Darius swallowed as she approached, and she reached out a slender hand to caress his face. When she spoke, her voice was a purr. "A gentleman concerned for my reputation — that hasn't happened for years!"

She slinked towards the bar, helped herself to another drink, and with a smile turned back to the gathered party, one of whom was staring at her as a rabbit stares at a snake.

She drank deeply, relishing the attention, before her smile slid away. "Yes, we did go out to the starboard deck together after dinner, but after a few short, short moments you left and headed aft. So, Mr Darius Damant, I'm afraid I am not your alibi for your mother's murder!" She finished her drink and banged the coupe down on the mahogany table. The port side door slammed shut behind her as she left the room.

Elliott shook his head. "Thorne."

Thorne walked over to the door and checked that the dancer had left the immediate vicinity before nodding at Elliott.

Elliott returned his attention to the flustered young man before him. His voice was silky as he addressed Darius. "Attempting to use a lady's reputation as an alibi is rather a caddish thing to do, Mr Damant. Attempting to do so during the investigation into your mother's brutal murder is quite something else again. That suggests either fear, or a guilty secret. So, Mr Damant, which is it?"

Darius's mouth opened and closed as he looked at Elliott. He jumped as Aquilleia spoke from her chair by the door. "He *is* hiding something…he is more upset by his mother's death than he wants people to know. He—"

"Stop!" Darius leapt to his feet; his face twisted as he glared at them. "I loved her…even after everything she had done, and all she was, she was my mother, and I still loved her!" He covered his face and began to sob.

Elliott ran a hand through his hair as he stared at the distraught young man. "Mr Damant—"

"No!" Darius leapt from his chair and bolted from the room.

Elliott looked at his friend with an exasperated expression. "Follow him, Thorne!"

Thorne dropped his notepad and thundered after the weeping young man. He returned a few minutes later, rather short of breath. "He ran to his cabin, fumbled with his key, and bolted the door behind him. I hope he doesn't do anything foolish…"

Aquilleia raised her voice again. "He won't hurt himself."

Elliott nodded. "Good. Carolyn Nolloth left the lounge for her cabin a little before Darius, so I doubt there would have been time for him to have left the fragrant Dona Carla on deck and arrive at his mother's cabin to set up the lye before she arrived…but he *was* alone in his cabin before the cocktail hour, which could have given him the time required. Hmm…food for thought. Next interview?"

Thorne flipped to the cabin layout he had been given by the steward Trevenniss. "Next is…ah, yes, Thornton Rust, and according to the manifest, his good lady, Sophie, who we know doesn't share his room…"

Elliott smiled. "In that case, we shall call Thornton Rust and his real roommate, Colten Kayfield. Bearing in mind the letter and the book we found in their room, this could be very interesting!" He placed another seat beside the one Darius had recently vacated and sank back into his chair, his fingers propped like a steeple before him as Thorne went to call the two men for interview.

○

### Interview with Thornton Rust and Colten Kayfield
### The Snug
### 3:25pm

After several minutes had passed, Thorne finally reappeared in the doorway and rolled his eyes at Elliott. He knew he didn't have to announce their two guests: Elliott would have heard Thornton's bluster from several yards away.

As the three men entered the room, Colten saw Giselle

and Aquilleia, poked Thornton in the ribs, and bowed in their direction. Thornton paused in his monologue, his mouth gaping slightly as the prod caught him off guard. He almost snapped his heels together as he inclined his head in their direction before returning his full and slightly myopic attention back towards Elliott.

Colten closed his eyes and groaned silently as Thornton squinted through his monocle and drew himself up into his best mixed-company buffoon — which wasn't so far from his true personality. He addressed Elliott with pompous self-righteousness as he leant his not inconsiderable weight upon the walking stick he had chosen to affect in his act. "I insist on knowing what this is about! I agree with Sir Wesley; who and what are you, sirrah? Attached to the forces of Empire? Poppycock! Show me your warrant card!"

Elliott smiled, grateful that they had kept the cards that had served them so well for many years. He reached into his breast pocket and produced a battered leather case. Colten's sharp grey eyes caught the initials E.V.C. on the front before it was flipped open to reveal the warrant card within.

Thornton, thrown a little off guard by the alacrity in which his impolite demand was met, covered his uncertainty with aplomb, glared at Elliott and threw himself into his chosen role with relish. Screwing his monocle in a little tighter, he took the proffered article and looked down his nose at the legend printed therein: Elliott V. Caine, badge number 1.D.C.I.B.E. He paused in his act; there was no rank given, and no title, just the name, followed by a nonsensical number and initials. Thornton turned the full weight of his glare upon Thorne. "And yours, sir! Quickly now!"

Thorne hid his own smile, reached into his inner pocket and produced a matching leather case with the initials A.S.T. The letters were underscored by a neat hole caused by a knife thrust from a long-forgotten fight, which ran neatly through the leather from front to back. He handed it to the irate man before him.

Thornton flicked the case open and glared at the inoffensive piece of card within, which bore a legend almost the same as the first: Abernathy S. Thorne, badge number 2.D.C.I.B.E.

Thornton handed the card back to Thorne and refocused his glare on Elliott. "Very well, they appear to be in order."

Thorne grinned. If Thornton believed that, he didn't have a clue what he was looking at. The first badge numbers for the British police had been issued in 1829, the same year the Espion Court had accepted a request for assistance from the newly created police force. Elliott and Thorne had been the two operatives sent to support the police and work as liaisons between them and the Court in its secretive and occasionally messy work for the Empire. 1 and 2 were the first badge numbers released, and the initials denoted their rank: Detective Chief Investigator for the British Empire. They were equal in position, pretending to differ solely for the benefit of those outside their inner circle. Both Elliott and Thorne had kept the same badges throughout the seventy-one years of their service within the police...simply leaving and rejoining under the same names, but in different departments, every fifteen or twenty years. The more recent police badges were slightly different from theirs, and that had caused one or two little hiccoughs and not a few pointed questions during the course of their last appointment in Scotland Yard.

Thornton continued to bluster. "I don't understand, young man; surely you should be interviewing us with our wives?"

Elliott nodded his agreement. "Yes, Mr Rust, we should — but it's rather difficult when your wife, if indeed you actually have one, isn't here with you. Now, our question is this: what is Sir Wesley Eade, another guest, doing hiring a troupe of actors without informing his host of his intentions?"

Thornton's jowls flapped as he stared at Elliott. Then a sudden bark of laughter came from Colten. "Well caught, sir…I congratulate you, truly I do." He turned to the older man and slapped him on the shoulder. "I think we're going to have to come clean, old chap."

Thornton winced and dropping his bluster, addressed his friend in a tone of mild reproof. "I do wish you wouldn't use such vulgar vernacular, dear boy…if I had your voice, the parts I could play!" He removed his monocle, tucked it back into its little pocket and nodded at Elliott. "I suppose my young friend is correct, I daresay you found certain…pertinent information while you were searching our room. Very well, please allow me to introduce my colleague, Mr Colten Kayfield, and I am Thornton Havelock Rust, Esquire. The others in our little troupe are Mrs Josephine Carter and Miss Sophie Havercroft, and we are indeed actors."

Elliott raised his eyebrows. "Esquire?"

Thornton spread his hands in a self-deprecating manner. "My dear mother was a gentlewoman. Alas, it broke her heart when I left the family home and the settled life of the gentry for a life of financial uncertainty and hardship treading the boards."

Colten looked at him, a slight smile flickering around his lips. "Your dear old mum ran a tobacconist's shop on Hunter Street in Sydney!"

Giselle exchanged glances with Aquilleia, who giggled and bit her lip as Thornton tried desperately to smooth his ruffled pride. He ran a manicured finger around the suddenly tight band of his neatly tied cravat. "Well…it's the thought that counts!"

Elliott gestured to the two seats opposite him. As the men

sat, Thorne whipped out another pencil and opened his notebook.

Thornton cleared his throat. "Back to the issue at hand. I take it you found the letter from Sir Wesley in our cabin?"

Elliott smiled. "Yes, and the book."

"Well, we are, as you have rightly said, a small acting troupe. We were contacted by Sir Wesley — he does a great deal for those who seek out the joys of the stage, and especially for those of us who occasionally find the remunerations somewhat…lacking. He contacted us in the hope that we would accept an offer of employment. He wished us to accompany him to this outpost of civilisation and act out a scene or two from a book he thoughtfully furnished for us."

Thorne looked up from his notes. "How were you invited to this weekend's event if the host didn't personally know you?"

Colten spoke from the depths of his armchair. "Sir Wesley told Mr Damant that we were investors in a mining concern he was interested in, so Mr Damant extended the invitation to the four of us. I believe Mr Damant was also interested in the idea of the mine. I understand that's how he made his fortune — funding mining concerns — and Sir Wesley wanted to talk with him about investing in it."

Elliott tapped his fingers against his lip and leaned forward. "Out of interest, regardless of the falsehood of describing the four of you as his 'business partners', was the mine he offered to Mr Damant real?"

Thornton tapped the floor with his cane and looked at Colten, who nodded. "I believe it was, yes, and quite local."

Elliott frowned. "How do you mean?"

"I remember because it was straight out of a Thousand and One Nights: the Sinbad Mine, Sinbad Gully — it's here in Milford Sound." He looked at Elliott and Thorne. "I don't know how they managed to get permission to reopen it, though."

Elliott stared at him. "Reopen? What do you mean?"

Colten pulled a face. "I research my roles; most of us do. I discovered there had been an attempt to mine in Sinbad Gully many years ago; it was an illegal concern as no land had been purchased…" He paused before continuing. "And then there was the disappearance!"

Elliott leant back and gestured. "Please continue."

"A young surveyor by the name of Thomas Nibbs had been given the task of travelling to the Sound and creating a more detailed map of the area. Upon arrival, he set out to map the entire length of the Sound from Milford City to the mouth of the sea. One day he travelled by boat to Sinbad Gully and found something that should not have been there. He was chased by a large number of men, but he managed to return to his hotel where he wrote two letters: one to his half-sister, explaining what had happened, and the other, which was little more than a postcard, to the proprietor of that hotel, who I believe still runs it to this day."

Elliott's eyes flickered slightly, showing a faint glimmer of green. "Coll Langen?"

Colten looked surprised. "Yes, the very same. Nibbs took his pack and left the hotel. He was last seen heading not for the Milford Track towards Te Anau, but the far more difficult, almost non-existent track to Queenstown, at the same time as a large group of heavily armed men arrived in Milford City looking for him."

Thorne looked up from his notes. "What had he discovered? An illegal mine wouldn't be worth killing over, surely?"

Colten shrugged gracefully. "All I know is what I found while conducting my research. The newspapers reported the salient details and they also contained photographic replicas of the letters; both of which alluded to the presence in the gully of a mining camp, which had, in his opinion, been in use for several years." He looked at Elliott, "Nibbs also stated that he had managed to — procure, shall we say — a sample from the mine, and that he would take it with him to Queenstown as proof, but neither he nor the sample were ever seen again. His half-sister was desperate to get word of him."

Giselle sat forward. "What was the sample?"

Colten turned to look at her. "An uncut ruby...which is a very rare find in this area; apparently New Zealand isn't the usual place to find them because the strata is wrong: garnets yes, rubies no. After his letters were delivered and the police informed, they and not a few reporters headed to the gully; there were signs that a mine *had* been worked there, but all the mining equipment had been removed and the workers had vanished."

There was silence, and Giselle nibbled on her nail. Gemstones, always gemstones.

Elliott folded his hands into a steeple and tapped his lips before beginning in much the same manner he had with Darius. "Very well, shall we move on? Gentlemen, we need to know your whereabouts between the hours of six and ten o'clock yesterday."

The two men looked at each other. Colten nodded, and began. "We, that is, Mrs Carter, Miss Havercroft, and our good selves, had enjoyed a fairly quiet afternoon resting on deck until just after five o'clock. The ladies disappeared to begin their ablutions and Rust and I headed to the bar for a little, ah, light refreshment. We withdrew to our cabin to dress for dinner a little before half past five—"

Thorne held up his hand. "You began your preparations for the evening so early?"

Thornton coughed. "I am a little older than my friend, and it therefore takes me a while longer to tend to such things." He harrumphed. "At maybe a little after half past five I bathed, and shortly after six o'clock I began my routine."

Thorne raised his eyebrows. "Your…routine?"

Thornton gripped his monocle and frowned at him. "We were to perform the play after dinner. Most if not all actors have certain…quirks that they must attend to before a performance."

Thorne nodded and continued his notes as Thornton grumbled quietly under his breath.

Elliott looked at the younger man. "And you, Mr Kayfield?"

"When Thornton had finished in the bathroom, I too ran a bath — I think I was in the tub by about six o'clock. Thornton was dressing in the main cabin—"

"How do you know Mr Rust was still in the cabin?" asked Aquilleia.

Colten shrugged. "Because the door was partly open: I could hear him rehearsing."

Elliott nodded. "Pray continue, Mr Rust."

Thornton shot him an annoyed look. "I dressed and was ready at a little after a quarter to seven."

Colten mused. "I left the tub at half past six…I usually soak for half an hour. I dressed, and at a few minutes before seven, we went next door and collected Mrs Carter and Miss Havercroft, then we went down to the lounge for the cocktail hour."

"Did you get all that, Thorne?"

Thorne added a few more scribbles to his notes and nodded.

Elliott paused. "Just two more things, gentlemen; firstly, if Josephine is Mrs Carter, then where is Mr Carter?"

Colten looked at Thornton and the older man replied. "Josephine Carter has been a widow for nearly twenty years now. Her husband was killed in Egypt, at the battle of Tell El Kebir."

Elliott nodded. "And secondly, Mr Kayfield, in your background research for your role, you said that one letter was sent to Coll Langen and the other to Mr Nibbs's half-sister. Correct?"

"Yes, that is quite correct."

"Can you remember the name of his half-sister?"

Colten thought for a moment and then nodded. "I believe her name was Lattimer, Ngaio Lattimer."

A faint green swirl appeared in Elliott's eyes. "Thank you, gentlemen; I would ask you not to speak with either Mrs Carter or Miss Havercroft until after we have interviewed them."

Thornton puffed himself up. "Of course."

As the two men left the room, the four who remained looked at each other. Giselle was the first to speak, her tone thoughtful. "Ngaio Lattimer is the name of Carolyn Nolloth's maid…"

Thorne nodded. "The book I found on her bed was a gift from her brother, Thomas." He stood and looked at Elliott. "I'll go and gather the other half of Sir Wesley's acting troupe."

### Interview with Josephine Carter and Sophie Havercroft
### The snug
### 3:45pm

A faint sound of swishing came from the port-side deck. The door was pushed open by Thorne, who stood aside and politely encouraged the next two offerings into the snug.

Josephine, her enthusiastic embonpoint rigidly contained

within her simple green day dress, entered half-dragging a terrified-looking Sophie behind her. The younger woman was wearing a blush-pink and rather frilly frock deliberately chosen to embody her self-imposed role as ingénue, but which unfortunately simply highlighted her as a woman trying desperately to appear younger than she was; that particular shade of pink doing very little for her deathly pale complexion.

As the two ladies settled themselves into their seats, Elliott took a swift sip from a small glass of brandy, replaced the glass on the table beneath an exuberant aspidistra and began. "Mrs Carter, Miss Havercroft, in the words of Mr Kayfield, it is time to come clean! We know you are both actresses in the pay of Sir Wesley Eade, and we need to know exactly what you were doing between the hours of six and ten o'clock last night—"

Sophie gave a sudden small scream and bit her hand. She looked desperately from Elliott to Josephine before her eyes rolled back in her head and she gracefully slid to the floor in a dead faint.

Elliott raised his eyebrows at Josephine, who sighed and spoke, her voice calm and level. "After dinner, I was sitting with Lady Carlton-Cayce and Miss Merry Damant in the lounge. Sophie and Mr Van der Linde went for a wander on deck. She found him charming…a little too charming, perhaps, and she accompanied him to his room. Nothing happened, but an unchaperoned woman acquiescing to a request to be alone with a man, and in his rooms…If you will excuse my bluntness, gentlemen, she's afraid you will think her a whore." Josephine's mouth twisted slightly. "It is how a great many people think of actresses, simply because we are on the stage."

Elliott and Thorne lifted the recumbent Sophie from her prone position on the floor and placed her back in her armchair. As Giselle rummaged in her reticule for smelling salts, she looked at Josephine. "Forgive me for asking, but are you?"

The older woman looked at Giselle in silence for some time before responding. "I trust I can speak honestly here?" At Giselle's nod, she continued. "Some of us are and some of us are not — Sophie and I are of the kind who most definitely are *not*! Sophie may occasionally have her head turned by a charming man; it does happen, but it is usually innocuous and no harm done. Certain theatres are willing to accept…extremes of such behaviour, but they aren't picky when it comes to their productions or their casting, and as such the performances are somewhat shoddy and lacklustre…" She paused and grimaced. "As are most of the patrons. Such places almost double as brothels, whereas the more salubrious theatres that are prepared to pay more, expect a certain level of…ability and good conduct, shall we say?"

Giselle nodded in understanding as Josephine continued. "Those types of theatres are safer for us as single women: no gentlemen visitors allowed backstage, a decent level of acting ability required as standard, along with the willingness to work hard…and they demand absolutely no black marks against your name. If it were revealed that Sophie had actually allowed a man to charm her into his rooms, it would destroy her prospects for a good livelihood by denying her access to the more quality establishments." Her eyes swept over Giselle. "But I'm sure that in your career, you have also been judged for daring to refuse the path our mothers and grandmothers were forced to tread…they had no choice and we do, but we are still judged, and usually most vehemently by our own sex."

There was a faint moan from the armchair as a slightly crumpled Sophie slowly came to. She looked up at Elliott and paled further, the colour on her already white face ebbing into a deathly grey.

Elliott held up his hand. "It's quite all right, Miss Havercroft. My associates and I will not judge you on the temporary lack of a chaperone. However, you must be absolutely honest with us about your exact whereabouts before, during, and after Carolyn Nolloth's death."

Sophie took in a shuddering breath and nodded; she rested her trembling hands in her lap and plucked at the gold ring on her thumb.

Josephine looked at her tremulous cabin-mate and sighed. It had been a very long day, and it didn't appear to be improving. "What do you need to know?"

Elliott sat back in his chair. "As I said earlier, shortly before Miss Havercroft fainted, we need to know exactly what you were doing between six o'clock and the time Carolyn died, which we know to be a few minutes after ten o'clock."

Sophie looked at Josephine and cleared her throat. Her voice, when she spoke, was higher than usual. "We, that is to say Josephine, Mr Rust, Mr Kayfield and I, were resting on the deck a little before five o'clock. We left to begin our preparations for dinner. I am not sure of the time…" Her voice faltered; she looked helplessly at Josephine who continued in a much firmer tone.

"Yes, we both went to our cabin…I think it was a little after five o'clock. Sophie ran a bath, she was in there for a good half an hour, and then it was my turn—"

Elliott leant forward. "If Miss Havercroft was in the bathroom, how are we to know that you didn't leave the cabin, Mrs Carter? Or vice versa?"

Josephine looked surprised. "Well, we spoke to each other through the door, both while Sophie was in the bath and when it was my turn."

Elliott looked at the younger woman; the colour was finally returning to her cheeks. "Is this correct, Miss Havercroft?"

She nodded, blinking rapidly. "Yes. We talked about our parts in the play we were to perform after dinner; how we saw our characters, that sort of thing. I came out of the bath, Josephine ran hers, and we continued our discussion through her ablutions. We dressed…Josephine's gown had some awkward stays and she needed my assistance, then we rested until Mr Kayfield and Mr Rust came to collect us for the cocktail hour."

Josephine looked at Elliott with an earnest expression. "It's true, Mr Caine; we were in each other's company from just after five to shortly before seven o'clock, when the others in our troupe came for us. After that, we were in the lounge and dining room for the rest of the evening until… until the events in Mrs Nolloth's cabin."

Elliott inclined his head. "Very well. Now tell me a little about this play you were to perform after dinner. I understand Sir Wesley provided you with the material himself?"

Josephine sat forward slightly; her face eager. "It was very good: a short melodramatic mystery about a gentleman whose wife falls out of love with him and in love with his friend. A touch scandalous perhaps, but not too racy. She plans to leave him, but the fates conspire against her and the two lovers are killed, leaving the widowed husband to the tender care of his housekeeper who has loved him for years."

Thorne caught Elliott's eye. "Do you have any idea who wrote it?"

Josephine nodded. "There was no name on the cover — it simply bore the title: 'A Price Above Diamonds'— but when Sir Wesley suggested the book, Mr Rust was concerned about getting the author's permission. That was when Sir Wesley said that *he* had written the book and he granted permission for it to be used." She caught the look Elliott shared with Thorne. "He was quite adamant that Mr Rust was to play the husband, Mr Kayfield the friend, Sophie the wife, and I the housekeeper. It would have been very neat and tidy as a short play, requiring only one set, but Sir Wesley didn't want the entire play."

Elliott raised his eyebrows. "He didn't?"

"No, just from the point where the wife and her paramour decided to kill her husband —"

"Mr Caine!"

Elliott's head snapped round as O.D walked into the room. The philanthropist expression became slightly rattled as he realised he was now the focus of attention for six people. He nodded at Sophie before stopping in front of Josephine. "Mrs Carter, I trust this interview is not too onerous for you?"

Josephine looked up at him, faint surprise on her face. "I understand that it is necessary, Mr Damant. And it is always best to get unpleasant things over and done with as soon as possible."

O.D nodded, then paused. "May I…may I show you the roof garden? There is quite a lovely view from the aft terrace."

Josephine smiled and stood up, gathering her skirts. "That would be lovely, Mr Damant. There are some things I feel I need to tell you." She stopped suddenly and looked at Elliott. "I take it we have finished, Mr Caine?"

Elliott looked from Josephine to O.D and back, a faint flickering of green visible in his eyes. "Yes, Mrs Carter, I do believe we have…enjoy your perambulations. Miss Haver-croft, thank you for your time; you may also leave."

As the three of them left the room, Thorne turned to Elliott, his eyebrows raised. "That escalated!"

Aquilleia smiled. "He cares for her. It has happened

suddenly, but he is quite aware of his feelings towards her and has become very protective."

Elliott grinned. "Hasn't he, though! Well, looking at the time frame it would seem that none of the troupe could be guilty of putting the lye in Carolyn Nolloth's wash jug…they are each other's alibis for the only possible window of opportunity."

Thorne shook his head. "They could all be in on it!"

Elliott pinched his nose and groaned. "Oh, I really hope not! Who's next?"

Thorne looked on the list. "Marjorie Lee Colville."

"I wonder…Thorne, would you do your collecting thing again, old chap?"

As Thorne left to collect their next victim, Elliott, Giselle, and Aquilleia quickly went over the clues to hand, in particular the unveiling of Sir Wesley as the author of the little melodrama.

Elliott shrugged. "It makes damn-all sense at the moment, but let's keep going; you never know what might happen next!"

○

### Interview with Marjorie Lee Colville
### The snug
### 4:10pm

Thorne waited by Mar's door as she went back into her room to retrieve her shawl. As she emerged and closed her cabin door, the sound of raised voices and laughter made them both turn, just in time to see O.D escorting Josephine Carter up to the roof garden, with Merry and Fleur following a few paces behind.

Merry smiled at Mar, but her smile faltered at the expression on Mar's face as she looked at O.D and Josephine. Thorne, too, caught the look. As the others made their way up to the roof garden, he politely held out his arm to Mar, and after a space of some moments where he thought she wouldn't take it, she finally did and they walked down to the snug.

As they entered the cosy little room, Thorne held the door open for her. Elliott looked up and smiled. "Mrs Colville, please take a seat."

As she sat down, Elliott took the opportunity to observe her. In her late forties, he would say, well but not expensively dressed in a suitably muted black tweed day dress. Her smooth, pale face bore no sign of the artifice of make-up, her dark eyes were watchful, and her hair was neatly pinned. She was the epitome of the respectable governess turned capable lady's companion.

The ghost of a smile touched her face. "I hope I meet with your satisfaction, Mr Caine?"

He laughed, his canines flashing. "I do beg your pardon, Mrs Colville. I trust you understand that we need to ask you some questions about your whereabouts yesterday evening?"

She nodded, turning to look at Giselle, Aquilleia, and Thorne. "I understand. O.D informed me of your arrival, and the truth of your purpose here. I will freely admit to being afraid for Merry's life, but the Fates conspired to take another in her stead. How may I assist you?"

"Where were you between the hours of, say, shortly before six o'clock and ten o'clock last night?"

She thought, her dark eyes flickering. "Between the hours of five and six I was with Merry and Fleur, helping Fleur with her German verbs. At a little after six o'clock, I returned to my cabin to prepare for dinner. I left my cabin at five or ten minutes to seven to meet with O.D and Merry in the lounge. Shortly after you arrived, Captain

Peach, Fleur, Torrance, Mr Ellis, and I left and made our way to the staff quarters for our meal. We dined at much the same pace as those in the main dining room, and we lingered over our coffee. At maybe a little after a quarter past ten we heard…something, but we were not sure what it was."

Thorne looked at her, a faint expression of incredulity on his handsome face. "How could you not have realised what you were hearing?"

Mar paused before responding. "The servants' sitting room has no external walls, and backs onto the engine room…we hear some very strange noises there." Thorne nodded as she continued. "We finished our coffee and then, as we made our way back to the lounge, Vasily informed us of what had happened."

"Thank you, Mrs Colville, for your succinct rendition of last night's events. I have one more question: where on this boat would I find lye?"

"Lye?"

"Yes – it is what was used to kill Mrs Nolloth."

She paused, then took a deep breath. "I think we used most of what was in the cupboard…" She faltered as Elliott turned his flickering eyes on her, then continued. "We — that is to say Merry, Fleur, and I — we use it to make soap, and the servants use it to clean the cast-iron pots."

Elliott nodded thoughtfully. "Where is it kept?"

"Some is kept in a cupboard in the kitchen and some in the storage cupboard next to Mrs Nolloth's cabin — I mean, the room that was…Mrs Nolloth's cabin."

"Are the doors to either cupboard locked?"

She shook her head. "No, there was no need." She smoothed the front of her dress. "With hindsight, obviously there was need, but how on earth could we have known that something like this would happen?"

Elliott smiled. "Indeed. Thank you, Mrs Colville, that will be all for now."

She stood up and paused for a moment as though about to speak, before turning and leaving the room.

Elliott looked at Aquilleia and raised his eyebrows. "Anything?"

Aquilleia frowned. "She hides things even from herself: I find her difficult to read."

Thorne helped himself to a drink from the bar. "Well, she has no alibi for the time between approximately six o'clock and ten minutes to seven." He took a sip of his drink. "And she certainly wasn't happy when she saw O.D taking the air with Josephine Carter!" He explained Mar's painful reaction to seeing the pair together.

Giselle nodded thoughtfully. "So…is she in love with O.D?"

Elliott retrieved his brandy from under the aspidistra and took a sip, scanning the guest list as he did so. "It certainly sounds like it, and it would appear that Sir Wesley knew enough to write a book about it! Right, Thorne, the next guest is — oh, this should be interesting! Be a good man and request the presence of Lady Leonora Carlton-Cayce, please." He turned to Giselle and Aquilleia. "Very interesting indeed!"

Several minutes passed, then Thorne reappeared in the doorway, a look of irritation on his handsome face.

Elliott raised his eyebrow. "You appear to be lacking something, my friend!"

Thorne's mouth twisted. "With the compliments of Sir Wesley Eade: Lady Carlton-Cayce will not be giving any interviews until such time as she can be interviewed by one of suitable character and rank, as becomes a high-born lady!"

Elliott's eyes gleamed, the green lights swirling slightly.

"Oh, really?" He turned to his wife and Aquilleia. "To the good lady's chambers!"

○

### Lady Carlton-Cayce's cabin
### 4:30pm

Elliott knocked briskly on the door; not for him the deferential light tap. The door was flung open and Elliott came face to face with Sir Wesley Eade in fighting mode. His expression as he gazed down his nose at Elliott and the others was at once supercilious and condescending, suggesting exactly how Sir Wesley fought in the Courts of Law, and also how he would look after stepping in something unpleasant.

He held up a peremptory hand and glared at the four in turn. "My client has taken legal advice from her counsel and decided not to participate in this ridiculous and futile charade. She will acquiesce to an interview once we have returned to Auckland and the proper authorities can begin their official investigations. In the meantime, you and your coven of interfering, self-aggrandising Nosey Parkers will leave my client alone, on pain of prosecution for slander, libel, and anything else I can throw at you!" He leant forward, the tip of his nose almost touching Elliott's. "We will also be bringing a personal case against you and your cohort over the theft of one of Lady Carlton-Cayce's jewels and the removal of several personal photographs from my private collection. If that diamond or those photographs are handed to anyone other than me or my client, I guarantee that you and your associates will be disposed of — permanently!"

Before Elliott could speak, Sir Wesley slammed the door shut. They heard his voice through the door. "And that, my dear, is how you deal with jumped-up enquiry agents!"

Outside the cabin, Elliott stared at the door for several seconds before turning to his friends. When he finally spoke, his voice was deathly quiet. "Well, that is how one who presumes to have power speaks to those they presume to have none. I have had enough interviews for one day; I suggest we procure one of Mr Damant's finest bottles of champagne, retire to a cabin, and go over what we have learned so far. We can continue with the interviews tomorrow after breakfast, starting with the good Sir Wesley and Lady Carlton-Cayce. Regardless of the good lawyer's opinion of his own abilities, they won't escape me!"

In the cabin, Lady Carlton-Cayce reclined on a chaise in an advanced state of glamour. Clad in a sumptuous astrakhan-trimmed grey silk peignoir, she studied her lover with a slightly distant expression as she stroked the platinum and diamond choker that graced her white throat. "Aren't you concerned about those photographs having a wider audience? They were meant solely for us…it cost a fortune to find a discreet photographer!"

Sir Wesley shook his head. "I know their type, my dear: popinjays, the lot of them! A good threat, and they melt back into the shadows that spawned them. If they do try to continue with their ridiculous act, I'll orchestrate charges of theft and of faking libellous photographs. They will live to regret the day they thought they could ruin us!" He rubbed his hands together with a laugh. "I think this calls for a drink, my dear."

As he headed to the drinks cabinet, Leonora spoke again. "But aren't you just a little concerned about the murder?"

Sir Wesley opened the chilled bottle of champagne, poured two coupes, and handed one to his companion with a smile. "Ah yes, about that…well done! I never would have thought of lye in the wash jug; you do have rather a flair, my dear! I couldn't have managed it better myself. As for being concerned about the murder…why on earth should I be, my darling? When I, more than anyone here, have absolutely nothing to fear from Carolyn's killer!" He raised his glass in salute and took a sip, and an expression of enjoyment appeared on his face as he savoured the wine. Say what you would about O.D, the man did have an excellent cellar!

Leonora turned her huge blue eyes to Sir Wesley's face. "But it wasn't me…I thought it was you!"

Sir Wesley's face froze. "It certainly wasn't me…it had to have been you!"

Leonora laughed, and her small white teeth flashed. "Oh, but it wasn't at all, darling!" A thoughtful look crossed her perfect face, and she tapped her polished nails against the side of her glass as she mused. "So, there is a killer whom we must fear. It must be someone else whose little secrets she knew; that could be rather interesting, and certainly more entertaining than this weekend threatened to be. Yes, I know it was murder and I know she had certain…personal information, but frankly, darling, her death has certainly livened things up. Trust Carolyn to be the life and soul of the party, even in death!"

Sir Wesley stared at his drink, gulped it and refilled his coupe rapidly. "If it wasn't you, and it certainly wasn't me — well, we will need to be very careful, my dear, and not just because there is a murderer wandering around. I have the added protection of my valet in my suite, but is your maid enough to protect you?" Before Leonora could respond, he took another gulp of his drink, and continued. "I also have to say that I *am* rather concerned that there will be an official investigation, and certain highly personal information might appear in the public domain. Not the photographs — I can deal with that little upset — but the possibility of something hidden amongst Carolyn's papers; anything to do with your little…secret, you understand? Or the fact that our affair began while you were still married to the Baron von Schmetterling!"

Leonora shook her head and took a sip from her coupe. "Carolyn knew nothing about that side of our relationship, darling. Van der Linde did and he kept it from her. I doubt very much that he told her a thing; he's very good at keeping his little blackmail business secret, even from associates." She paused with a smile. "As to my very well-hidden secret, my husbands were all very highly regarded, extremely discreet…and utterly terrified of anyone uncovering their private lives. They all excelled at taking their little secret, and mine to their graves…those dear, dear men." She laughed; the platinum set diamonds at her throat sparkling in the flickering gaslight. "Going back to your concerns, darling: Van der Linde likes money, especially other people's money, but he doesn't like to share information or the spoils of his labours. We were really rather lucky; If one were forced to choose a blackmailer, he is quite the right type as he is very discreet and unwilling to share! No, I doubt very much that Carolyn would have known anything desperately damaging about us." She paused thoughtfully. "Intriguing that they were each blackmailing us, and the other never knew." She settled back into the chaise and smiled as she ran an elegant fingertip around the rim of her glass. "In answer to your earlier question, you need have no fear for my safety, darling. Besides my maid, one of the stewards is very…attentive to my needs; you have no reason to be concerned about my safety."

Sir Wesley's expression darkened. "I do wish you wouldn't—"

Leonora's eyes flashed. "And I do wish *you* wouldn't, Wesley! You are not yet my husband. And now I have a headache; leave me." Her eyes narrowed dangerously as she looked at the man she had considered making husband number nine. Perhaps she should reconsider: he was getting a trifle needy!

Sir Wesley set his coupe down on the little table, a faint tremble in his grip his only show of emotion. He bowed from the neck and walked stiffly to the cabin door.

"Oh, and Wesley?"

He turned. "Yes, my dear?"

Leonora took a sip of her champagne, a faint but spiteful smile on her rouged lips. "Send the steward Trevenniss to me. I require his services for the rest of the afternoon."

Sir Wesley's face paled; two high spots of colour appeared on his cheeks as the confused jumble of emotions on his face set into harsh lines. He walked over to his smirking lover and bent down so that he could look directly into her brilliant blue eyes. When he spoke, his voice was smooth and tightly controlled. "My darling Leonora, you push me too far. Please remember, my dearest, that Van der Linde is not the only person on this vessel with highly damaging personal information about you."

Leonora continued to smile. "Why, my darling, whatever can you be referring to?"

Sir Wesley's thin lips peeled back from his teeth in a caricature of a smile. "Perhaps it is time for a little…honesty between friends. I never told you, my darling, but when we first met, I was well aware of your reputation. As discreet as you have been in covering your past, you *are* known to those of us who *know*; indeed, it was the reason I sought you out. When forming our subsequent attachment, I realised that I needed to know more about your background: your family and associates, that sort of thing. The associate I hired…a Mr Morten Van der Linde, found some interesting information. He destroyed most of it on my orders, but I kept one or two salient items for my delectation, and he made copies for his! I didn't tell you at the time, my dear, but a few months ago someone broke into my home and several documents were removed. I have undertaken the recovery of my own paperwork; however, certain other documents in my possession, including the birth certificate of one Signor Aurelio Azzurro, remain missing."

Leonora's ruby lips parted with a gasp as she gazed up at him. Her perfect face was frozen, the only sign of life a vein pulsing in her throat.

Sir Wesley's smile widened as he saw his strike had hit home. He straightened up, walked towards the door, and turned to face her. "But I'm sure you'll be pleased to hear that before that particular document vanished, I had a copy made and hidden in a place of great safety. And if you wish it to remain there, my dear, you will not request the presence of the steward this afternoon, or at any other time again." His smile settled into a malicious and triumphant smirk. "Come to think of it, my dear, that rule now applies to any playmate, other than those *I* choose for you! That particular entertaining little trait of yours is now at an end until I wish it to occur. I wish you a good rest, Leonora. We will continue our discussion after dinner, when perhaps my offer will appear, in the cold light of day, to be the best — indeed, the *only* hope you have of protecting your reputation…for if you attempt to turn against me, I will bury you! Good evening, my lady."

He closed the door quietly behind him as Leonora stared blankly at the far wall.

**Several minutes later**

Leonora was still sitting where Sir Wesley had left her. She took a shuddering breath, her face deathly pale. How dare he! How dare he threaten her?

Her head snapped round at the sudden tapping on her door. She gathered her thoughts. It couldn't be Wesley, not after what he had just threatened her with. She took a deep breath. "Who is it?" She was pleased that her voice didn't tremble at all.

"It is I, Morten Van der Linde."

Leonora closed her eyes and took a deep breath; she gripped the stem of her coupe so hard the brittle glass cracked. She stared at the little beads of red forming on the fingers of her right hand before discarding the pieces of glass on the table before her. Removing a small, lacy handkerchief from her décolleté, she dabbed at her bloody fingers as she raised her voice. "Enter."

The door opened and the immaculately dressed diamond merchant entered the room. Morten pushed the door shut with a silky smile and approached her, his expression showing his appreciation of her outfit.

She ignored his lascivious stare and waved a languid hand from the chaise longue. "What do you want?"

Morten smiled as he approached the gilded lily before him. "My dear Lady Carlton-Cayce, I merely wish to be in your glorious and unique presence! Must there be another reason?"

She turned her huge blue eyes on him. "Money!"

Taking in the cold expression on her face, Morten rethought his approach. With an elegant shrug, the light in his eye became less appreciative and more judgemental. "I agree, it is tawdry…but it must be broached. The death of my darling Carolyn changes nothing, you understand? Our… agreement will continue as before." He paused, looking at the beautiful creature before him with a derisive eye before continuing. "What people choose to do with their lives, time, and money is their business, my dear lady. But you really shouldn't be surprised when others take advantage — or judge."

Leonora gazed at him silently; a few moments passed before Morten realised she wasn't looking at him, but through him. She parted her ruby lips. "I understand." She turned away and waved her hand towards the door.

Morten immediately understood that he had just been dismissed. He pursed his lips, then decided the gentlemanly option would be best under the circumstances. He bowed towards the back of her head and showed himself out of the room. As he began to shut the door she suddenly called, "Send the steward Trevenniss to me; I have need of him."

Morten paused. "As you wish, my lady."

Once the door had closed, Leonora moved swiftly to her writing chest and wrote a short note. Signing it, she lit one of the small candles on the desk and sealed the paper with green wax, pressing her metal seal depicting a small chrysanthemum into the molten wax before placing it on the table before her.

She sat in silent thought until she was roused by a deferential knock at the door. "Who is it?" she called.

"Trevenniss, my lady."

Her lips twisted into a spiteful smile. "Enter!"

### The lounge
### 7:00pm

Elliott, Giselle, Thorne, and Aquilleia entered the lounge for the cocktail hour. O.D, Merry, and Josephine were sitting in a quiet group in the middle of the room, and there was no one else to be seen.

O.D looked up at them, an irritated expression on his face

with a mixed expression. "They have all requested supper trays. My daughter's birthday weekend, and they are all hiding in their rooms!"

Merry patted his hand. "It's all right, Papa, really it is." She turned to look at them, an uncertain smile on her lips. "To be honest, I had wondered about a supper tray too!"

Elliott smiled back. "I doubt anyone would have complained, Miss Damant. Are Mar and Darius not joining us?"

O.D shook his head. "Mar has a severe migraine and is resting in her room. Darius — well, Darius is suffering in his own way; he has spent nearly all day in his cabin and has refused to join us. He even refused a supper tray! Captain Peach and Fleur are dining in the captain's cabin, and Torrance is dealing with the things that Darius should have dealt with today, and has taken a supper tray into his office." Running a hand through his hair, he glared at Elliott. "I'll be the first to admit that I despised my odious sister-in-law and it was very much a mutual loathing: no love was lost between us, Mr Caine." He shook his head. "But what was done to her was just so utterly…I am at a loss for words! How is your investigation going? Have you any idea who could have done such a hideous thing, or their possible reasoning for it?"

Elliott paused. He didn't want to inform O.D of Carolyn and Van der Linde's plans for Merry until after they had interviewed the diamond merchant. He shook his head. "We are only halfway through the interviews. We have one or two interesting leads, but I'm afraid I cannot say more just yet. Rest assured, Mr Damant, as soon as we know, you'll know."

O.D nodded abruptly. "I understand." He looked at Josephine and smiled, then leant towards Elliott. "Mrs Carter has been telling us of her exploits on the stage; she has acted with some of the best names in theatre." He paused, and a slightly mulish look crossed his face. "But I shall still speak to

Sir Wesley about inviting guests under false pretences." He paused. "I would like to thank you and your associates, Mr Caine. After this hideous situation developed, at least you were here and able to begin your investigation immediately: searching the cabins, gathering clues, and questioning the guests. Hopefully, this entire mess will be over and done with by the time the engines are fixed, and we can hand the evidence and the person responsible to the proper authorities in a neat and tidy package."

Elliott smiled. "That is my hope, Mr Damant. How goes the attempt to fix the engine?"

O.D waved his empty glass. "The engineer is hopeful that he and the stoker should be able to cobble something together — his words — to replace what was removed. We shall simply have to wait and see, I'm afraid."

Vasily appeared at the door to the dining room and announced that dinner would be served at half past seven. He bowed his head to Elliott. "May I interest you in a cocktail, sir?"

Elliott smiled. "Yes, Vasily, you may indeed!"

The butler bowed and walked towards the bar, as Elliott, Giselle, Thorne, and Aquilleia followed him into the snug.

Merry turned back to her father. "Papa, I'm concerned about Mar…she truly looked unwell earlier."

O.D frowned. "When was that?"

"When we four went up to the roof garden. We walked past Mar and Mr Thorne…they were standing outside her cabin. I think it was just before her interview. She looked so pale; I wonder if her migraine had already started?"

O.D caught Josephine's eye; she looked both concerned and slightly guilty. He patted his daughter's hand. "That must be it. I am sure she will feel better tomorrow."

Merry nodded and smiled. "I think I will have a little champagne. Would you like some Josephine? Papa?"

Josephine nodded with a bright smile. "A glass of champagne would be lovely, thank you, Merry."

O.D nodded. "The same for me please, my dear."

As Merry headed towards the bar, Josephine leant towards O.D. "Octavius…"

He took a deep breath. "I know, I know." He sighed. His feelings for Josephine had arrived rapidly — from the first moment he had seen her on Friday, to be exact — but he knew there might well be an issue with Mar. She had run his home for years, caring for Merry from birth, even when Cordelia was still alive. Her ability to organise the day-to-day running of everything that was not part of his business empire was outstanding. She might have believed that he would never marry again — or that if he did, it would be to her. He sighed. He cared for Mar and always would, but a home could not have two mistresses.

He looked at Josephine with a rueful expression. "I will talk with Mar in the morning…that may prove to be a rather upsetting conversation."

Josephine's expression was understanding; she leant forward and in a rather daring display of affection, placed her hand over his. "I will be here if you need me." She sat back in her chair and passed a hand across her eyes. O.D frowned slightly. "Are you all right, my dear?"

Josephine grimaced. "Sophie has been somewhat…clingy. I understand that she is frightened and concerned, as are we all, but last night she was in an almost constant state of hysterics — I barely slept for dealing with her. I truly hope she settles this evening; I need to sleep!" She frowned. "I didn't think to bring any sleeping powders with me."

O.D leant forward with a smile. "I may be able to assist. I have a box of Dr Morpheus' chloral sachets upstairs; you would only need to take one."

Josephine looked relieved. "That would be marvellous,

thank you." She paused. "I hope you don't think me presumptuous, but may I take two? I think Sophie would also be helped by a good night's sleep."

O.D smiled and stood up. "Yes, of course. I shall go and get them." He bowed to her and made his way back to his suite, where he removed two sachets from the full box on his bedside table before returning to the lounge. He handed the small paper envelopes to Josephine, who placed them in her reticule with a smile. As she did so, Merry returned to their table with Elliott, Giselle, Thorne, Aquilleia, and Vasily; the butler carrying a tray bearing seven full champagne coupes.

## Sunday morning
### 2:50am

The cabin door opened slowly in the dim moonlight; the silence of the early hours broken only by the faint slap of water against the side of the vessel.

A robed figure paused on the threshold of their cabin, they cast a sharp eye around the still deck, before quietly stepping out and closing the door behind them. They winced at the click of the latch, loud in the still and misty early morning air.

Gathering up their voluminous attire, they crept in an elaborate and exaggerated fashion towards the stairs, where they attempted to make their way down to the main deck in silence. Luck, however, was not on their side as they caught their foot in the capacious robe and slid down several steps before arresting their momentum at the foot of the stairs with several hissed oaths.

As they pulled themselves upright and straightened their

garb, a soft noise caught their ears. Turning to look along the deck, they saw the door to the snug slowly closing.

They froze, then considered the options available: it could be the killer, but they had taken care of that threat by simply ensuring they were armed at all times; it could be the person they were meeting, making sure they were on time; or it could be one of the servants. They dismissed the latter thought out of hand — even the hardest-working servant would be in bed at this ungodly hour of the morning!

Deciding it must be the person who had sent them the note requesting they meet, they hurried towards the doorway and stopped on the threshold to check no one was following them, before sliding into the snug and shutting the door behind them with a faint click.

Delving into one of their robe's many pockets, they removed a box of matches and a piece of paper covered with a rough sketch. Placing the map on one of the tables, they struck a match and scanned the piece of paper to see where they were in relation to their destination…ahh yes, there it was. Of all the perfectly ridiculous places to meet; when there were private cabins, why choose the kitchen? Blowing out the match, they dropped it into one of the pot plants and stuffed the map back into their pocket as they continued through the dim room.

Reaching the doorway, they darted a quick glance around the silent and dingy dining room. Excellent: empty. Walking past the massive table, they headed to the door that led to their final destination.

Gritting their teeth, they tried the door to the kitchen and breathed a sigh of relief when it soundlessly swung open. Hurrying inside, they carefully closed the door and surveyed the kitchen, its dark wood and marble surfaces scrubbed and gleaming in the glow of the gaslights. They paused to wonder why the gaslights were on, then dismissed the thought;

perhaps the servants preferred it that way, with a body lying in state in one of the storage rooms. As they considered their proximity to a murdered body, they turned, almost against their will, to look at the closed door at the far end of the kitchen: the door that led to the pantry, and beyond that, the meat locker…the final resting place of Carolyn Nolloth.

Shivering in spite of themselves, they hurriedly pulled their mind away from the shroud-wrapped contents of that cold room and instead focused on waiting for their highly anticipated discussion.

A sudden noise came to their attention; a slight clicking sound, as of something hot cooling down…or fingernails tapping on metal. Turning to see where the noise was coming from, they looked again at the door to the pantry and realised with a sudden jolt that the door was now ajar.

Swallowing hard, they looked at the door that led back out to the dining room, then turned back to the open door that led to the pantry and the meat locker. They must have been mistaken…the door had probably been left ajar by a careless maid desperate for her bed, then the movement of the boat had swung the door open and that had caused the sound. Yes, that must be it.

Standing by the now cold range, a sudden and slightly unwonted thought worked its way into their mind: in their entire life, they had never actually seen a corpse. A small oversight, perhaps; the opportunity to actually create one had presented itself on several occasions, but they had never taken that chance, for fear of professional reprisals and unwanted questions. Now, however, the opportunity to see one in the flesh, as it were, had suddenly presented itself without the risk of an audience. Far be it from them to look a gift horse in the mouth!

A furtive smile touched their face as they walked towards the far end of the kitchen. Passing into the pantry, they turned up the dim gaslights and looked towards the door to the meat locker. It stood wide open, the flickering light barely extending into the darkness of the cold, lead-lined room beyond. Hesitating, they turned to cast a faintly yearning look back at the warm, bright lights of the kitchen before shaking their head at their sudden faint-heartedness; the dead couldn't harm the living. They took a deep breath and entered the sparse and frigid room. It was furnished only with empty metal shelves, a sizeable wooden crate, and four wrapped sides of beef too large to rehouse elsewhere and which had been moved as far as possible from the room's centrepiece: a massive marble butcher's block that held Carolyn Nolloth's mortal remains…the still form wrapped in a white sheet that ensnared what little light there was, her covered body almost glowing in the middle of the shadowy room.

Seemingly against their will, the figure slowly approached the marble slab and reached out a trembling hand towards the covered form. As they reached the makeshift bier, a soft breeze seemed to caress the surface of the shroud.

A shiver began at the base of their spine and crept its way to the top of their neck, setting their hair on end as they realised there was no way a breeze could enter the sealed and windowless room.

They turned sharply at a sudden noise behind them: a harsh metallic clang as the door to the meat locker was pushed shut. The next sound was the sharp click of the bolt being thrown from the outside.

Realising their only escape route was now barred, they turned back to the corpse. Their breath caught in their throat as the shrouded shape on the butcher's block slowly began to move, the linen sheet falling away to expose the ruined form as it slid from its bier and slowly walked towards them.

Sir Wesley leapt from the approaching horror with a

scream and flung himself against the locked door, his manicured fingernails ripping at the lead lining in his desperation
to escape. Gibbering in terror and searching frantically in the
folds of his voluminous dressing gown for his revolver, he
turned back to face the bloodied corpse. Just as her slender,
ruined fingers fastened around his throat, his shaking hands
finally found his gun. Pulling it from his pocket, he lifted it to
his temple and pulled the trigger.

○

**A few moments later**
**The Meat Locker**

Twitching the shroud back over Carolyn's remains,
Phoenixus stood by the slab and ran a smoothing hand over
the remains of their face and hair. Their body slowly transformed from the double of the damaged corpse before them,
back into the form of the guest they had killed some months
earlier, and whose place they had taken.

Turning, they smiled at the added corpse in the room,
pausing to admire their handiwork. Things had gone mostly
to plan, but they hadn't expected the appearance of a gun at
their little meeting; how very fortunate they had chosen the
one room on the vessel that was lead lined…no one would
have heard the gunshot.

They paused, a feeling of uncertainty came over them as a
sudden ripple passed across their face and another expression appeared in their eyes: one of utter horror, sorrow, and
despair. Seemingly against their will, they walked to the wall
and violently struck their head against it. As blood began to
seep from the self-inflicted wound, the fearful expression
faded, to be replaced by one of anger and contempt. Gently
stroking the weeping laceration on their temple, they smiled

as the wound healed rapidly under their soothing hand. Turning, they faced the door and tapped a rhythmic tattoo. The door was swiftly opened by their subordinate: one they had managed to bring to their way of thinking, and it hadn't taken much persuading. Finding a participant willing to assist them in return for money and…other considerations had been a lucky and timely discovery.

Their helper smiled at them and handed them their clothes. While their employer dressed, the associate saw the gun on the floor and raised their eyebrows. Phoenixus thought for a moment, then nodded, and the revolver was slipped into a pocket. Locking the door behind them, they silently returned to their separate cabins.

### Sunday morning
### O.D's office
### 9:00am

As Elliott and Thorne entered the room, O.D looked up from his discussion with Darius.

Elliott nodded at the young man, who looked very pale and rather unwell: the death of his mother, though she had been rather a poor parent, had obviously affected him deeply.

"Mr Damant. I don't suppose either of you have seen Lady Carlton-Cayce or Sir Wesley this morning? We need to continue with our interviews and they are next on our list."

Both O.D and Darius shook their heads. Darius spoke; his voice lifeless and lacklustre. "I haven't seen either since… since the night my mother…excuse me!" The young man clamped his hand to his mouth as he ran from the room. O.D looked after him, then turned to Elliott and Thorne in some concern. "I never realised he might still feel some affection for his mother, not after everything she did to him! In answer to your question, gentlemen, no. I haven't seen Lady Carlton-Cayce since yesterday…although I do believe she is in her cabin as Vasily informed me her maid had requested a breakfast tray this morning. I haven't seen Sir Wesley since… well, before dinner last night." He fiddled with a piece of paper. "Why do you ask?"

Thorne scratched the bridge of his nose. "That seems to be the last time anyone saw him, It appears that we have misplaced Sir Wesley."

O.D frowned. "The Taniwha is a sizeable vessel, but not big enough to lose a person…he must be here."

Elliott nodded. "Our thoughts exactly, so we intend to organise a search from the bilge to the top deck. I suggest we start—"

"In the kitchen!"

The three men swung round to stare at Aquilleia, who had suddenly appeared in the open doorway. She nodded, her face deathly pale. "He is in the meat locker!"

The three men hurried out of the room, then Thorne paused by her side. "I'll take you to Giselle's cabin—"

Aquilleia touched his hand, a faint smile on her face. "I shall be fine; you go."

She watched him run out of the room, before turning her unblinking violet gaze on the door that led to O.D's private rooms.

○

## The Kitchens
### 9:10am

Desdemonia glared at the pile of washing up; would it never end? As she set about organising her staff to manage the seemingly never-ending task, they were joined in the kitchen by O.D, Elliott, and Thorne.

O.D looked at her. "Mrs Ainu, I am sorry to interrupt you at your work, but I'm afraid we need to check something."

Desdemonia looked concerned. "I can assure you, Mr Damant, Vasily and I looked into it at the time, and we could find nothing untoward."

O.D frowned at her. "What are you talking about?"

Desdemonia looked at him. "One of the engineers thought he heard a noise in the kitchens early this morning: their sleeping quarters are just the other side of the dividing wall. My husband and I checked and could find nothing wrong in the kitchen or the pantry—"

Elliott held up his hand. "What about the meat locker? Did you check the body?"

Desdemonia shook her head. "No. The door was bolted on the outside, so we thought it was just engine noise."

Elliott gripped his cane as he walked towards the door at the far end of the kitchen. "The engines aren't running, Mrs Ainu." He pushed the door open and the three men entered the pantry; on the other side of the dim room sat the large, lead-lined door to the meat locker. Elliott frowned; he really didn't like lead-lined rooms…or kitchens in general, for that matter. They tended to contain things that some might find upsetting: a butchered murder victim, the frozen remains of a corpse, or worse — a meal that was perhaps not quite up to snuff. He caught Thorne's eye and realised his friend was feeling the same. With a nod, Thorne turned on the gaslights in the pantry, giving them a slightly clearer view of the solid door sitting between them and the room beyond. As they surveyed the door, they were joined by Vasily who followed silently behind O.D, his face set.

Elliott took note of the heavy metal bolt locking the door from the outside. He turned to Thorne and gestured at the lock. "I think we might need your kit down here, Thorne. Don't touch the door please, gentlemen, I'll open it." Removing the red silk handkerchief from his breast pocket, Elliott carefully pulled back the bolt. Turning back to the door, he looked at Thorne. "One…two…three!" On the third count he pulled the door open and the four men rushed into the cold room, Elliott and Thorne turning swiftly to ensure no one was hiding against the wall. O.D approached the shrouded figure that still lay prone on the marble slab, then looked at Elliott. "I suppose we should make sure…?"

Elliott nodded. O.D took a deep breath and was reaching for the sheet when Vasily held up his hand. "I'll do it, Mr Damant. I saw what was done to her and, being honest, I have seen worse. She was a part of your family, welcome or not. Please, allow me."

O.D nodded gratefully and stepped back, allowing Vasily to lift the cover and check the body. Elliott and Thorne also approached, and the three men agreed it was undoubtedly the corpse of Carolyn Nolloth.

The butler stood to one side and scanned the little room as Thorne carefully smoothed the material back over the bier. Vasily's green eyes suddenly flicked from one side of the room to the other as he realised something was amiss. Turning, he called to his wife in the kitchen. "Desdemonia?"

The statuesque woman appeared in the doorway; a questioning look on her handsome face. "Yes, husband?"

"How many sides of beef were in here yesterday?"

Desdemonia paused before she responded. "There were four. Why?"

Vasily gestured towards the far end of the meat locker. "Because now there are five."

Elliott, Thorne, and O.D turned towards the sides of beef hanging under their canvas sheets, or rather, to the one bare side of meat, and the four that were covered.

Elliott's eyes flashed. "Four sides there were, yet five there are, and one without a cover. Well, let's check, shall we? Mrs Ainu, if you would please leave us?"

Desdemonia looked at her husband, nodded and walked back into the kitchen.

Back in the meat locker, Elliott approached the nearest of the covered sides. With a sharp movement he whisked the cover away to reveal…a large side of beef.

O.D exhaled sharply, as Elliott looked at him with a grin. "One down! Ready?" He pulled down the next cover. Vasily swore violently and O.D recoiled as the corpse of Sir Wesley Eade swung before them; his cold corpse hanging from the end of a thick length of hessian rope strung between the wooden ceiling beam and the steel butcher's hook embedded in his back

Elliott looked disappointed. "I was hoping he would be somewhat further back…oh well." He frowned as he peered up at the hanging corpse. "He's been shot…right temple; that probably explains the sound that woke the engineer." He looked at O.D, who had a nauseous expression on his face. "We know Sir Wesley had a gun with him, a Browning; we found it during our search and put it back where we found it — more fool us! I trust you knew he had brought a gun aboard?"

O.D swallowed and nodded jerkily. "Yes, although he didn't actually ask my permission. I should let you know that…well, I know about the gun because he threatened me with it on Friday night, shortly before Carolyn's death."

Elliott nodded. "Well, he could have shot himself but he certainly couldn't have hung himself up afterwards. Now he is here, so…where is the gun?" He stepped away from the body and looked at the floor under the hanging corpse, but he could see no weapon. He rifled through the pockets of the voluminous robe the dead lawyer was wearing, also to no avail…which could only mean one thing: the killer was now armed!

He frowned at a sudden rustling noise. Rummaging in the folds of material, he discovered a pocket containing a slip of paper with a message and a scribbled map. He smiled and turned to Thorne, who was examining the empty wooden crate in the corner of the room. "Anything there, Thorne?"

His friend paused before answering. "There is a lot of blood inside this crate. It's on all five sides *and* the lid, as though something that had bled a great deal was stored within it. But not for too long, as it hadn't started to pool. The bloodstains are also quite dry, and there are several strands of golden-brown hair, quite long and wavy." He looked at the covered remains of Carolyn with a thoughtful expression before turning back and gesturing at the hanging lawyer. "What the hell was he doing down here?"

Elliott held up the piece of paper. "I think this might have something to do with it. How very intriguing…listen to this, chaps."

> I need to talk with you about what she knew. Meet me in the kitchen tonight at 3:00am. Burn this note.

Thorne looked at the note with a practised eye. "I would say this was not written by the same person who sent the threatening letters; neat handwriting rather than blocked capitals, and the paper is different. This is more a personal note suggesting a meeting: 'I need to talk with you about what she knew'. Is it referring to Carolyn Nolloth? Lucky for us that he disobeyed the instructions to destroy it." He held up the roughly drawn map and frowned. "There are no markings on the drawing, other than a little X in this area here. It's simply a plan of some rooms, but I don't recognise them…what does the map lead to?"

Vasily spoke from behind them, his demeanour silent and almost angry as he glared at the piece of paper. Reaching out, he took the map and turned it ninety degrees before handing it back to Thorne. "The X is in the kitchen; this shows the layout of the dining room, kitchen, pantry, and meat locker." He looked up at the hanging corpse and touched his head. "If you gentlemen will please excuse me, I must leave!" Without waiting he turned and left the room. Entering the kitchen, he saw Desdemonia seated at the kitchen table and sat beside her. She turned to him and held out her hand; as he gripped it, a single tear fell down his cheek.

### O.D's office
### 11:30am

Elliott, Giselle, Thorne, and Aquilleia entered O.D's suite and presented the tired-looking philanthropist with the news that they had photographed, printed, and searched the meat locker and pantry, and the rooms could now be reopened. All the evidence had been taken to Thorne's cabin and was now under the watchful eye of Veronique, who had accepted a large mutton bone and several biscuits as a retainer for guarding duties.

O.D nodded, his face grim. His morning had not gone to

plan: Mar's migraine had worsened to the point where she couldn't leave the sanctuary of her curtained room, so his attempt to explain the future presence of Josephine had been temporarily abandoned. The lack of enforced learning of German verbs, however, had been a gift to Merry and Fleur, who had decided to spend their morning swimming in the chill waters of the Sound before Merry's special birthday luncheon.

As Elliott, Thorne, Giselle, Aquilleia, and O.D sat around his desk, a firm knock echoed from the door. O.D paused before raising his voice. "Come in."

The door opened, and Vasily and Desdemonia entered. Vasily looked at O.D, a strangely compelling expression on his face. "Mr Damant, I think the time has come for the truth, don't you?"

O.D raised his eyebrows and leant back in his chair before nodding. "Yes, yes of course you're right. Tell them… tell them everything."

Vasily ran a hand over his short hair, squared his shoulders and addressed Elliott. "I regret to say that my wife and I are not who you think we are. We approached Mr Damant with a business proposition and after a fashion, he agreed to our proposal."

Elliott blinked, and an expression of interest crossed his face as he sat up in his chair. He looked from Vasily and Desdemonia to a slightly shamefaced O.D. "If you aren't who you said you were, then who are you, and why are you here?"

Desdemonia spoke. "Much like you, we had a reason to be here…just not the reason you and the others were led to believe." She looked at her husband before continuing. "We needed to get close to Eade."

Thorne raised an eyebrow. "Did you kill—"

"No!" said Vasily. "No, we did not. In fact, his death has rather disrupted our plans: we needed him alive rather than dead. The Devil take my brother for escaping me even at the last!"

Elliott's eyebrows shot up. "Your brother?"

Vasily nodded. "In truth, my half-brother. My name, the name my mother gave me, is Malachy Featherstone-Eade, and this is my wife Simone. My father was Sir Harbottle Eade, the 2nd Baronet of Eadeford, who was also Wesley's father. He travelled to India in 1848, where he tried and failed to set up a tea business in Upper Assam. He met and married my mother there, but his father had the marriage annulled on the grounds that my mother was not of quite the same class." Malachy took a deep breath and continued. "He ordered my father's return to England, where he was swiftly married off to a rich debutante and matters were…smoothed over, shall we say? Unfortunately for them, my mother produced me some nine months after her marriage, and with the assistance of a solicitor demanded my birthright, which they swiftly denied on the grounds of what they claimed was my illegitimacy. My mother produced both marriage and birth certificates and her solicitor took them to a meeting with my grandfather's associates in Guwahati, from which he never returned — and neither did the documents." Simone held out her hand, and Malachy grasped it. "We followed my brother's career for years, trying to find the proof of my birthright, and last year we finally found a way!"

Thorne flipped open a new notepad and continued his almost unnoticed shorthand.

"A member of his household agreed to get me into my brother's home and furnish me with the combination to the safe…for a price. It was a reasonable amount, so I paid it, and on New Year's Eve I found myself in his house on Cricket Hill in Sydney. I opened the safe and discovered some rather interesting things within: my birth certificate, yes, but also both our father's marriage certificates and other papers, proving not only my legitimacy, but also that my father's family had taken those documents from my mother's solicitor, whom they had then paid to disappear. Perhaps more damaging still to my brother's reputation, the documents also provided incontrovertible proof that my father had married Wesley's mother while he was still married to mine!"

Elliott sat upright. "Bigamy?"

Malachy nodded, a vicious smile pulling at his mouth as looked at Elliott. "Yes. It would seem that my paternal grandfather lied, my father was still very much married to my mother when he was himself married off to the young woman whose dowry our grandfather desired."

Elliott settled back in his chair. "So, Sir Wesley was not a sir, after all?"

Malachy shook his head. "The title goes to the eldest legitimate heir…and I now have the proof to show I was born legitimately, and to a mother in wedlock, more than a year before Wesley's birth in 1850. My brother's father and grandfather both lied to the authorities. I was going to confront him with the evidence this weekend and demand his utter humiliation before the highest court in the Empire, but the bastard — and I can now legally call him that — the bastard is dead, and all I can do is take back that which was stolen, which is now, finally, mine!" His green eyes flashed with emotion as he gripped his wife's hand.

Thorne looked up from his notes. "May I ask…who was the helpful insider who assisted you in obtaining the information you sought?"

Malachy and Simone exchanged glances; Malachy cleared his throat. "He's actually aboard the Taniwha: it was my brother's secretary, Robin Ellis, he has access to Wesley's house and safe. He furnished me with a spare key and guaranteed me free and safe passage." Malachy gave a short bark of laughter, "I would have given anything to have been there when my brother discovered what had been taken!"

Giselle spoke from the settee. "Rather a generous and kindly act, considering his livelihood was at stake in assisting you…I take it he was never discovered?" Malachy shook his head as Giselle continued. "I wonder what was in it for him, other than the agreeable sum you mentioned?" She studied her nails. "You said you found 'other interesting things' in your brother's safe, Mr Featherstone-Eade. May I enquire what they were?"

O.D looked at Malachy. Pointing to a settee, he moved towards his drinks cabinet and without bothering to ask, poured everyone a very stiff whisky.

Malachy and Simone accepted the drinks and sat down. Taking a gulp of the liquid, Malachy continued. "There were three packets of information kept separate from my brother's main papers. One contained two copies of a birth certificate belonging to a young man whose name I didn't recognise, an Italian by the name of Aurelio Azzurro; he was apparently born in Verona in 1865. A second package contained several personal photographs of a particularly lurid nature, and a third package contained a gemstone of a particularly vibrant shade of purple."

Giselle choked on her drink. Elliott hurried over and gently patted her on the back; she waved him away and spluttered, "The Larkspur Diamond?"

Malachy nodded. "That is what I took it to be. The stone is infamous."

Elliott and the others shared a glance, knowing that the real Larkspur Diamond was hidden away in a little pot of face cream in Thorne's bathroom, guarded by the inimitable Veronique.

Elliott sat back in his chair and looked at the man before him. "Where is the gem?"

Malachy smiled. "It's safe. As they were all in a safe belonging to my brother, who had wrongly claimed my inheritance, I decided that those items belonged to me. They're in a lock box in our cabin."

Elliott smiled from his position on the settee, his canines flashing. "There is the slight problem that the photographs, however distasteful or amusing they are, depending on your personal preference, are the property of the person who either appears in them, or staged them."

Malachy's face darkened. "They were in my brother's possession, so now they are mine!"

Giselle shook her head. "Elliott is correct, Mr Feather-stone-Eade. I take it that it was Sir Wes— excuse me, *Mr* Wesley Eade in those photographs?"

Malachy nodded, and his glance flicked towards the ladies in the room. "There was also someone else in the photographs. I cannot state the true nature of the images in mixed company, you understand?"

Giselle looked at Elliott, who continued. "We understand, Mr Featherstone-Eade; we found similar images in our search yesterday. They are of Mr Eade with a certain other guest, I take it?"

Malachy nodded, and Simone smiled. "I was not too surprised; in our previous life we owned a rather prestigious private club. We witnessed a great range of human behaviour, and so we viewed the images with a somewhat less…scandalised eye. Such a person could charge the earth for their appearance and services…they really are quite stunning."

Elliott ran a long fingernail along his lower lip. "Yes, that brings us to the matter of the birth certificate…now that would definitely belong to the person whose birth it regis-tered." He paused. "1865…that would make them thirty-five years old now." He turned to Giselle. "How old would you say Lady Carlton-Cayce is, my dear?"

Giselle gazed at her husband and nodded. "I would say she is in her mid-thirties, so yes, it is possible. If the truth were to come out, the photographs and the birth certificate would stand as very strong evidence against her in a court of law."

O.D held up his hand. "I have absolutely no idea what you are talking about, and quite frankly, I don't think I want to know!"

Aquilleia spoke quietly from her chair. "The photographs are of Sir Wesley and Lady Carlton-Cayce."

O.D looked slightly embarrassed. "I'm afraid I still don't quite understand. Lurid personal photographs are rather foolish, but they are in fashion these days. Their relationship isn't…or rather, wasn't, quite the done thing either, as they weren't married, but most people turn a blind eye to that little issue these days, especially if the people involved are discreet. Certainly, this far away from the Motherland, the occasional little moral quirk is rather easy to ignore."

Aquilleia spoke again. "And the birth certificate is also that of Lady Carlton-Cayce."

Elliott leant towards the shocked philanthropist and murmured a few words in his ear. O.D's somewhat bushy eyebrows described an immediate arc, he sat back in his chair and nodded slowly. "I understand now how those photographs would cause a grievance. In the wrong hands, such images would cost them everything. They would both have been cast out of society…social standing or no, even down here." He looked at Elliott. "Absolute discretion is the only refuge for such relationships, and the photographs would have utterly destroyed even the most well-crafted, carefully lived lie. As to the birth certificate…well that could well be the final nail in the coffin! if Lady Carlton-Cayce cannot provide reputable proof of her sex, that would be her undoing. Not just for the more obvious reasons, but because her many husbands obviously knew what she was when they married her!" He took a gulp of his whisky. "All the heirs to the fortunes she has taken over the years would demand their day in court and the retrieval of their family estates. That would lead to several unpleasant months in court, and not a few years in gaol!"

Elliott nodded. "Back to the subject of the diamond. It was stolen from its rightful owner some years ago, and both it and he have never been seen again — at least until the reappearance of the gem on this vessel." He looked at Malachy. "But I regret to inform you, Mr Featherstone-Eade, that the genuine stone is safely hidden until it can be returned to its owner. The gem you have is simply a paste copy."

Malachy's eyes narrowed. He stood up suddenly and limped out of the room. Elliott looked at Simone. "I didn't mean to upset your husband, madam; we found the stone during our search and it is most definitely the Larkspur Diamond."

Simone took her time in answering. "My husband and I have a great deal of knowledge from our previous existence, Mr Caine. We know our gemstones…believe me when I say to you that what we possess *is* the Larkspur Diamond."

After some minutes had passed, Malachy reappeared in the doorway. Closing the door none too gently behind him, he stomped to the table and carefully emptied the contents of a small velvet pouch onto the malachite surface. There was a sharp intake of breath from Giselle, who approached the exposed gem. She looked at Malachy. "May I?" At his nod, she gently lifted the vibrant purple gemstone and gazed at its multi-faceted surface. She turned incredulous eyes to Elliott. "I don't understand…this is also the Larkspur! It's identical!"

Elliott, a thoughtful expression on his face, turned to Thorne. "Thorne, would you mind awfully popping back to your cabin and bringing the other diamond here, please?"

Dropping his notebook on his chair, Thorne left the room and hurried along the deck to his cabin. Opening the door, he was almost knocked over by an ecstatic and very waggy Veronique who accepted a head scratch before following him into the bathroom where he picked up the small pot and a face cloth. The happy Labrador's tail drooped and she whined softly as Thorne walked back towards the door. He paused on the threshold, turned to look at her and dropped the pot onto the bed before gently squeezing her silky ears and giving her another handful of biscuits before returning to O.D's office.

Entering the room, he approached the malachite table, opened the pot and removed the jewel, wiping the cold cream away with the face cloth. He handed the now thoroughly moisturised purple gem to Giselle, who held it up alongside the jewel Malachy had brought; they were indeed identical.

Aquilleia looked at the two diamonds, her violet eyes almost matching the diamonds' exquisite shade, as she whispered. "One gem, twin souls. What does it mean?" She looked at the others. "There is something…something to do with these jewels, I cannot see it, but it is important."

Elliott looked at her sharply, before turning back to Giselle. "These are both flawless diamonds; neither are paste. You saw the original stone in New York before it was stolen; how large was it?"

Giselle shook her head. "It was a long time ago, Elliott, but I'm sure it was the same size as these gems. It couldn't have been cut down again; it was already perfect, there would barely be any diamond left!" She paused. "Unless…"

Elliott looked at her. "Unless?"

Giselle continued. "Shortly before Nathaniel De Coeur and the jewel went missing, there was a slight mistake in arrangements to display the diamond. It had been booked to appear in both London and Paris — on the same day. The day came, and the diamond was on show…in both cities! There was an uncharitable suggestion that De Coeur had a paste copy made, and that was the gem he loaned to Paris. It caused a bit of a problem for the two museums…the French refused to send anything across the Channel for years."

Thorne looked up from his notes. "What are you suggesting?"

"What I'm suggesting is this: what if he never made a copy? What if there were always two stones, both known as the Larkspur – or the Lark, and the Spur?"

Giselle handed the gem back to Thorne, who carefully stowed it back in its little pot. She placed the other stone on the velvet pouch and returned to her chair as Elliott paced up and down by O.D's desk. "I can't place these diamonds in this investigation at the moment; Wesley had one and Lady Carlton-Cayce had the other…"

Aquilleia spoke quietly. "Lady Carlton-Cayce wanted them both, but Wesley was not willing to give her his, even though they were both hers to begin with."

Elliott paused in his pacing and looked at the psychic. "Why?"

O.D spoke from his chair. "Lady Carlton-Cayce is a known collector of gems. The Larkspur is, or rather, are, perfect examples of their kind."

Aquilleia shook her head. "There is another reason why she wants these stones. She desires to give them to someone…but I can't read her to find out who, or why."

Giselle looked at her. "Do you see the Fox interfering at all?"

As Aquilleia shook her head, O.D's jaw dropped; he

seemed to be having difficulty keeping up. "The Fox! That would be impossible, my dear. The Fox isn't aboard the Taniwha — only my crew, invited guests and their servants are here."

Giselle smiled faintly. "The Fox is one of your invited guests, Mr Damant, and they have been on the Taniwha since Friday."

O.D suddenly looked hopeful. "Then it must have been the Fox! The Fox is the murderer!"

Giselle shook her head firmly. "No. The Fox has never killed or attacked anyone; indeed, they pride themselves on their ability to liberate certain little trinkets from their careless owners without the use of violence."

O.D took a much-needed sip from his drink and looked at her over the rim of his glass, his eyebrows firmly set over his patrician nose. "May I inquire…who?"

Giselle's smile grew wider. "You may inquire, but I shall not tell! I was there when the Larkspur was taken from De Coeur, and the Fox was there too. But they didn't take the gems: no one knows who did. All we know is that somehow one stone ended up in Wesley Eade's private collection, and the other in that of Lady Carlton-Cayce." She settled into her chair and frowned. "De Coeur's event was the pinnacle of the social year; for such a hermit, he threw incredible parties—" She suddenly sat bolt upright in her seat. "Good Gods! *She* was there, Elliott, *she* was there!"

Elliott stared at his wife. "Who?"

"Lady Carlton-Cayce — she was De Coeur's companion at the time!"

Thorne raised an immaculate eyebrow. "Between husbands, was she?"

Giselle grinned at him. "Don't be a cat, Thorne! I remember there was quite a stir at the event. Because of his insistence on privacy, they were never actually seen together during their courtship, but she was there at the party…and both De Coeur and the diamonds disappeared that same night." An intense look crossed her face. "I've just had an incredible thought…this might sound strange, but just listen. De Coeur was of a similar height to Lady Carlton-Cayce, he was also slender, with brilliant blue eyes and pale-blond hair, and he wore a beard and moustache. Lady Carlton-Cayce was there at the party, but Nathaniel De Coeur ostensibly stayed in his suite the entire time. The event was in full swing; music, acrobats, and plenty of wine. Suddenly there was a scream, and when everyone rushed into his private rooms, he and the diamonds had vanished. Here is my suggestion; what if Nathaniel De Coeur never actually existed, and it was Lady Carlton-Cayce as her male self? As Thorne said in jest, she was between husbands at the time…what if she assumed a male identity between marriages?" Giselle turned to look at Aquilleia. "That's what you meant when you said 'they were both hers to begin with', isn't it? Lady Carlton-Cayce is the rightful owner of both stones…she *is* Nathaniel De Coeur; or rather, she was, until she remarried and that identity no longer served its purpose."

Aquilleia smiled as Elliott nodded. "It works…we will have to talk with Lady Carlton-Cayce, and now that her counsel has left us to wander other lofty, vaulted corridors, she will have no voluble supporter to thwart us."

Giselle took a triumphant sip of her drink as Thorne scribbled furiously in his notebook. Simone caught Malachy's eye and raised her eyebrows. And they thought that their little plan had some interesting twists!

O.D looked at Elliott and Giselle, expressions passing over his face as he tried to understand the various and rather scandalous items of information that had been brought into the light over the last few minutes. Eventually he settled on something that Giselle had said earlier. "You say that you actually know the Fox?"

Giselle nodded as she took another sip of her drink. "I have had some dealings with them in the past. They assisted me on one or two cases where I needed to…leave a place with extreme haste, shall we say? They are very, very good at what they do. They have their own morality and absolutely no qualms whatsoever about acquiring things that belong to others…especially if the original owner is arrogant. If they realise the diamonds are on the Taniwha, they won't be for very much longer — and neither will the Fox, wrecked engine or no!"

Thorne looked up from his prolific notes. "Mr Damant, you agreed to invite Malachy and his wife aboard, masquerading as servants. May we ask why? What was there in their little charade for you?"

O.D took a sip of his drink and cleared his throat. "Well, I suppose there is no harm in telling you now: Wesley Eade had been blackmailing me to the tune of several thousand pounds a year. His financial demands began shortly after the events I told you about in Brazil. How else could he afford such an expensive mistress? Even on his income as a lawyer and a member of the landed gentry he couldn't manage such lavish spending without additional income."

Giselle looked at him with sympathy. "Could you not have pipped him to the post, so to speak, and informed the authorities about what truly happened?"

O.D shook his head. "Oh no, my dear, you misunderstand me. He never threatened to inform the authorities: that would have been too easy. He instead threatened to tell my daughter. Not the truth, you understand, but rather his bastardised account of what he believed had occurred that day. Needless to say, due to his chosen profession, his idea of the truth and the actual truth were never one and the same thing: he was exceptionally gifted at twisting reality and making others believe his creations. He threatened to go into nauseating and heavily embroidered detail about both my wife's affair with Alexander and the money I paid out thereafter to protect my reputation." He looked at Elliott, a disgusted expression on his face. "He also made several disparaging and rather obscene comments about Mar! He was a deeply unpleasant man, whom I had no choice but to keep paying. So, to answer your question, Mr Caine, I was prepared to do anything to destroy the man who tried to destroy me and my family while serving his own best interests! When Malachy Featherstone-Eade approached me, I knew it was the best chance I had of bringing Wesley down."

Elliott nodded thoughtfully. "And killing him?"

O.D stared at Elliott before shaking his head vehemently. "No, you misunderstand. When the truth about his family and his origins could finally be proved, I admit that I was planning a party with fireworks! But as Malachy and Simone have said, it had to be legal. Knowing he was a bastard wasn't enough, begging your pardon, ladies. Finding that proof and destroying him…that was our aim. We wouldn't have to kill him; the destruction of his standing, his ruination in society, *that* would have crushed him. We didn't have to kill him to destroy him, Mr Caine…the proof of his birth was all we needed."

Elliott looked at the philanthropist. "If you had known of the photographs and the truth about Lady Carlton-Cayce, would you have used that to destroy him?"

O.D paused, his eyes searching Elliott's face before he shook his head. "No, because that would have destroyed Lady Carlton-Cayce too. Our target was Wesley Eade, not his mistress. Her standing would have been damaged enough by her association with such a morally reprehensible man: a man who knew of his own illegitimacy and who willfully hid proof of the rightful heir to his family's estate. Releasing the photographs and the birth certificate would destroy her, purely over an accident of birth that made her what she is." He paused. "Besides, I wasn't informed as to the actual content of the photographs, only that they were pornographic in nature...and the birth certificate was never mentioned."

Elliott addressed the silent couple sitting on the settee. "And you? Mr Featherstone-Eade, would you have used the photographs and the birth certificate to destroy your half-brother?"

Malachy paused before replying. "If he had chosen to fight me in the courts, then yes, I would have used the images as ammunition, but not before then...and I would have scratched out the other person's face in those photographs! I would not, however, have used the birth certificate; Lady Carlton-Cayce shouldn't be condemned because of her alliance with him, or because of what she is." An amused expression appeared on his face. "We employed people like her in our club. If we condemn her for what she is, we would be hypocrites."

O.D looked at Malachy and Simone, then turned to Elliott. "We didn't need to kill him, Mr Caine, and we didn't...please believe us."

Elliott, Thorne, Giselle, and Aquilleia looked at each other in silence. The door to the outer office, which had been ajar, moved gently, but no one in the room noticed.

Elliott sighed. "Very well. I trust I don't have to tell any of you not to share the information divulged here with anyone else?"

The three nodded, and O.D smiled wryly. "Although I'm not sure how the other guests will take the butler and house-keeper suddenly taking their correct places at table as Sir and Lady Featherstone-Eade!"

Malachy looked at his wife, who smiled and addressed O.D. "If you don't mind, Mr Damant, we would prefer to stay unknown. We will continue to serve until the airship returns to collect us."

O.D looked incredulous. "That is most irregular, I must say! But if that is what you wish, then so be it."

Malachy stood up and gathered his possessions from the table. He hesitated, then reached into his inner breast pocket and removed a thick envelope, which he handed to Elliott. "These are the photographs and the birth certificates; I trust you will dispose of them in the correct fashion." The ghost of a smile appeared on his lips. "It would appear that we no longer need them." His eyes narrowed. "But I will be keeping the diamond I found in my brother's safe! Good afternoon, ladies, gentlemen." And he escorted his wife from the room.

### Merry's cabin
### Private Birthday luncheon
### 2:00pm

Merry looked up at her father and smiled tremulously. "Thank you, Papa…it's lovely!"

O.D beamed as his daughter clutched the yellow and somewhat frilly Paris day frock and held it up in front of the mirror; it was always nice when a gift turned out to be the right choice. "You're very welcome, my dear." He turned back to the ladies on the settee. "Perhaps a little more champagne, Mrs Carter. Mar?"

Mar shook her head. Josephine looked up from her study of the birthday girl and nodded with a smile. She turned to Mar and said brightly, "Such a lovely colour too. She has the right complexion for yellow; so many aren't that lucky." She thought of Sophie and her unfortunate penchant for choosing the wrong outfits, the wrong colours, and the wrong men...and her most recent habit of taking things entirely the wrong way. Josephine sighed; she truly had no idea how to deal with her cabin-mate. She had offered her friend the chloral sachet O.D had provided the previous evening, and been immediately and hysterically accused of attempted poisoning! Josephine had taken her own sleeping draught in an ill temper and fallen asleep rapidly, leaving the fearful Sophie, who was hiding under her eiderdown, to search for sleep without her roommate's offer of chemical assistance.

Next to Josephine, Mar sat in pale silence, her carriage rigid, her very proper politeness a stiff retort to the younger woman's cheerful attempts to engage in small talk.

O.D winced as he left the two women together in the slightly chilly atmosphere and walked to the little drinks table to refresh the glasses. The discussion he had finally managed to have with Mar about Josephine had been as unpleasant as he had feared. He had managed to speak with her in the privacy of her darkened cabin only a few minutes before Merry's birthday luncheon was due to start. Mar's calm, matter-of-fact, but wounded statements, followed by her utter refusal of his offer of continuing financial support, had rendered him quite speechless. The emotional issues he was not prepared to face, but the financial issue he could deal with, whether she wanted the money or not. After all the years she had spent looking after both Merry and their home, he was damned if he would allow her to become destitute!

On the opposite side of the room, Merry's maid Jane carefully lifted a small tray of canapés and began the first round of the slightly unusual birthday luncheon that had been organised after the debacle over the previous day's dinner. Everyone had again insisted on lunch trays in their cabins. O.D had at first been furious, but then decided that in the circumstances, he was just as happy without the presence of what were, in all honesty, bought and paid for guests. More importantly, Merry had been quite accepting of the change. She seemed a little preoccupied, but that might have been due more to her aunt's unseemly passing than the effect on her birthday weekend of a few no-shows at her luncheon.

He scowled as he filled up Josephine's glass. Hopefully Caine and his associates would get to the bottom of this hideous business and have everything wrapped up neatly for the police on their return to Milford City.

Turning, he was joined suddenly by a rather pale Darius, who shot him a slightly twitchy smile and poured himself a large brandy. Emotional small talk was not one of O.D's virtues. He was loath to ask his nephew if he was well because he simply couldn't understand how Darius could be so affected by his mother's passing after everything she had done to him…unless it was the manner of her death that caused him such grief. He realised that he had to say something, anything. Just as he was about to speak, Darius nodded at Merry. "Rather an odd twenty-first birthday party, uncle. None of the invited guests being present, I mean, but Merry seems to be managing well. Stiff upper lip and all that, I suppose."

O.D nodded. "Yes, it seems to have become a simple, private birthday luncheon. Perhaps not quite the done thing, socially speaking, but between you and me, none of the other guests would leave their cabins." He scowled. "They can damn well stay there for my daughter's birthday luncheon, but by God, they will present themselves for dinner and earn their keep tonight!"

Darius smiled his odd, twitchy smile again, and looked pointedly at Josephine and Mar. "Mrs Carter seems to be enjoying herself very much away from her husband…but is everything all right with Mar? She seems very quiet."

O.D stopped dead, then placed the two glasses back on the table and turned his full attention to his nephew. Darius looked quite ill: his face, pale at the best of times, was sallow and unhealthy-looking, his dark eyes were dim and red-rimmed, and as he lifted the large brandy to his lips, his hand shook.

O.D addressed Darius in an undertone. "Mar is suffering from a migraine which has lasted for more than a day. The shock of your mother's death has made her rather unwell; it was extremely good of her to leave her cabin and come to this little gathering. As for Mrs Carter…her name is Josephine; she and Mr Kayfield…and Mr Rust and Miss Havercroft for that matter, are not married to each other, nor to anyone else. They are actors whom Wesley Eade hired to entertain us for Merry's birthday." He paused, realising how much Darius's pointed comment had irritated him. "And you had better get used to her continued presence aboard this vessel, Darius, because I have asked her to marry me, and she has said yes! We will be announcing our engagement tomorrow morning. Now if you will excuse me, I shall take these drinks to my daughter and my betrothed!" He picked up the glasses and walked away, leaving his dumbstruck nephew staring after him.

⟡

### Lady Carlton-Cayce's cabin
### 6:30pm

Leonora, draped over the chaise in her cabin, looked at the man opposite her, the extreme blue of her eyes pinning him in place as he informed her of what he had overheard in O.D's office.

When she spoke, her voice was like ice. "I want my personal belongings returned to me; do you understand? The photographs, the birth certificates…and the gemstones: both of them!"

The man before her nodded silently, his eyes fixed on her as she flexed one elegant, slender foot.

"I trust I do not have to go into detail about just what I am prepared to do to see that my demands are met?"

He shook his head as he stared at her and licked his lips.

She gestured violently towards the door. "Get out!"

He turned and stumbled out of her cabin, pausing to close the door quietly behind him. He took a deep breath and smoothed the front of his jacket with a slightly trembling hand, before slowly making his way along the deck.

Back in the cabin, Leonora wearily closed her eyes and sighed. As she did so, the door to her bathroom opened noiselessly. A figure approached and stopped directly behind her; a pair of smooth hands silently reached for her white neck…

Leonora jumped, half-turned on the chaise, and laughed. "I almost forgot you were in there…I take it you heard?"

The figure started to massage her neck and shoulders. "Yes, I heard…can he be trusted to retrieve the items?"

Leonora shrugged gracefully, her shoulders rising and falling under the supple hands gently easing the stress from her muscles. "He's about as useful as a duck, and as intelligent, but yes, he can be trusted." She paused, turned to her admirer and said in an arch tone. "He's rather taken with you, though…"

Her companion laughed softly as they caressed the white-blonde curls at the nape of Leonora's neck. "I must tell him I am not that way inclined!"

DEATH IN THE SOUND

Leonora burst into peals of laughter, her small, pearly-white teeth flashing. "Don't hurt his feelings too much, darling. We still need him…for a little while, at least."

She closed her eyes to better enjoy her neck massage, then flinched. Reaching up, she caught at the guilty hand. "I do wish you would remove that thing!"

Her admirer smiled. "Why?"

Leonora smiled back. "Because it's rather coarse. No one wears rings on their thumbs!"

"I do. Would you like me to take it off?"

Leonora's smile deepened. "That will do — for a start!" She laughed again as she reached up to caress the face above her.

### The lounge
### 7:00pm

"I don't give a damn, Torrance!" O.D bellowed. "These people have accepted my hospitality, my food, and enough wine to sink an ironclad since they arrived here! Yes, I am aware that the guests were allowed dinner last night, and breakfast and luncheon today in their cabins. I am also well aware that we have had a murder or two! However, none of them may request a supper tray tonight. It is my daughter's twenty-first birthday, and by God, they will damn well turn up for dinner! Their presence this evening was the sole purpose of their invitations! I am issuing the order, and it is your job to see to it! The cocktail hour will begin now! Get them down here: all of them!"

O.D strode into the snug and poured himself a generous whisky as Torrance left the room at a run to see his orders were carried out.

### The kitchen
### 7:00pm

Simone sat in a quiet corner of the busy kitchen and supervised as one of the kitchen maids carefully made a basic stock for soup. The girl had some skill in the kitchen, and Simone was enjoying teaching her the rudiments of cooking. She looked up as her husband approached, and her smile of welcome vanished at the expression on his face. "What's wrong, husband?"

Malachy looked at Mary and the other staff bustling round the kitchen before gesturing at the door. "There's something I need to show you."

Simone looked at the curious maid with an encouraging face. "Keep going, Mary, you're doing very well. I'll be back in a few moments. Don't forget, never let it boil! Slow and steady."

Malachy took her elbow and the two of them left the crowded kitchen. Entering the lounge, they nodded at a rather flushed O.D, who had been joined by Merry and Josephine.

O.D addressed them both. "I have issued an order that all meals tonight will be served in the dining room only. No supper trays; everyone will be dining together in that room." He jabbed his finger towards the door leading into the dining room.

Malachy frowned. "Do the guests know?"

"Torrance is dealing with it now. I trust this will cause no issues with the meal?"

Simone shook her head. "Not at all. Miss Damant has already given me her menu choices for this evening, and that was to be the only option for the supper trays. The only requirement is the dining table be set and that can be dealt with speedily. It will be quite easy to see to."

O.D looked relieved. "Thank you. Thank you both…for everything." He turned back to Josephine and Merry.

Malachy went back into the kitchen and gave the order for the table to be set before rejoining his wife in the lounge where they made their way out onto the deck and walked towards their cabin. As they approached the door, Simone made a sudden exclamation; the lock was badly damaged and the door stood ajar.

Malachy nodded. "This is what I wanted to show you." He carefully pushed the door open. Their room had been very tidy when they had left it earlier that day, but no more: it appeared that an extremely thorough and very violent whirl-wind had sped through the small cabin, dedicated to creating as much destruction as possible in the enclosed space.

Malachy looked at the remains of the small iron-bound chest that had contained the items from his brother's safe in Sydney. "I don't think they found what they were looking for. We should let Caine and his associates know."

Simone nodded slowly as she took in the wrecked cabin, then gasped. "Mal, the marriage certificates and the diamond!"

Malachy grinned and patted his inner pocket. He took her hand and kissed it. "I'm not leaving those items hanging around, my love. I shall keep them on me until this mess is over."

Simone looked worried. "Perhaps you're right." She gestured at the room. "This will take a while to tidy, and we have our duties to attend to…"

Malachy nodded. "We'll have to deal with it after dinner. We can clear the bed and worry about the rest in the morning."

Simone looked at the little brass clock on the wall. "After

O.D's orders, I think dinner will be served on time. People tend to drink their cocktails rather rapidly these days, and after a double murder they will probably be drinking twice as fast! I'd go and make sure all is ready."

Malachy nodded. "I need to assist with the table. These deaths are going to make it rather tricky to place the guests!"

Simone smiled and patted her husband's cheek. "At least it was one of each…in appearances, if nothing else. That makes setting the table somewhat easier than if it were two of the same sex, does it not?"

Malachy grinned. "You may be right. Come along, wife… just a few more hours to go, and then home!"

They smiled at each other as they left the cabin and headed back to the kitchen. As they walked past the empty staff cabin next to theirs, the door cracked open and a face appeared in the darkness beyond.

So, the man had the gem. Well, there was still a little time to be had – they would simply have to make that time count!

**The dining room**
**10:00pm**
**After dinner**

The assorted guests began to make polite noises about heading to their respective cabins, each taking great care not to make eye contact with each other, or their host, who cast his gimlet-eyed glare on all of them as they refused coffee in the lounge for the far safer territory of their cabins…and the company of their watchful maids and valets.

O.D, nodded at Elliott, Giselle, Thorne, and Aquilleia as they left the room. They were followed by Josephine, who smiled gently at O.D before she escorted a nervous Sophie back to their cabin.

Sophie had spent most of the day hiding in their room. The younger actress had thrown a screaming fit upon being told she was expected to leave the safety of their cabin and be present at dinner. Her hysterics had ceased only after she was promised a chaperone in the form of a very irritated Josephine, who had envisaged spending a pleasant few hours in the lounge after dinner with O.D…and, of course, any other guests who remained in the sumptuous surroundings. Instead, she had been forced to settle for an evening playing nursemaid to an unstimulating and jittery conversationalist who had also doubled as a gooseberry, followed by an unwanted early night! Josephine sighed as she left the room. She just hoped she could sleep again tonight; after the events of the last few days, she wasn't sure whether she should be laughing, crying, or terrified! Betrothed! To Octavius Damant! Amidst birthday celebrations, murder and a hunt for a killer! A hysterical giggle rose in her throat; feeling Sophie's panicked eyes on her, she turned it into a cough. A sudden thought crossed her mind: she still had the chloral that Sophie had refused. If her roommate was still unsure, she would take it instead.

O.D, his daughter's arm through his, watched as Josephine guided the silent and nervous Sophie back to their cabin. He sighed and patted his daughter's hand. "Bedtime, my dear. Come along."

Merry shook her head. "I think I shall just take a turn on deck first, Papa, and then I shall retire."

O.D frowned at his daughter. "I should feel happier if you were in your cabin."

Simone suddenly appeared in the lounge and Merry saw her chance. "Mrs Ainu?"

Simone smiled at her; O.D had made good on his promise not to reveal their identities. "Yes, Miss Damant?"

"Would you send my maid down to me, please?"

"Yes, of course."

"Mrs Ainu," O.D called, "It would be best if all the servants went to their rooms at the same time — to act as escorts to each other, you understand. I don't think anything will happen to them, but better safe than sorry."

Simone nodded. "I understand, Mr Damant, I'll see to it." As she left the lounge, Merry turned to her father. "There: Jane will be with me, and then we may both retire in safety."

O.D nodded, with a look of uncertainty on his face. "Very well, but I shall wait until she comes down."

Merry smiled. "Of course, Papa."

After a short interlude, Simone reappeared with the young maid. O.D kissed his daughter on the top of her head. "Goodnight my dear, pleasant dreams."

"Goodnight, Papa, and you."

They both jumped as a sudden boom vibrated up from the waterline. The craft juddered violently in the water as the long-dormant engines burst into life.

O.D closed his eyes and smiled in relief. "Oh, thank God, we have engine power! I shall tell Captain Peach to take us to Milford City with all haste. Goodnight, my dear."

The magnate hurried to the captain's cabin; his spirits somewhat lighter. With the return of the engines came the return of hope.

He arrived at Captain Peach's room and hammered on the door. After a few moments the door was flung open by a slightly dishevelled Marcus, who pushed a hand through his dark hair, opened his mouth and paused, listening to the sounds thrumming from the engine room. He looked at O.D hopefully. "The engines?"

O.D beamed at him. "Yes, Captain…the engines!"

Marcus grinned back. "I'll get dressed and meet you in the wheelhouse!"

As O.D turned to leave they were joined by the young stoker, Timmy, who had run from the engine room. The young lad caught his breath as he stopped at the captain's door. "Beggin' your pardon, Captain, the engineer says he reckons to have half power, an' we can turn to Milford City as soon as you fancy — she'll just be a mite slow."

O.D slapped the stoker on the back. "Damn good work, young man, damn good! Captain Peach, I'll go and let Caine know, and then I'll meet you in the wheelhouse."

Captain Peach addressed the young stoker. "Timmy, wait for me here and then come up to the wheelhouse with us. We shall need you to untie us, then we'll be ready to leave." He looked at O.D. "Bearing in mind the time, Mr Damant, instead of heading straight for Milford City, it might be an idea to head over to the far side of the channel and anchor there for the night." He paused. "It's the one thing about the Taniwha's design I was never sure about: not having front-facing lights. I'm loath to travel at night without them; it's extremely unsafe."

O.D frowned. "Yes, yes, I suppose you're right…I just want to get this boat back to civilisation and wash this blasted mess off our hands and decks!"

Marcus nodded. "I understand, Mr Damant…it'll be over soon enough now." He thought for a moment. "When the Taniwha was built, we had gas lamps fitted on the outer decks, to enable you and your guests to retire to your cabins in safety. What if we light all the lamps, on all the decks? That will show us to any other craft in the Sound. We could crab a little way to the shallower part of the Sound, anchor overnight, and continue to Milford City at daybreak. What do you say?"

O.D nodded firmly. "Do it!"

Marcus grinned. "I'll just get dressed."

O.D, waiting by the door with Timmy, had a sudden thought. He leant towards the stoker. "I'll be right back." He headed towards the lounge, and entering, smiled at his daughter, who was still sitting with her maid. "My dear, we now have partial power to the engines. We shall begin our return to Milford City shortly."

Merry smiled. "Oh, Papa, that's excellent news!"

O.D again kissed her cheek. "Goodnight, my dear."

Merry watched her father leave, and waited a few moments before turning to her curious maid. "Will you run a bath for me please, Jane? I'm just going out for a bit of fresh air on deck; I'll return in a few minutes."

The young maid looked a little worried, but bobbed and headed to her mistress's cabin. Merry waited until she had left and sank back into her cushioned armchair with a sigh. If this weekend was what she could expect from her future birthdays, she would cease ageing immediately. What an absolute nightmare! Of all the gifts for a twenty-first birthday, murder, mystery, and mayhem were perhaps not the best. To think she used to enjoy reading Poe — never again!

She heard sudden movement in the dining room as the servants, leaving their work to be finished in the light of day, left the kitchens and took themselves to their beds. As various serving maids, stewards, tweenies, and cleaners bade her a happy birthday and goodnight, Merry smiled and nodded as they headed to the safety of their shared accommodation. When the last had gone, she stood up with a groan, gathered her stole, and wandered through the lounge towards the snug and the port-side deck.

As she approached the door to the deck, Merry paused. Morten Van der Linde was standing by the steps, smoking a cigar.

Merry shivered. The strong possibility that he was not

the man she had thought him to be had been gently but firmly put to her by Mar earlier that very afternoon. Mar had illustrated her position with some rather unsavoury information about Morten's true relationship with her Aunt Carolyn. As Merry watched him smoking by the rail, he turned suddenly; with a gasp, she ducked back into the snug. Pressing herself tightly against the wall, she stared at a framed hunting print and listened in silence as he looked around sharply.

He was sure he'd heard something...ach, dolt! The events of the weekend were playing on his nerves, that was all; his ears were playing tricks on him. He took a deep breath of the evening air and smiled. Never mind: it was nearly time for his promising little appointment.

He stubbed his cigar out in a small, lidded silver ashtray he carried with him, slid it back into his pocket, and wandered back into the snug, passing inches from Merry. He headed back into the lounge, letting the doors swing shut behind him.

Merry wrapped her stole around her shoulders and headed outside to the foot of the stairs. She stood where Morten had a few moments earlier and watched the fast-flowing water. Her young mind turned to the private discussion she'd had with her father shortly after lunch, where he had brought up the possibility of his remarrying. Merry felt torn: Josephine was nice, but Mar had been with them for years...

Merry sighed. Perhaps, since Papa was pondering such a huge change in their household, he would also consider moving the Taniwha somewhere a touch more accessible. From what little she had seen in passing, the Marlborough Sounds had been lovely. The town of Picton had everything they could need, and the scenery was breathtaking; soft, rolling hills, sunny inlets, and little beaches that were lovely to paint; yes, perhaps now, after everything that had happened and in the light of possible future events, Papa would consider a move somewhere a little less brooding. She shivered in her flimsy stole. The weather in the Sound always turned sooner than in the north; the chill autumn air was definitely making itself felt tonight.

In the stillness of the evening, broken only by the hum of the engine, the whooshing of the paddles, and the rhythmic slap of the water along the hull, Merry felt herself being lulled into sleepiness. She smiled: perhaps it *was* time for a bath and bed. As she put her hand on the railings, there was a sudden movement behind her. Before she could turn, Merry's waist was grasped by powerful hands and with one sharp movement she was lifted and thrown over the side.

Merry opened her mouth to scream, but nothing more than a terrified gasp came out as she plunged downwards, her hands grasping instinctively at the rail to stop herself falling into the thrashing water below. Her cold fingers scrabbled desperately at the wet wrought iron — she could feel herself slipping!

Suddenly she heard someone calling her name, and sobbing she looked up to see Darius standing on the deck above her.

"Merry?"

"Darius! Oh, Darius, please help me…I can't hold on!"

He reached out and grasped her wrists. "It's all right, Merry. Let go; I've got you!"

Merry felt Darius's grip tighten around her wrists, and with a sob, she let go of the rail. But as she braced herself to be lifted, Darius smiled. "This is for my mother, you thieving bitch!" He opened his hands and Merry plummeted into the squalling waters of the open channel. He left her to scream as the Taniwha began its slow journey back towards Milford City.

## Two hundred feet away

Outside the small fishing hut that was his home during the walking season, Manu sat in the flickering light of his small campfire and removed a clay pipe from his pack. His dark eyes took in the brilliance of the stars above and the towering shadows of the sea cliffs around him. He breathed a happy sigh; what more could a man want?

In the act of filling his pipe, he raised his eyes from the bowl and stared at the brightly lit vessel that steamed slowly past him. She was heading away from the mouth of the Sound and up towards Milford City...but in the thrashing water of the vessel's wake, Manu's sharp eyes picked out a small shape flailing desperately in the churning water.

Leaping to his feet, he jammed his pipe between his teeth, ran to his little boat and pushed off. Pulling on the oars, he headed towards the weakly moving figure in the water.

## The Lounge
### 10:30pm

Morten Van der Linde stood by one of the display cases in the lounge and polished his gold-rimmed monocle. It was of course for show; his eyesight was perfect.

He fixed the little glass into his right eye and leant towards an ornate, glass-fronted cabinet that held a selection of Japanese opera masks. One in particular caught his eye; dark-red skin, impossibly wide white eyes, black horns, and a sneering, open mouth filled with sharp, red-tipped ivory teeth.

The deep crimson curtains next to the case billowed as a chill breeze came through the half-open door leading to the deck on the starboard side of the boat. Morten straightened up and shivered; again, he thought he heard a faint noise... shaking his head, he pushed the door shut and pulled the curtains across. The weather was definitely turning; it would be good to return to the heat, society, and happy enterprise of his life in Australia, even if it would be without his companion and partner in crime.

His mind slid to Carolyn's dreadful death. Poor Caro, she would be a hard woman to replace, but he would certainly try!

Since the death of his paramour, he had spent most of the last two days wondering whether he should continue their plan for him to cajole Mereanthy into marriage. She was wealthy, not unattractive, and young enough to mould into a suitable wife...at least until her money ran out. Then, well, perhaps Carolyn's idea of a little accident would be the best option!

He had decided to try his hand at organising a rendezvous with the young woman before dinner, but quickly realised that both Merry's father and the worthy companion had their eyes fixed firmly on him. They had made it impossible to attempt any form of contact with the young heiress, so he had come to the conclusion that returning to Sydney unaccompanied was the only option available to him.

He frowned, remembering the awkward and somewhat heavy handed pre-dinner discussion. They still hadn't explained what they meant by "the letters you have sent Merry" — he hadn't sent the blasted girl anything!

He huffed slightly as he smoothed his orange silk cravat. Pah! If that particular door was now closed, it would not inconvenience him too much. He was not one to rest on his laurels, and so always kept several options open at once. Part of the amusement gained from his endeavours was the planning and juggling of such schemes...and of course the money was always welcome! The smile that appeared on his lips had a satisfied, feline quality. There were several other plans he could turn to...not quite as profitable individually, but he nursed the hope that his many and varied little sidelines might prove just as fruitful when added together.

Thinking of which, he pulled out his pocket watch; they were definitely running late. He would give them until a quarter to the hour and then, well, certain information and photographs in his possession would be made public. A shame, really; their little secret was one of his more lucrative arrangements.

His smile widened. The guaranteed income from such people was a lovely thing, but then the taking of personal information and the destruction of a victim was also very much a part of the game he enjoyed, and Carolyn had understood that very well. They were quite similar creatures in their tastes, habits, and games. She had been both astute and entertaining over the last few years. As a society hostess she had access to parties, families, and those in the know...in spite of her abusive treatment of the servants. She also had a nose for searching out trifling little peccadillos and fleecing their desperate owners accordingly. The small amounts of money earned from this had quickly mounted up...and had quickly been spent! He smiled — they had both truly enjoyed the high life!

But Carolyn had been unaware of certain aspects of his little sideline. Oh, he had fed her a handful of juicy titbits here and there, purely for the entertainment value of watching her work the victim...but he had kept the scandalous, the dubious, the truly obscene, and the most financially rewarding seams of information for his own mining and delectation.

As a diamond merchant of fairly affluent standing, he too had access to society parties, families, and people in important positions. And as one of his feet was planted firmly in the criminal underworld of several nations, Morten also had access to other things that some of his clients, who spluttered over his diamond prices, had been more than willing to pay through the nose for: namely, information…both about themselves, and others. Watching the so-called 'great and good' working themselves into fits of outrage over having no choice but to invite him to an event because of the work he had undertaken for them was yet another perquisite he found most enjoyable.

He smiled. So much naughtiness in the world! Photographs, letters, and other information were so easy to come by if you knew the right, or indeed the wrong people. And if copies were made and kept safe — purely to protect oneself, you understand — the fear of exposure ensured no danger to him from those stalwart, upstanding members of society so willing to be separated from sizeable amounts of money to preserve their own social standing…or destroy another's.

Including, it had to be said, dear Sir Wesley. Several very interesting opportunities for paid work, and various items of a salacious, intriguing, and highly profitable nature had come from that particular gentleman.

There were also two other people aboard this peculiar vessel who had personally paid towards his and Caro's very high standard of living. He allowed himself a chuckle. Yes, life was very good, if you were prepared to grasp it and shake it till the guineas rattled!

And now another victim had fallen into his trap. Such

wanton behaviour, too, visiting a servant in their rooms… quite shameful!

His smile widened in anticipation of what his most recent acquisition could offer him. As he speculated, his attention was caught by a rather exquisite diamond and platinum set, incorporating earrings, necklace, and what appeared to be a ten-carat solitaire ring. Putting his wandering fancies back to bed, he twisted his monocle in a little tighter and bent to read the italics-laden card beside the display. So absorbed was he in his reading that he failed to notice the Maori mannequin behind him begin to move. It silently stepped down from its plinth and walked towards him, its footfalls sure and silent, gripping the heavy pounamu mere. Eventually, the figure stood behind the unaware Van der Linde.

The mere swung through the air with sudden, shocking violence, its arc ending with a sickening crunch at the base of Morten's skull.

The little golden monocle dug sharply into the flesh around Morten's eye as he fell to the floor. He landed on his side, his eyes flickering desperately around the dimly lit room as he realised with a horrifying jolt of panic that he couldn't move — or breathe!

The figure walked to the door leading to the servants' sitting room and turned the key in the lock. Moving to the doors to the dining room, the snug, and the starboard deck, they did the same until the lounge was closed off from the rest of the boat…and they had the privacy they desired.

The last things Morten saw as his sight began to fade were the grinning face of the red-toothed demon mask leering at him from its plinth…and the far more horrifying sight of a faceless mannequin standing over him, the dead-white linen body draped in a kahu kiwi.

As he gazed at the figure in helpless, paralysed fear, it

crouched down and began to whisper in Morten's ear, the linen fingers slowly stroking the smooth white material that covered their mask-like face. Confusion, then mind-numbing terror appeared in Morten's wild eyes as the blank, linen covered visage of the mannequin slowly transformed into that of one of the guests, and he realised just who had killed him, and why.

The figure straightened up and smiled as they placed the mere on the little pie crust table next to Morten's corpse and carefully removed the deathly sharp katana from the samurai armour. This would take a little time, but presentation was everything…they had taught that to John Stable many years earlier.

### Aquilleia's cabin
### 10:35pm

Aquilleia sat up with a gasp, the dim moonlight shining through the curtains barely lighting the little clock on her bedside table.

She pressed a hand to the pendant at her throat and took a deep breath. The feeling that had affected her when Carolyn had died had returned: a soul was no longer available to her mind.

### The Lounge
### 10:40pm

The figure placed the sword back in the samurai warrior's scabbard without bothering to wipe it clean. Walking around the room counterclockwise, they unlocked the doors before turning back to look at the oddly lifelike mannequin with a strange smile.

They hoped Versipellis would understand and enjoy the little joke…their dear brother did so enjoy solving mysteries.

### Wesley's cabin
### 10:50pm

Robin Ellis wiped down the typewriter and folded the carefully worded missive that had taken him several attempts to perfect. He tucked it into an envelope, gripped the fountain pen tightly in his left hand, and printed a name on the front.

Leaving Wesley's cabin, he checked for witnesses before moving quickly to one of the other cabins and thrusting the note under its door. He rushed back to his late employer's rooms, closed and bolted the door, leant back against it, and breathed a sigh of relief. Another opportunity! He smiled. Anonymous blackmail was a wonderful thing: any amount of money could be requested, and picked up from a point of his choosing without any chance of discovery. He shook his head; how on earth they thought such sordid goings-on could be concealed in the close confines of a private boat was any one's guess — and with a servant, too!

A sudden knock on the door sent him flying across the room. His heart hammering, he stared at the door as though it had suddenly sprouted snakes. He cleared his throat. "Yes?"

There was a pause, then a low voice responded. "It's the steward, sir, I have a message for you."

Robin let out a nervous laugh, then walked to the door, took a deep breath and opened it. He stared at the messenger. "You're not the steward—"

The figure lashed out and caught Robin in a violent right

hook that knocked him to the floor. They walked into the cabin and closed the door behind them. The blackmail note was flung in Robin's face as he stared up in confusion. All he wanted was money — this wasn't what he had planned!

His attacker moved to the bed and picked up one of the feather pillows. Turning, they pulled out a revolver, placed the pillow over Robin's startled face, and pulled the trigger.

### O.D's suite
### 11:00pm

O.D paused in his ablutions at a noise from his sitting room. Wiping the soap from his neck, he walked out of his bathroom, stood by his armchair and listened. The sound came again: a very soft tapping at his cabin door.

He walked to the door and opened it. His daughter's maid, Jane, stood on the threshold, a concerned expression on her face.

O.D hurriedly tightened his dressing-gown belt. "Jane? Is everything all right?"

The young maid bit her lip. "Oh, sir, I don't know! Miss Merry told me to run her a bath before bed and said she would come up after taking the air…oh sir, I'm that worried! It's been nearly an hour and she hasn't come back!"

O.D's eyebrows lowered. "She said you were going to walk with her…" He saw the panicked look that appeared on the maid's face and closed his eyes. "It's all right, Jane. Well, maybe she went for a wander and fell asleep in one of the armchairs—"

The maid shook her head. "No, sir, I checked. When I saw her last, she was in the lounge, so that's where I went first, but she wasn't there, sir, nor the snug…" She frowned. "But there was an odd smell in the lounge, sir, sort of metallic… and one of the mannequins was all smashed up, and some of the rugs have been moved."

O.D's face turned deathly pale. He hurried into his office and blew down one of the speaking tubes on the desk. As he waited for a response, he opened one of the drawers in his desk, removed the revolver from within, and took out a box of bullets.

A high-pitched whistle came from the desk as Torrance, who had been on the edge of sleep in his cabin, responded to his master's call. His voice sounded tinny and high-pitched as it travelled down the narrow pipe. "Is everything all right, Mr Damant?"

O.D raised the speaking tube. "No, Torrance, it is not — Merry has gone missing! Please inform Caine, Thorne, Mlle Du'Lac, and Madame Aquilleia, and bring them here immediately. And let Mar know."

There was a sharp intake of breath at the end of the tube. "Yes sir!"

O.D headed back into his sitting room, where Jane was still standing by the door, wringing her hands. He gestured to one of the armchairs. "Please sit down, Jane, and leave the door open; I will be right back." He hurried into his bedroom and dressed, throwing on the evening wear he had only just removed and tucking the revolver and bullets into his pocket.

As he re-entered his sitting room, Elliott, Thorne, Giselle, and Aquilleia arrived, closely followed by Mar, and Torrance, clad in his dressing gown. Thorne was also accompanied by a yawning Labrador, her leash gripped in his left hand.

Mar was the first to speak, an expression of deep concern on her face. "O.D, what's this about Merry being missing?"

O.D gestured to the maid. "Jane is concerned, and so am I. Merry said she would go for a walk on the deck with Jane before bedtime; indeed, the only reason I agreed to her whim was because she said she would take Jane with her. It turns out that she instead sent her maid to draw a bath and went for a walk on her own — and now she is missing!"

Elliott frowned, and addressed the frightened maid. "How long ago did you leave your mistress?"

"Oh, sir… I left her in the lounge at ten minutes past ten — it now stands at an hour!"

O.D stepped forward. "Caine, Jane said there was an odd metallic smell in the lounge."

Without a word, Elliott turned and ran to the flight of stairs, rapidly followed by the others.

As they arrived at the deck entrance to the snug, Elliott paused; reaching into his dinner jacket, he removed his revolver from its holster. Thorne caught his friend's eye and did the same as Elliott slowly opened the snug door and checked inside before entering the small room, followed closely by Thorne and Veronique. Elliott advanced to the lounge door and paused again as his nostrils flared; he could already smell it. He turned at the faint growl behind him. Veronique was staring at the door, her hackles rising. Elliott looked at Thorne, who nodded, his face set; he, too, recognised the smell.

Elliott took a deep breath, placed his hand on the ornate brass knob, and with a sharp twist on the handle, flung the door open. As he, Thorne, and Veronique entered the sumptuous room, they realised that several things were out of place; not least the decapitated linen head of the samurai figure which sat several feet from its armour-clad host. The damaged remains of the mannequin lay propped like a boneless drunkard against one of the velvet settees, the prone figure still bearing its ornate leather and lacquer-work kabuto — though that ornate helmet, instead of resting upon the severed head of the blank mannequin, now graced the equally decapitated, and silently screaming head of Morten Van der Linde, which his killer had jammed onto the mannequin's neck to replace the cleaved original.

Giselle, Aquilleia, Mar, and Jane entered the room behind O.D. Torrance, on entering, choked out an oath and ran for the open window. Giselle took in the revolting display and swallowed hard; she reminded herself firmly that she had seen worse — much worse!

Mar, her hands pressed to her mouth, stared at the severed mannequin's head in utter horror. Her gaze darting from the dead-white countenance on the rug to the bloodied head of the diamond merchant and back again, before she suddenly crumpled to the floor in a dead faint.

Giselle, Aquilleia, and Jane hurried to her side and between them, managed to get her onto a chaise. Giselle walked to the bar and returned with a bottle of brandy and four tumblers on a tray. She poured a stiff measure and handed it to the pale, shaking maid. "Drink this."

As the young woman gulped the drink and coughed, Giselle poured a glass for Aquilleia and another for herself, which she drank in one go, before pouring a fourth and pressing it onto the now-awake, deathly pale, and shaking Mar.

O.D stared at Elliott, his face grey, his voice hoarse and shaky. "Where's — where's the rest of his body?"

Elliott waved his hand at the display. "The easiest way to get rid of a body on a boat is to throw it overboard; that's probably what happened here." He gestured to the open window where Torrance was busily reacquainting himself with his previous meal. "Most likely through that window."

Torrance redoubled his efforts as Thorne cleared his throat. "Ah, actually, Elliott, it's under this settee." Elliott looked under the plush piece of furniture; the mortal remains of Van der Linde had indeed been violently forced underneath.

Thorne handed Veronique's lead to Aquilleia, and he and Elliott carefully lifted the heavy settee and placed it against the wall before turning back to view the rest of Van der Linde. Elliott affected the dry investigative technique that had served him so well in the past, while Thorne went with his usual mode — a highly elevated eyebrow and a slightly nauseated expression — as they took in the damage done to the unpleasant man they had dined with only a short time before.

Elliott looked down at the floor and lifted one foot, then the other, experiencing a repellent, squishy sensation. With a grimace, he realised the rug he was standing on was saturated with blood; the Persian pattern concealed the redness, while the thick wool absorbed the liquid…he stepped off the rug and stood next to Thorne, who looked down and wrinkled his nose.

Giselle looked up at her husband. "Elliott, I think we should get Mar to her cabin; she's had quite a shock."

Elliott nodded. "Of course."

O.D turned concerned eyes to Elliott. "My daughter…you don't think she could have witnessed this, and been—"

Elliott seized his arm. "No! Do not follow that train of thought, Mr Damant! We will find her."

O.D wrung his hands. "But where?"

"She's alive."

They turned to stare at Aquilleia, who was standing quietly by the chaise her thick woolen shawl draped around her shoulders, and Veronique sitting by her side. She turned her violet eyes on O.D. "She's alive, and safe…she's simply no longer on the Taniwha." She paused, thinking. "But there is something else…another has disappeared: I can no longer feel their presence."

Thorne looked at her, an intense expression on his face. "Who?"

Aquilleia pulled the shawl tightly around her shoulders. "Robin Ellis." She took a deep breath. "And someone else is not what they seem."

Elliott frowned. "What do you mean?"

A look of distress appeared on her face. "It feels as though there is an additional person here with us, trapped inside another. Subjugated...and they are afraid, so very afraid!"

As they stared at Aquilleia, Mar struggled to her feet. Jane went to help her, but she brushed the young maid's hand away. Her voice was weak and faltering, "I... I think I will go to my room. No, Mlle Du'Lac, I will be quite all right alone, but thank you for your concern." She turned to O.D. "Octavius...I am sorry."

O.D shook his head, his face pale. "You have nothing to apologise for, Mar. If, as Madame Aquilleia states, Merry is no longer aboard but safe, then all is well; we will find her in time. Go to your cabin and rest. I shall see you in the morning."

Mar gazed at O.D for a long moment then turned and slowly left the lounge, walking through the snug to the portside stairs.

O.D turned to his daughter's maid. "Jane, you too...you have had a nasty shock; go to your room and rest. Torrance, will you please escort her."

Torrance straightened up, dabbing at his lips with his handkerchief. "Of course, Mr Damant." As he and the young maid left through the starboard door. O.D sat down abruptly, his head in his hands.

Aquilleia walked towards Thorne and held out her hand, which Thorne took and kissed. He turned to Elliott and Giselle, and lowered his voice. "Someone trapped inside another. Could it be…? Is Phoenixus here, pretending to be one of the guests?"

Elliott looked perturbed. "I honestly couldn't say, Thorne. When we change our appearance we can take on the memories of the person we imitate, but we don't keep any part of the person trapped inside us, whether they are alive or dead at the time of our imitation."

Aquilleia took a breath; the time had finally come. "Two names are coming through to me. Phoenixus is one; the other is Chymeris. Does this name mean anything to you?"

Elliott's eyes flared with a green light. He stared at her, and his voice, though tightly controlled, trembled slightly. "Chymeris was the name my mother had chosen for my sister; she, Phoenixus, and I were to be born on the same day…but both my mother and my sister died the day my brother and I were given life. My father only told me about her after Phoenixus killed you and Angellis."

Aquilleia's eye's glistened with tears and she touched Elliott's hand. "I'm so sorry—" Her voice caught in her throat and she began to crumple.

Thorne caught her and carried her to a settee, where he held her hand and looked on helplessly as she moaned softly, "One that died, yet three there are; two skin-changers and the reborn!"

O.D, realising that what was happening in his lounge was way beyond his ken, spoke in a deceptively calm voice. "I cannot claim to understand what is going on here, but I do know that my daughter has gone missing, a psychic has insisted that she is safe, and the head of a freshly murdered guest has been skewered onto one of my display mannequins. Therefore, I will talk with the staff about closing this room until you feel prepared to remove said remains and place them with those of Carolyn and Sir— damn it! I mean *Mr* Wesley Eade! The Featherstone-Eades should be in their cabin. I will arrange it now, and then I do believe I shall take a dose of chloral and go to bed! Goodnight, ladies and gentlemen." He walked through the starboard-side door.

Giselle looked at her husband. "That is a gentleman teetering on the edge!"

Elliott nodded. "A great deal has happened over the last few days…I don't think now is the time to tell him about the Featherstone-Eades' cabin being ransacked, either!" He turned to Aquilleia who seemed to be waking from her trance. "Are you well, Aquilleia? Well enough to talk?"

Thorne frowned. "Elliott—"

His friend held up a hand. "I have no intention of pushing, Thorne, I just need to ask."

Aquilleia patted Thorne's hand. "It is all right…there are things that must be said." She looked at Elliott. "Please ask me what you need to know."

Elliott looked at the psychic. "You mentioned Robin Ellis; you can no longer feel his presence?"

Aquilleia nodded.

"Is it similar to Merry? Is he no longer on the boat?"

"No, it feels different. I can still feel Merry's presence, even though she is not here. Robin Ellis is gone completely… just like Carolyn Nolloth, Wesley Eade, and Morten Van der Linde."

"Dead?"

She took a deep breath. "I believe so." She looked at them each in turn. "I am not a medium; communing with the dead has never been my gift. I see and feel for the living: who they truly are, their past, their present, and their future…I feel their presence and their emotions: happiness, sadness, fear." Her violet eyes grew large. "At least two here wallow in their feelings; one in love, the other in hate. Both are gifted at cloaking themselves and their emotions; they have both

293

killed before, and will do so again! But of the deaths on the Taniwha, one is not responsible for the murders of Wesley Eade, Morten Van der Linde or Robin Ellis — only for that of Carolyn Nolloth!"

Thorne's blond eyebrows rocketed upwards. "Two murderers? God's teeth!"

Aquilleia was about to respond when Elliott sat next to her on the settee. "Can you see them? Can you see who either of them are?"

Aquilleia shook her head. "As I have said, they are both clever at cloaking, but in different ways. It is possible they have lived a lie for so long that they now believe it themselves…people can persuade themselves of anything if they expend enough effort."

Giselle looked thoughtful. "Are they aware of each other, or are they separate?"

Aquilleia frowned. "They are separate. Their reasons, their justification for killing, are completely different; one kills for love, the other for hate." She paused. "And yet love can sometimes turn to hate…"

Malachy and Simone entered the lounge by the starboard-side door. Malachy looked at Morten's remains, his green eyes bright as he scanned the injury to the neck. "That was certainly not caused by a kitchen knife!"

Elliott pointed to the samurai sword attached to the rest of the armour. "Methinks that was the instrument of his demise: razor-sharp, and to hand."

As the group paused to look at the wicked looking instrument and their minds turned to just what had happened to the odious diamond merchant, the heavy door to the lounge was suddenly flung open; the carved wood slamming against the panelling as O.D strode purposefully back in. The tired, defeated man who had left just a few moments ago had been replaced by a man who would brook no nonsense. Elliott suddenly understood what he must be like to deal with in business.

O.D glared at the group of startled people. "Damn it all, I'm not resting until my daughter is safely back with us and the perpetrator of these obscene killings is handed over to the authorities!"

Elliott nodded. "Most excellent, Mr Damant…but I'm afraid we're looking for two killers now, not one!"

O.D closed his eyes and rubbed the bridge of his nose. "Good God!"

Thorne went to the bar, returning with a tray bearing several more tumblers and a decanter of whisky. O.D sat down next to Thorne and quietly poured several healthy doubles.

Elliott turned to Malachy. "I take it Mr Damant has told you to shut down this room?"

Malachy nodded, looking at the dishevelled and bloody display. "And I can certainly see why!"

"Is there any way to do so without obstructing the use of the kitchens and dining room?"

Malachy nodded. "We can lock the lounge starboard door and the doors that lead into the snug, the dining room, and the service corridor to the staff quarters. That would still leave a clear route for the kitchen staff to access the dining room and their own sitting room through the kitchen."

Elliott nodded in a satisfied manner. "Good, then do it, please. Now, Thorne, we have a great deal of work on our hands in here; we must bring the trunk down and start investigating the room. But let's see about Mr Ellis first, shall we?"

Elliott, Thorne, Giselle, and Aquilleia, accompanied by a tired and slightly grumpy Veronique, followed O.D to the cabin that had been allocated to Wesley Eade's personal secretary.

O.D knocked firmly on the door. "Mr Ellis…Mr Ellis, we need to speak with you." There was no response from the room beyond. He turned to Elliott who shrugged, turned the handle and opened the unlocked door. Elliott looked around the silent room. "Empty…where the Devil could he be?" He tapped his lips for a few moments. "Let's try Eade's cabin." Turning, he marched to the port side of the boat and stopped at the door to what had been the lawyer's cabin. Lifting his hand, he knocked firmly on the door; there was no answer. Elliott flashed a glance at Thorne and opened the door. He paused, taking in the violent scene before him. "Aquilleia was quite correct; I think we will have to deal with this room next, my friend."

Thorne again handed Veronique's lead to Aquilleia, who took the tired Labrador to one of the loungers on the deck and sat stroking her ears as Thorne, Elliott, and Giselle entered the cabin, and O.D stood in some agitation by the door.

Elliott studied the figure lying on the floor next to the single bed. He took in the torn pillow left on top of Robin Ellis's face and frowned. "Smothered? It would take a great deal of strength to smother a healthy man."

Thorne lifted the pillow and grimaced. "Not smothered: shot through the left eye."

Giselle spoke from the dressing table, where she was rummaging through the open drawers. "No one reported hearing a gunshot…perhaps the killer used the pillow to muffle the sound?"

O.D entered the room, took in the corpse, and dragged a hand through his hair. "Good God, another one? First Carolyn, then Eade, then Van der Linde, and now Robin Ellis — we're going to run out of room in the meat locker!"

As he spoke, a sudden, brilliant explosion of purple light filled the room; the bolt of lightning was accompanied by a deafening boom that shocked them all into silence as the heavens opened; the rainfall was instantaneous and torrential as up in the wheelhouse, Captain Peach rapidly decided that their current location was as close to Milford City as he was prepared to go in the company of the sudden and powerful storm. The engine was thrown into reverse to slow the boat, the anchor was hurriedly dropped in the shallower depths, as the slow-moving vessel was brought to a halt in the violently churning water of Harrison Cove.

O.D left the cabin, nodding to Aquilleia who was trying to soothe Veronique. The Labrador had been as startled by the thunder as everyone else, and was sharing her displeasure at the noise by trying to drown it out with a chesty grumble of her own.

### The hotel
### 11:45pm

Coll wiped the bar and smiled at his wife. "Another quiet evening, my dear. I was thinking of taking the dog out for a wander, but I think the storm has put a stop to that!"

Before Rose could reply, the front door to the hotel was suddenly kicked open and a drenched Manu entered carrying a sodden and unconscious Merry.

## Monday morning
## The hotel
## 12:30am

Coll pulled the door shut with a muttered oath. "I'm sorry, my dear, the Taniwha still isn't answering. I will have to go out in the boat."

Rose got up from her seat by the now dry and sleeping Merry, and gestured to Coll to follow her outside. She quietly pulled the wooden door to and turned to her husband. "The storm is getting worse, Coll. You can't take the boat out and you know it — the Sound has her own ways…she could kill you! Merry is safe here, and the best thing for us to do is to keep her warm, stay out of the storm and wait for it to break. You know what the Sound is like; this could blow over in a few moments or linger all week. They will discover that Merry is missing at some point, and then they'll contact us."

Coll heaved a sigh. He knew his wife was right, but he had a bad feeling about what was coming this night — besides the storm.

He looked over at Manu who was sitting next to the fireplace, his damp clothing steaming gently in the heat as he gazed into the dancing flames and coddled his cup of tea.

Coll walked over and rested his hand on the mantle. "Why didn't you return her to the Taniwha, Manu? It would have been quicker and easier for you."

The Maori looked up at him and shrugged. "When I got her out the water, the only thing she said was that someone had pushed her overboard. It didn't seem sensible to return her to a place where someone had tried to kill her."

Rose stared at him. "Merry actually said that someone tried to kill her?"

Manu nodded as he sipped his tea. "She didn't say who; she fainted after she told me what had happened. I think she was just relieved I got her out…" He turned back to the fire; his dark eyes pensive. "She was terrified."

Coll looked at Rose, his face set. "The Taniwha are not answering my calls, and now we hear that someone has tried to kill Merry. I think something bad may have happened. I'm going to send a message to Versipellis' contact in London…I think we need official assistance!" He turned and headed to his little office, where he kept the telegraph.

Entering the room, he twitched the curtains back from the rain-soaked windows. In the distance, he could dimly make out the lights of the Taniwha as she lay at anchor in Harrison Cove. There came another rolling crash of thunder, and a massive flash of lightning almost blew him back from the closed window. The sudden illumination threw the small harbour, wooded hills and impossibly steep cliffs of the Sound into stark relief. Coll caught his breath; the beauty of the Sounds was at once glorious and terrifying.

Turning back to his desk, he uncovered the device. It had cost him a small fortune to have the hotel attached to the system, but due to the remote nature of the Sounds, and the many and various guests who wanted to send messages around the world, it had paid back its cost tenfold in fairly short order.

He began to prepare his message for transmission. Nothing too obvious; perhaps a polite 'it has come to my attention' type of thing might be best? He looked through the open door, and saw Manu, still steaming slightly, sitting by the fireplace drinking his tea. Coll shook his head. No, honesty was always the best policy. Lapotaire could explain it at his end; that was what he was paid for, after all! He began to write his message.

LAPOTAIRE STOP URGENT STOP ATTEMPTED MURDER ABOARD SHIP STOP ALL COMMUNICATIONS UNANSWERED STOP REQUEST ASSISTANCE STOP INQUIRE COLL AT MILFORD CITY HOTEL STOP

Coll read through it a few times and nodded; blunt, to the point and only one name…that would do.

He sent the message and waited for the response, which arrived twenty minutes later; the message had been received, and would be delivered to the given address shortly.

Hopefully Lapotaire would get that within the next few hours. Coll sat back in his chair and glared through his storm lashed window at the distant boat. What the hell was going on aboard the Taniwha?

○

## A private cabin
## 2:30am

With a shuddering breath, the dimly lit figure placed the fountain pen down on their writing chest and gazed at the letter it had taken them so very long to write. Picking up the pages, they reread their words before carefully folding the letter and tucking it into an envelope.

Pulling their warmest dressing gown tightly about them, they placed the envelope on their dressing table, and with what appeared to be a great and painful effort, they walked to their cabin door, opened it, and stepped onto the wet deck. Beyond the cabin door, the thunderous squall beat the waters of the Sound into a thrashing mass of liquid darkness that tugged at the Taniwha's hastily dropped anchor. The mixture of the water's violent movements and the heavy rainfall guaranteed absolute privacy as the gowned figure glanced up and down the empty, wet walkway.

The only people awake would be dealing with the abomination in the lounge; their breath caught in their throat… after all these years, their hopes and plans had been dashed by the cruel actions of another.

Closing the door behind them, they headed slowly towards their destination: O.D's cabin.

As they reached the main door that led directly into O.D's living room, they paused. If he were there, it would be difficult. There were no words to explain everything that had occurred, no argument that could justify what had been done…but it was far too late for that now; there was only one way through this, and they knew what must be done.

Reaching out a trembling hand, they turned the handle and the door swung open. They entered the dim and silent room, approached the desk from which O.D ran his domain, and gently swept one hand along the carved, dark wood.

As they turned, they saw gaslights flickering in the bedroom. Summoning the courage to continue, they entered the empty room. Placing a trembling hand on the edge of the bed, they paused, and were about to cross into the bathroom when they caught sight of a small box on the bedside table. How very opportune: no need to search.

They stared at the box in silence before catching it up in a sudden movement and putting it in their pocket. As they were about to leave, they caught sight of a photograph on O.D's desk. They took a shuddering breath; tears stinging their eyes as they turned away and left the room. The lock clicked with an ominous finality as they returned to their cabin without looking back.

## Thorne's cabin
## 2:55am

The small figure paused on the threshold and peered into the nearest window. They knew the man whose cabin it was would be downstairs dealing with the body in the lounge, but they didn't know just how long he would be there. They also knew he had a dog; a faint snuffling sound coming from under the door to the man's room, the figure gripped the heavy bag they were carrying a little tighter. Closing their eyes, they willed themselves to be strong...they needed to prove to their mistress that the interloper, though pretty, was not up to the wonderful task of looking after *all* her needs.

Taking a deep breath, they slowly pushed open the door and came face to face with Veronique, who had hoped the noises on deck were her master returning with midnight treats. Instead, a young woman whose smell she did not recognise appeared in the doorway and hurriedly closed the door behind her.

Ana gave the curious dog a tremulous smile, lifted the heavy bag and opened it. Reaching in, she pulled out two shortbread biscuits and placed them on the floor. Veronique looked at her, looked at the biscuits, sniffed them carefully, looked back at her again, and then pounced on the shortbread.

Ana breathed a sigh of relief as she dropped another few biscuits and began her search. Having spent so long in Dona Carla's employ, she had taken her mistress's instructions on eavesdropping to heart, and followed them on many occasions, including some when her mistress might not have appreciated her maid's assistance!

One such had occurred just a few hours earlier. Her

mistress had been visited by *her*, and informed that the gem had been removed from her keeping and hidden somewhere in this cabin. Ana allowed herself a smile. She would find the gem and give it to her mistress, and that would be the end of that particular little redhead!

Finding nothing in the main cabin but a collection of strange and esoteric-looking paraphernalia comprising of various brushes, coloured powders, and a sizeable collection of photographic equipment including several bottles of strong-smelling liquids, she turned her attentions to the small bathroom. It was neat and tidy, with an open wash-bag on the side, the contents of which she carefully probed; soap, always a good start…a shaving brush, scissors, and a cut-throat razor. She frowned; the gentleman who slept here had a very neat beard. Then she shrugged. She had never had to deal with a master, so perhaps a cut throat razor was normal. A small pot of cold cream…she removed it from the bag; how many men used face cream?

Twisting the lid off, she caught her breath as she gazed at the purple gem within. Allowing herself a triumphant smile, she screwed the lid on and tucked the pot into her pocket. Leaving the bathroom, she quietly pulled the door to, then spun round in shock at the sudden, frighteningly polite sound of someone clearing their throat.

The smiling woman standing before her held out her hand. "That belongs to me, and I want it back…now!"

Ana jumped at the raw tone in the woman's voice, her heart pounding in her throat, and she put her hand in her pocket to remove the pot. Her eyes flicked to the snoring dog under the table. The valerian tincture she had used on the biscuits had worked rapidly; she would have to tell her mistress it was a success.

As the other woman approached, her right hand outstretched, Ana caught sight of a strange ring on the woman's right hand: a gold band in the form of a snake eating its own tail, with the design turned inward, towards the palm.

Ana flung the pot in the air and launched herself forward, her sharp fingernails aimed at the woman's face. But as she reached out her wrists were caught in a steel-like grip. "I really don't think so, my sweet!"

With one sudden movement, the woman lifted Ana off her feet and threw her against the far wall. As Ana hit the wall and fell to the ground, the immaculately manicured hands reached for her throat. As they began to grip, Ana realised with sudden cold certainty that her mistress would never hear about the efficacy of valerian drops on the Labrador.

After several minutes, her attacker stood up and looked at the body of the young maid. Dead brown eyes gazed blankly through the mass of thick, dark hair that had come free from its pins during Ana's desperate fight to survive.

Her killer turned from their most recent victim and scanned the room for the little pot, finally spotting it by the unconscious Labrador's paw, where it had rolled to a halt.

Walking slowly towards the dog, they stooped to pick up the pot and check the contents. As they tightened the lid, they reached down and lightly ran a slim finger along the Labrador's silky ear. Smiling, they moved closer to the sleeping dog.

## The snug
## 3:00am

Aquilleia suddenly gasped and pressed a hand to her chest.

Thorne placed his camera on one of the tables and hurried to her side. "Aquilleia, are you all right?"

She took a deep breath and shook her head. "It's happened again...another death..."

Helping her into a chair, Thorne knelt before her. "Who? Do you have any idea?"

Aquilleia shook her head again. "It's someone I don't know...they are aboard the Taniwha, but I don't recall meeting them."

Elliott and Giselle entered the room. They had been dusting for Galton's details in the lounge and it had rapidly had become a complete nightmare! The entire area was now covered in Thorne's best number six green powder, and there were hundreds of prints to be checked.

Giselle nudged Elliott and nodded towards them. "What's wrong?"

Thorne looked over his shoulder. "Aquilleia believes there's been another murder, but she doesn't know who it is."

Elliott closed his eyes and pinched the bridge of his nose. Giselle walked behind the bar and reached for the brandy and some tumblers. She allowed herself a wry smile; at this rate, by the time they arrived back in Milford City, they would all be in an advanced state of alcoholism. She poured Aquilleia a drink before settling on the seat next to her. On the other side of the room, O.D, still in his evening dress, snored faintly in one of the armchairs by the port-side door.

Giselle leant forward. "Can you describe them?"

Aquilleia took a sip of brandy and closed her eyes. "A young, small female...her life revolved around—" Her eyes snapped open. "Dona Carla!"

Giselle's mouth fell open. "Dona Carla's dead?"

"No, the girl; her life revolves around Dona Carla..."

Elliott's eyes flashed as he thought. "Dona Carla's maid is a small, young girl. She was with Dona Carla at the aether-drome in Auckland."

A strange expression suddenly appeared on Aquilleia's face and she shuddered violently. Turning to Thorne, her eyes became huge and pinpoints of silver light appeared in her violet gaze. "Veronique!"

Thorne leapt to his feet and charged out of the room, closely followed by Aquilleia, Elliott, and Giselle, the two women throwing propriety to the wind as they hitched up their gowns like cancan dancers and ran.

Thorne arrived at his cabin door, flung it open, and stopped in shock on the threshold. The body of a dark haired girl was huddled against the far wall, whilst under the dressing table, Veronique lay on her back, her jowls flapping gently in time with her rhythmic snoring.

As Thorne and Aquilleia hurried to Veronique, Elliott and Giselle turned their attentions to the young girl. Sightless brown eyes gazed up at them and they realised that Aquilleia's vision had been quite right...there had indeed been another murder.

Elliott looked over his shoulder at Thorne. "Is Veronique all right?"

Thorne pulled Veronique out from under the dressing table and gently patted at the damp snout. Veronique snuffled, belched, and continued to snore. He turned to Elliott, a look of concern on his face. "I can't wake her."

Aquilleia leant closer to Veronique's nose and sniffed.

"Valerian… if she was given a small dose, she should be all right…she'll sleep, and be fine in the morning."

Thorne stared at her. "And what if she was given a large dose?"

Aquilleia looked at the worried man before her, and was suddenly taken with a feeling that all would be well: both for Veronique, and for them. She caught Thorne's hand and squeezed it tightly. "She will be well. I suggest we try to wake her and give her fresh, clean water and perhaps a little food; that should help get rid of the effects of the valerian."

Thorne nodded and gently moved Veronique onto her side, the Labrador grumbled faintly but continued to sleep. Thorne went to the trunk that contained all Veronique's foodstuffs, removed a sizeable mutton bone that he had planned to give her as a morning snack, and placed it directly in front of her nose. The snoring continued, but the edge of a pink tongue appeared. As Thorne gently prodded the damp black nose with the bone, the snoring stopped and Veronique's eyes opened…she gazed up blearily at Thorne, and her tail began to thump the floor as she realised who was sitting in front of her, and just what the nice smell was.

As Thorne got Veronique to her feet, Aquilleia emptied the water bowl and refreshed it. Placing the full bowl of clean water in front of the unsteady dog, she watched with relief as the dog drank, and drank, and drank. She refilled the bowl again as Veronique sat down heavily and began to lick the bone.

Thorne sat next to Veronique and blinked rapidly. He reached out to touch Aquilleia's face; she took his hand and kissed it.

Over by the far wall, Elliott and Giselle were taking in the young maid's more obvious injuries while trying not to look too closely at her face; victims of manual strangulation were never a pretty sight.

Elliott gestured to her neck. "Marks where long nails have dug in…could a woman have done this?"

Giselle looked up at him, her face inches away from the dead girl's throat. One of her delicately drawn red eyebrows arched. "Of course a woman could have done this; not all women are physically weak. A strong woman could easily have killed her…or it could have been a man with unusually long fingernails." She looked pointedly at her husband's hands before gesturing to one particular mark on the girl's neck. "It looks like her killer wore a ring of some kind…" She raised her hands, and without touching the corpse, held them just in front of the marks. "On the right thumb…an unusual place for a ring."

Elliott frowned and drummed his fingers on the floor. "For the last few hours I've had my hopes pinned on one suspect…but they don't wear any rings on their right hand."

Giselle sat back on her heels. "Lady Carlton-Cayce?"

"Exactly! She had a great deal to lose –—more than most — but this just lacks, I don't know…class!"

Giselle turned back to the rapidly cooling corpse. "Well, we have been working on the basis that the killer is someone already aboard the Taniwha; could it possibly have been an outsider?"

Elliott grimaced. "I sincerely hope not! That would put the absolute bloody kibosh on our investigation so far, and no mistake!"

He glared at his wife, who smiled sweetly. "So, Elliott, are we saying that it is someone already aboard?"

His head fell forward and he groaned. "I hope so…what say you?"

Giselle lifted her husband's chin and grinned at him. "Well, it's far more plausible than suggesting that someone sailed after us, climbed aboard without anyone seeing them, went on an unwitnessed murderous rampage for no apparent reason, and then disappeared without a trace during severe weather. Don't you think?"

Elliott nodded. "And we think it's…?

Thorne raised his voice as he stroked Veronique's ears. "I would have said Lady Carlton-Cayce too, but it looks like this victim *was* killed by someone wearing a ring on their right hand; Lady Carlton-Cayce only wears rings on her left hand…and her right hand lacks the marks that one gets when wearing rings, even for a short while. Which rases an interesting suggestion…could she have a helper?"

Elliott groaned again. "One killer who only killed Carolyn, and another who may or may not have an assistant. Not counting Carolyn's unknown confederate! Oh Gods!"

Aquilleia looked at them both. "And the added bonus of someone hiding inside someone else."

Elliott turned to face her; the soft brown of his eyes touched by faint green lights. "So Phoenixus is here?"

She nodded. "As is Chymeris."

Elliott's eyebrows furrowed over his nose and the green lights in his eyes began to swirl faster, rapidly consuming the brown until his eyes were pools of green. When he spoke, his voice was deathly quiet. "What exactly do you mean?"

Aquilleia took a deep breath. "I can see them both, in their true forms. When you were born, Chymeris should have died. Her physical form did; but her desire for life was so strong, she took over your brother's body, forcing him to dwell trapped, as a prisoner, in his own mind. It is not Phoenixus we should fear, Versipellis — it is Chymeris!"

Elliott shook his head violently. "No! No, you're wrong! My sister died before she could be born! It is Phoenixus who is responsible for the murders…including those of Angellis and you, in Astraea all those years ago!" He turned to leave the cabin.

Aquilleia held out her hand. "Elliott, please listen, our names indicate our abilities, yes?"

"Yes! What is your point?" snapped Elliott.

"Please hear me, Elliott. Versipellis means 'Skin Changer', Shadavarian means 'Shadow Shifter', Angellis means 'Messenger', Aquilleia means 'Water Diviner', Phoenixus means 'Firebird', and Chymeris can mean either "False Skin" or 'Bird of Discord'. Phoenixus has exhibited abilities that are not within his name…" Aquilleia paused and looked at Elliott. "But those abilities *are* within Chymeris' names! She has the same abilities as you, to change her skin and become someone else, she also has the ability to sow discontent and strife. Those are not Phoenixus' gifts. He has been overthrown, trapped within his own body and mind! We may never know what he has been forced to endure in his confinement — and we don't yet know what his abilities may be. If we don't try to help him, we will all regret it…but it may already be too late…"

Elliott stared at Aquilleia, trying to take in what she was saying. If she were right, over a thousand years of hatred would have to be rethought.

Thorne took a deep breath, crossed his legs at the ankle and continued to stroke Veronique's ears. The Labrador snuffled at his hand before continuing her bleary-eyed attempts to destroy the mutton bone before her. "Well, this has certainly been an eye-opener…" He looked at the woman he loved, who had been murdered, so they had thought, by his friend's brother all those years ago. "You are quite sure?"

Aquilleia nodded. "I am absolutely sure. I don't yet know which guest Chymeris is imitating, but I know she *is* here, and guilty of several of the murders committed aboard."

Elliott looked at her sharply. "And you have already said which…do you know how?"

Aquilleia took a deep breath and closed her violet eyes.

"She transformed into the corpse of Carolyn Nolloth in the meat locker, and Wesley Eade took his own life in terror at the approaching horror."

Giselle blenched. She had seen Carolyn's corpse; it was no wonder Eade had killed himself...that vision approaching would have turned anyone's mind!

Aquilleia continued. "She also killed Morten Van der Linde and Dona Carla's maid while searching for the Larkspur, and she killed Robin Ellis because he had witnessed something and was trying to blackmail her."

Giselle cleared her throat. "Can you see the accomplice at all?"

Aquilleia sighed and shook her head. "It's strange; Chymeris must be shielding them. I can usually read people quite quickly, but here...we know the crimes have been committed, and I should be able to see the guilty one, but it is still very unclear. I can see a man, easily led by certain desires. He believes himself to be Chymeris' helper, but another also believes they are an accomplice. They are aware of each other, and their presence in Chymeris' life on the Taniwha, but they are each unaware of the other's true place within Chymeris' plan."

Elliott bit savagely at his nail. "Playing one off against the other, perhaps...like Carolyn, Van der Linde, and the third in their grubby little clique!" He paused. "Can you see who they are yet?"

Aquilleia shook her head, and a wry smile appeared on her lips. "I'm not living up to my reputation, am I? What I said a while ago still stands, especially in the case of the third person in the Carolyn Nolloth and Morten Van der Linde trinity; I still cannot see who they are, they are very good at hiding their mind. Some people become so bound up in the false story they weave for others that they too begin to believe it, and that is the point where I have absolutely no way of reading them. They believe their own lies, and nothing can part them from that belief. When such people are finally faced with the genuine truth, it can cause them great harm."

Elliott groaned quietly. "Did Phoenixus — I mean Chymeris — did they attack Merry?"

Aquilleia shook her head firmly. "No, they were not involved. And neither Chymeris nor her assistants were in any way party to Carolyn Nolloth's plans to harm her niece."

Thorne looked up from his silent study of Veronique's ears. "What is Chymeris doing here?"

"She wants the Larkspur…it is my belief that she needs the diamonds to get her brother out of what she now believes to be *her* mind. She seeks to imprison him within one of the diamonds, to free herself of what she sees as his constant interference in her plans. Every now and then he tries to fight her, to take back control, but she's far too strong for him."

Elliott looked at her sharply, the green swirls in his eyes spinning faster as he spat out a sudden oath. Leaping to his feet, he ran into the bathroom and emptied out Thorne's wash bag. The pot was gone! He ground his teeth. Damn and blast! He walked back into the main cabin. Four pairs of eyes, one set still rather bleary, looked at him. "It's gone…bloody hell!" He stood with his back to the bathroom door and fumed.

"Oh, of course!" said Thorne.

Elliott glared at him. "What?"

Thorne blinked. "It's just come to me…I know who sent the threatening letters to O.D."

Elliott paused in his self-flagellation and raised an eyebrow. "Who?"

Thorne sat back with a sigh. "Lime blossom!"

Elliott looked nonplussed. "Explain!"

"We searched all the cabins, and only one guest uses lime blossom, I don't know quite how I missed it at the time, but…think, Elliott."

Elliott sat back in the armchair and pondered, moving through the various bathrooms they had searched. "Darius Damant doesn't wear scent, Rust uses hair oil but not lime blossom, and Kayfield doesn't wear any. Mrs Carter uses jasmine, Miss Havercroft has several bottles, but not that particular scent, Mar uses lavender, and Lady Carlton-Cayce uses…everything but lime blossom! Eade had no hair oil in his cabin, Merry uses lily of the valley, Van der Linde used highly scented hair oil but not the right one. Burrows…" He paused and nodded. "Torrance Burrows uses lime blossom hair oil! Ellis was a blackmailer but did not use that scent, Dona Carla wears Jicky, and O.D's beard oil is lemon. By a process of elimination, it has to be Torrance Burrows!" He grinned at Thorne. "Excellent, but does that make him a murderer as well?"

Aquilleia shook her head. "We have nothing to fear from him. He has already realised that he made a terrible mistake; he is no threat."

As they sat quietly, Giselle looked at the others and sighed. "Well, I can't really put this off any longer."

Elliott looked at her. "Put off what, exactly?"

"I have to do something rather unpleasant."

Elliott raised an eyebrow. "Oh…what?"

Giselle looked at her husband. "I have to tell Dona Carla that her maid is dead." She stood up and smoothed the front of her slightly tired-looking frock.

Aquilleia stood up too. "Would you like me to come with you?"

Giselle thought for a moment. "Yes, it might be an idea… you may pick something up. I might have a quick wash and a change of clothes first, though."

Aquilleia smiled. "I agree. Shall we meet on the deck in ten minutes?"

Giselle nodded. The two men stood up as their better halves left the confines of the small cabin, leaving the two men in the company of a drugged Labrador and one very dead maid.

Giselle and Aquilleia paused outside their respective cabins, unlocked the doors and entered their rooms at the same time.

Aquilleia headed straight to her bathroom, removing various items of clothing and depositing them on the floor as she went.

In the cabin next door, Giselle headed to the little bedroom where Lilith slept. Ordinarily she would have left her maid to rest, but one or two of her stays were rather tricky to undo, unless you happened to have a spare pair of hands that were fitted on backwards.

She tapped gently on the door; Lilith was a light sleeper… but there was no answer. Giselle frowned and tapped a little harder…still no response. Giselle pursed her lips, grasped the handle and pushed the narrow door open. As she entered the dim little room, the first thing that caught her eye was the narrow bed: neatly made…and very empty. Giselle frowned and headed back into the main cabin. As she began her attempts to undo the more awkward stays, she started at a light tapping on the cabin door. She moved to the window and flicked the curtain out of the way; Elliott was standing on the step.

She unlocked the door and stepped aside as he entered and flung himself into one of the small armchairs with a groan. "Well, I've just been down to the snug to inform O.D that there has been another death. I think he's drunk most of a bottle of whisky on his own, and I'm not even going to try to count what Malachy has put away in the course of this evening!" He looked at his wife, then reached for her hand. "What is it?"

Giselle looked both concerned and irritated. "Lilith isn't in her room…I think we can both guess where she is."

"Ah…well, shall I assist you in getting changed? There are rather a lot of loops, buttons, and whatnot in the back of that very attractive evening frock."

Giselle nodded and turned her back. As Elliott carefully undid the multitudinous fastenings that kept his wife within her gown and the satin creation fell to the floor, he grinned. "I don't suppose there's time…?"

Giselle smiled back and slapped lightly at the wandering hand. "No, husband, there isn't!"

She entered the bathroom and returned a few minutes later, her face scrubbed to pinkness. She opened the wardrobe and skimmed through the contents before selecting a simple grey tweed skirt, a matching jacket, and a cream silk blouse. Several minutes later she was escorted to Aquilleia's cabin, where the door was opened almost before she had the opportunity to knock.

Aquilleia pulled her door shut and the three of them walked down the deck towards Dona Carla's cabin, the last suite before O.D's private rooms.

### Dona Carla's cabin
### 3:45am

Giselle knocked firmly. A few moments passed before the door was opened by a somewhat dishevelled Dona Carla, wearing a skimpy red peignoir. She looked at Giselle with surprise and not a little irritation. "Giselle, darling, it's rather late for social pleasantries, don't you think?" She paused. "Is everything all right?"

Giselle shook her head. "No, Dona, it isn't. May we come in?"

Dona Carla tugged her peignoir tighter around her shoulders and shook her head. With a disarming smile, she pulled the door closer to behind her. "I don't think so, my darling. Whatever the urgency, I'm sure it can wait till some decent hour of the morning…sometime after lunch, perhaps."

She stepped back into the room and began to push the door shut. Giselle moved forward and caught the door. "No, Dona — it can't wait!"

The dancer looked at the two women on her threshold, her face uncertain.

Giselle leant forward, exasperated. "We'll make this easier, shall we? *You* know that *I* know you are the Fox, we know Lilith is in your cabin, we know you asked her to steal the Larkspur, and you have always made your personal predilections obvious. Now, may we come in?"

Dona Carla folded her arms across her chest and looked at her curiously. "What is this about?"

Giselle took a deep breath. "It's about your maid; I'm sorry, Dona."

Dona Carla opened her mouth, realisation dawned on her

mobile face as she looked from Giselle to Aquilleia. "No…not Ana! Please God, no!"

As she began to slide down the door, Giselle and Aquilleia caught her, and helped her back into her cabin. As they entered the room, Lilith, who had been lying on the bed, had leapt up on hearing Dona Carla's cry and swiftly helped them place her back into bed. As she pulled the thick comforter up around the sobbing woman's shoulders, Lilith looked at Giselle, her expression defiant. "You wish for me to give my notice, yes?"

Giselle studied the woman who had been her friend and companion for so long. She shook her head. "I think Dona Carla needs you far more than I do right now, Lilith." She looked at her earnestly. "I know she promised to help find those responsible for our parents' murders if you gave her the jewel, but you could have come to me, Lilith…you could have come to me."

Giselle turned and left the cabin. She was followed by Aquilleia, who quietly closed the cabin door behind them.

◯

### The hotel
### 4:00am

Rose poured boiling water into the teapot, swirled it round, emptied it, and began the morning ritual of the pot of tea. True, it was few hours earlier than the usual time, but they had found it impossible to sleep.

Setting various items on a tray, she carried it through to her husband's office, closing the door behind her with a practised flick of her foot before placing the tray on his desk and lifting the pot to pour. Manu was fast asleep in one of the chairs by the fireplace, having refused the offer of a bed to instead wait for news with Coll. Rose turned to look at her husband, who was standing by the window, his tired eyes fixed on the dimly lit and distant boat that bobbed in the still-choppy waters of Harrison Cove.

There was a sudden sound of running feet behind her; the door was flung open as Merry launched herself into the room, almost knocking the teapot out of Rose's hands in her hurry. "Please, Mr Langen, I have to get back to the Taniwha!"

Coll blinked at her as Rose hurriedly placed the teapot back on the tray. Manu opened one tired eye, stretched, and reached for one of the oatmeal biscuits on the tea tray.

Coll's tone was gentle. "Merry, the weather is still quite bad—"

"You don't understand!" said Merry. "Darius pushed me overboard!"

Coll stared at her in shock. "Darius! Manu told us what you said when he pulled you from the water — Merry, are you sure? Could you not have simply fallen—"

"Aunt Carolyn is dead!"

Coll frowned. "What?"

"She was murdered! And Sir Wesley Eade...oh, Mr Langen, you have to help us!"

Coll stared at the tearful young woman before turning to the telegraph. He had sent several messages during the night, most of them to Lord Lapotaire in England. He had finally received a message in response, granting Caine and Thorne carte blanche to investigate as they saw fit.

Coll thought hard, tapping his lips with a pencil stub, and suddenly remembered an airship that should already be heading in their direction. He sent up a plea that its captain was in the wheelhouse as he hurriedly scribbled a short message.

CAPTAIN MARCHESTON STOP URGENT STOP
MURDER ABOARD THE TANIWHA STOP RETURN
ARMED STOP COLL STOP

He sent the message. After a few short minutes that felt
like a lifetime, there was a response.

COLL STOP UNDERSTOOD STOP ALREADY ON WAY
TO COLLECT GUESTS STOP ARRIVAL TIME 2PM
TODAY STOP NO ARMS ALLOWED ABOARD PRIVATE
AIRSHIPS STOP

Coll looked at the frightened young woman. "Well,
they're unarmed, but they're on their way."

### Thorne's cabin
**06:45**

Aquilleia eyes snapped open. Faint silver lights swirled in her
violet eyes as the vision faded. She looked at Thorne who
was feeding Veronique a light, pre-breakfast titbit before
dealing with the contents of the lounge and Robin Ellis'
cabin. She took a deep breath as she sat back in her chair and
thought about what she had just seen: someone else had
disappeared from her sight…but not by another's hand.

○

## The Lounge
### 8:30am

Thorne glared out of the rain-streaked window, then turned back to begin his inspection of the samurai armour. After several minutes, he paused and sat back on his haunches. "Elliott, this armour has been put back wrong. There's also blood on the scabbard." He took a closer look at the arm of the samurai warrior and ran his hands over the mannequin. Interesting: it was a linen body over a solid frame, but where the right hand was firm, the left hand felt a little…squashy.

After some thought, Thorne walked over to a fine display of kukri knives. Removing one, he returned to the samurai, and working carefully, cut open the stitching on the left hand. Large quantities of combed wool immediately poked through the split in the seam. He pressed the material… nothing but stuffing. Moving behind the samurai, he removed the ornate cuirass covering the torso and slit a few inches of the stitches down the back of the mannequin. Placing the weapon on the floor, he removed some of the stuffing and looked inside, his eyes widened as he realised just what he was looking at. He cleared his throat. "Elliott, I think you had better come over here!"

Elliott looked up from his study of the mutilated remains of the diamond merchant. "I'm a little busy right now, Thorne."

Thorne looked at him, pools of violet light sparkling in his green eyes. "Elliott, now!"

Elliott's head snapped round at the tone in his friend's voice. Without another word, he walked towards Thorne and stood next to him. "Right…what am I looking at?"

Thorne nodded at the mannequin. "Feel the right hand."

Elliott gripped the strangely firm hand and let it go. "Now what?"

"Now feel the left."

Elliott took the left hand and frowned. "It feels soft."

Thorne nodded and pointed to the back of the dummy. "Now look at what's inside."

Elliott peered into the incision Thorne had made in the back of the mannequin. He stared at the exposed contents in silence before turning back to his friend, the green light in his eyes matching the violet flashes in Thorne's. "Bones! It looks like a complete human ribcage!" Elliott pointed at the hands. "Right hand firm, left hand soft...now, who do we know who was missing a left hand, and who hasn't been seen for ten years?" He pulled out more of the wadding that had been stuffed in and around the bare ribcage, and as he did so he heard a faint rustling. He looked at Thorne. "There's something else in here." Reaching inside the mannequin, his searching fingers found a small, linen wrapped pouch. Elliott's face drained of expression as he opened the package and looked within. Without a word he turned and poured the contents onto the malachite table; myriad cut diamonds spilt across the polished green table top, their glittering brilliance sparkling in the morning sunlight.

Elliott shook his head as he stared at the stones. "Diamonds, diamonds, everywhere; the Larkspur twins, gem collectors, a very dead diamond merchant, and now these... stuffed inside what appears to be the corpse of someone who went missing ten years ago." He shook his head irritably. "We need to check the other mannequins first, but I do believe we shall have to inform O.D that although we have temporarily misplaced his daughter, we may well have found the body of his former business associate, Alexander Burrows!" He paused. "And Darius told us who made the mannequins…we need to speak with her immediately."

○

**Mar's cabin**
**Five minutes later**

Elliott glared at the door and knocked louder. "Mrs Colville, please open the door."

Giselle held up an admonishing hand. "It is still quite early, Elliott. Perhaps she is still asleep?"

Aquilleia looked up from her petting of Veronique's ears and shook her head. "She is not asleep."

Elliott looked at her sharply, and turning back to the door, he reached out and turned the handle. As the door swung open, the dim room beyond appeared empty but for a low fire in the grate and the silent, huddled form under the blankets on the bed.

Elliott approached the bed and placed his hand on Mar's shoulder. He shook his head. "She's gone…" He looked at the bedside table. Next to a photograph of Mar with Merry and O.D sat a glass with a layer of powdery residue in its dregs, and a small box bearing the legend "Dr Morpheus' Chloral Sachets". He took a deep breath. Damn!

Giselle called out in a low voice. "Elliott, there's an envelope on the dressing table…it's addressed to you." She handed the note to her husband who sat next to the fire and began to read. Several minutes passed in total silence as he worked his way through the lengthy missive. Giselle sat next to the bed, Thorne and Aquilleia took the chairs by the doorway and waited, the dim, flickering light from the fire the only source of illumination.

Elliott finished the letter and sat back in his chair. "She has confessed to the murder of Carolyn Nolloth."

Thorne's eyebrows shot up. "Why?"

"She was being blackmailed. Apparently, Carolyn had already taken all of her money…so she demanded a different kind of payment for her silence. Carolyn sent Mar a note telling her to come to her room shortly before dinner; Mar burned the note…which explains the charred paper we found in her wastepaper bin. When Mar arrived for the meeting, Carolyn demanded that Mar encourage Merry to accept Van der Linde's offer of marriage. Mar would not do anything to harm Merry, so when Carolyn entered her bathroom to finish her ablutions before dinner, Mar went into the neighbouring linen store, removed the lye and mixed it in the wash jug on Carolyn's wash stand."

Giselle slowly tapped her finger on her lip. "But why was she being blackmailed?"

Elliott sighed. "Because Carolyn knew that Mar had murdered Cordelia Damant and Alexander Burrows."

There was total silence in the cabin. Giselle looked at the huddled form on the bed. "Did O.D know?"

Elliott shook his head and held out the letter. "Here — you read it."

Giselle opened the letter and began to read aloud.

Dear Mr Caine (if that is indeed your real name, which I doubt, but I digress),

I wish to tender my confession to the willful murder of Carolyn Nolloth. Of the deaths aboard the Taniwha, that is the only one to which I am willing to put my name.

Carolyn was blackmailing me over two crimes I previously committed in Brazil: namely, the murders of Cordelia Damant and Alexander Burrows.

I was there when Cordelia decided to begin her plan to replace O.D with Alexander. She did not want a divorce, and she was not prepared to leave empty handed. As a wife who had committed adultery, she would get nothing — nor would she be able to take Merry with her — but she wanted it all…

She and Alexander planned the 'kidnapping', and wrote the ransom note together. Unfortunately for them, I had been unable to sleep and saw her leave the note on O.D's desk early that morning. Her behaviour was so furtive, so unusual that I'm afraid I read the missive in a state of bewilderment…how could the note say she had been kidnapped if I had just seen her leave the house a few moments earlier…a free and safe woman?

I couldn't understand what it meant, so I followed her when she left the house. She went straight to Alexander's residence and I'm ashamed to say that I committed the most unladylike crime of eavesdropping…but I was very glad that I had! They planned to kill O.D when he arrived with the ransom, then place his body in the mine and set off the explosives Alexander had himself previously stolen…yes, Mr Caine, apparently Alexander himself had been behind the acts of vandalism, setting the final scene for their evil plans. By doing this they would be free, and after the necessary period of mourning, they would marry and get everything. I simply couldn't believe what I was hearing…they were so brazen about their plans, I felt sick! After all O.D and Alexander had been through together, to allow that vicious harlot to come between them…make no mistake, Mr Caine, that is exactly what my sainted friend was, a greedy, money-grubbing whore, just like her sister.

I knew immediately what I had to do to thwart their diabolical scheme. I went back to the house and took my husband's service revolver from my trunk, I then returned to

Alexander's house and entered without knocking. I caught them in an embrace. They leapt apart when they saw me...I shot them both without a word.

Giselle paused, and looked at the silent form in the bed.

Next to where they had been sitting was a note detailing where to 'find' Cordelia at the abandoned mine. I decided to take it with me, as I thought it might come in useful.

I was in a quandary as to what I should do with their bodies. I am not a very strong woman physically, and knew I could drag, but not carry them. Then I remembered the trouble we had been having with the Marabunta: army ants, awful things. They can strip the flesh off an adult human within twenty-four hours...and they had proved useful to me before. I dragged the bodies to the part of Alexander's Garden where Marabunta had been spotted. I knew the children would never go there as they had been warned about the ants. Merry never could stand insects, and neither Darius nor Torrance would ever leave her on her own.

I tied their bodies down with wire, tidied up the area where I had shot them, and returned home just as O.D and the others were beginning to wake. I said I would go into town and take the children to Alexander's house.

I dropped them off, with a warning about avoiding the Marabunta, then returned to O.D's house, set the horse and trap behind one of the old barns, took a fast horse and rode to the ransom drop at Viagem Valley. Luckily, I arrived just before O.D and managed to see the game through; he threw the package of diamonds they had demanded at me, and I threw him the note detailing which mine he should make for. I rode like the wind to get there ahead of him.

Once there, I tied the horse behind one of the sheds and checked the entrance to the mine — it had been rigged with explosives. I found the detonator and waited for O.D to arrive. I had to make sure that he would witness the explosion, but not be injured.

As he approached the mine, I pressed the plunger. The noise will stay with me forever…it was beyond sound!

O.D was flung to the ground and it took all my reserve not to fly to his aid. I ran to my horse and began the trek back to the house, where I set the tired beast in the stable, collected the horse and cart, and fairly flogged them into town to establish my alibi…

Unfortunately for me, the one occasion where Carolyn deigned to wake early was the same day that I had to deal with Cordelia and Alexander's attempt to destroy the man I loved. She witnessed me return from the mine and change the horses before she left for her boat to Europe; her first demands came later that evening by telegraph. Just money: she didn't know about the gems. I toyed with the idea of giving her the diamonds, but decided that as Cordelia and Alexander had desired the stones so much, they shouldn't be parted from them.

You should by now know what I did with their bodies. I waited for the ants to strip their flesh down to dry bone, then I wired their skeletons, using wadding and linen to turn them both into mannequins which I found amusing to keep. The samurai armour contains the remains of Alexander, and the mannequin in the Maori chieftain's cloak contains the skeleton of Cordelia…I am telling you this, so you can give them the proper burial they attempted to deny O.D, with their plan to seal him into his mine.

Carolyn continued to blackmail me on and off. I had a little money of my own put aside, and she delighted in taking it all, little by little.

After she and that revolting man Van der Linde arrived on the Taniwha, Carolyn sent me a note, which I subsequently burned. The note demanded a meeting in her cabin where she demanded a different kind of payment for her silence. She demanded that I encourage Merry to accept Morten Van der Linde's grotesque offer of marriage!

I would never countenance such an evil thing…Merry is an innocent. I could not, *would* not do anything to harm her, and so when Carolyn entered her bathroom, I went to the linen store next to her room, removed the lye, and mixed it in the wash jug on Carolyn's washstand…the effects were quite spectacular, and no doubt painful — but she deserved it all and more!"

With the attack on Mr Van De Linde (which I hasten to say was not carried out by me…though had I been physically stronger, he would also have died by my hand) and the subsequent damage to the mannequin, I realised the truth of its origin would be impossible for me to conceal any longer. Therefore, I have decided that the time has come to end my journey.

O.D never knew what I did in Brazil, Mr Caine, and that is the truth. Did I do it for him, and Merry? If I were being completely honest, I would have to admit that I did it mostly for me. I couldn't face the thought of him being taken from me. Their decision to kill him gave me no choice, and led to their own execution!

I will wait to see one more sunrise in this place. I have travelled to many lands, Mr Caine, both as a lone traveller, and with O.D and Merry. I have witnessed many beautiful things, but nothing comes close to the beauty, joy, and simplicity that I found in these waters. The happiest days of my life have been here, surrounded by the cliffs and the untouched forests…with O.D and Merry.

I regret nothing, except perhaps my foolish inability to tell the man I have loved for so long of my great affection for him. Informing him of my crimes may assuage the guilt he currently feels about his feelings for Mrs Carter. I trust they will both be very happy together.

Au revoir, Mr Caine; we shall not meet again.

Yours sincerely

Marjorie Lee Colville

Post Script.

If you choose to look inside the third mannequin, the one wearing my husband's uniform, you will discover his mortal remains. He attempted to force me to leave Brazil and return with him to India. He was disposed of by means of the same gun, and the same Marabunta nest which I used to take care of both Cordelia and Alexander.

MLC

Giselle took a deep breath, placed the letter back in the envelope, and handed it to Elliott. She shook her head, and pulling a small handkerchief from her sleeve, she dabbed at her eyes.

Thorne looked at the form on the bed. "A woman with steel in her bones! When she felt something needed to be done, she certainly didn't shy away from it."

Elliott ran his fingers through his hair and glared at Thorne. "Five murders, a suicide, two stolen diamonds — and we are still no closer to discovering the killers!" He threw himself into the small armchair and grimaced.

Aquilleia nodded. "That is true about one of them, but we do now know who killed Carolyn, and we know she didn't kill anyone else on the boat."

Giselle looked at her. "Playing devil's advocate for a moment, are you absolutely sure? Mar *could* have killed the others."

Aquilleia shook her head. "But she didn't…she willingly confessed to the murders she had committed. If she were guilty of the other deaths, why not add them to the list? Might as well be hung for a sheep as a lamb. And remember what I said before: there are *two* killers. One murdered Carolyn Nolloth, and we now know that that was Mar…she was the one who killed for love. The other is Chymeris: we know she murdered Wesley Eade, Morten Van der Linde, Dona Carla's maid Ana Luiza Santos, and Robin Ellis…and she definitely kills for the sake of hate!"

Elliott pressed his hand to his chin and thought. "You said that Chymeris has two assistants…could one of them be Lady Carlton-Cayce?"

Aquilleia shrugged hopelessly. "I honestly couldn't say. I still can't see. She's kept a powerful secret almost her entire life. She is either incredibly gifted at covering, or she simply believes her own version of the truth. Either way, if she is one of Chymeris' helpers…I cannot see past her walls."

Elliott stood up. "In the interest of trying to find out who the hell is guilty, I think Lady Carlton-Cayce's cabin should be our first port of call."

Giselle gestured to the bed. "What about Mar…how are we going to tell O.D?"

Elliott eyed the huddled form under the blankets. "The only way we can; we will give him Mar's letter…yes, under the circumstances, perhaps we should do that before we corner Lady Carlton-Cayce—"

The sudden sound of a gunshot echoed around the room, shocking them into silence. Elliott and Thorne stared at each other before running out onto the deck and looking up and down the deserted corridor. As they stood there, they heard a man's voice shouting from the deck below. "Mr Caine? Mr Caine?"

Running down the stairs, they found an agitated Malachy standing outside the cabin he shared with his wife, a gun in one hand and a bloodied handkerchief pressed against a deep gash in his temple. His choice of language was colourful. Several guests had run out of their own cabins on hearing the gunshot and were now gathered in assorted varieties of night attire around the swearing man. He was midway through a picturesque description of the parentage of the person who had attacked him when Elliott cut in. "I had no idea that cross-species procreation was possible, Mr…Ainu. Now, what has happened?"

Malachy took a deep breath. "I was just in our cabin; we haven't slept, so I decided to freshen my appearance before dealing with my duties. I heard the door to the deck open, and as I turned some bastard struck me and knocked me to the floor. They rifled through my pockets and found the pouch with the Larkspur…it's gone!"

Elliott closed his eyes. "Did they also take the documents that prove your legitimacy?"

Malachy paused in the middle of another stream of vitriol. "No, they left those."

"The same pocket as the gem?"

"Yes."

"Well, we know what they were after — and now they have both diamonds!"

Thornton opened his mouth, caught Colten's expression, and closed it with a snap as O.D pushed his way through the crowd to Elliott's side. "What in God's name has happened now?"

Elliott hastily informed the weary man about the second diamond theft, then looking at him with sympathy, he produced the letter. "This was trusted to me this morning;

take it to your cabin and read it. Please don't judge too harshly."

O.D took the envelope and paused. "This…this is Mar's writing…" His face paled as he slowly turned from Elliott and walked back to his suite. As he approached Josephine and Sophie on the stairs, he paused and held out his arm; Josephine, an expression of deep concern on her face, took his arm and walked with him, leaving a jittery looking Sophie to find her own way back to their cabin.

Elliott took a deep breath, and gesturing to the others, led them back up to the cabin deck. "Was I the only one to realise who was missing from that little gathering?"

Giselle thought. "Dona Carla and Lady Carlton-Cayce."

Thorne nodded. "Well, Dona Carla took to her cabin after the death of her companion, and Lady Carlton-Cayce hasn't left her cabin since the death of Wesley Eade." He looked at the others. "Or has she?"

Elliott smiled. "Time for a discreet conversation, I think."

### Lady Carlton-Cayce's cabin
### 9:15am

They walked around the aft of the boat and arrived at Lady Carlton-Cayce's door. When Elliott knocked, the door was opened a crack by Lady Carlton-Cayce's maid, who glared at them and snapped, "My lady will not talk to you; she will only speak with the correct authorities—"

Elliott bent his face close to the waspish maid, and snapped. "We have had enough of your mistress's refusal to co-operate in this murder investigation. Kindly inform her that we have both her birth certificates and the photographs, and that we are prepared to be discreet. She may find the authorities she seeks are less likely to be quite so polite!"

There was a slight sound behind the door. The elderly maid turned to look, then opened the door grudgingly. "My lady bids you enter."

Elliott, Giselle, Thorne, and Aquilleia entered the heavily perfumed boudoir to be confronted by a silent Lady Carlton-Cayce lounging on her chaise. Resplendent in a confection of deep-crimson silk and marabou, she gazed at her guests without expression. "Michaels, you may leave us. Return in ten minutes."

The maid looked from her lady to Elliott before nodding abruptly and leaving.

Elliott turned to the baroness. "We need you to answer some questions—"

Leonora glared at him. "That birth certificate and the photographs are my property, and you have no right to keep them from me." She gave a short bark of laughter. "Wesley was right. You are nothing more than a jumped-up Nosey Parker — or worse, a common blackmailer!"

Her fury turned to icy fear as green pools appeared in Elliott's eyes. She stared at him in shock as he leant down and allowed her to see the swirling lights in his eyes. "You are not the only person on this vessel who has secrets, my lady. If you and those documents are part of our investigation, then we shall investigate, and whatever we discover about you and your past will be judged on whether or not it is germane to our investigation. If it is, we will investigate with or without your permission; if it is not, those items will be returned with tact and discretion. I trust I make myself clear?"

Leonora looked up at him, her blue eyes shockingly wide, then gave a jerky nod and settled herself back against the plump cushions on the chaise

Elliott stood up. "We will begin by searching your rooms...again."

They began their search, Leonora watching in silence from her plush throne. Giselle went straight to the jewellery case and worked her way through it; Thorne rummaged in the bathroom; Aquilleia searched the drawers and wardrobe, but the Larkspur was not there.

Elliott stood by the door, watching the silent woman's face as they searched; he suddenly raised his voice. "Stop!" As the others turned to him, he looked at Aquilleia and gestured at the baroness. "Look at her...what do you see?"

The psychic sat in the chair by the dressing table and faced Leonora. She sat in silence for some minutes before responding. "She's afraid. Not of us, but of one of her companions; she knows they have at least one of the diamonds."

Elliott looked at the baroness. "This person you trust has killed before...I ask you now, who are they?"

Leonora's perfect face twisted sharply. "I don't know what you are talking about!"

"Did you assist them in the murders of Wesley Eade, Morten Van der Linde, Robin Ellis, and Ana Luiza Santos?"

A look of shock appeared on the mask-like face. "No!"

Aquilleia nodded. "They used you to get to the diamonds...they knew you had given one to Wesley Eade. They insisted you get it back, but it had already been stolen. You couldn't get it back...so they did. You are afraid of them." She turned to face Elliott. "The gems are not here; Chymeris has them both." She gestured at the baroness, a frustrated look on her face. "She won't speak, and I can't see who she's hiding...she loves the person she *thinks* Chymeris is."

Leonora looked at the psychic warily. "Who is Chymeris?"

Elliott looked at her, his face set. "Chymeris is the true name of the person you are protecting. They have killed before, and your utter naivety in protecting them means they will be free to do so again! I ask you again, baroness: who are they?"

Leonora pressed her lips together and shook her head.

Elliott dragged a hand through his hair. "Thorne, please go and ask the butler to come here. We will place Lady Carlton-Cayce under arrest and keep her confined to her rooms until we return to Milford City and hand her over to the authorities she is so desperate to meet!"

Thorne left the room, returning a few minutes later with Malachy and Simone. They glared at the baroness as Elliott explained the unusual situation.

Malachy nodded firmly. "We will lock her in. She won't get away!"

○

**A cabin**
**9:25am**

Chymeris smiled at her companion. "One more little detail, and we shall be ready to leave. We simply need to wait for them to make their move." She laughed. "And they are so very easy to read." Her assistant smiled and placed a small valise on the bed, Chymeris opened the case and looked at the contents, pausing to run a slender finger across the glowing purple facets that winked up at her before she locked the case and her confederate placed it by the door.

She looked at them with a smirk. "Ready yourself."

Her accomplice smiled, checked the Browning revolver they had taken from Wesley Eade, and left the cabin.

334

○

## O.D's private deck
### 10:00am

The changeable weather of the Sound had finished making its presence felt, the severe storm of the previous evening disappearing almost as swiftly as it had arrived. The bright autumnal sunshine bathed the Sound in shades of gold as O.D poured several cups of tea and handed them round, then settled himself in one of the folding chairs on the deck and rubbed his eyes. His face was grey, and he was unshaven. "So, you're saying that Lady Carlton-Cayce knows who the killer is, but will not name them?"

Elliott took a sip of his tea and added a few more sugar lumps. "I'm afraid so. And to make it worse, she doesn't actually believe they *are* the killer...she has fallen completely under their spell. We've placed her under lock and key in her cabin; her maid is with her, and the door is being guarded by Malachy and his wife, Simone. She will not escape." Elliott ran his hand through his hair. "I just wish she'd tell us who the blasted killer is!"

Thorne stood by the rail and smiled as Jane brought the young pup Manaia down for her second perambulation of the morning. The small dog made a beeline for Veronique and an immediate tail-wagging session began. Thorne gripped the leash tightly; he had no desire to drag a sodden Labrador out of the Sound.

The sound of footsteps came from above them as Captain Peach and his daughter Fleur descended from the wheelhouse. The captain looked at O.D. "We can continue to Milford City as soon as you give the order, Mr Damant."

O.D nodded. "Thank you, Captain." He paused as he

realised that Fleur was staring over his shoulder. Shading her eyes with one hand, she looked out across the Sound towards Milford City before turning to her father. "Is that a boat?"

The others immediately turned. A small rowboat was indeed approaching the Taniwha. Captain Peach hurried back to the wheelhouse, and returning with his telescope, trained it on the approaching vessel. "It's Coll Langen and Manu, Mr Damant — and your daughter!"

O.D leapt up and took the proffered telescope from Peach. Looking through the brass instrument, he saw Merry wave to him from the boat. He waved back and headed for the stairs, where Aquilleia placed her hand on his arm. "Quietly, Mr Damant...there is one aboard who should not yet know that she lives. Hide her in your quarters, and keep her away from the port side of the boat." As O.D stared at her, she stamped her foot and glared at him. "Do what I say, or all will be lost!"

Thorne stepped forward. "I would do as she says, Mr Damant."

The philanthropist nodded and descended the stairs, followed by Captain Peach and Fleur. As they reached the gangway, the captain dropped the short rope ladder quietly over the side.

The little vessel pulled alongside. Coll helped Merry climb up the ladder and O.D clasped his daughter fiercely. As Merry opened her mouth, O.D held his finger to his lips and whispered in her ear. Merry blinked and nodded as she and Fleur, escorted by Captain Peach, hurried up to her father's suite.

Back on deck, O.D, Coll and Manu were talking in hushed tones. Coll nodded at Manu who turned to O.D and spoke a few short words. The effect on the philanthropist was instantaneous; his grey-tinged skin paled to the colour of chalk before slowly turning a deep puce. As he turned back to the stairs that led to his suite, Coll caught his arm. "Marcheston will be here at two o'clock. He knows!"

O.D's expression hardened. "Thank you, my friend. You'd better return to the hotel…we'll deal with this."

As the small boat pushed off and headed back to Milford City, O.D stood and watched it for a moment, his fists clenched, before making his way back to his suite. As he arrived on his private deck, Merry threw her arms around him. He held her close, and looked over her head at Elliott. "My daughter and I need some time together…there are things she must know, and I must be the one to tell her."

Elliott nodded. "Of course, Mr Damant. May I suggest we reconvene in your suite at midday? There are many things that need attention."

He and the others all stood up as O.D led Merry back into his suite and firmly closed the door.

Thorne raised an eyebrow. "Midday?"

Elliott sipped his now-cold tea and grimaced. "Yes, midday. We need to head back to the cabin and think — we have two hours!"

### O.D's suite
### 12pm
### The Denouement

Elliott looked at the gathered men and women and cleared his throat. "Ladies and gentlemen, may I have your attention?"

The low murmur disappeared as the people in the room turned their attention to the man standing by O.D's desk.

"Thank you. We have decided that due to the rather unusual circumstances of these murders, some things are too personal and simply too strange to share with the other guests. That is why only you have been invited to this explanation of the murders that occurred aboard the Taniwha this weekend."

O.D, Merry, Fleur, Torrance, Josephine, Giselle, Thorne, Aquilleia, and Veronique gazed back at him in silence.

Lady Carlton-Cayce was in her room, under the watchful eyes of Malachy and Simone; Dona Carla was still refusing to leave her cabin, and was being watched by Lilith; shortly after returning to their shared cabin following the attack on Malachy, Sophie had finally given in to an extremely dramatic fit of hysterics and had locked Josephine out of their room…as far as Josephine knew, she was still there, hiding in the bathroom; Rust and Kayfield had taken up temporary residence in the bar, and were slowly working their way through the Taniwha's supply of Champagne and whisky; Darius was still lingering in his cabin, and Captain Peach was on duty in the wheelhouse, watching for Captain Marcheston's arrival, while the majority of the servants were in the staff room, having a much-needed break from their employers.

Elliott cleared his throat and began. "We were originally called in to investigate a series of poison-pen letters and threats against Mr Damant and his daughter. These threats began when O.D and his daughter visited England last year, and had been quite threatening — especially in relation to Miss Damant."

A sudden noise came from the corner as Torrance covered his face with his hands.

Josephine raised a hand. "Are you saying it was the poison pen author after all… that they were the person who tried to kill Merry?"

Torrance sat up straight and shook his head vehemently. "No! It wasn't the poison pen writer!"

Merry opened her mouth, but a sudden movement from Elliott caught her eye, and she paused. O.D turned to look at his secretary; Torrance was pale, the skin of his face an ashen grey as he tried to avoid his employer's eyes.

An unreadable expression appeared on O.D's face, and in a very quiet voice, he inquired, "What makes you so sure, Torrance?"

Torrance wrung his hands, and with a sudden sob he whispered, "Because I sent them…I sent them!" He fell back into the armchair, a look of revulsion on his gaunt face. "I thought it was you! All these years I thought you had killed them and got away with it. I had to punish you! Then on Friday I overheard your conversation with Mr Caine, and found out that it wasn't you. All those years I hated you, threatened you and Merry, and for nothing! I'm sorry…I'm so sorry!" He began to weep; deep, tearing sobs that tore at Merry's heart.

Elliott looked at the weeping young man, and inquired. "How did you come to the conclusion that O.D murdered your father, Mr Burrows?"

Torrance coughed and tried to wipe his face. Josephine held out a handkerchief, delicately embroidered but sensibly sized, which he took gratefully. After a few moments he answered, his voice husky. "Darius told me. He said that his mother had seen Mr Damant leave the house early on the morning my father and Mrs Damant were killed, that she had heard gunshots, and that she saw Mr Damant hiding a lathered horse behind the house…I now know it wasn't true, none of it was true!" He looked up at Elliott. "But why tell me such an awful lie? I don't understand!"

Elliott looked at Torrance. "In a way, Mr Burrows, it *was* true…" He held up his hand as O.D leapt to his feet with an outraged expression. "His mother told him exactly what she had seen that morning. When Darius told you, he simply changed the identity of that person to make you despise O.D…it was all part of a plan, years in the making. But I digress. The person Carolyn witnessed that morning wasn't Octavius Damant: it was Marjory Lee Colville. It was Mar she witnessed leaving the house early, and it was Marjory Lee Colville whom she saw hiding a lathered horse behind the house. Mar was the one who killed Cordelia Damant and Alexander Burrows…for reasons we shall not go into here." He looked at O.D and Merry with an understanding expression; the magnate had spent the last two hours comforting his daughter after breaking the news of both Mar's death, and her confession to the murders of Merry's mother and Torrance's father, the murder of her own husband, and the more recent death of Carolyn Nolloth.

Elliott turned to Torrance. "To answer your question, Mr Burrows, it rather has the air of an attempt at divide and conquer. Pardon my saying so, but you are not a man who enjoys confrontation; you are quiet, introverted. Carolyn and Darius knew you would sit, and think, and think, and one day explode; but in a manageable, bookish way."

O.D looked at his tearful daughter, then walked over to where Torrance was sitting. As Torrance coughed and mopped at his face, O.D spoke. "Torrance, Torrance…listen to me, my boy; let's get this settled and then we can begin again. A clean slate…what do you say?"

An expression of terrible hope appeared on the young man's face as he looked from O.D to Merry. "I — I don't know what to say…after what I have done, you still want me to stay?"

Merry nodded firmly. "You're family, Torrance. What you did, how you behaved, it was based on a lie…it wasn't really you."

O.D poured a large amount of whisky into two tumblers and handed one to the young man. "I think you need this, Torrance — I know I do!"

He sat back down and nodded to Elliott, who continued. "Darius told you the lie his mother told him to tell because *he* was her accomplice. All the time he has lived under your roof, Mr Damant, Darius has been in cahoots with his mother to bring about your downfall — and that of your daughter!"

O.D looked at him over the rim of his tumbler. "The money, I take it?"

Elliott nodded. "What else? It was the only thing Carolyn cared about, and she passed her greed and fury at being on the outside of so much wealth to her son. Between them they came up with the idea of a suitor: someone who could charm a young woman into situations that could be twisted to suit their needs."

Merry shifted slightly in her chair; Josephine reached out and gently patted her hand.

"They chose, for the wooer, Carolyn's long-term business partner, Morten Van der Linde. If he knew about the wooing, I doubt he knew about the ending Carolyn and Darius had planned; the murders of both Van der Linde and Miss Damant as part of a failed love affair."

Merry pressed her hand to her mouth as she realised how close she had sailed to utter disaster.

Elliott looked at her with an understanding expression before continuing. "But before their plans could come to fruition, Carolyn Nolloth was murdered. This saved Miss Damant, and gave Van der Linde more time — but not very much more! The following day we began our searches and discovered an abundance of clues and information, some of which turned out to be red herrings. One genuine clue was a note found in Carolyn's cabin." Elliott produced the note from his pocket and placed it on the desk. "It simply states: 'All is going to plan. Hold steady and all that you desire will soon, rightfully, be yours.'" Elliott surveyed his audience. "But all was not going to plan; Carolyn's death threw both her accomplices into panic. Her partner had no idea what to do next, and her son knew that their plans for revenge were now void. He couldn't continue without his mother's input, so he sat and waited for the right moment to arrive…"

Elliott took a sip of his drink. "While he bided his time, someone else took the opportunity to follow through with their own wicked game. This person, who is known to us as Chymeris, was in search of two diamonds known as the Larkspur. The diamonds had been owned by one man, but had been separated, and were now in the hands of Lady Leonora Carlton-Cayce and Wesley Eade. Mr Eade became the next casualty, lured to the meat locker and forced in terror to take his own life."

A sharp snap from the little fire in the grate made people jump, so deep was the silence in the room.

Merry shook her head. "But what do you mean, 'forced in terror'? How do you frighten someone enough to make them do such a thing?"

Elliott paused, they had decided that some of the more unusual aspects of the killer should be kept quiet; the truth of Chymeris' abilities was something that very few humans would be willing to accept, and so it would be best to simply not mention it at all. "It is possible that the killer sought to frighten information out of Mr Eade on the whereabouts of the diamond by masquerading as your murdered aunt. We found evidence that they hid her body in the large wooden crate in the meat locker; we found blood and several strands of chestnut-coloured hair within it. It is not yet clear to us why they did such a thing, and we may never know." Elliott paused, gauging the effect of his statement…it seemed to be accepted without question. "In the course of our interviews, we discovered two other people on the Taniwha who had good reason to want Wesley Eade dead; the true heir to the Eade family estate and his wife. They arrived with a plot to remove Mr Eade — not from his life, but from his wealth and estate. They had the proof, and were planning to confront him with it…but the killer reached him first."

"Who is the rightful heir?" asked Merry, looking very confused.

O.D looked at his daughter. "They asked that their names are not released until after they have returned to England to claim their rights." He smiled. "But if I said that he never did behave like a butler…"

Merry's jaw dropped, she turned back to Elliott who continued.

"As I said, Mr Eade killed himself. Whether this was part of Chymeris' plan we may never know…but it meant that they and their accomplice now had a gun: the very weapon Mr Eade had used on himself—"

"Has that weapon been found?" asked O.D.

Elliott shook his head.

There was a collective intake of breath, then Josephine spoke. "An accomplice?"

"Yes," said Elliott. "Chymeris could not have succeeded in their plans without the help of another." A wry look appeared on his face. "They actually have two helpers…"

Josephine looked incredulous. "Two? Do you know who they are?"

Giselle spoke from her chair. "We know who one of them is; the other is still unknown to us."

Josephine looked from Giselle to Elliott and back again. "Well? Good grief, don't keep us in the dark…who is it?"

Elliott paused; he knew how to make an announcement. "The one we know of…is Lady Leonora Carlton-Cayce."

"Good God!" Josephine exclaimed. She looked taken aback at her own words. "Oh, I do beg your pardon. Will she not say who the other is?"

Elliott shook his head. "She won't tell us who Chymeris is, let alone their second. We believe the other accomplice is responsible for the damage to both the engines and the telegraph machine. Lady Carlton-Cayce will not reveal the identity of the killer; she still refuses to believe they are guilty of the murders committed on this vessel and that is why she is under arrest in her cabin. We shall hand her over to the authorities and she can plead her case with them…though that may not go well for her, for several reasons."

O.D caught Elliott's eye, flicked a glance to his daughter and shook his head slightly. Elliott understood; any allusion to Lady Carlton-Cayce's true sex was not for discussion in the present company.

"Then yesterday evening, things…escalated somewhat. Merry was attacked after dinner and thrown overboard. She saw who did this; it was Darius. there was no one else on the deck. He had finally decided how to best punish his cousin and uncle for what he saw as their rejection of his mother's claim to the family wealth. But as Darius was throwing Merry overboard on the port side, Morten Van der Linde was being most disagreeably murdered in the lounge. Again, we know this murder to have been committed by Chymeris, because of the method used; I shall not go into details here."

Merry and Fleur looked slightly relieved, while Josephine looked not a little disappointed.

"Chymeris arranged the crime scene, and left…but their work was still not done. Shortly after killing Van der Linde, they also killed Robin Ellis, whom we believe was attempting to blackmail them. We believe that through their accomplices, Chymeris had discovered where the diamonds were hidden. One was held by the true heir to the Eade family estate, and the other was in our possession...so they went to Thorne's cabin, took the gem and murdered Dona Carla's maid, Ana Luiza Santos, who was also searching for the stone."

"Why?" Elliott looked at Fleur, who blushed slightly, but continued. "Why did she want the gem if it wasn't hers?"

Elliott frowned; more matters he couldn't explain properly in the present company. "Ana Luiza Santos wanted the diamond to try to...persuade someone that she was worthy of them; she was simply in the wrong place at the wrong time. Chymeris then decided to go after the other jewel, and sent their second to do this; they attacked the butler and took the stone. Chymeris now has everything they came here for – and we still don't know who they are!"

Aquilleia moved suddenly in her chair. Elliott raised an eyebrow, and she nodded; the one they had been waiting for was approaching.

There was a soft tap at the door. Elliott nodded to O.D, who called, "Who is it?"

A slightly muffled voice responded. "It's Darius; may I come in?"

O.D's eyes blazed and he leapt to his feet, but Merry and Josephine each placed a calming hand on his arm. Merry shook her head at him. "No, Papa...Mr Caine has a plan, and we must see it through." She rose, went through the door to her father's bedroom, and pulled the door to behind her, leaving a slight gap so she could continue to listen.

Elliott surveyed the people in the room and spoke in a low voice. "It is imperative that no one mention that Miss Damant is here...do you understand?"

As the assorted people nodded, Thorne opened the door

with a smile and gestured into the room. "Do come in, Mr Damant."

An ashen-faced Darius entered quietly. He took in the room's occupants, including the dishevelled Torrance, and turned to O.D. "I'm sorry, Uncle, I see you're busy...I'll return later."

O.D held up a hand, and when he spoke, his voice was firm. "Darius, please stay! Mr Caine and his associates believe they have finally solved these hideous crimes."

Darius raised his eyebrows, and a muscle twitched under his left eye. "Oh, yes? Oh, that's good news. But if you will excuse me, I have rather a lot to do."

Elliott smiled at the twitchy young man. "Darius, it would be helpful if you could stay. This does, after all, involve your mother's murder."

Darius swallowed hard and looked at his uncle. "Do we know...who?"

O.D nodded, and his eyes were hard as he gazed at his nephew. "It was Mar."

Darius stared at him, then burst into peals of laughter, the sound becoming higher and higher in pitch, until tears were running down his face. He leant on the desk and paused to catch his breath as he looked at O.D. "You can't be serious! Old Mar? Rubbish!"

"I am in deadly earnest!" O.D replied. "Mar killed your mother because she was being blackmailed—"

"Would you like to take a seat, Mr Damant?" Elliot interjected, waving Darius to an armchair. "I'm afraid you've arrived too late to hear the opening fireworks, but I'm sure you will find the rest of the show most entertaining."

As Darius sank into one of the plush chairs, he looked at Elliott, and the tic in his left eye became slightly more pronounced. "I, um, I thought I saw a small boat approaching earlier this morning. Is there any news...anything at all?"

Elliott swore to himself, but maintaining a suave expression, he shook his head. "I'm afraid not, Mr Damant. That was the stoker taking the opportunity to do a spot of fishing, nothing more."

Darius nodded, a faintly relieved look on his still-ashen face.

Elliott took a sip of his sherry. "For the benefit of the younger Mr Damant, I shall sum up our findings. The death of Carolyn Nolloth has been solved; Marjorie Lee Colville confessed to the murder shortly before taking her own life early this morning."

Darius stared at him, the whites of his eyes gleaming silver in the sunlight that streamed through the windows.

Elliott continued. "But in her written missive, she makes it perfectly clear that she did not commit any of the other murders that have occurred on the Taniwha. In the letter she left, Mar also confessed to three other murders which she committed ten years ago…if she was prepared to admit those, why not the others? We believe she was telling the truth. Mar killed Carolyn, but the remaining murders were committed by another person. We do not know their current alias, but their true name is Chymeris, and they have killed many times before."

Darius stared at him, a faint light in his eyes. "Are you saying that this Chymeris murdered the others…and Merry?"

Elliott smiled. "No, Mr Damant. I'm saying that Chymeris killed Wesley Eade, Morten Van der Linde, Robin Ellis, and Ana Luiza Santos. I'm accusing *you* of the murder of your cousin Merry…or rather, the attempted murder." He turned to the bedroom door. "Miss Damant, you can come in now."

The door swung open and Merry walked back into the room, her eyes sorrowful as she looked at her cousin. Darius' face turned white; he shrank into his chair as his cousin approached him.

She shook her head. "Oh, Darius, how could you? How could you?"

Darius curled into a ball in the chair, avoiding her eyes. Aquilleia looked from him to Merry, frowning, then sudden understanding appeared in her eyes. "Stop him!" she cried.

Before anyone could move, Darius leapt from his seat and grabbed Merry by the hair. He swung her round and pressed the muzzle of a gun against her temple, then looked at his uncle, a too-wide smile on his face. "I've got you now, you bastard! I'll kill this bitch, then you — and it will all be over!"

Josephine stood up; her face was the colour of paper as she held out her hand. "Please, let Merry go; take me in her place."

Darius turned to look at her, the gun still pressed firmly to Merry's temple. His wet lips pulled back in a rictus grin. "You don't understand, my dear Mrs Carter…after I have killed my cousin and my uncle, I shall kill you too!"

Thorne slowly stepped back into the shadow of the wall behind him, seeming to blend with the darkness there.

Darius, still holding Merry, pointed the gun at his uncle. The grin on his face was ugly to behold. "And with you dead, the entire family fortune will come to the wonderful, kind, heartbroken, and oh, so patient nephew."

Elliott spoke from his armchair. "Aren't you forgetting a few things?"

Darius laughed. "Do you really think that after what I have done, I would blench at killing the rest of you? Fools!" He paused suddenly, and darted a glance to the corner where Thorne had been standing. "Where did he go?" His voice rose. "Where did he go?"

Elliott smiled, his canines flashing as the shadow between the cabin door and the now-unnerved young man darkened rapidly. He raised his voice. "Wherever he wants to!"

Thorne suddenly materialised out of the shadows behind

348

Darius and with a hard swing, slammed his clenched fist into the young man's right ear.

Darius dropped the gun with a squeal. Throwing his cousin to the floor, he clutched at his ear and turned in time to experience the full force of a furious uppercut from Thorne. Darius reeled, and caught an equally thundering right hook from O.D.

The outer door crashed open and Captain Peach ran in, a determined expression on his face and a loaded revolver in his hand. He stared at Darius, who was prostrate on the floor. "I heard raised voices," he said, "and after the events of the last few days, I was a little concerned!"

O.D gripped his arm. "Thank you, Captain Peach...your timing was most opportune. Thank you."

Captain Peach nodded. "Not at all, sir."

Elliott turned to look at Thorne who moved back to the corner he had originally been standing in. Merry stared at him in shocked silence.

"But you were there...I saw you!"

Elliott caught Thorne's eye and smiled. "The Bowyer brothers are not the only ones gifted in the art of illusion, Miss Damant."

○

## The Airship
## 2:00pm

The airship that had first brought them to the Sound finally puttered into view. Several guests had gathered on the deck to observe Lady Carlton-Cayce's transfer to Captain Marcheston's airship, and on to the police station in Picton for further questioning.

Captain Marcheston carefully lowered the airship into

the water by the Taniwha and a gangplank was hurriedly set between the two vessels; it had been decided that using the launch would not be necessary as only a handful of people and some few items of luggage would be crossing the narrow walkway.

As Captain Marcheston stepped out of his wheelhouse, he shivered; it may have been sunny, but the weather was definitely turning in the Sound. He climbed aboard and was greeted by Captain Peach and O.D, his eyes flicked across the gathered guests until they met the soft grey eyes of Ngaio Lattimer. He smiled at her, and was greeted with a gentle smile in return.

Arriving at Lady Carlton-Cayce's cabin, Captain Marcheston nodded at Malachy, who knocked at the door, grim-faced. It was opened by Lady Carlton-Cayce's maid, Michaels, who silently stepped back as the young captain removed the baroness from the cabin. They were joined by Trevenniss and two of the ship's maids who collected her luggage from where it had been placed outside her door, and conveyed it down the gangplank and onto the waiting airship.

As the guests turned to watch the removal of one of their own, a faint scuffle sounded from above as Elliott and Thorne guided a handcuffed and furious Darius down to the main deck.

Elliott nodded at Captain Marcheston, keeping a firm grip on the violently struggling young man. "Room for one more?"

Captain Marcheston nodded. "What's the charge, just so I have something to say to the police?"

Thorne handed him a piece of paper. "This is a written statement from Miss Mereanthy Damant; in it she states that her cousin, Darius Damant, made an attempt on her life. He also threatened the life of Mrs Josephine Carter, a guest aboard this vessel. The necessary details will be passed on to the authorities in due course; all we ask is that you remove Mr Darius Damant and Lady Carlton-Cayce to the police station in Picton at your earliest convenience."

Captain Marcheston took the report, scanned it and looked at Elliott and Thorne, his eyebrows raised. "This is rather irregular—"

He was interrupted by a sudden scream from the baroness as Dona Carla, who had been standing quietly by the stairs, suddenly swung her tightly clenched fist in a short arc that connected painfully with the side of the baroness's face. Lady Carlton-Cayce fell to the floor, a look of total shock replacing her usual smooth impassivity. She huddled in a ball and screamed in pain as Dona Carla rained blows down on her unprotected head and back. "Puta! You bitch — you killed Ana!"

Giselle ran to her friend. "Carla, no! Carla, stop — please!"

Dona Carla twisted away from Giselle and kicked out viciously at the sobbing baroness. She continued her onslaught until Lilith managed to push her way through the shocked throng and grasp her arms. "Dona, Dona... stop, stop!" Dona Carla looked at Lilith, tears streaming down her face. She looked down at Lady Carlton-Cayce and spat at her; then began to sob. Lilith led her back to her room, passing a shocked-looking Sophie who had decided to wrap herself up in a warm overcoat against the chill weather and leave the safety of her room just in time to witness the short-lived and somewhat one-sided catfight on deck.

Elliott and Thorne raised their eyebrows at each other as Giselle and Aquilleia helped the battered baroness to her feet. Giselle turned to Elliott. "I know she has to go to the police station for questioning, and I understand that she knows more than she is saying about the murders, but she should see a doctor first…I think Carla has injured her ribs."

As Elliott was about to respond, he was violently pushed from behind. He spun round and came face to face with Trevenniss…who was holding a poisonous and familiar looking revolver aimed straight at Elliott's head.

Trevenniss smiled. "Everyone will back away from the gangplank. Further, further…thank you. All is planned and ready, my Queen!"

Giselle and Aquilleia looked at each other, then turned to stare at Lady Carlton-Cayce. The baroness stood upright, though her pain was evident on her battered but still beautiful face. As she straightened her back, her mask of impassivity returned. She stared at the steward, who grinned at her.

A polite voice broke the silence. "Excuse me, please."

The guests parted like the Red Sea as one of their number nudged their way to the front. Josephine's mouth dropped open. "Sophie!"

The actress smirked at the older woman. Making her way towards the steward, she paused before Lady Carlton-Cayce. She gently caressed the beautiful face before removing the golden snake ring from her right thumb and tossing it at the silent baroness. "A parting gift, my sweet — to replace the two items I've liberated from your gem collection!" With a smile she walked towards the steward. "Is everything set?"

Trevenniss nodded, the gun still trained on the others. "I replaced her bags with yours, my Queen; all is ready."

"Well done!" Sophie purred.

Darius, still handcuffed and gripped by Elliott and Thorne, realised they were no longer concentrating on him. Wrenching himself free, he flung himself towards the actress and steward. "Take me with you! I can pay—"

The gun fired and Darius fell to the ground, his hands still cuffed together. A look of blank shock on his dead face.

O.D took a step forward. "Darius!" He stopped dead and slowly raised his hands as the steward trained the gun on him.

Sophie smiled brightly. "Well, it has certainly been amusing. I can't say I'll be seeing any of you again…" She turned to face Elliott, and a faint yellow light appeared in her eyes. "But you never know…brother!" She looked at Giselle and her smile twisted. "I did say you should have chosen me, my sweet."

Trevenniss kept his gun trained on the people on the Taniwha as he assisted Sophie onto the airship and ordered the airship crew onto the Taniwha.

As they pulled away, Sophie turned and smiled at Elliott, then threw off her coat to reveal a man's tweed travel suit beneath. With a gentle movement she stroked her face, and before the stunned guests, she began to change. The ripe, feminine figure stretched in height and slimmed to an athletic build, while the carefully coiffed hair became shorter, darker, and curlier as the young woman who had once been Sophie Havercroft returned to the form and the smirking face of the one they had known as Phoenixus, but who they now knew to be Chymeris.

Elliott swore violently as the airship pulled away, lifted into the air, and headed towards the mouth of the Sound. The Taniwha's engine was still under half steam, and had only small lifeboats with no engines – it was hopeless!

As he stood in impotent fury, the swirling green lights in his eyes were mirrored by those in the eyes of Giselle, Thorne, and Aquilleia; green, gold, purple, and silver pools that followed the path of the airship as it carried their enemy to freedom.

Chymeris raised a hand in farewell, and laughed. A shame

she'd had to lose the more preferred female form, but it had been worth it purely for the look on her dear brother's face!

Turning her back on the Taniwha, Chymeris smiled as the airship carried her towards the blue and silver light of the open sea…and the final stage of her master plan.

**THE END**

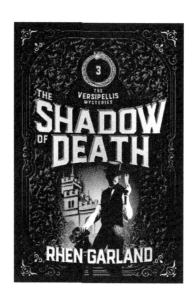

**The Shadow of Death**
*Book 3 of the The Versipellis Mysteries*

**PREVIEW**

**The Isle of Cove**
**February**
**Midnight**
**1825**

The dark winter waves swelled and crashed along the bleak coastline as the full moon, peering through racing storm clouds, cast its shifting light upon a small, windswept island.

Resting just off the southern coast of Westrenshire, the tiny, wooded island sat at the end of a narrow causeway, assessable only at low tide, that led from the mainland village of Penwithiel, to the island's tiny harbour village of Cove.

Down in the harbour, under the cover of protean clouds and dappled moonlight, a small group of men bearing swords were silently disembarking from one of the fishing boats. The leader of the group nodded his thanks to the young fisherman who had used his father's boat to smuggle them into the village earlier that day. The young fisherman, who was barely thirteen, nodded back and watched as the armed men left the jetty and followed the narrow, winding lane that led away from the harbour and up to the hill beyond.

The group made their way along the lane and came to a halt at one of the small cottages that lay on the outer edge of the village. Their leader walked silently up the tidy, well-kept path and tapped lightly on the front door with a gauntlet clad fist. After a few brief minutes, the door opened and they were joined by a quiet, unarmed young man dressed in black; a young man with hazel eyes. He nodded silently at the men, closed the door behind him, and joined them as they continued along the lane to the top of the hill.

They arrived at a point where the path diverged; one path leading right, towards Cove Castle, and the other heading left, towards the cliffs and Horseman Falls.

Taking the left-hand path, the men finally arrived at an ornately carved door, seemingly set into the side of the hill itself; a door that would lead them to the heart of an evil that had tormented the islanders and their children for many years.

The leader paused at the doorway and gestured, the young man with hazel eyes moved to the front and knocked a strangely rhythmic tattoo on the solid barrier. Moments later, the door slowly swung open.

The red-robed figure on the other side of the threshold looked at the hard faces of the gathered men and swallowed hard. "They are all here. I have done as you instructed, I have betrayed my brethren…" He looked at the quiet young man, an expression of fear on his face. "But have I done enough to be forgiven?"

The young man nodded. "Yes, you have done enough. Now go, and never return to this place."

The doorkeeper nodded jerkily and hitching up his robes, ran past the quiet man, and down the path that led to the village as the troop of armed men silently entered the torchlit passage and made their way to a chamber, hidden deep within the hill, that was their final destination.

As they descended, the distant sound of chanting became apparent. The young man caught the eye of the leader of the mercenaries he had hired and made a gesture. The leader nodded, and tapping two of his men on the shoulders, pointed at the doorway. The armed men settled against the wall and stood guard as the others continued down the torchlit passageway towards the distant voices.

○

## The Temple of the Inner Sanctum

The black-robed figure slowly lifted the bejewelled and wickedly sharp knife from its velvet bed; light from the flickering braziers placed around the opulent chamber caught the gleaming edge of the blade as the figure turned their burning gaze upon the grey-clad acolyte kneeling before them, and in a rich, strangely gravelly voice, intoned, "Who entreats entry into the sacred upper echelons of this most devout order of the Priory of Cove?"

The acolyte pushed back their heavy cowl, revealing a tumbling mass of dark hair surrounding a proud, cruel face. The young woman raised her voice for the words she had spent many months practising. "I, Josephina of the

House of Burgoyne, do entreat entry into this most sacred order."

The dark figure leant forward; their eyes fixed on the young woman's face. "And by what vow do you entreat entry from your Master?"

The young woman smirked, the ugliness of the expression at odds with her fey beauty. "By the vow of blood, and by the offering of a sacrament, do I entreat entry from my Master."

The Master smiled back. "And do you swear fealty to this order, to keep its secrets, and those of our Brothers and Sisters?"

The acolyte smiled. "I do!" She held out her open hand.

As the glinting blade paused over the centre of her palm the figure spoke again. "And do you wholeheartedly promise to imbibe to excess, to feast to excess, to fornicate to excess, and to bring rich offerings to our altars?"

Josephina nodded proudly. "I do!"

The blade was placed against her palm, and slowly drawn to her index finger. As her blood welled up and dripped onto the floor, the black-robed figure enveloped her bloody hand in his. "Then, my daughter, we bid you welcome. Welcome to the Temple of the Inner Sanctum!"

Cheers rose from the massed brethren lining the smooth walls of the huge cave that was home to the debauched Priory of Cove. Men and women clad in robes of white, grey, and red roared their approval as the Master removed her grey apparel and dropped it to the floor, revealing a sheer white cotton gown beneath. He removed a deep red robe from the altar and draped it around her shoulders.

The Master raised his voice. "Let it be known that Josephina is now and forever a Sister of the Holy Inner Sanctum; the highest of the high within the Priory of Cove." He ran a burning eye over his rapt congregation. "Let it also be known that Sister Josephina will replace the blasphemer Jerome as my right hand!"

Josephina turned proudly to face the thirty men and women whose cheering echoed around the massive, ornately decorated chamber as each man and woman drank a toast from their full goblets of deep-red wine. Judging by their bleary eyes and slurred words, these were not the first draughts of the evening.

Josephina snapped her fingers at a white-robed acolyte kneeling next to the altar. "Fetch the offering!"

As the acolyte stumbled out of the room in their haste to perform her bidding, their cowl fell away, exposing the face of a young girl; her light blue eyes and pale face framed by a mane of silky, white blonde hair that spread across her shoulders as she flew to one of the side chambers to retrieve the gift Sister Josephina had brought as sacrifice.

Josephina turned back to the Master with a look of exultation. "If it would please the Inner Sanctum, I have brought a suitable offering for the altar."

The white-robed female returned to the hall, carrying a terrified young child in her arms. The little boy's wide-eyed stare took in the proud young woman and the huge black-robed figure next to her; as the Master approached with a searingly unpleasant smile, the little boy began to cry.

A murmur rustled among the spectators, and several stepped forward, ugly gleams in their eyes, as the Master took the child and placed him on the ornate stone altar.

"No!"

Josephina and the Master spun round as one of the red-garbed monks pushed back his dark-red cowl to reveal a face very similar to Josephina's. He held out his hand to the Master. "No! Father, you swore after what happened last time: no more children!"

The black-robed figure glared at the younger man. "How

dare you, you impudent brat! I banished you from this order for your insubordination, and you defy me again to enter this hallowed space. How dare you raise your hand to me! I spared your life the first time your impudence raised its head, Jerome, and only then because you were my son — but no more! From this day on, you are no son of mine! Guards, remove this blasphemer!"

As two grey-robed men grasped his arms, the red-robed monk shouted, "This has gone beyond what this place was supposed to be, Father! This was to be as the Hellfire Club: nothing more than drinks, frolics, and play! What you have done here is sacrilegious to the very nature of this club!" He turned to the proud young woman beside the Master. "Josephina, how could you?"

The Master laughed. "Did you really believe that I would be prepared to stop at just one child? After the wealth of ages of our family's true nature had been revealed to me? *We* are the rulers here, Joseph…not the cattle who serve us! That child was only the most recent of our offerings…and he will not be the last! Take him!"

As the guards dragged the still-shouting man out, Josephina turned to the Master and held out the jewelled blade he had just used on her. "Father?"

The Master smiled and stroked the side of her face, the similarities in their features all the more apparent in their identical expressions of expectant, exultant cruelty. "No, my daughter…this is your offering, and your gift to possess."

As the white-robed acolyte tied the mute child to the altar, another of the red-robed monks stepped forward. "Brother Jerome is right! Thomas…my lord, you cannot do this!"

The Master snapped his fingers at another grey-robed follower. "Prove your fealty and destroy this usurper!"

The young man, swaddled in his too-large robes, stared at

the Master and shook his head. The Master's eyes opened wide, the whites gleaming in the flickering orange glow from the braziers. He crooked his finger at the fearful young man and crooned, "You dare refuse a direct order from me? Come here, Brother Phillipe…come to your Master…"

As the terrified young man again shook his head, shouting came from the long corridor that led to the doorway: from the direction in which the protesting Jerome had been dragged.

The Master's head snapped round as the sounds became clearer: shouting, mingled with the sound of sword play. Gritting his teeth, he turned back to his daughter and gestured at the bound child on the altar. "There is still time for you to prove your allegiance, my daughter! Kill the child!"

Josephina nodded; a rictus grin that was a travesty of a smile disfigured her face as she rushed to the altar. Standing beside the feebly moving little boy, she gripped the dagger with both hands and began the ritual. "I, Josephina, child of the House of Burgoyne, and Sister of the Inner Sanctum of the Priory of Cove, make this sacrifice of flesh, blood, and fear—"

As she raised the dagger above her head to strike, Jerome suddenly appeared in the doorway. Running across the cavernous room, he wrenched the blade from her grasp, and threw it onto the altar. As Josephina screamed in anger, he dragged her towards the far wall.

Several bloodstained, armed men ran into the room, and paused to take in the sight of thirty unarmed, drink-sodden men and women cowering against the walls. The armed men faced the brethren, swords drawn, all except one man who stood by the door, a heavy sack on the ground next to him.

The young man with hazel eyes slowly mosed his way through the crowd until he stood before the black-robed lunatic whose followers called him Master.

The Master turned his burning eyes on the troop of armed men and bellowed, "Infidels! Blasphemers and usurpers hear me — I shall have vengeance upon you all!" His fiery gaze rested upon all in the room; but when it came at last to the hazel eyed man before him, he paused for several moments before bursting into incredulous laughter. "Popplewell? Well, I'll be damned if it isn't my good and true friend the Reverend Popplewell! Have you finally decided to join us and throw away your foolish desires for love and harmonious dwelling, old friend?"

The Master grinned as he drew himself up to his full height, head and shoulders above the silent man before him. "And how is your delightful wife? Oh, of course, how could I forget? She's roasting in hell because she stole her own life… such a shame about your faith condemning her, old friend. And your son only just buried — well, what little they could find after we of the Inner Sanctum had finished with him!" He roared with laughter as several of the younger acolytes stared at him in horrified revulsion.

Josephina echoed her father's laughter, then turned her burning dark eyes on the vicar and sneeringly sang, "Lullay, thou little tiny child. Bye bye, lullay, lullay. Lullay, thou little tiny child. Bye bye, lullay, lullay." Her eyes flashed. "A song for dead children in your sacred book, Reverend!" She screamed with laughter as she twisted against her brother's tight grip. Jerome's face was deathly pale as his eyes flickered from his father, to his sister, before resting on the gentle face of the quiet man.

Newton Popplewell, the Burgoyne family vicar, turned his steady hazel gaze from the sadists before him and walked to the altar. He looked at the terrified child with kind eyes and gently patted the boy's bound hands, then paused as he noticed the discarded blade. He leant down to the little boy's ear. "Close your eyes, my child."

As he stepped back, the vicar reached up and removed the neatly wound white cravat from his throat. He kissed it and placed it on the altar before turning back to the Master, a faint smile on his lips. "Thomas Burgoyne, Earl of Cove…you shall not take another child as you took mine." And with a sharp lunge, the young man plunged the bejewelled dagger straight into the Master's heart.

Josephina's laughter ceased, and there was a sudden dead silence before her screams began. She writhed against the grip of her brother, who gazed in stupefied shock as their father, Thomas Burgoyne, Master of the Priory of Cove, gaped at the knife in his chest. His black eyes burned as he looked into the intent, hazel eyes of his killer, then he dropped like a felled tree.

As the vicar untied the mute child, a man appeared in the passageway, desperately pushing his way through the fighters; he stopped next to the altar and Popplewell handed the child to him. "Look after your boy, Samson; he will take some time to heal." The man clutched the child to his chest, and nodded. "Yes, Reverend…and thank you, sir."

The vicar shook his head. "Go to your wife, my friend; return your child to the safety of his home."

As the relieved man left with his son, Popplewell turned his attention to the rest of the Monks of Cove, who stood flinching from the swords of the armed men before them. "Now, apart from Thomas Burgoyne, who else was a part of the Inner Sanctum? Come along now, gentlemen…ladies, don't be shy — we know for a fact that none of you are!"

Jerome shook his head, a stunned expression still on his face as he held his sobbing sister. "I was unaware of the existence of an Inner Sanctum until the…events of last month were made known to me. Reverend, I am so very sorry."

Popplewell nodded to him. "And I believe you, Jerome; however, the murder of my child was not the first carried out by this diabolical coterie…several children have gone missing from Cove, Penwithiel, and further afield over this last year. Your father was the instigator of the heinous crimes committed here, and he did not act alone. I know this, I also know that I am willing to be…merciful to those who admit their crimes and tell us where they hid the bodies, so that we may give those innocents a Christian burial. So, members of the Priory of Cove, tell me: there were four members of the Inner Sanctum present on the night my son was murdered, one was the Master; who are the other three? And where are the bodies of the children you murdered?"

There was silence.

Popplewell raised his voice. "Remove your cowls, and let us see who inhabits this place of death."

No one moved. Popplewell looked at Fellwell, who raised his sword.

The cave was suddenly filled with the sound of rustling, as several hoods were lowered, and one in particular caught his eye. The white-robed blonde stared silently at the floor as Popplewell stood in front of her. "Well, well, Nanette, and you not yet sixteen. Whatever will your parents say?"

The young girl turned her tear-streaked face to glare at him, her blue eyes blazing with hatred. Then she tossed her head and stared at the floor.

As Popplewell scanned the room, one of the red-robed men sneered, "You have no power here, Popplewell. You're a vicar, not an avenging angel, and Brother Grimstone will enjoy teaching you that in due course!"

Popplewell moved to stand before the arrogant man. "And is Brother Grimstone here?"

The sneering man cast a supercilious glance around the room. "No," he muttered.

Popplewell nodded. "I'm not surprised." He called over his

shoulder to the leader of the mercenaries he had hired. "Fellwell?"

"Yes, sir?"

"What did you do with Grimstone?"

Fellwell paused. "Grimstone?"

"Yes, Grimstone."

Fellwell shrugged. "I couldn't rightly say, sir, but Feldspar might know. Feldspar!"

The man lounging by the doorway with his sack looked up from cleaning his nails with the tip of his dagger. "Sir!"

"Do we have Grimstone, Feldspar?"

Feldspar paused. "I don't rightly know, sir. Shall I check?"

Fellwell nodded. "Please do."

Feldspar saluted. "Yes, sir!" He tucked his dagger back into his belt, lifted the heavy sack and emptied its contents across the floor. Several of the robed men and women cried out, and not a few were violently sick as the severed heads of their more bloodthirsty friends bounced free from their material confines and rolled across the floor, leaving bloodied, gory streaks on the rough stone.

"Do any of these belong to the man you're looking for, sir?" asked Feldspar.

Popplewell nudged the head nearest to him with his foot, and the unmistakable features of Sir Grimstone Covey stared blindly back at him through glazed eyes. He nodded at Fellwell. "This is he." He turned back to the red-robed man, who stared at him in horror. "I am very much in the way of being an avenging angel, Markham. Yes, I know who you are, and I know that *you* were present on the night my son was murdered."

Fellwell dragged the complaining man to the altar. Popplewell cast his gaze over the silent room as he walked towards Jerome and Josephina. "There was at least one more whose identity I know, and one who is unknown to me; speak now, or suffer the consequences."

Josephina spat at him in rage. "Rot in hell with your wife and brat, you bastard!"

Popplewell stood before the struggling woman. "And here is the third of the Inner Sanctum; take her with Markham."

As Fellwell took her by the arm Jerome stared at the vicar. His face turned grey as he realised the implication of Popplewell's words. "What are you going to do with my sister?"

Fellwell pushed Josephina against the altar, next to Markham. He stepped back and nodded at another of his men, who silently raised his crossbow and fired. The bolt left the machine with an oily twang, followed almost instantly by a meaty thud as it hit the sneering Markham in the heart. The deathly silence erupted into screams from the monks as another member of the Inner Sanctum died before them.

Popplewell looked at Jerome. "You were there when we discovered my son's body; you saw what had been done to him. He was five years old, Jerome. You were there when I had to tell my wife her only child had been murdered; you were there when we discovered her body at the foot of Horseman Falls. You tell me, Jerome: what do you think I should do with your sister?"

Jerome stared at him in horrified silence before turning, almost against his will, to look at his sister. "Are you truly saying that — that Josephina was…oh my God!" He fell back against the wall and raised his eyes to Popplewell's. "But she only entered the Inner Sanctum tonight — I don't understand!"

Popplewell looked at the young man with gentle eyes and patted his shoulder. "Your sister has been a dedicated follower of your father's perversions for quite some time, Jerome. I'm truly sorry to be the bearer of such news." He turned back to the tear-streaked, yet still proud and arrogant woman before him. "I will say it again: there is one more of the Inner Sanctum whose identity is unknown, speak now and mercy will be shown...but if you hold your tongue, you will suffer, Josephina!"

The dark-haired woman laughed at him, hysteria evident in her high-pitched, screaming laughter. She ignored the corpse at her feet and propped herself against the altar as she spat her contemptuous response. "You presume to threaten me? You fool, you ridiculous preaching fool, with your words of love and brotherhood! We have brotherhood here, bathed in blood, and fear, and power! You and your pathetic wife and brat...what did you have that we couldn't take from you whenever we wished? Answer me that!"

She continued to laugh as Popplewell bent towards her. But when he whispered in her ear, her laughter stopped dead and her face froze. She shook her head, her dark eyes wide and tinged with fear. "You cannot do that; it is impossible!"

Popplewell studied her. "Is it, now? With all your self-proclaimed power, can you not do it? It is a simple thing, an easy thing...for those of us who have the ability." He raised his hand to Fellwell, who nodded and gave the order for his men to remove the monks from the cavern. As the terrified hedonists were marched from the room, Popplewell looked at Fellwell. "Now that they have seen what can and will happen if they do not speak, see if any of them are willing to divulge the whereabouts of their previous victims." Popplewell paused, his hazel eyes thoughtful. "Feel free to use any and all methods you feel suitable under the circum-stances to...extract that information."

Several of the monks cried out in both fear and protest as they were dragged from the chamber. A slight smile crossed Fellwell's face; he and the reverend had talked about what would be acceptable...and what would not, but none of the monks had been privy to that little conversation; it would be enjoyable watching them squirm. His smile widened. "It will be my pleasure, Reverend."

Popplewell nodded. "I will join you shortly."

Fellwell turned and left the chamber, slamming the iron-bound outer door shut behind him as he left the three people in the opulent, treasure strewn room to stare at each other in silence.

Jerome took in a shuddering breath. "I will ask you again, Popplewell: what are you going to do with my sister?"

Popplewell smiled faintly. Moving away from the altar, he removed his coat, threw it across what had been the Master's throne, and began to roll up his sleeves. "Don't worry, Jerome, I will not kill her; she will be punished in a rather different manner than eternal damnation in hell. I will make her an unwilling ally in my fight against the evil nature that festers deep in the heart of your family!"

Josephina stared at him in silence, an expression of genuine fear on her tear-streaked face.

Taking a deep breath, Popplewell turned back to the altar, and the silent scions of the House of Burgoyne.

He raised an eyebrow. "Shall we begin?"

○

**Find *The Shadow of Death* and other great reads from Rhen Garland at www.rhengarland.com**

# ABOUT THE AUTHOR

Rhen Garland lives in Somerset, England with her folk-singing, artist husband, 4000 books, an equal number of 1980's action movies, and a growing collection of passive-aggressive Tomtes.

"I thought when I finally started writing that my books would be genteel "cosy" type murder mysteries set in the Golden Era (I love the 1920's and 30's for the style, music, and automobiles), with someone being politely bumped off at the Vicar's tea party and the corpse then apologising for disrupting proceedings. But no, the late Victorian era came thundering over my horizon armed with some fantastical and macabre plotlines and planted itself in my stories, my characters, and my life, and would not budge."

I enjoy the countryside, peace, Prosecco, and the works of Dame Ngaio Marsh, Dame Glady Mitchell, John Dickson Carr/Carter Dickson, Dame Agatha Christie, Simon R Green, and Sir Terry Pratchett. I watch far too many old school murder mystery films, TV series, and 1980's action movies for it to be considered healthy.